COLLECTION

VOLUME

—4—

THE *Regency* COLLECTION

VOLUME
—4—

The Outrageous Dowager
by
Sarah Westleigh

Devil-May-Dare
by
Mary Nichols

First published in Great Britain 1999 by
Harlequin Mills & Boon Limited,
Eton House, 18–24 Paradise Road,
Richmond, Surrey, TW9 1SR.

ISBN 0 263 81710 5
106-9908

Printed and bound in Spain
by Litografia Rosés S.A., Barcelona

THE OUTRAGEOUS DOWAGER

by

Sarah Westleigh

Dear Reader

The Outrageous Dowager was great fun to write. I loved inventing the main characters: Lexie, a young widow willing to flout convention to enjoy her new-found freedom while seeking a younger, suitable husband with whom to share the rest of her life; and Storm, a bachelor Marquess possessed of a rakish reputation carefully nurtured as a defence against the mamas hoping to trap him into marriage with one of their daughters.

Lexie and Storm are attracted to each other, but have different agendas. Who would be bold enough to wager on the outcome of the relationship?

Happy Reading!

Sarah Westleigh

Sarah Westleigh has enjoyed a varied life. Working as a local government officer in London, she qualified as a Chartered Quantity Surveyor. She assisted her husband in his Chartered Accountancy practice, at the same time managing an employment agency. Moving to Devon, she finally found time to write, publishing short stories and articles, before discovering historical novels.

Other titles by the same author:

The Inherited Bride*
Set Free My Heart*
Loyal Hearts*
Heritage of Love
A Most Exceptional Quest
Escape to Destiny
A Lady of Independent Means
Chevalier's Pawn*
Felon's Fancy
Seafire
A Highly Irregular Footman
Jousting with Shadows
The Impossible Earl

* linked

CHAPTER ONE

LONDON seethed with joyous, cheering crowds celebrating peace. With Boney safely incarcerated on Elba, twenty years of war had ended. The day before, on June the sixth 1814, six weeks after the last shot had been fired, the Allied Sovereigns had landed on English soil, come to visit the people who, by their unflinching determination to oppose Napoleon, had contributed so much to the allied victory.

At the port of Dover, detachments from the most famous regiments of the British Army had been there to greet Czar Alexander of Russia and the King of Prussia, the latter accompanied by his young sons and old Field Marshal von Blücher, his Chancellor. Prince Metternich, the Chancellor of Austria, was among other famous names to come ashore with them.

Today they were due to arrive in London as guests of the Regent, and the people of the capital thronged the streets to cheer them. Coaches, carts and wooden stands lined the route from the south-east suburbs to St James's Palace. Word went round that the Regent's scarlet-and-gold-clad postilions would not be needed, for the exuberant, swamping multitude planned to unhorse the coaches and drag them in triumph over London Bridge.

Lexie had not ventured into the suburbs to view the procession but the seething excitement in the capital proved too much for her and, ignoring the protests of Mrs Caroline Baldwin, a remote cousin by marriage who lived with her, she had donned her oldest and plainest garments, intending to walk from her house in Bruton Street to St James's to see what she could see.

'Really, Alexia!' Mrs Baldwin had exclaimed. 'I sometimes think you quite forget your position! What your poor dear husband would have said I cannot imagine!'

'Amber would have understood,' Lexie had retorted as she tucked the last wisp of her fair hair out of sight beneath an old chip bonnet and tied the black ribbons beneath her determined chin—coupled with the washed-out grey muslin gown she had worn in the garden at Porthewan, the Earl of Amber's estate in Cornwall, it rendered her inconspicuous.

Colourless might have been a better description, she had mused wryly, with her pale skin and fair eyebrows and lashes. All the better. She had had no wish to be recognised. As a finishing touch she had fastened a plain white fichu about her shoulders, since the neckline of the dress was a little low for walking out and it would not be prudent to carry a parasol to protect her from the sun.

She could have been sitting in one of the stands erected for the privileged, but she hadn't wanted that. What she craved was freedom from the constraints of convention, the opportunity to take risks. Amber had understood that—why else had he bought her a sporting curricle and a splendid pair of matched blacks with which to race about his cliff-top estate?

He had watched and applauded her expertise with the ribbons and, despite his age, had accompanied her on many of her more sedate excursions. She had heard it said that it was better to be an old man's darling than a young man's slave. Certainly, it had not been unpleasant to be the first but she had no intention of ever becoming the second. If and when she married again—

'Well, I do not!'

Cousin Caro's usually fluttery voice cut firmly across her thoughts. She must be upset, thought Lexie with a secret smile. It took little to agitate the elderly widow whom she had discovered living in reduced circumstances. Lexie had needed a gentlewoman like her cousin, related however distantly to the Earl, to give her establishment respectability, and so had installed her as her companion.

Cousin Caro fluttered about making life more comfortable for her young cousin and made few demands. But she did have strict ideas about what was and was not done in polite society. Mixing with the noisy, sweating mob was something that was definitely not.

'Why you wish to expose yourself to molestation by those common people I cannot imagine!' went on Mrs Baldwin when Lexie did not reply.

'Because they are so joyous, so excited, and are truly enjoying themselves for once,' Lexie explained soberly. 'It is not often they have a holiday. I would like to share in their happiness. They will not harm me.'

'I sincerely hope not,' sniffed Mrs Baldwin. 'I would not trust myself—'

'But you are not me,' Lexie pointed out. 'If you are to be happy here with me, Cousin, you must learn to accept my rackety ways. I cannot live the restricted life convention demands. I did during my come-out year and I loathed it after the freedom I had enjoyed in Ireland. For years I have been incarcerated in the depths of Cornwall and more recently have been forced to lead a retired life in mourning for Amber. Now I intend to live a little. He told me I should, and left me the means to do so.'

Cousin Caro shook her grey head in its elaborate lace cap and sniffed again. 'I would not have thought it of my cousin!'

'He understood me,' said Lexie dreamily, remembering the indulgent peer, old enough to be her grandfather, who had recently lost his only son. She had been coaxed into marrying him because he was an earl and could offer her security. She had not managed to provide him with an heir but he had not held it against her, admitting that it was probably his fault, he was too old to beget a child.

Because he had loved her, he had left her the unentailed estate of Merryfield in Hertfordshire and the town house in Bruton Street—from which she was about to depart on her adventure—not to mention more than enough money invested in the Funds to enable her to live exactly as she liked. His nephew, the new earl, had been furious to see so much of his uncle's fortune left elsewhere.

'At least take Chalker with you,' pleaded Cousin Caro, referring to Lexie's personal maid, Florence Chalker. 'She knows London better than you do!'

'She never liked it in Cornwall and was glad to

return,' grinned Lexie. 'She has already gone out. I sent her off an hour or more ago.'

'Then I must—'

'No, you must not, Cousin.' Lexie regarded the plump figure of her companion with tolerant affection. 'You would become faint in the heat and be of no use at all. Wait for me here. I shall not remain out for long.'

She left Mrs Baldwin reclining on the *chaise longue* in a flutter of anxiety and made her way from her house by the servants' entrance. Most of the staff had already been given permission to go out to join the celebrating crowds, leaving Mrs Walker, the cook, and Mr Dymock, the butler, to look after things.

She managed to make her way to St James's without too much trouble, for she knew the nearby streets well by now, having lived in London for several weeks. The King of Prussia, with his sons, arrived almost as Lexie joined the throng outside the palace. The cheers, she felt certain, would be heard in the City.

Not that the King seemed to appreciate them much, his air of gaunt melancholy never lifting. He left the coach before the doors of the palace. His short coat and white pantaloons enabled the distant, straining crowd to admire his large bottom. The princes, fair, upstanding youngsters, followed him down.

But where was the Czar? Patiently, the good-humoured crowd waited, calling, shouting, laughing and singing.

They did not yet know it but, in the face of the

size and enthusiasm of the unpoliced populace, the coaches had scattered before crossing London Bridge. The Czar's coach had skirted London to the south, crossing the Thames by Battersea's wooden toll bridge.

Word spread like wildfire that he had entered the capital by the turnpike at Hyde Park Corner and had gone straight to the Pulteney Hotel in Piccadilly, where his sister, the Grand Duchess of Oldenburg, was already installed. And, once there, he had refused to travel on to the state apartments reserved for him in St James's Palace, declaring that his sister had persuaded him to remain with her for the duration of his visit.

A heaving mass of spectators began to flood along St James's street towards the Pulteney, Lexie swept along in their midst. A stout, sweaty woman caught at her elbow as Lexie stumbled and would have fallen.

'Must keep on yer feet, ducks,' she advised, revealing blackened teeth as she grinned.

Lexie nodded and smiled, not trusting herself to speak for fear of giving herself away by her accent. For the first time she felt fear. Had she fallen she would have been trampled to death. But fear simply hardened her resolve to remain upright and to see her adventure through to the end.

She arrived at last before the hotel, deafened by the cheers and calls for the Czar to show himself. At length he did, waving from a first-floor window, a round-faced individual in bottle-green. His head rose from the high gold collar of a tunic so padded and laced that he had difficulty in moving his arms beneath the gold epaulettes.

But he was the greatest Russian of all, leader of the soldiers whose defence of Moscow had led to Boney's disastrous retreat from which his army had never recovered. The cheers echoed all the way back to St James's Palace and beyond.

But suddenly, distant jeers could be heard as a lavish coach, escorted by outriders wearing the red and gold uniforms of the Regent, attempted to force its way along St James's Street towards the hotel. The Prince, who had been waiting on his own ground to greet the Czar, had been forced to make his way through a hostile throng of his father's subjects to pay his respects to his important visitor.

But the crowd thwarted his intention. Lexie could hear the hoots and cat-calls, the cries of 'Where's yer wife, then, Prinny?'

'Serves Prinny right,' howled the stout woman who, somehow, still remained at her side. And although he would never hear her, she screeched abuse at the royal personage now being forced to turn back.

Lexie felt sorry for a man she knew to be lonely and unhappy. His marriage to Caroline of Brunswick had been forced on him for political and financial reasons. Of course, he should have resisted more strongly before entering into the disastrous alliance, for he was already wed to Mrs Fitzherbert at the time. But the Crown and Parliament refused to accept the legality of that marriage.

He had hated Princess Caroline from the start and tales of his mistreatment of his wife abounded. Having met that stout, crude woman, Lexie did not blame him. But on the other hand, having married her and begotten a daughter by her, he should have treated her more kindly.

'Can't even fight for 'is country,' the woman was screeching. 'Not fit for nuffing 'e ain't, 'cept finking up new uniforms!'

Lexie opened her mouth to defend the Regent, but thought better of it. Prinny, she knew, had pleaded to be allowed to fight with the army but the Constitution would not allow the heir to the throne to risk his life. So he had comforted himself by designing uniforms, wearing one himself when he went to inspect his own regiment, the 10th Hussars. It was the nearest he would ever get to action, but through no fault of his own.

However, she soon forgot the discomforts of the Regent in her own. The press and stench of unwashed bodies in the heat, the foul breath of the woman who seemed glued to her side, had begun to overcome her. She wasn't used to it, that was her trouble. Lexie knew she must escape the crowd and began to edge her way to its fringes. Easier said than done, she found, progress was slow, but eventually, by a determined effort, she did reach a spot where the crowd had thinned. She paused for a moment to draw deep breaths of the slightly less malodorous air.

That proved a grave mistake. Two rough-looking men noticed her fighting for breath and, friendly enough, asked her if she was all right.

She nodded and incautiously answered, 'I'm feeling better now, thank you.'

'Cor, a nob!' They glanced at each other and then

looked her up and down, reaching out to feel the quality of her gown, evident despite its age, and eying the snowy whiteness of the fichu about her shoulders. 'Wot yer doin' 'ere, yer 'ighness, mixing wiv the loikes of us?'

'The same as you are,' said Lexie, keeping calm. They did not mean her harm. 'I wanted to greet the Allied Sovereigns.'

'Did, did yer?' The leader and spokesman's eyes suddenly gleamed. 'Nice bit of gold. Werf a bit, that.' Lexie's hand flew protectively to the pin fastening her fichu. Another mistake she'd made. Amber had given it to her on her twenty-first birthday and she valued it for sentimental reasons. But she should not have worn so finely chased and valuable an article on the streets.

'Got anyfink else under there?'

A great dirty paw shot out to grasp the thin muslin and tear it off her. Lexie gasped and struggled to escape but the second man, smaller but wiry, held her arms from behind while his companion carried on unimpeded.

'Let me go!' shrieked Lexie, beginning to panic.

'Shut yer gob,' hissed the big man, his hand still clutching at her fichu, 'or it'll be all up wiv yew. Nice sport it'd be, taming yew afore we cuts yer throat.'

'No!' she cried. 'Take the brooch and let me go!'

Her last words became a muffled croak as the man behind clasped a grimy paw over her mouth, making Lexie heave with revulsion. One or two people glanced in their direction but their interest was slight. Such incidents took place every day and it was best not to interfere. The girl might be the man's wife or daughter and it wasn't wise to get mixed up in family quarrels.

Lexie began to struggle in earnest. The good humour with which the incident had apparently begun had turned sour. The men were determined to have her brooch and her, too, if she read them correctly. That such a thing could happen in a crowded street without anyone coming to her rescue! She would never have believed it!

She stamped on the foot of the man behind her but her soft shoe failed to make any impact—he scarcely seemed to notice. The big man had torn the fichu from her shoulders and was taking the opportunity to reach down the neck of her dress, hoping to find something valuable, if only a coin, nestling between her breasts. When he failed he began to fondle her flesh instead, sending tremors of disgust streaking through Lexie.

'We'd better get going,' suggested the man behind her. The big man nodded. 'Find somewhere's quiet.'

Lexie made a supreme effort to tear herself free and managed to emit a strangled scream.

The effect seemed instantaneous, though afterwards she realised that help must already have been on its way. The big man took a cracking blow on his chin; a thin cane inserted between his legs tripped him up and he collapsed at her feet. A long, blue-clad arm flashed past her ear to land a bunched fist on the smaller man's jaw. His grip on her broke as he slid to the ground.

'Oh!' gasped Lexie, trembling and almost giving way to the waves of faintness washing over her. 'Thank you! I called, but no one else. . .'

'Come,' said her rescuer brusquely, bending down to retrieve her torn fichu, the pin still attached, and scanning the crowd quickly as he rose again. 'The mob may turn upon us. Besides, these men will revive in a moment and it would be better if we were not around at the time. Come, miss. Take my arm.'

Lexie had recovered slightly. For the first time she looked at her deliverer. Her eyes widened before she quickly lowered her head.

Lord Stormaston! It surely could not be! Where had his lazy drawl and languid manner gone?

But she knew that it was, and remembered him and his reputation when she had known him seven years ago. How scornful she had been of his excessive indulgence in all the so-called gentlemanly pleasures of wine, women and gambling. She had not had occasion to speak to him since her return to Society but she had heard the gossip which always surrounded his activities.

The years had moderated his behaviour somewhat: he drank and gambled rather less than of old, but he kept an actress in a love nest near Drury Lane and had lots of other willing women available when he felt like it. He was also rumoured to visit Jackson's gymnasium to practice the noble art of self-defence. After his recent performance she no longer doubted the truth of that information.

It was indeed Stormaston, but a different man from the one who frequented the salons and ballrooms of polite society.

He had given no sign of knowing her. She desperately did not want him to recognise her. It was so many years since they had last met and she had changed. She was no longer the unsophisticated young girl who had been brought from Ireland by her parents to secure a husband. She was now a widow, a mature woman of experience. He would think her a foolish child still if he discovered that the erstwhile Lady Alexia Hamilton had got herself into such a stupid predicament.

She had not taken his arm as requested and kept her head bent as she felt herself dragged unceremoniously from Piccadilly into a less frequented side-street.

'That's better,' he commented as he slowed his pace, released her arm and began to massage his broken knuckles. 'I could deal with two of them by taking them by surprise, but I would not back myself to win a brawl against both together. How are you feeling, Miss. . .er. . .?'

'Much better, thank you,' murmured Lexie, ignoring his hanging enquiry as to her name, staring steadily at the silver button fastening his cut-away coat at his midriff. 'I am most sensible of the service you have rendered me. . .sir, but I shall be all right now. If I may have my fichu. . .?'

'Ah, yes, your fichu.' He stared down at the piece of cloth in his hand as though seeing it for the first time. He inspected the gold pin through narrowed eyes and Lexie resolved never to wear it in any company of which he might form a part.

But next moment, startled, she was looking up into that dark, dangerous face she remembered so well, at the livid scar which scored his cheek, a mere thread now, which scarcely marred the symmetry of a remarkably handsome face dominated by a long, finely chiselled, arrogant nose.

He swung her fichu aloft on the end of his cane. His black brows lifted and with them his lazy lids, revealing brilliant blue eyes which blazed down at her filled with mischievous merriment.

'I think I deserve a prize for delivering you from those rascals and recovering your property, my dear.'

His words had caught her off guard. But she might have expected such unchivalrous behaviour from a man with his reputation! Especially as, despite the gold pin, he probably thought her nothing more than a lady's maid, dressed as she was.

A strange smile curved his lips as she jerked her head up in response to his taunt. His free hand came out to tilt her chin, so that he could study her features more closely. But still he did not recognise her. At least, she did not think he did, for the smile became a grin as, still holding her property out of her reach, he lowered his face towards hers.

'A kiss, I think,' he murmured, and before she could protest he had covered her mouth with his own.

He held her only by that hand under her chin yet Lexie stood paralysed as he tasted her lips, gently at first, teasingly. Then as, involuntarily, hers began to respond, he deepened the kiss, stirring strange, foreign feelings in Lexie's mind and body.

Abruptly, as quickly as it had begun, it was over, leaving her bemused. He seemed rather breathless as he handed her her fichu, the precious brooch still firmly stuck in the material.

'An ample reward, my dear,' he murmured.

'Would you accept my escort home? It would be safer for you.'

'No!' gasped Lexie, coming to life again after her stunned acquiescence to the kiss. And added a belated, 'Thank you. I shall be perfectly all right now. The crowd has moved off and I do not have far to go.'

He bowed, correctly and yet somehow mockingly. 'They have gone to mob old Blücher, I believe. If you are certain I can be of no further assistance we must part. A pity, my dear. I feel we might deal well together were you—'

'Oh, no! No, please. I must go. Goodbye.'

In her confusion Lexie almost stumbled over her own feet in her hurry to escape. She knew the way but did not want to make straight for Bruton Street. He might try to follow her. But although she looked over her shoulder several times on her way back she saw no further sign of the disreputable Marquess.

Stirred to admiration, James Graham, Marquess of Stormaston, watched her trim figure making its hurried yet graceful retreat, a small, satisfied smile on his fine lips. Did she really believe that he had not recognised her? He had done so the moment her eyes had lifted and widened in recognition. No man could mistake those beautiful green orbs in their nests of gold-tipped lashes, the elfin beauty of her small face. He had felt her allure all those years ago when she had captured poor old Amber. She had been out of bounds to him then, but now. . .

Now, Lady Alexia Hamilton was the Dowager Countess of Amber and an unconventional countess, too, it seemed: a young woman of spirit not given to swooning at the least thing. He should have realised her gallant, imprudent nature, given that he had watched her galloping indecorously in Hyde Park, indifferent to the scandalised gaze of other ladies of fashion who never went faster than a trot, and had seen her driving her curricle about town, quite unescorted apart from a youthful tiger up behind.

Amused, he had observed her as she fielded the attentions of half a dozen eager suitors and an even greater number of gentlemen with more dubious motives for their pursuit. He had not joined the throng surrounding her, preferring to watch and wait, to study the way she coolly but charmingly held them all at bay, to attempt to discover the chink in her armour.

He had done that today. She liked to be free from constraint, would take a risk, rise to a challenge. Were they not the very reasons he himself had left his grandmother and sister sitting in a window overlooking the route, had decided against returning to his own window overlooking St James's Street and had skirted the edge of the crowd to discover what was going on at ground level?

Lady Amber had ventured into the midst of the crowd. Even he had not dared that much, dressed as he was in a superfine jacket, pantaloons and shining beaver, until the sight of a young woman being molested had drawn him deeper into the throng to attempt a rescue. Jackson had told him he possessed a useful bunch of fives; today he had proved it.

Absently, he rubbed his sore knuckles again, watching as Lady Amber glanced over her shoulder before turning a corner. Had he not known where she lived he would have followed her to find out, as she no doubt feared. But he had discovered something else about the delectable Countess.

That kiss, stolen more to punish her for her instant withdrawal, her refusal to acknowledge their acquaintance—did she still hold him in the disdain which had so diverted him all those years ago?—had been a revelation. Lady Amber's cool looks and charm hid depths of passion he had contrived to stir. Her response had been instinctive, untutored—what the devil had Amber been about all those years?—and had shaken her as much as it had him.

He grinned to himself as she turned not into Berkeley Street but into Clarges Street; and he began to cover the distance to the corner with long, far from languid strides which quickly ate up the distance. He would follow her on her devious route anyway, keeping out of sight, to make certain she met with no more trouble.

He now watched from the corner where Bruton Street entered Berkeley Square, saw her descend the area steps of her house and vowed that, before long, the Dowager Duchess of Amber would become his new mistress. Once, of course, he had dismissed Miss Hermione Green, the pretty little actress who currently occupied the discreet flat he owned in one of the less fashionable areas of London.

When Lexie arrived back she took a last look over her shoulder before descending the area steps but could still see no sign of Lord Stormaston. He did not appear to have followed her, for which she was thankful. She would never be able to face him again if she thought he knew who she was.

She lost no time in going up to her room, passing by the door to the small drawing-room where she had left Mrs Baldwin, on tip toe to avoid being heard. Cousin Caro was bound to notice the state she was in, spot her torn fichu, and she felt in no condition to answer her cousin's questions at the moment. She was still trembling as a result of the assault. Stormaston's kiss could have nothing to do with her state, for she was no green girl who had never been kissed before.

On the other hand, she had never been kissed quite like *that* before, in a such a way as to lead her to kiss him back without meaning to. She blushed at what he must have thought. No delicately brought up young lady would have dreamed. . .

But no delicately brought up young lady would dream of doing half the things she did, she reminded herself. For a start, they would never have defied convention by entering St James's Street, where so many gentlemen of the Town had rooms and where no lady of repute would be seen driving, let alone walking unescorted or masquerading as a servant in the midst of a crowd.

What was a kiss, after all? No more than the rather intimate touching of lips, which, on the rare occasions when a suitor had dared to kiss her in the past, had meant nothing or had filled her with faint distaste. Amber's caresses had been fatherly, warm and affectionate, rather than passionate.

Stormaston's kiss had roused new and untried feelings to swamp her mind and body and render her weak and helpless while it lasted. Even to herself she could not deny that she had enjoyed the experience. But it was never likely to be repeated, thank heavens, for surely if it was he would know it had been she whom he had rescued.

Though, on second thoughts, why should he? All women were the same to a man like him. To him that kiss had been nothing more than a momentary diversion. She need not flatter herself that the effect for him had been as shattering as it had been for her.

She roused herself enough to rise from the blue brocaded cover of her four-poster bed on which she had sunk on entering the room, and crossed to sit before the satinwood kneehole table that served for both dressing and writing to look in its mirror.

She scrutinised her face carefully before deciding that, however much she felt it must, her recent experience did not show. Even her lips, which felt tender to the touch, showed no sign of excessive pressure: they were always full and faintly pink. But she could not sit trembling and staring at herself for ever. She must pull herself together and dress for dinner.

Luckily Chalker returned as she was attempting to divest herself of the old gown. 'Oh, my lady,' she panted, flinging off her bonnet and rushing forward to help her mistress. 'I'm sorry to have been so long, but the crowds were that thick! There now, that's the last hook undone. Will you be taking a bath? Shall I ring for hot water?'

'Yes, I need one.' A slight shudder passed through her as she remembered her ordeal before Stormaston had come to her rescue. Chalker did not know how much she needed to rid herself of the feel of those awful creatures who had molested her. Only Cousin Caro knew she had gone out into the streets alone, though Chalker had wondered at her choosing to dress herself so dismally. 'Did you see the King and the Czar?'

'Oh, yes, my lady!'

As Chalker undressed her, Lexie heard all about her maid's adventures, which it seemed had been far less exciting than her own. By the time she had bathed, dressed, and descended to the drawing-room to await the announcement of dinner, she was able to greet her cousin quite naturally and give an entertaining if expurgated account of her sighting of the King and the Czar.

'And no one recognised you?' demanded Mrs Baldwin anxiously.

'No, Cousin, you need have no fears for my reputation!' Lexie assured her gaily. 'I would not have missed the experience for the world!'

Strangely enough, now she had completely recovered, that pronouncement was true.

If she dreamed of strong arms and gentle, firm lips that night it was, she assured herself next morning, much better than suffering a nightmare involving her attackers.

CHAPTER TWO

NOT belonging to the most exalted ranks of the nobility, Lexie had not received an invitation to the banquet at Carlton House the following evening, given by the Regent in honour of the victorious allied leaders. Instead, she had attended a rout, a poor affair since all the chief exemplars of the *bon ton* were necessarily absent.

At least, she had consoled herself, it saved her from the embarrassment of meeting Lord Stormaston so soon after their encounter. But she would certainly have to endure the sight of him the next evening, at his sister's coming-out ball at Downshire House.

His lordship's brother, Lord Hugo Graham, had been at the rout, but not his sister Fanny. Fanny, Lexie had surmised, could not venture out into Society by herself and the Duchess, like the Marquess, would be at Carlton House. She could have come with me, she had thought with a wry smile, relishing the idea that, as a dowager, she would be considered a suitable chaperon.

The esteem in which Lexie held Lord Hugo was considerably lower than that in which she held the Marquess. For all his gazetted wickedness, Lord Stormaston had an engaging manner that his demeanour only served to enhance.

Green young ladies, flattered and excited by any

attention he showed them, ignored as far as possible the admonitions of mamas and chaperons who were forced to snatch their charges from his dubious company—for to become embroiled with the Marquess of Stormaston would shred a girl's reputation beyond repair.

The mamas would have taken Lord Hugo's attentions to their charges no less seriously but, in fact, found no need to warn the young ladies against him, for they held *him* in abhorrence. For one thing, he was possessed of neither title nor fortune but, crucially, he lacked his brother's aristocratic address, his charm and the natural authority the dangerous Marquess exercised with such ease. He also lacked his looks and taste, thought Lexie, dispassionately eyeing Hugo across the room set aside for the younger set to dance.

One of a group of noisy, extravagantly apparelled young men whose striped waistcoats dazzled the eye and whose extraordinarily high collars prevented their turning their heads, Hugo had his hair brushed up *á la Brutus* and held a quizzing glass to his jaundiced eye while a cynical smile sat uncomfortably on his rather plump features.

Like his face, his figure spoke of excessive indulgence in food and wine. He had a name for attempting to outdo his brother's deplorable reputation, whoring and gambling with reckless abandon. Some went so far as to brand him profligate and depraved.

Yet no one had ever considered Lord Stormaston either profligate or depraved. Disreputable, disgraceful, scandalous, but not depraved. Despite his faults he was well-liked; besides, his ascetic features and athletic build denied the truth of any real descent into depravity.

Whereas Stormaston's popularity could not be denied, his brother's was doubtful even amongst his cronies. They, it was rumoured, tolerated Lord Hugo as a hanger-on rather than because they liked him.

Thank goodness she had no need to acknowledge him, thought Lexie, for although she had recently exchanged cards and visits with his grandmother and sister, he had not been present. And unlike his elder brother, he had not been in Town seven years ago when she had her come-out.

Earl St Clare, an older admirer who was waiting to escort Lexie into the concert room, followed her gaze and shook his head. 'Young fools,' he grunted, 'making such cakes of themselves. There they go, confound 'em, can't think why they had to annoy us with their presence in the first place. Wouldn't receive 'em myself.'

'They are all scions of impeccably noble families,' Lexie reminded the widower drily.

'Should still be ostracised,' grunted his lordship. 'Off to some gambling hell, no doubt, where young Graham will attempt to restore his fortunes.'

'Does he play that deep?' wondered Lexie.

'Pockets to let, last I heard. Depend upon it, someone will have to settle his debts and honour his vowels soon or the world will fall about his ears.'

'That badly fixed, eh?' murmured Lexie as they walked through to take their seats in the music room. 'Surely he has an allowance and the Duke would. . .?'

'Don't want the Duke to know,' she was informed. 'Scared of the old fellow, I gather; besides, it's

Stormaston he wants to annoy. Storm will have to settle his brother's debts if he wants to save the family name from disgrace.'

'I rather thought Lord Stormaston had done quite enough himself to sully the name of Graham—'

'Not badly, never got into a scrape he couldn't get himself out of. His fortune is so vast—'

It was Lexie's turn to interrupt this time. 'That does, of course, colour people's perceptions,' she commented drily, 'but gentlemen have squandered larger fortunes.'

'True, Lady Amber, but Storm never threatened to be such a halfwit as to do anything of the kind.' There was amused affection in his lordship's voice as he ushered Lexie into a seat and sat in the one beside her. 'A little wildness is to be expected in a young man who escapes the bonds of tutor and trustees to find himself master of his own destiny and possessions. There never was any real harm in Storm.'

That had not been the impression Lexie had gained seven years ago. However, since his lordship's own son, Felix, Viscount Dexter, was one of Lord Stormaston's closest friends and every bit as much of a rake, she declined to argue with her partner. She merely remarked, 'But why should Lord Stormaston feel obliged to settle Lord Hugo's debts? Surely it is for the Duke to rescue the family name?'

'Storm was made his guardian you see, until the boy reached his majority.'

'Not the Duke?' queried Lexie, rather surprised.

'No. Young as he was at the time, Stormaston was named guardian to both his younger siblings in his father's will. The Marquess didn't expect to die while his heir was so young, you see.'

'But his son needed a guardian himself!'

'Had trustees instead. The Duke and Duchess and a firm of solicitors. They looked after it all, of course. But once Stormaston reached his majority, Lord Hugo became his problem. Lady Fanny, too. He has to see her settled.'

'I do not envy him,' murmured Lexie.

The musicians struck up at that moment and, since the subject of the conversation was no longer in view, Lord Hugo faded from Lexie's mind. Thoughts of facing Lord Stormaston the next day she found more difficult to banish. To her increasing annoyance she found them disrupting her enjoyment of the evening.

Lexie took great care over her appearance as she dressed for the Downshire ball. It seemed important that she should in no way resemble the dowdy individual Lord Stormaston had rescued from the mob a couple of days earlier.

Eschewing the pastel muslins fashionable amongst the hopeful young ladies enjoying their come-out Season, she had chosen to wear a gown made of jewel-like silk in a shade of emerald that enhanced the colour of her eyes. Over it floated a gauze of a lighter, softer green, ruched and gathered at the hem and decorated with intricate pink and silver embroidery. The low neckline, similarly embroidered, revealed the swell of her breasts, emphasised by the gathering-in of the high waistline. Long matching evening mittens reached above her elbows towards tiny puff sleeves. Diamonds set in filigree silver graced her slender throat.

A circlet of pink silk flowers with silver leaves surrounded the soft, smooth, fair knot arranged on the crown of her head. The use of curling-irons had coaxed the wisps of fine hair about her face into becoming ringlets. Lexie hoped they would retain the curl all the evening but if they did not Chalker would be on hand to restore them.

Chalker put the finishing touches to the coiffure and stood back to admire the effect.

'Thank you, Chalker,' smiled Lexie. 'A touch more powder to cover my freckles, perhaps. That Gowland's lotion does not a scrap of good!'

'You should not have ventured out into the sun the other day without a parasol,' reprimanded Chalker with a smile as she dabbed a puff over Lexie's nose and cheekbones.

'I wore a bonnet,' grumbled Lexie. 'Thank you. You had better bring the powder and curling-irons with you. I fear I may need both before the evening is over.'

She rose and went down to the small drawing-room where Cousin Caro reclined in her favourite position on the *chaise longue*; draperies, which suited her vague manner but not her plump figure, trailing to the floor. She held a piece of neglected needlework in lax fingers.

'Will I do?'

Caro's several chins wobbled as she nodded approval. 'You look fit to be a duchess!' she declared.

'You prefer me looking this way?' teased Lexie,

remembering Cousin Caro's criticism on that other occasion.

'It is as you should look, my dear Alexia. You will be the belle of the ball—'

'No,' denied Lexie quickly, allowing a slight frown to mar the perfection of her brow. For a moment she wished she had not taken so much trouble over her appearance. 'Lady Fanny must be that. She is such a sweet child.'

And how did Lord Stormaston come to have such a delightful sister? she wondered rather sourly. Fanny's excellent if rather unassuming looks were understandable since she was very like him, but her character was altogether more admirable. She would never take advantage— But she would not think of that.

Quelling her unruly thoughts and her consequent attack of nerves, 'You will be all right while I am gone?' she asked her cousin. 'You could have accompanied me, you know.'

'I much prefer to remain here, my dear. Maria Seacombe is coming round once she is free. We shall enjoy a comfortable coze.'

'And exchange all the latest scandal, if I am any judge!' teased Lexie.

Mrs Seacombe was in a similar position to Cousin Caro and the two older ladies had become friends. Neither hankered after the excitement and glitter of the occasions which Lexie adored. They would have found full participation in the social round too exhausting. Only occasionally did Caro encase her plump figure in a fashionable gown, cover her greying hair with a pretty lace cap and take her place amongst the matrons and chaperons to listen to a recital.

The butler knocked and entered to announce the arrival of the carriage.

Lexie nodded. 'Thank you, Dymock. I'll see you tomorrow,' she said, turning to Caro and planting a kiss on her round cheek. 'Not before nuncheon, though!'

Dymock took her cloak from Chalker, who was waiting quietly nearby, and Lexie allowed him to place it around her shoulders. He then led them downstairs and opened the front door for her himself, since the two footmen were both on duty outside with the coach, dressed in the impressive Amber livery of blue and silver, powdered wigs and all. They escorted their mistress to her carriage. Chalker, knowing her place, hurried ahead to squeeze herself into the far corner. One footman helped Lexie to mount and removed the step, the other indicated to the coachman that he could move off. The groom released the horses' heads and both he and the footmen quickly mounted the swaying vehicle as it moved off.

Lady Amber was making a show that evening. And Lady Amber knew that she had taken extra trouble over her appearance and ordered the two footmen in full fig and a groom as well as Jethro Pascoe, the coachman, both wearing black topped by tall hats, to escort her, simply because she wished to impress a certain marquess with the difference between the shabby young woman he had rescued and the wealthy Dowager Countess of Amber. Not, she surmised, that he would see her arrive, he would be too busy inside. But he would be bound to hear the gossip.

She smiled up at Jethro as she descended from the conveyance at Downshire House. Jethro it was who had improved her riding skills and taught her all she knew about driving a curricle. He was, she supposed, in his forties and had gladly left Cornwall to accompany her to London.

'I shall probably be leaving at about two,' she informed him.

'I'll be waiting for your call, my lady,' he assured her, with a dignified inclination of his head. But his eyes twinkled down at her as she stood, illuminated by the last rays of the sun. He was enjoying himself in London, not least because his spirited young mistress was so evidently blossoming into the great lady he had always considered her.

In the busy receiving cloakroom Lexie greeted acquaintances while Chalker removed her cloak, brushed a tiny speck of dust from her silver sandal and tweaked a recalcitrant curl back into position. The ball would probably go on until dawn but she felt fresh and energetic. She anticipated an enjoyable evening and might stay even later than two. In which case Jethro and the other servants had a long wait. But they had their own ways of passing the time.

By now Lexie was used to arriving at this kind of function alone. It did not concern her in the least; she had made no close friend as yet and would rather that than join some party of acquaintances she would feel obliged to remain with all the evening. It left her free to circulate, to sit with anyone she liked between dances. She never lacked for partners and usually became the centre of a throng of gentlemen jostling for her attention. Some considered her a flirt but that did not concern her either.

Lexie was enjoying herself and knew she was not seriously breaking any hearts. Her success did, however, diminish her popularity with some of the hopeful mamas and their charges. Young men who should have been offering for the young ladies' hands sighed instead over the undisputed charms of the flighty Dowager Duchess of Amber.

Slowly, one step at a time, Lexie mounted the marble staircase, moving beneath the glittering chandeliers towards those waiting to receive her. Like most others she had arrived neither early nor late and the queue stretched before and behind her, which meant that the guests were being passed quickly along the receiving line just inside the ballroom.

It was ridiculous to feel so nervous. Lord Stormaston would scarcely look at her. She wished he would not be there but he must be, since he was Lady Fanny's guardian and standing in for his absent grandfather as host.

She knew neither those above nor below her on the stairs and could not therefore enter into conversation with either party. But she had to keep her mind occupied, so she studied the marble of the entrance hall and staircase, the wine-coloured drapes, the gold fringes and tassels, the paintings of august Downshire ancestors, which reminded her uncomfortably of the present heir, and the brilliance of the huge chandeliers.

All this splendour would be his one day. Did he

deserve such an inheritance? The indolent rake of salon, ballroom, card room and gambling hell, in her opinion, did not. Perhaps responsibility would change him.

And then she remembered the strong, athletic, far from indolent gentleman who had snatched her from the hands of two thugs in the middle of what could have turned into a hostile crowd, and wondered. *That* Lord Stormaston had been alert, resourceful, forceful, full of vigour. And, she reminded herself before she forgot, instinctively touching with her folded fan lips which still remembered his kiss, just as loathsomely rakish as his reputation had painted him.

That encounter had spoilt everything for her. She had been enjoying the Season so much. Her come-out, apart from a natural seventeen-year-old's enjoyment of parties and balls, had proved a wretched experience, for the need to secure a husband had been hanging like a threat over her head, with her mother nagging her unmercifully and her father taking little interest in proceedings, just wanting her off his hands with a favourable settlement.

And she had met no one really suitable, certainly no one who had offered for her. She had so hoped to fall in love! Her parents, of course, had scoffed at that idea and reminded her of her duty. So she had accepted Amber.

Dear Amber. He had been the kindest of husbands yet she had never felt able to call him Edward. It would have been like calling her father—even her grandfather—by their given names.

This time she was free to please herself, choose a

husband or not. Of course, she had grown up in the interval and no longer cherished romantic dreams about marriage, but she would not wed simply for the sake of it again. She had security, the will to enjoy life to the full, the flattering attention of many admirers. What more could she want?

Affection, companionship, a family. And why not love? asked a plaintive voice in her head.

She shook it impatiently. Love! Was it love that had made her tremble when Stormaston had kissed her? Certainly not! That had been a purely physical reaction over which she had had no control. Lust, then? She had not believed herself capable of that. Yet that single kiss had stirred her in startling ways, ways the consummation of her marriage never had.

And the memory of it made the thought of coming face to face with the Marquess again unsettling to say the least. For she could not be absolutely sure he had not recognised her. If he had, would he be base enough to mention their encounter? And, she thought ruefully, in future there would be no escaping Lord Hugo, either. Since he was family they were bound to be introduced.

At last she approached the double doors opening into the ballroom. Her turn soon. She kept her eyes firmly fixed on the throng milling beneath yet more grand chandeliers, saw pale gauzes and butterfly colours counterpointed by the darker garb of the gentlemen and enlivened by more scarlet coats than she had ever seen gathered together, except on a parade ground.

The presence of some green coats of the Rifles and blue of the Dragoons confirmed that

Wellington's battered but victorious army was already returning from the Peninsula, although the newly created Duke had himself still to arrive in London.

She was next in line. She settled her gauze scarf more neatly across her forearms, fidgeted with her fan, opened it and snapped it together again. Then she was curtsying before the Duchess who was regal in purple silk despite her tiny size, though the feathers in her headdress added a good foot to her height, and being greeted warmly, even kissed, by a radiant Fanny floating in a cloud of white, and passing on to curtsy formally to a black-clad Lord Stormaston at his most top-lofty and impressive.

He took her hand and bent over it. Lexie had to know. She looked up, trying to catch any gleam of recognition in the blue depths of his eyes.

There was none. His lids drooped, almost obscuring them. 'Enchanted, Lady Amber,' he drawled. 'Delighted to renew our acquaintance...after so many years. Recognised you immediately.'

Lexie inclined her head, lowering her eyes quickly to prevent his seeing the uncertainty in them. Had he really hesitated? Did his words hold a double meaning? 'Thank you, my lord,' she managed to say without allowing her voice to quiver.

'Devilishly sorry to hear of your loss, don't you know.'

'Everyone,' said Lexie, 'has been most kind.'

'Must present my brother.' His lordship waved a limp hand towards a stout figure resplendent in blue satin. Since he could not turn his head because of the height of his collar, Hugo turned from the waist, his quizzing-glass before his eye. 'Lord Hugo Graham. Hugo, may I present Lady Amber. We were introduced years ago—' he lifted a negligent shoulder '—before you came to Town, my dear fellow, and before she became a countess.'

He was, if anything, more languid than ever. Except that, with a speed which denied his lazy air, while she and Hugo were making their devoirs, he had taken her dance card from her nerveless fingers and scribbled his name thereon, using the little pencil attached.

Hugo made an elaborate leg. His plump, moist hand held hers while he uttered some extravagant compliment to which Lexie made an abstracted reply.

'Grandmama is becomin' quite *risqué* in her old age,' Stormaston confided as he returned her property, a slight smile lifting one corner of lips whose touch had had such a devastating effect on her. 'Allowed a couple of waltzes to be included, in honour of the Czar, who is exceptionally fond of the dance. You can waltz, I collect?' His voice held an intolerable undercurrent of boredom as he made the enquiry.

'Of course,' said Lexie as haughtily as she knew how, sweeping past Hugo before the next in line trod on her heels and he, too, demanded her card and stole a dance.

Because the insufferable Marquess *had* stolen a dance. She would never have agreed to stand up with him had he afforded her the chance to refuse. Given five minutes in the ballroom she could have protested her card to be full. It probably would have been, too.

Her hand was shaking—with rage—as she looked down to see where he had written. And then she nearly exploded. He had claimed two dances, both waltzes! One before supper and one much later, in the early hours.

He had never taken the slightest notice of her until tonight. Had kept his distance while even his friend Felix St Clare, Lord Dexter, had often solicited her hand for a dance and spent its duration shamelessly flirting with her, to her amused enjoyment.

Now, suddenly, he was making a spectacle of her. People would begin to talk, for to stand up twice with her, and both of the dances waltzes, must suggest that he was paying her marked attention. And marked attention from the Marquess of Stormaston was undesirable to say the least. She must make her displeasure plain or she would quickly be tarred with the same brush as he!

Quietly seething, she greeted her usual court of admirers as they and others gathered round to initial her card, keeping her smile bright and her voice light, laughing and flirting as she always did, until one youthfully persistent and disappointed suitor voiced his displeasure.

'Divine Lady Amber! How can I bear it? I was countin' on leading you out for a waltz! Storm don't usually dance with you at all, do he?' protested the young man, who had not yet reached his majority, in a rather less dramatic but more truculent tone. 'Doin' it because he's host tonight, I collect, doin' the pretty by his guests. But he oughtn't to waltz with you *twice*! I shall strike his second initial out!'

'No!' Quite why she stopped the Honourable

Oswald Cresswell from inserting his name instead of Stormaston's, Lexie could not have said. To cover her impatient denial—for dancing with Oswald would be more of a trial than with Stormaston and perhaps that was why—she made a joke. 'He might take exception and call you out, and you know his reputation with pistol and blade!'

Oswald paled. He had forgotten the Marquess's superior rank, how high in the instep he could be, how easily he climbed up on his high ropes and, lastly, how much most men feared being called out by him. Oswald considered himself a poetic young man to whom violence was anathema. Courage was not his long suit.

'Well. . .' He hesitated.

'Put your name against this one,' suggested Lexie pacifically. Slender and poetic Oswald might be, but he had clumsy feet and a country dance with him as partner would be much more the thing.

Others were clamouring to claim her hand and Oswald reluctantly gave in, muttering that he could not even claim the supper dance, either, as he passed the card to a young Captain of Hussars.

As Lexie had anticipated, every dance on her card had been initialled long before Lord Stormaston was able to relinquish his post at the door. As the orchestra struck up, he took his sister out to open the ball. Dancing with one's sibling was, of course, considered bad form but when had the Marquess ever considered form? In any case, since he was standing in for their grandparent, all would be forgiven.

Lexie could not help but notice the easy grace with which he executed the steps and bows of the minuet, the proud, fond smile he bestowed on his sister as she curtsied. Flushed and glowing with excitement, Fanny's looks had improved out of all recognition. Her latent attractions had surfaced. She was undoubtedly the belle of this particular ball.

Not long after this a great stir ran around the ballroom and a cheer went up from the younger members of the company. The Czar himself had arrived, together with the elderly Marshal Blücher. Both men, epaulettes and stars gleaming under the candles, were immediately besieged. Fanny's come-out had become a glittering occasion.

Although she danced and laughed and enjoyed herself, chatting with friends between the dances, the prospect of her waltz with Lord Stormaston hung heavily over Lexie's head. As usual, his lordship's social behaviour was impeccable—tonight he was the perfect host. Lord Hugo's loud-mouthed cronies, she noted, were not present. He himself had disappeared to the card room almost immediately.

Most of Stormaston's own friends, however, had been invited. Despite their high spirits and bouts of devilry, which they kept well away from ball or drawing-room, they were welcome guests, gracing any assembly with their exquisite presence and impeccable manners.

Although some had already repaired to the card tables, others remained in the ballroom, Lord Dexter, among them, presumably to lend their friend moral support in the doing of his duty. Dexter had secured the supper dance with her and she quite looked forward to it. She found him an entertaining, relaxing companion. She liked Felix St Clare, despite his dubious reputation, and had no qualms about dancing with him.

For some reason she did not hold him in the same disgust as she had always held Stormaston, perhaps because, being almost as young as herself when first they had met seven years ago, his reputation had still to be earned. While Stormaston, enjoying his freedom after reaching his majority a couple of years earlier, had already managed to make himself notorious and had therefore become a gentleman to be shunned.

Dexter was dancing a cotillion with Fanny at the moment, Lexie noticed, she blushing and confused but looking extraordinarily pretty. It was not unusual for the attentions of such men to cause green girls to colour and simper, but Fanny must know Dexter, since he was her brother's friend. Although perhaps not.

Fanny had only recently come to town and Dexter had no reason to do more than leave a card at Downshire House since Stormaston did not reside there. Lexie wondered, and wondered too whether the Duchess had noticed Fanny's reaction to Lord Dexter's attentions and whether she would be warned against him.

Thank goodness she was free of all the limiting restrictions by which young girls were bound. If Society thought the worse of her for standing up twice with Lord Stormaston, and engaging with him in barely respectable waltzes at that, so be it. Any man she would even consider marrying would account it of no consequence. She would *not* refine over it but enjoy the novelty of being partnered by a gazetted rake. Her pulses quickened with excitement as she prepared to meet the challenge.

The only thing was that, although she had spoken the truth when protesting that she could dance the waltz, it was not the whole truth. She knew the steps, had practised them with a dancing master in her own drawing room, but had never had occasion to use her skill in public, for the waltz had only been introduced to English ballrooms the previous year and was as yet seldom danced, except at Almack's under the strictest of supervision.

Which reminded her that she had not yet received vouchers granting her entry to those august assembly rooms. She must make herself pleasant to the patronesses, she thought, inclining her head and smiling sunnily in the direction of Lady Jersey and Lady Castlereagh, sitting together watching the dancing. Although no doubt it had been Stormaston's idea to include waltzes in the programme, the Duchess had acquiesced, risking the censure of more conservative elements in Society. But then, a duchess of Lady Downshire's standing could afford to.

And Stormaston intended to dance both waltzes with her. Why?

He must surely have recognised her. Well, he said he had, but from years ago. Something had brought about the change in his attitude.

'Thought it about time I ousted that bunch of young sapskulls and fortune hunters who have been throwin' themselves at your feet these last weeks,' he informed her as he led her out on the floor. 'Your reputation to think of, y'know.'

Lexie's pulses beat even faster. So he had noticed

her, despite his keeping his distance, and had offered an explanation for his sudden attention.

'You account it a kindness to dance with me, my lord?' she demanded sweetly. 'Others might think that to partner your lordship—twice—*and* in the waltz—posed a greater threat to my reputation.'

She thought his lips twitched. She could not see his eyes, hidden as they were beneath those drooping lids. Like so many men, he possessed enviably dark, sweeping eyelashes.

'But you don't care a fig for your reputation,' he drawled as he placed a hand on her waist and with the other took hold of one of hers, much to Lexie's hidden agitation. 'Do you, Lady Amber?'

'Of course I do! Every female must!' Her breathlessness was caused entirely by indignation, Lexie knew. It was uncomfortable, just the same, since the music had begun and she had been forced to place her hand on his arm as he swung her into the fast, spinning steps of the waltz. She needed to concentrate on them but could not. He was far too near, although he held their bodies the correct foot apart.

'No lady can afford to lose her reputation!' she asserted firmly. 'That is what is so unfair! A man can do what he likes—well, almost,' she amended as his lordship lifted a sardonic brow. 'Anything short of being caught cheating, anyway—without being cold-shouldered by Society, but a lady— Well!'

'As you say. "Well!"' he mimicked, his face straight, his eyes now regarding her in just the way they had in Piccadilly. 'They would be ostracised. But only should they be *discovered* in their unconventional behaviour. Believe me, my lady,' he whispered in her ear, having bent his head forward the better to do so, 'there are many ladies present tonight whose private lives would not bear close scrutiny.'

Lexie stumbled over his feet. The import of his words, the innuendo behind them, had not been lost on her. Recovering from the shock, she struggled to take up the steps once more. He, of course, was as accomplished in the waltz as in everything else he did and thanks to his expertise and strong lead she had been managing fairly well until momentarily stupefied by what he had said.

Having recovered herself, she glanced up to find his blue eyes watching her confusion with amusement. She glimpsed again the vital, charming gentleman who had rescued and teased her in Piccadilly.

And because the memory brought a rush of pleasure, 'I have no desire to engage in scandal-mongering,' she informed him tartly. 'Your own disreputable behaviour is no secret, my lord. No doubt you are responsible for the dubious if hidden reputation of the ladies of whom you speak—'

'You flatter me, ma'am,' he murmured, whisking her round a corner and twirling and dipping to the strains of the Viennese waltz with the utmost aplomb. 'My tally of conquests is considerably exaggerated. Felix, now—' he glanced across to where his friend was dancing with Fanny again '—has made far more conquests in his shorter life than I in mine.'

'You keep tallies, my lord?' Lexie made her tone honey-sweet. 'No lady, I collect, would be flattered to discover herself upon such a list. Most would assiduously avoid the likelihood of such a fate, were it known.'

He chuckled, deep in his throat. A sound which had a strange effect upon Lexie's nerves. A challenge had been thrown down and accepted. 'We keep no tally, my lady. Our secrets are our own. But one knows one's friends—'

'And discusses one's conquests,' uttered Lexie in deepest disgust.

'Do the ladies not boast of theirs?' he enquired, all innocence.

Lexie blushed. Of course they did, but it wasn't the same thing at all! The ladies only crowed over the number of offers they had received, not. . .

'Ladies do not indulge in seduction!' she declared indignantly.

'No?' he purred, remembering a certain matron who had initiated him, at an early age, into the mysteries and pleasures of sexual adventures. 'You allow your inexperience to show, my dear Lady Amber.'

Lexie compressed her lips and refused to be drawn further. But she knew that a battle of wills had been joined.

He had determined to make her his mistress. He hadn't said so, but she knew it. She suspected that the languid, rakish air he wore when he was not rescuing damsels in distress was probably a mask behind which he hid a more dynamic personality. It was fashionable to appear bored. Perhaps he was. Perhaps that was why—but if so, why did he remain in Society?

Oh, it was of no use trying to decipher the

Marquess of Stormaston's motives! But if she ignored his notable excesses—of which he could probably be cured if she could discover the reason for them—she had to admit that he was, in other respects, a man she could tolerate as a husband. Well born, educated, rich and—she almost blushed at the thought—exciting.

At least, in the absence of any other, he would make a stimulating target at which to aim! The Season promised to become excessively entertaining.

CHAPTER THREE

AFTER the waltz Lexie retired to the room where Chalker waited, ready to fuss over her appearance. A fresh dusting of powder on her nose, a quick twirl of her curls with irons kept hot in the brazier for the purpose, and Lexie was ready to face her partner for the next set. She had not particularly needed Chalker's attention but while her maid worked Lexie had time to recover her composure and plan her next move.

He had, for some reason, decided to seduce her. She had to admit that being pursued by Lord Stormaston was, if nothing else, enlivening. Upon consideration, she decided that she would not set him down. He was, after all, a very rich, personable gentleman.

At seventeen she had not looked beyond his disreputable reputation. At four and twenty, older and wiser, she felt able to form her own judgement. A rich, young, apparently desirable widow, she had an alibi for behaving with less regard for convention than the young virgins on the marriage market.

After all, she had become slightly notorious herself for no good reason that she could see, and so had begun to doubt Society's verdicts. Its rules imposed a strait-jacket no spirited young man or woman could help but rebel against. Young gentlemen were forgiven the sowing of a few wild oats but. . .

She surprised in herself a sudden fellow-feeling for the Marquess. Did his additional sowing of poppies and thistles mask a greater degree of rebellion? It would be pleasing to discover what did, even now, make him indulge in undoubtedly scandalous behaviour. And since Society accepted him, how could it possibly ostracise her simply for enjoying his companionship while in company?

When she danced with him again she would, she decided, seek to engage rather more than his passing fancy. She had to charm and intrigue him into wanting to know *her* rather than simply her body. Friendship was, after all, the best basis for marriage. And if he thought her agreeable to anything less, he had a surprise in store.

Restored in appearance and mind, Lexie returned to the ballroom to find the young Hussar waiting anxiously to lead her into the next set.

Supper was two dances away when a stir at the door announced the arrival of the Prince Regent and his party. The Duchess, the Marquess and Lady Fanny immediately went to greet their royal guest. The honour of His Royal Highness's presence set the seal on the success on Fanny's coming-out ball.

Everyone swept bows and curtsies as, with the Marchioness of Hertford—for whom he had abandoned his morganatic wife Mrs Fitzherbert and his former mistress Lady Jersey—on his arm, the Prince Regent waddled his portly figure the length of the ballroom. Despite the grotesque figure he cut, Lexie could not, as usual, help feeling sorry for him when she remembered his spoilt life.

However much he might imagine otherwise, had

he been allowed to lead his army, he would have been quite out of place on campaign, let alone on a battlefield. She simply could not envisage a man who had always so enjoyed his food and drink and who, reputedly, never rose before noon and then took hours to dress, being at home on some scorching plain or frozen hill top sharing the discomforts of his men. And, she thought, suppressing a chuckle, re-designing every uniform in sight!

Stormaston, though, the attentive host strolling by the Prince's side, would have made a fine officer. The uniform would have shown off his physique admirably and she wondered fleetingly why he had not chosen to escape the confines of English Society by purchasing a pair of colours and following the drum despite his lofty expectations.

Lord Dexter came to claim her hand for the supper dance. He was, she thought, as they executed the steps of the cotillion, rather abstracted. He scarcely attempted to flirt with her at all. But he would be bound to ask her to allow him to escort her to supper and she prayed he would not prove to be dull company tonight. He had been all attention while partnering Lady Fanny.

A sudden suspicion made her remark, 'Lady Fanny looks charming tonight, does she not?' when the steps of the dance allowed.

His brown eyes lit up, serving to confirm her notion. 'Indeed she does, Lady Alexia.'

Lexie had let it be known among those she considered her friends that she would not object to returning to the form of address which had been hers before her marriage. Lord Dexter had quickly asked permission to address her so.

'The Duchess is such a stern chaperon,' he went on, 'that I had not spoken to her before tonight.'

'Did not Lord Stormaston introduce you?'

Dexter grimaced. 'He is as jealous of his sister's reputation as any matron. I do not believe he considers me fit company for so innocent a young lady.'

'He,' said Lexie with asperity, 'should be the last to criticise or condemn! Does he not lead you and others in the paths of iniquity?'

The music stopped and Felix offered her his arm. 'Shall we proceed to supper?' She nodded and placed her hand under his elbow. As they trod through to the supper-room, he continued with the interrupted conversation. 'Indeed, he does lead his friends, and because of that he unfortunately knows all our faults and misdeeds! There is no cozening Storm! He himself will not deal with the young beauties brought to the marriage market.'

'Yet one day you will all need to wed.'

'Ah!' He looked down at her, a wry smile on his lips. He was not as attractive as the Marquess, she considered, yet his features were regular and pleasant, his eyes a warm brown, and his face held a certain strength which those of many of his contemporaries lacked. No wonder his attention had flustered Fanny. 'But even the worst of rakes may reform!'

'Ah, but persuading a prospective bride and her family of such an excellent intention may prove difficult,' teased Lexie, smiling back.

'Would *you* believe me, dear Lady Alexia?' he

asked, and there was more than a hint of seriousness in his voice.

Lexie studied his face for a moment and then nodded. 'I think I would. But you would have to prove it by exhibiting reformed behaviour, my lord!'

Before they had time for more, a familiar voice hailed them.

'Felix! Join our party, will you?'

The Prince Regent was circulating prior to taking his leave. He had other functions to attend that evening and had not been expected to remain long at Downshire House.

'As host I must wait upon His Royal Highness's departure,' explained the Marquess. 'I'll be back in a moment. Fetch supper for Grandmother, there's a good fellow.'

'Delighted,' murmured Felix, his eyes immediately seeking out Fanny, who, absurdly, had been escorted in by Oswald Cresswell.

How that young gentleman had managed to obtain the supper dance with the person in whose honour the ball was being held Lexie could not imagine. Except that it suddenly dawned upon her that Oswald's father, a viscount, was heir to an earldom and a vast fortune which would one day come to Oswald. Did the Duchess—even the Marquess—consider him a suitable match?

Fanny leapt upon the arrival of Lexie and Felix with obvious relief. Lexie sympathised. Oswald was not the most enlivening of companions for all his expectations.

'Lady Alexia!' she cried, blushing prettily. 'How

delightful that you are able to join us! And Lord Dexter, too!'

Felix bowed to the Duchess, who twinkled at her grandson's friend over her fluttering fan.

'Fetch me a glass of wine and something substantial to eat, Dexter. Otherwise I vow I shall swoon for lack of nourishment! I feel that I have not eaten this age, despite the banquet last evening. I declare, at my age I find two such occasions coming so close together quite exhausting.'

She sank back, fanning herself vigorously.

'At your age, ma'am?' smiled Felix. 'I vow you look not a day over thirty.'

'Away with your flummery, sir! I am over seventy and sometimes I feel it! Bring me that refreshment immediately!'

Felix grinned. He clearly knew the Duchess rather well. 'And for you too, Lady Fanny?' he enquired.

'I shall fetch Lady Fanny's supper,' insisted Oswald, not to be set aside even for Lord Dexter.

'Please, do not come to cuffs over me,' pleaded Fanny rather breathlessly. 'I require little to eat and lemonade to drink. Between you, you should be able to manage to bring enough for all of us.'

'Storm can look after himself,' declared Felix. 'But you, Lady Alexia, what may I bring for you?'

Lexie asked for an ice cream and a glass of lemonade, though in truth she would have preferred wine. But to ask for it would only serve to add more shot to the gossips' armoury and she felt they had quite enough already.

As the gentlemen disappeared, Felix heading the slighter Oswald by at least six inches, Lexie asked the Duchess if the previous evening had been a success.

'The Regent put on a magnificent show, splendid food and wine, all his gold plate on the table, thousands of candles, he himself the most affable host, but conversation was petrified. No one knew enough languages, y'see. Then afterwards, the stupid fellow insisted on introducing his mistress to the Czar.'

'Lady Hertford?' prompted Lexie.

'Aye, the ageing grandmother just departin' our door over whom the fool swoons like a love-sick youth! Alexander nodded, but refused to speak to the woman. She curtsied and withdrew in the haughtiest manner. The evenin' was doomed from that moment on.'

'How unfortunate,' murmured Lexie.

Before she could probe further into the previous evening's disasters someone else engaged the Duchess in conversation.

Fanny remarked, 'It is such a pity we did not know of the Regent's banquet until long after the date for my ball was fixed, but I do hope you are enjoying it. Do you think it a success?'

'Undoubtedly,' responded Lexie. 'What more could you wish for, having received both the Czar's and the Regent's blessings on the occasion? Not only is the ball a success but you have taken in Society, believe me. You are looking so charming tonight that it is small wonder the gentlemen are falling over themselves to serve you!'

'Do you think so?' Fanny fluttered her fan to hide

her nervous agitation. 'I know I do not normally impress gentlemen, not as you do, dear Lady Alexia.'

'Only because you needed to gain in self-confidence. If you do not possess it after tonight, then I hold out no hope for you!'

Fanny laughed, as she was meant to. 'You do me so much good, Lady Alexia, I wish we had met before! I must admit I have never felt so confident in my appearance. Do you not admire my gown?'

At this point the Duchess rejoined their conversation and, having heard Fanny's question, 'I should hope she does!' she declared. 'After all the trouble Madame Aristide went to to design and make it exactly right!'

'Indeed, Your Grace, Madame Aristide has excelled herself,' confirmed Lexie. 'White was exactly the colour to throw up Lady Fanny's excellent complexion and the darkness of her hair.'

'I feel a little like a snow queen,' muttered Fanny, still not absolutely certain of the rightness of the choice, having held a preference for pink herself.

'And what is wrong with that, eh?' demanded her grandmother, nodding her plumes. 'Pity there ain't any eligible princes about to make a real queen of you one day!'

'There are the young Prussian princes,' murmured Lexie naughtily.

The Duchess snorted, her eyes twinkling, but before she could reply their refreshments arrived and in the confusion of sorting out plates and glasses and then sampling what the gentlemen had brought, the conversation died.

Before long Lord Stormaston rejoined them,

apparently eating nothing but carrying a glass of claret.

The Duchess bestowed a fond smile upon her grandson.

'The Regent has departed, James?'

'He has,' Stormaston confirmed, taking the chair between Lexie and Fanny which Oswald had just vacated in order to fetch another glass of lemonade for Fanny. 'Sent his congratulations on a splendid evenin'.'

He turned his lazy smile on Lexie, who felt quite hemmed in by gentlemen of dubious reputation and great charm but rose to the occasion by exhibiting her not inconsiderable wit and fascination, directing the latter at Lord Dexter until she caught Fanny's hurt eyes fixed upon her.

She did not imagine that Fanny's *tendre* for Felix St Clare would last, but had no desire to be accused of entering into competition for his favours, so she turned most of her attention to Stormaston instead. After all, he was the one she wanted to ensnare and he did not seem in the least averse to being enchanted.

On his return with Fanny's refreshment Oswald scowled as he seated himself between Felix and the Duchess instead of Fanny and Lexie. Lexie could tell he was considerably put out: first Stormaston had stolen both the waltzes and now he had had the gall to take his seat!

'How is your mama?' the Duchess demanded of him. 'A great pity she is indisposed and unable to come tonight, is it not Fanny?' she said, turning to the girl, who was seated on her other side.

Fanny murmured, 'Indeed it is, Grandmama.'

'And your father, of course, never appears in Society.'

Oswald flushed, an embarrassment to which he was prone. 'M-mama sent her most s-sincere r-regrets, Your Grace. She has ate somethin' disagreeable, I f-fear.'

'Pity. I would have enjoyed a coze with her. Tell her so, young man.'

'C-certainly, Your Grace.' Oswald inclined his head in acquiescence.

Poor Oswald! The Duchess's attention had reduced him to a stuttering idiot, thought Lexie compassionately, seeing the despairing look he sent across the Duchess to Fanny, who gave the faintest of shrugs in return.

Lexie became convinced that the Duchess did have hopes of a match between the young people. But she was too engaged in parrying the attentions of both Dexter and Stormaston to give the matter much heed. Fanny, she felt certain, would not be forced into a match which was not to her liking. Meanwhile the Marquess, despite his grandmother's close presence, was passing the most audacious remarks.

'Ice cream and lemonade do not suit your temperament, my lady,' he murmured. 'They are not for one so full of fire and spirit.'

Lexie fluttered her fan and batted her eyelashes. Her heart had begun to thud in earnest. Would he admit that he knew they had met before? 'But how can you judge, my lord, after so short an acquaintance?'

'Ah!' His smile ravished her and she felt the heat

begin to mount in her veins. If only the ice cream were capable of quenching it! 'I can read it in your lovely green eyes, my dear,' he murmured. Felix had leant forward to speak to Fanny. No one could hear what they said above the general hubbub. 'They dance and sparkle, but in their depths I see promise—'

'Promise?' How she kept her voice cool and teasing Lexie did not know. But she must play her part in this charade. 'You mistake, my lord. I promise nothing.'

'Do you not, Lady Amber? I wonder.' And as he held her chair for her to rise, the Marquess drawled, 'Until our next dance, Lady Alexia.'

The caressing tone of his voice, the wicked look in his eyes, warned her that he indeed thought her manner an indication that she was acquiescing to his seduction. She smiled back, flirting her fan as she did so.

'I cannot wait, my lord,' she murmured, adding silently to herself, 'To return home.' For at that moment she changed her mind. She would plead a headache and leave before she was forced into the Marquess's arms again. She feared that too much of such intimate contact with Lord Stormaston might test her resolution beyond its limits.

Lexie was not afraid of him, but of his strange effect upon her senses. She had never known its like. Merely sitting next to him was almost a torture. She felt so drawn to him that if she was to achieve her end at the expense of his, she must keep him at arm's length meanwhile.

She danced as spiritedly as ever during the next

hour or two, a little knot of excitement gathering in the pit of her stomach as she thought of the battle to come, a mere glimpse of Stormaston across the room sending her pulses leaping. But as the time of the waltz approached she sent a footman to fetch Chalker and another to call Jethro, and made her adieus to the Duchess and Fanny. Luckily his lordship was occupied elsewhere, entertaining the Czar.

'Dear Lady Alexia, are you not feeling well?' asked Fanny. 'Or is it that you find the ball tedious after all!'

'I do not find your ball remotely tedious, Lady Fanny, it is the most famous occasion I have yet attended. But I must confess to having developed a most lowering headache,' Lexie went on, crossing her fingers behind her fluttering fan. 'The heat, I think, and the excitement. . .'

'You will call upon us,' instructed the Duchess imperiously, setting the seal on Lexie's acceptance into Society despite any scandal circulating, and even after watching her flirt with Dexter and her grandson. The words were accompanied with a gracious smile. Stormaston had inherited her eyes, recognised Lexie, and much of her aristocratic looks and manner. Fanny had most of the looks but had not yet developed the manner. Perhaps she never would.

Fanny excused herself as her next partner came to claim her hand for a dance. The Duchess watched her granddaughter's retreating back as she went on, 'We shall be at home on Monday, but no doubt we may meet you before that, in the park on Sunday. I believe all the visiting dignitaries intend to join us in our normal parade.'

'Indeed, Your Grace, I shall be there as usual. And I shall be delighted to call on Monday.'

'Good. And I will send you an invitation to my drum early in July, when I hope the Duke of Wellington will be in London and able to honour us with his presence.'

'I should be thrilled to meet the Duke, Your Grace,' murmured Lexie, curtsying respectfully. 'I should like that above everything.'

The Duchess nodded. 'This promises to be a gala summer. You'll be good for Fanny. She needs bringing out. I wish you a speedy recovery, Lady Amber.'

'Your Grace is very kind.' This was not the moment to suffer from either surprise or guilt. Lexie looked up into the eyes which reminded her so much of those others and said, 'Please convey my apologies to Lord Stormaston. I fear that I really could not endure long enough to dance with him again. As for my other partners—'

'They will soon find others to take your place, though perhaps not ones so pleasing to them as you would be. James was to dance with 'ee again, eh? Serve the young reprobate right to be stood up for once.'

The elderly woman's eyes were twinkling again. Lexie suspected that the Duchess was not deceived by her excuse to leave yet, staggeringly, seemed not to think any the worse of her for refusing to fall in with her grandson's whim, and had actually indicated that she approved of a friendship between her and Fanny. Lexie could scarcely credit her good fortune.

As the carriage trundled the short distance back to Bruton Street she mused on that first waltz with the

Marquess and found herself regretting the loss of the second. Half asleep, she was dreaming of twirling in Stormaston's arms as the footman opened the door and pulled out the step. Perhaps it was as well the dream had been interrupted, she thought wryly, as she mounted the stairs to her bedroom. Dreams had a tendency to wander into forbidden realms.

Caro would be in bed, thank goodness. By morning she would be calm enough to give her cousin a composed and edited account of the ball.

This she did over a late breakfast. Caro chuckled over her description of poor Oswald's frustrations and discomfort, poured herself another cup of chocolate and spread thick butter on a slice of fresh white bread.

'I met the Duchess once,' she remembered. 'Before poor Mr Baldwin died.' For a moment she faltered, the ready tears springing to her eyes, but then she pulled herself together and went on, though her voice quivered rather more than usual. 'Astonishing woman. Can put the fear of the Lord into better gentlemen than Mr Cresswell if she has a mind. High in the instep, sets a person down without mercy if needs be, yet can be as charming as you like. I collect she has taken to you, Cousin.'

'Perhaps.' Lexie was at a loss to know quite why the Duchess had been so gracious to her. There were, after all, many other young matrons she could have chosen to favour on Fanny's behalf. Possibly Fanny herself had had something to do with it, having shown such a frank willingness to treat her as a friend. But however it had come about, it seemed she was destined to become intimate with the Marquess's sister. She sipped her chocolate thoughtfully.

'I think she would like Oswald and Fanny to make a match of it. But Oswald fancies himself in love with me and Fanny with Lord Dexter.'

'Young people these days!' sighed Caro. 'In my day one wed the person one's parents or guardians chose without giving anyone else a thought.'

'In my day, too,' said Lexie wryly. Though not entirely without silent mutiny.

Breakfast was scarcely finished when a footman announced the arrival of the Marquess of Stormaston, who trusted that her ladyship was at home.

Lexie swallowed, tempted to say she was still indisposed or not at home. But she had to face his lordship sooner or later.

'Show him into the morning-room. Inform his lordship that I shall join him directly.'

She had donned a small cap that morning rather than have her hair dressed in a more elaborate style, intending to spend the morning writing letters. But her blue sprigged muslin gown looked well enough and the cap quite becoming.

'Fancy Lord Stormaston calling!' exclaimed Cousin Caro breathlessly. 'Whatever can have brought him here?'

Lexie had most carefully omitted all allusion to the Marquess from her adventures on the day the Allied Sovereigns had arrived, and done no more than casually mention his name in the list of gentlemen with whom she had danced the previous evening. Displaying an insouciance she was far from feeling, she turned from the mirror.

'I cannot imagine,' she retorted. 'Come, Cousin. I am certain you will wish to meet his lordship and I would prefer not to entertain him alone. His reputation runs before him.'

'Well, if you think so. . .you do not usually require my presence. . .'

'But this morning I do. You have no objection, I trust?'

'No, none! You are showing just that discretion I have been advising.' Caro rose to her feet, tweaked her skirts into place and carefully arranged a silk scarf with a long gold fringe about her shoulders. 'But all the same, it is unlike you to require a chaperon. Did you take him in dislike when you danced with him?'

'Oh no, but I would not trust his lordship a foot further than I could throw him. He regards widows as fair game, I collect.'

'Yet you will receive him?' cried Caro, aghast.

'Why not? Others do, and he cannot harm me while you are present. And he has most engaging manners. You will enjoy meeting him and find him quite charming, I am assured.'

Caro shot her cousin a shrewd glance, for Lexie had been unable to prevent a thread of excitement from entering her voice. He had called! To what end? She had not expected him to make his next move quite so soon.

Half a head taller than her companion, slender and exquisite, Lady Amber—Alexia—entered the morning-room slightly ahead of a much older woman of plump and flushed appearance, who tugged nervously at a length of fringed silk trailing from her shoulders rather than look him in the face.

To the Marquess, rising courteously to make his devoirs, the other woman might not have existed. He wished she did not. Did Alexia consider him a fool, to be taken in by her evasions?

He had hoped to have a private exchange with Alexia—he savoured the sound of her name in his mind—for beneath the languid air which he donned like a cloak whenever he wished—although his wild days were long over it suited him to cherish the reputation they had earned him—lay a prodigious volume of annoyance, made the more bitter because she appeared to be in the full bloom of her health this morning. And quite irresistibly desirable.

'Ladies.' He made his bow and suffered the introduction to Mrs Charles Baldwin, Lady Amber's late husband's cousin, Caroline. He wished the faintly ineffectual and disapproving Cousin Caroline to the devil. However, the knowledge that Alexia felt she needed a buffer between them gave him an odd feeling of satisfaction. He had not been wrong. Mutual desire did exist. Why else should she fear being alone with him?

And why else had she fled the ball before their second waltz? Memory of his sharp sense of loss and frustration on discovering her defection brought back the full force of his anger.

The ladies sat on a settee and he subsided back into the small, rather uncomfortable armchair from which he had risen.

'I trust you are quite recovered from your... indisposition, Lady Amber?' he enquired. 'You appear to be in splendid health this morning, what?'

Beneath the drawl Lexie detected the cutting edge in his voice and under his usual exquisitely lazy manner she sensed suppressed anger. He had disliked her leaving the ball before their waltz, then. She had, of course, known that he would.

'I am completely recovered, I thank you,' she returned, smiling, sitting quite at her ease. Caro was looking at her in an odd manner. Lexie had not told her cousin that she had left the ball pleading a headache. At the time it had seemed no more necessary than mentioning the Marquess other than in passing. But Caro, for all her *distraite* manner, was no fool. Lexie could foresee a need for uncomfortable explanations later. 'It is kind of you to trouble to enquire.'

'Not at all.' He waved aside any thought of thanks. 'I promised my grandmother and sister that I would call since they could not. They will be relieved to hear that you have made such a remarkably swift recovery.'

The anger was still there. Lexie doubted whether his explanation represented the full truth of the matter even if the Duchess and Fanny did know he intended to call. He had come because he wanted to set her down, but Caro's presence had foiled his intentions.

'It was only a headache, my lord, brought on by the heat and the stuffy atmosphere, I collect. The chandeliers give a brilliant light but the burning candles only add to the heat and their smoke combines with the presence of so many people engaged in energetic exercise to make the air thick. Once outside my headache soon evaporated.'

'Had I known, it would have given me great pleasure to escort you to the terrace for air,' purred his lordship. 'You had only to wait a few more moments for our waltz.'

'I had no wish to rob your lordship of the enjoyment of the dance,' said Lexie ingenuously, her hands folded demurely in her lap. 'You waltz so exquisitely and with such enthusiasm, while I am but an indifferent performer.'

'Did your lessons not serve, my love?' murmured Caro, glancing furtively from one to the other.

'Lady Amber has no need to fear lack of expertise, ma'am. She has the steps perfectly.'

Lexie shot Caro a repressive glance. 'But the concentration required of me quite spoils my enjoyment at present. When I left you were engaged in conversation with the Czar. I did not feel it necessary to interrupt.'

Storm inclined his head. She was clever, but she should not escape him. 'Since you appreciate fresh air, will you ride with me round the Ring in Hyde Park on Sunday afternoon? You would, perhaps, feel safer in the crush which is bound to prevail since our victorious guests are to show themselves, if you are accompanied by someone capable of defending your person.'

Wretched man! Reminding her of that other time again! Yet still not admitting that he had recognised her! One day she would find the moment to challenge him on the point. But not now.

'I regret, my lord, that I shall be unable to do so. I have already agreed to drive Cousin Caro so that she may catch a glimpse of the Sovereigns and our other important visitors,' lied Lexie.

Storm saw the startled and then agonised expression on Mrs Baldwin's face and smiled.

'If that is indeed Mrs Baldwin's wish then I shall be delighted to drive you both in my landau. The crush is bound to be considerable but I shall take every care to avoid disaster.'

Caro opened and closed her mouth but no sound came. She did, however, manage to clutch at Lexie's arm.

Lexie closed her eyes for an instant. How could she be so cruel? She knew perfectly well how much Caro feared crowds and crushes. Caro would never bring herself to set foot in a carriage destined to take part in such an outing. And Stormaston, the rogue, was playing upon Caro's undisguised fears.

'You dislike the idea of such an expedition?' he enquired solicitously. 'If so, and will entrust your charge to my care, I guarantee to return her to you perfectly safe. I am certain that Lady Amber would scorn to miss the occasion.'

'I shall accompany her, of course,' began Caro faintly, finding her voice at last and screwing up her courage only to be interrupted by a furious Lexie.

'I am not in Cousin Caro's charge,' she gritted.

'No, my love,' murmured Caro, 'but I do pray you not to venture out alone as you—'

Lexie cut her off sharply. She wanted no references to previous occasions! 'I should be perfectly safe, I assure you, but if it would calm your mind,

Cousin, then I will agree to ride with Lord Stormaston.'

Storm stood up and bowed, his mission accomplished. 'We could drive should you prefer—' he began.

But Lexie was in no mood to vacillate. 'You asked me to ride, my lord, no doubt having already ascertained my preference in the matter. I am happy to accept your escort.'

'Then I shall wait upon you on Sunday, Lady Amber.'

Lexie remembered that she wished to charm the man into matrimony. She smiled her most bewitching smile.

'I shall look forward to it.'

'And will not, I trust, suffer from another indisposition?'

'I am normally extremely healthy, my lord.'

'That is what I thought.'

CHAPTER FOUR

STORMASTON took his leave. A relieved Mrs Baldwin eyed her young cousin suspiciously.

'I did not realise you were so well acquainted with his lordship, Alexia. You will take care, will you not? His reputation. . .'

'Is perfectly well known to me, Cousin. I am no foolish chit, I am entirely aware of what I am doing. Simply because I engage to ride with his lordship does not mean that I intend to succumb to his blandishments.'

'I should hope not!' cried Caro faintly. 'Alexia my dear, you cannot risk your own reputation. . .'

Lexie sprang to her feet and began to pace the turkey carpet, irritated with Caro for putting her own doubts into words. 'Why not? He is the most eligible gentleman in town.' She spread her hands. 'All the mama's would be hanging out for him for their daughters were it not for his reputation, and even so some of the less scrupulous disregard it. I, on the other hand, am free to do as I like!'

She had no wish to invite keener opposition by exposing her real intention to her cousin. Besides, Caro might gossip, and if word of her purpose were to reach Stormaston's ears, Lexie must fail. She came to a halt before the settee and addressed her cousin with great seriousness.

'But, Cousin Caro, I enjoin you not not to gossip

about my dealings with his lordship. Promise me, not a word to Mrs Seacombe or anyone else. I should not like to become an exhibition.'

'Oh, no! My lips are sealed! But others will talk, my dear. He is certainly an exceptionally fine-looking gentleman. Handsome—elegant—' Caro's flushed face became a deeper shade of pink '—and he must be most attractive to a young woman such as yourself, despite his indolent, affected manner—'

'Which I believe to be an affectation, Cousin.'

'Well, yes, it must always be, I collect. No one could be born with it except perhaps the most vacuous of creatures, which I am persuaded his lordship is not. But you are so impetuous, my love! There must be other eligible gentlemen who would make more suitable escorts.'

'None that I have so far met,' declared Lexie firmly. 'I shall not discourage his admiration, for I have found no other gentleman at present in Town able to offer such agreeable company.'

This was true, for although Lord Dexter amused her considerably, he was inclined to admire Lady Fanny, who cherished a *tendre* for her brother's disreputable friend. And Stormaston himself possessed a remarkably compelling personality he shared with no other. She already had a reputation for flouting convention in other ways so she might just as well outrage the *ton* still further by flirting with someone whose activities they loved to denounce.

Caro shook her head in helpless acknowledgement of her inability to dissuade her wayward cousin, and sighed. 'If you are determined on it I must advise you to be cautious, my dear Alexia. Some gentlemen are not always honourable in their dealings and the Marquess. . .well, you have said yourself that his reputation is of the worst kind.'

Lexie laughed. 'I believe I can handle the Marquess, Cousin Caro. Forewarned is forearmed, is it not? I shall behave with the utmost discretion. You need not fear for me on Sunday, for I intend to take a groom right into the Park with me instead of leaving him at the gate as is my normal practice. His lordship will not, perhaps, expect that, having seen me riding alone in the morning. I was used to do so all the time in Cornwall and I find the slow company of a groom tedious when I desire to gallop.'

Cousin Caro gave another faint cry of protest. 'It is so unladylike to gallop!'

Lexie chuckled. 'I know, dear Cousin! But I cannot give up every pleasure simply to please the stuffy dames who lead Society! But I do take a tiger up behind when I drive my curricle about Town.'

'You make such a spectacle of yourself, my dear Alexia! And a deal of use that lad Jeffs would be in an emergency, except to hold the horses! And to think I imagined you were learning discretion at last! But I must allow that Lord Stormaston seemed a most agreeable young man,' Caro admitted rather wistfully. 'I wonder he is not yet wed.'

Lexie chuckled. 'Because he is determined not to become leg-shackled, I dare say. He enjoys his bachelor freedom too much. Wish you were a few years younger, Cousin?'

'Well, if I were, I must confess I might be tempted. . .' Mrs Baldwin flushed and smiled rather guiltily. 'But I never had the chance to fix the interest of so fine-looking a man, even as a flirt.'

'I do consider myself fortunate,' admitted Lexie with another chuckle. 'I did not anticipate enjoying myself half as much as I believe I shall!'

Crowds already jammed the streets when Lord Stormaston presented himself in Bruton Street the next day to find Lexie waiting, dressed in a splendid leaf-green costume and with a saucy bejewelled and feathered hat perched firmly on her head. Her magnificent chestnut gelding stood at the door.

From her parlour window Lexie saw him arrive astride an expensive grey stallion, a superb figure in an exquisitely cut snuff-coloured jacket, buff pantaloons and shining hessians. Her nerves tightened in anticipation. She could scarcely have wished for a more impressive escort.

Caro, who had been watching with her, exclaimed over the perfection of his lordship's appearance and retired to her *chaise longue*, where she carefully arranged her draperies ready to receive him.

'Do take care,' she admonished after he had been shown up and made his bow. 'Such crowds! I wonder that anyone should venture forth.'

'There are thousands waiting in Piccadilly outside the Pulteney Hotel to catch a glimpse of Czar Alexander,' Stormaston agreed, offering Lexie his arm. 'We will take all care, ma'am, never fear.' To Lexie, as they descended the stairs, he remarked, 'We had best avoid passing that way.'

'I know,' said Lexie, 'they are there every day, I have seen them.'

'Of course, you must have,' he responded gravely as he offered her a lift to mount. But, meeting his eyes for a brief moment as she placed her foot in his clasped hands, Lexie became aware of amusement lurking in their depths.

Regretting her rash remark, she took refuge in settling herself in her saddle but soon, edging her horse along Mount Street to Tyburn Lane and the Grosvenor Gate into Hyde Park through the throng of carriages, carts and pedestrians, she forgot her discomfort in the excitement of the moment.

'The people have gone mad over him.' Stormaston took up the conversation again as he walked his horse at her side. 'It seems all London will gather in the Park this afternoon to watch him parade with the leaders of the other Allied countries.'

'I must confess that I myself am agog,' Lexie told him. 'I long to see Marshal Blücher and Prince Metternich.'

He smiled. 'I conceived that you might be.'

Jethro Pascoe had insisted on accompanying Lexie himself that afternoon instead of Jeffs and he rode ahead, clearing the way, making certain no pedestrian got trampled underfoot. In the Park itself chaos reigned. Storm and Lexie joined the splendid cavalcade of silk, gold lace, splendid carriages and glossy horses being ridden or driven there, only to discover that their part in the assembly was less to see than to be seen and cheered.

The Master of the Horse, wearing his garter ribbon, led the official parade, comprising the carriages carrying all the important visitors together with their escorts.

'All I can see,' grumbled Lexie as they trotted with other equestrians round the Ring in their wake, 'is Alexander's bodyguard, or at least their waving plumes and the flash of their cuirasses in the sun.'

'A pity, I agree,' murmured Storm, smiling down on the eager, lively face beneath the amazing thing she wore on her golden curls. 'But I would not have missed the occasion for the world.'

'Oh, nor would I! Look, everyone is following the Sovereigns towards the private gates into Kensington Gardens!'

'Then so shall we, if you wish it?'

'Why not?' said Lexie.

But she had not realised that the mass of riders, almost all men, many in uniform, would urge their mounts into a gallop, fan out to overtake the carriages and surge towards the bridge across the Serpentine. Their progress developed into a disorganised charge and, caught up in the middle of it, Lexie needed all her skill to remain in her saddle, even with Storm protecting her on one side and Pascoe on the other.

As they pounded over the narrow bridge Pascoe gave a sharp cry and Lexie turned her head anxiously to see his boot fly into the air, torn off by the impact of another rider barging into him. But he quickly recovered his stirrup and kept his place beside Lexie while Storm pressed close on her other side, their knees clashing from time to time. Lexie was too occupied in controlling her horse to do more than vaguely register a familiar tingle in her nerves.

Now they had crossed the bridge she must avoid being pushed against a tree, or, worse, crushing a pedestrian against one, as was happening to a woman screaming just ahead, as a wild-looking animal butted into her, its rider quite out of control. And surely that was the Master of the Horse scrambling to his feet after having been thrown to the ground!

'We must extricate ourselves from this,' called Storm, his voice grim. Without further ado he took hold of Lexie's bridle and edged his own mount towards the grass, pulling the chestnut with him.

Lexie's lips compressed in annoyance—did he think her incapable?—but she merely murmured 'Steady, Danny,' soothing the animal, whose staring eyes and flattened ears bore witness to its agitation. And somehow Storm manoeuvred both horses out of the throng without getting them pinned against a tree or trampling any sightseers.

Once free of the mass of riders and halted on a comparatively uncrowded stretch of grass Lexie dismounted, the better to soothe Danny. Storm swung out of his saddle and laughed a reckless, joyful laugh which set her nerves tingling afresh.

'You did not need my aid to dismount, I perceive!' he observed, taking her reins from her grasp.

'No, my lord, and neither did I need your help to escape the throng,' retorted Lexie with spirit. 'But we have lost Pascoe, and he is without one of his boots!'

'Is he, indeed! I dare swear he is not the only one to have accoutrements dragged off in that stampede! But it seems he could not escape with us. No doubt he is now before Kensington Palace with all the other sightseers! Do not concern yourself, Lady

Amber, your groom is well able to take care of himself, he will come to no harm.'

'I hope you are right,' said Lexie, her anxiety for Pascoe turning to wry amusement that, for all her care, she was now alone with Stormaston. If you could call being in the midst of a seething mass of people in Kensington Gardens alone!

Standing at the heads of their horses beneath a spreading tree they were, however, screened from most of the people still attempting to catch a glimpse of anyone of consequence who might be passing. If they themselves were the focus of a few inquisitive stares this did not seem to concern the Marquess.

'But if you will not admit to needing rescue,' he went on, 'I cannot claim a reward.'

Lexie thought she might suffocate, for the breath stopped in her throat. 'Indeed you may not, my lord!' she managed, sharply if a trifle faintly.

'A disappointment, I must confess. A kiss would have been a fitting end to our adventure.'

His tone of mock affront brought the colour flooding to Lexie's face. He knew! She had suspected as much from the first. Odious man!

'No such thing!' she exclaimed. 'And I collect that you perceived all along that it was I you rescued from the throng in Piccadilly that day! You behaved abominably, treating me as you would a servant! Why did you pretend not to recognise me?'

'You seemed to prefer to remain incognito, my dear Lady Amber. Who was I to force you to admit your identity?'

'Do not play the innocent with me, Lord

Stormaston! You did it for your own amusement and have been laughing at me ever since!'

'You do me an injustice, Alexia. . .Lexie.' His pained voice yet held a thread of laughter in it but very little drawl. 'Since you were masquerading as a lady's maid I felt justified in treating you as such.'

Lexie, uncomfortably aware that she had left herself open to rough usage by her rash behaviour, took refuge in indignation. 'I have not given you permission to address me so, my lord!'

He grinned unrepentantly. 'No, you have not, my delightful child. I have taken the liberty upon myself. And I wish you would call me James. If we are to be intimate—'

Lexie suddenly relaxed. He was teasing, flirting with her. Two could play at that game. 'Are we to become intimate, Storm? Despite your thinking me a child?' she purred. She could not possibly call him James, not yet, not while she still felt so at odds with him. She hoped he would accept the compromise.

'Hmm,' he mused, 'At least that is an advance on "my lord". One day, though, I swear you will call me James. For although you may occasionally harbour childish notions, in every other respect you are a most captivating woman. We shall become intimate, you know.'

She tapped his arm with her riding crop in mock admonition. 'You presume too much, my dear Storm. However, I am not averse to your pursuit, it will enliven what might otherwise become a tedious round of pleasure—'

'Tedious, with all the pageantry we are promised, the balls, the galas, the dinners to be attended, the museums, the galleries, the theatres and the opera to be visited? You amaze me, Lexie.'

'But lacking an escort. . .' She allowed the sentence to trail off, looking down in what she hoped appeared to be demure confusion.

Storm was not deceived. He scented victory and plunged headlong into the final stage of the chase. 'Then I must offer mine, my dear Lexie. I cannot have you languishing, bored, during such a joyous, triumphant summer as this!'

'Your escort, Storm?' Lexie, having achieved her purpose, lifted her eyes to his wickedly smiling face then quickly lowered her lashes, suddenly, inexplicably, shy. 'But my reputation. . .' she managed to murmur, achieving without difficulty just the right tone of uncertainty.

'In public I shall behave with the utmost propriety,' he promised, amusement still lurking in his voice. 'I can, you know.'

'Yes,' acknowledged Lexie. 'You reserve your most scandalous behaviour for gaming hells, mills, cockfights, curricle races and boudoirs, I am informed. You played the perfect host at your sister's come-out. Apart from your stealing of my two waltzes.'

'From that accusation I beg to be absolved,' he protested mildly. 'I stole nothing. I was perfectly at liberty to engage for any dances I chose.'

'But why?' demanded Lexie, and then, as the blue eyes swept her features and the grin spread widely over his face, wished she had not.

'Because, my dear Lexie, I desired to enjoy your delightful company and hoped to taste your delicious lips again. Had you remained for our second engagement. . .but you did not.'

His gaze narrowed and for an instant Lexie sensed again his anger at her defection. But almost instantly the smile was back in place and he murmured, 'Do you know, I believe we are private enough here for me to claim both vengeance and reward—'

'No!' gasped Lexie, stepping back and coming up against the trunk of the tree. 'No, Storm, indeed you must not. Look,' she cried in desperate relief. 'Here come your brother and his friends.'

Storm glanced idly over his shoulder to the carriage-way leading to Kensington Palace. The procession had long since passed on and people were beginning to straggle back. 'So they do. But do not think you have escaped, Lexie, my dear. I shall claim what I am owed, never fear.'

Hugo and his cohorts reined in. Hugo left the path to halt his horse beside them.

'I thought it was you I saw in the mêlée, brother.' He eyed Lexie speculatively and made an elaborate sweep of greeting, though without dismounting. 'When you disappeared I thought you might have come a cropper,' he added unpleasantly.

'I regret to cause you disappointment, but no such luck, brother,' drawled Storm, all his languid airs back in place. 'I merely escorted Lady Amber from what had become a dangerous game with little point to it.'

'Dashed fine run, though a deuced stupid fuss everyone is makin' over these creatures. Demmed if I can see why.'

'Mind your language, if you please, brother! Or had you forgotten the presence of a lady?'

Storm's sharp reprimand startled Hugo but he smiled, none too amiably. 'Forgive me, Lady Amber. I am not used to finding Storm alone in the company of a *lady*.'

'Were you not my brother I would call you out for that,' remarked Storm, his lazy mantle back in place. 'But perhaps not.' He shrugged dismissively. 'Such a slur from you would scarcely warrant the effort.'

Lexie, though, could see his eyes, cold blue steel, the way his jaw clenched, moving the thin line of the scar across his cheek, the whitened knuckles of the fist clenched about the reins of their horses. She thought she had never seen him look more dangerous.

Hugo's red face whitened. He wheeled his horse and rode off, his companions following after. He, too, had glimpsed the fury hidden beneath that careless exterior. And was afraid of his brother's wrath.

'You do not like him,' said Lexie without thinking.

'On the contrary,' disclaimed Storm. 'I like him well enough when he is not behavin' like an ass. But he resents bein' a penniless younger son, you know. Liked it even less when I was his guardian and still hates havin' to rely on me for an allowance.'

'Has he no money of his own?'

Storm shook his head. 'He will inherit a competence from the Duchess when she dies but not enough to live on in the expensive way he expects. He needs to marry a fortune.'

'But the mamas will not give him countenance.'

'Rather less than they give me,' agreed Storm with

his wicked grin. 'But come, Lexie my love, do you wish to ride further? Or shall we return through the Park? The crowds appear to have dispersed somewhat.'

He had dropped the question of the kiss. Lexie, while noting his new and even more scandalous method of addressing her, relaxed still further and reached for Danny's reins.

'Return, I think. I shall better enjoy a ride early tomorrow morning when Hyde Park is less crowded.'

Storm relinquished the reins without demur. 'And should we meet then, I may ride with you?'

'Gladly, Storm,' agreed Lexie, allowing him to assist her into her saddle. She had mentioned riding the following morning, intending them to meet; he had not been slow to realise it.

Jethro Pascoe returned to Bruton Street limping but otherwise unhurt, greatly distressed at having failed in his duty to keep close to his mistress. Lexie, receiving her bandy-legged, apologetic coachman in the morning room, assured him that she fully sympathised with his difficulties and had been perfectly safe with Lord Stormaston.

'I am greatly pleased to hear it, my lady,' said Pascoe, his weathered face under its thatch of greying hair all smiles in his relief. 'If anything had happened to 'ee, my lady, I would never have forgiven myself.'

'None of us expected such an exhibition of misplaced enthusiasm,' said Lexie, 'and just think, if you had not been beside me, Pascoe, I would have suffered the knock you took! Soon after that the

Marquess managed to extricate us from the press and escort me safely home.'

'Aye, my lady,' nodded Pascoe, 'his lordship be a mighty fine horseman. But I doubt he has a better seat or hands than you.'

'You are prejudiced, Pascoe,' laughed Lexie. 'And if what you say is true, then I have you to thank! I shall ride tomorrow morning. Tell Jeffs, will you?'

Jeffs, as usual, waited at the gate for his mistress's return. Lexie had not gone far before meeting Storm, who turned to accompany her. He made no objection to a gallop and soon they were racing along beside the Serpentine, slower riders, hearing the thunder of their hooves, moving aside to allow them to pass. Storm's stallion Brutus, with a heavier rider aboard, had difficulty in keeping up with Danny, who was exceptionally fleet of foot.

'You have a prime piece of horseflesh there,' Storm acknowledged as they paused, allowing the horses to regain their wind.

Lexie patted Danny's steaming neck. 'Pascoe chose him for me. He chooses all my horses. He is an excellent judge.'

'And a devoted servant, or I miss my guess,' smiled Storm. 'He returned safely yesterday?'

'Yes, though his slashed leg pains him and he was upset to have failed in his duty. He considers you an excellent horseman,' she added mischievously.

'I am obliged.'

Lexie chuckled. 'I thought you might be!'

'Imp!' declared Storm. 'I dare swear you are teasing me!'

He raised his hat to a middle-aged gentleman riding by, who bowed to them both but did not stop.

'Thomas Creevey,' he murmured. 'The news of our riding together will be all over town by this evening. He is an inveterate gossip.'

'It will prepare Society for our appearing together at the Countess's rout tonight.'

Storm raised his brows. 'I was about to enquire as to your intentions. You are to attend?'

Lexie nodded, the mischievous smile still on her lips. 'But not without an escort, I trust?'

He bowed from the waist. 'I shall be honoured, Lady Amber. At what time may I wait upon you?'

With the details settled they rode amicably side by side to rejoin Jeffs, who fell into place behind them as they continued on to Bruton Street.

Later in the day Lexie made her promised visit to Downshire House in Grosvenor Square. People were used to seeing her about Town alone in her curricle by now but her arrival still caused a stir of admiration for the remarkably fine horseflesh, the elegant carriage and the skill displayed by its driver.

Jeffs jumped down to hold the matched pair of black horses while Lexie gathered the skirts of her stunning violet carriage gown about her, mounted the steps and entered the hall, where the heels of her half boots clicked resoundingly upon the marble floor.

Lady Fanny ran forward to greet her when she was announced at the door of the receiving room and the Duchess welcomed her graciously. Several other ladies were already present. Mr Oswald

Cresswell, the only gentleman there, looked decidedly embarrassed. He bowed elaborately over Lexie's hand and gazed devotedly into her green eyes before glancing nervously in the direction of the Duchess.

Lady Jersey, Mrs Drummond Burrell and Lady Cowper, all distinguished Patronesses of Almack's, were already sipping at dishes of tea. Lexie, persuaded to share a small settee with Fanny, accepted hers, together with a small slice of Madeira cake. Lady Jersey, as was usual, chattered away while the others nodded, smiled and made small interjections, until the lady ironically known as 'Silence' was finally interrupted by the entrance of Stormaston and Dexter.

Lexie inclined her head and then looked steadfastly into her teacup while the gentlemen made their devoirs. Fanny blushed. The Duchess, her small, aristocratic, silk-clad figure positively radiating pleasure, greeted her grandson with affection and Dexter with warmth.

Soon the talk somewhat naturally turned to the forthcoming assembly at Almack's, to be held as usual on the Wednesday evening.

'You have a voucher, of course, Lady Amber,' stated the Duchess, in such a definite tone that Lexie was almost ashamed to admit that she had not.

'I was admitted seven years ago, Your Grace, but since my return from retirement in Cornwall I have not yet been offered. . .'

'An oversight, no doubt,' drawled Stormaston. He bowed gravely in Lexie's direction. 'I shall look forward to escorting you there on Wednesday, my lady.'

There was a moment's astonished silence before Mrs Drummond Burrell smiled, murmuring, 'We shall be glad to welcome you both. To our regret you are not a frequent visitor, Lord Stormaston.'

And Lady Jersey exclaimed, 'Of course you must come!' almost at the same moment.

Lady Cowper, the most popular of the hostesses, having rummaged in her reticule, triumphantly produced a bundle of tickets. 'I have vouchers here, my lady! We do so look forward to seeing you at our assembly.'

'Thank you all,' murmured Lexie, receiving the ten-guinea vouchers conveyed to her by an outwardly solemn Storm, whose blue eyes laughed wickedly at her.

The Patronesses rose to leave and were soon followed by Oswald, who whispered that he should like to book a dance with her on Wednesday.

Lexie promised to keep him one. She could not dance with Storm all the evening; that would look far too particular and raise more eyebrows than she was inclined to tolerate. As it was she doubted whether he would be satisfied with the regulation two. The mere fact of his escorting her would set those tongues wagging which were not already engaged in the exercise.

Being even now the subject of much speculation, she had no doubt at all that the Patronesses would discuss the matter with all their vast acquaintance, wondering at Stormaston's interest, discounting, as she did herself, any honest purpose in the designs of a rake of his calibre, placing bets on whether the Dowager Countess of Amber would fall for his undoubted charm and accept a *carte blanche*.

She kept her head high as she drove home in her curricle. A reputation as the outrageously eccentric Lady Amber was not to be scorned, rather, to be encouraged if she wished to make her mark on Society, but she must show no hint of shame, no consciousness of having overstepped the mark. If one were bold enough, unconventional behaviour was often tolerated, whereas a single deviation by one who normally kept well within Society's strict set of rules could lead to ruin.

Not that she much cared if she were ruined socially. She would, on the whole, be perfectly content leading a retired life at Merryfield once she had experienced the freedom of a London Season not overshadowed by the urgent necessity of catching a wealthy husband.

The challenge Storm presented was irresistible. A small smile played round her lips as she flicked her whip over Pitch's ear and turned her pair into Bruton Street.

An indefinable radiance surrounded her as she ran upstairs, a glow which even Caro's expression of grim foreboding could do nothing to destroy.

CHAPTER FIVE

By Wednesday, when they appeared at Almack's together, Society buzzed with the latest *on dit*. The Marquess of Stormaston and Alexia, Countess of Amber, were quite openly conducting an *affaire*. How far it had gone none could tell, but as the tongues wagged, Lexie's reputation stood in some danger of being besmirched.

She did not greatly care. Her conscience was clear; she was having a splendid time, since Storm was proving a most attentive and amusing companion, and the old tabbies could say what they liked as long as Lady Fanny and the Duchess continued to believe the attachment innocent of vice. If the Duchess continued to receive her, so would most other hostesses.

'My dear,' murmured Storm as they presented their vouchers and were admitted, he having abandoned his normal trousers or pantaloons to don the knee breeches and silk stockings decreed by the Draconian rules of the Patronesses, 'how does it feel to be admitted to "the seventh heaven of the fashionable world"?'

Lexie chuckled. 'I have heard it described as an exclusive temple, though exactly what is worshipped here I cannot tell!'

'Vanity, my love. Nothing but vanity.'

'Yet to be excluded is looked upon as the worst

kind of ill-fortune.' She shook her head in amused disbelief. 'I am amazed all over again that we plot and intrigue and use all our diplomatic arts to gain admission and are ready to pay ten guineas for the privilege of entering so uninspiring a set of rooms and partaking of such indifferent refreshment.'

'It is the exclusivity of Almack's which makes it so desirable. Only think,' said Storm, idly fingering his quizzing glass while eyeing the cream of Society wandering about the room with a cynical eye, 'three-quarters of the nobility knock at its doors in vain!' He grinned down at her. 'Do you not feel honoured to be here?'

'I must confess there is a certain sense of satisfaction!' After the briefest of pauses Lexie went on, 'Yet denial now would matter so much less than it would have done seven years ago, when to find a husband was the object of my being brought to London. Mama regarded admission here as the key to my success.'

Unconsciously, she sounded sad, almost disillusioned. Studying her vivid face, the unusually pensive green eyes in their nests of tawny lashes, the finely arched dark-golden brows, the slightly concave line of her adorable nose, the all-too-kissable lips, Storm felt the familiar stir of desire.

'As I remember it, you were a great success,' he remarked as he led her out to take their places in a set. 'Quite beyond the touch of a rake like me, of course. But that does not mean that I did not notice how delectable a morsel you were. And still are,' he added, his eyes appraising the fetching figure outlined by the folds of her delicate blue gown.

'Really, Storm, you should not address me in such a manner! Should you be overheard—'

'But I was not, and you, my dear Lexie, were pleased with the compliment, is that not so?'

'I am long past being shocked by anything even you might say,' responded Lexie, throwing him a mocking glance. But her heart had begun to beat fast. She would be obliged to use all her wit to hold this dangerous, attractive lord to a virtuous course.

When the dance was over Storm led her from the floor.

'Shall we repair to the terrace?' he asked her, with such an air of innocence that Lexie was tempted to laugh.

'I do declare!' she exclaimed without answering him. 'There are the Duchess and Lady Fanny! I must go and pay my respects.'

Storm smiled sardonically and made no demur over escorting her across to his grandparent, dressed that evening in dark blue silk, who sat stiff and upright in her seat, dominating the small party gathered about her. She immediately commanded him to fetch Lady Alexia a chair, thus drawing them both into her circle.

The moment both Lexie and Fanny had accepted partners for the next pair of dances and taken to the floor, the Duchess patted the chair beside her with an abrupt, 'Sit down, James.'

Storm obediently lowered himself beside her and arranged his long legs, watching Lexie depart with marked displeasure.

The Duchess eyed him shrewdly before she spoke.

'You cannot monopolise Lady Alexia, James,' she

admonished sternly. 'It will not do. She is not one of the Cyprians or demireps with whom you are so wretchedly fond of consorting. I am quite sure that even you would not wish to shred her reputation beyond repair.'

'You amaze me, as ever, with your command of low language, Grandmama,' teased Storm, reluctantly removing his eyes from Lexie to meet his grandmother's critical gaze. 'But no, of course I do not. However, since she is of age and willing to accept my escort—'

The Duchess snorted, tossing her head, making the jewels in her turban flash. 'What young woman would not be dazzled by your attentions after years of marriage to an old man, years spent buried in the depths of Cornwall! Lady Alexia is a high-spirited filly but virtuous. I doubt she is willing to be seduced by you or anyone else, and I should think it a great pity should you see fit to attempt—'

'Grandmama,' interrupted the Marquess with rather more firmness than he usually used with his grandparent, at the same time laying a restraining hand upon her arm.

'You will allow, I trust, that I am not irredeemably lost to all sense of propriety, that I have never yet caused damage to any lady whose reputation had not already been sullied past redemption and that I am of an age when I may do as I please. I have always done my utmost to abide by Your Grace's wishes. But, much as I love you and hold you in respect, in the matter of my private life I must protest my right to conduct it as I please.'

The Duchess reached up to touch the scar on his

cheek with a knotted finger, her faded old eyes tender. 'I know, my dear. You have always had a keen, if sometimes misguided, sense of honour.'

Storm gently took her small, veined hand in his. He smiled cynically. 'I was young and idealistic then. I have since learned the true value of women of her sort.'

'But do not think all women unworthy of your regard.' The Duchess recovered her hand and tapped him on the shoulder with her folded fan. 'As for obliging me by following my wishes, I know how much it cost you to give up your ambition to purchase a pair of colours, my dear boy, and that much of your rackety behaviour since has stemmed from your obedience to my wish. But you are Downshire's heir and the thought of Hugo's inheriting almost gave your grandfather a stroke.'

She nodded solemnly at Storm, who had given a rueful half-laugh followed by a sigh. 'You have responsibilities, James, most of which I know you shoulder with determination and great skill. But you have not yet provided yourself with an heir—certainly not a legitimate one. Have you fathered many bastards?'

The question came out in the Duchess's best *grande dame* manner accompanied by another sharp tap with her fan and for an instant even Storm looked slightly taken aback by her outspokenness. But he quickly recovered himself.

'Two, to my certain knowledge,' he drawled. 'Both are well provided for.'

'They should be legitimate and gracing your nursery! You are depriving us of the joy of watching our great-grandchildren grow up! You must wed, James, and Alexia Hamilton would make you a fine wife.'

Storm crossed his legs and eyed the toe of one brilliantly polished pump.

'If I wanted a wife,' he agreed, lazily flicking a speck of dust from the black sleeve of his coat. 'But I do not, at present. It may surprise you to discover, ma'am, that I have every intention of avoiding marriage until I am certain that it will contain at least a measure of felicity. I have seen too many men in my position ensnared by some scheming chit for their title and wealth, only to serve long years of domestic warfare and unhappiness. I have no wish to be caught in that matrimonial trap.'

'God love you, my dear, I should not wish it for you—' began the Duchess, but at that moment the dance ended and their tête-à-tête with it.

Storm was not sorry. He was exceedingly fond of his grandmother and did not relish her strictures. But he only bent to her will when his conscience told him he must, as over the question of joining the army.

His own much-loved estates, attached to the marquessate of Stormaston, required considerable attention, and the extensive lands and fortune pertaining to the honour of Downshire would demand an efficient and conscientious hand to guide them on the demise of the present Duke.

Hugo would not do. Even at the age of eighteen, when Hugo had been a mere lad of twelve, Storm, like his grandparents, had been able to see the weakness and wildness, the envy in his younger brother, and to anticipate the probable dissipation of the family fortune were he ever to inherit.

At one and twenty, when Storm became entirely his own master and could have done as he pleased in defiance of his grandparents' wishes, Hugo's fifteen-year-old character had appeared even less promising. And so Storm had heeded his grandmother's pleas, shouldered his duty and forsworn the army as a career. But his high spirit of adventure had demanded other outlets and thus his reputation as a rake had been born.

He stood silently behind Lexie's chair, admiring the golden swathes of hair so ingeniously intertwined with pearls and ribbons, longing to touch, to kiss the tender spot exposed on the nape of her neck, and wryly admitted to himself that any hint of real wildness now was entirely for the sake of appearances.

Of course, like any other gentleman, he had kept a succession of mistresses. And soon, perhaps very soon, he would dismiss Hermione from his flat. Lexie filled his thoughts; he had no inclination to bed his mistress now. She would find no difficulty in securing another protector, of that he was assured.

He had won her generous favours in the face of stiff opposition and Storm, who was perfectly aware of his own ability to attract but did not suffer from any great degree of self-consequence, believed she had chosen him solely because he had the most money to lavish upon her. So she, like others before her, would suffer few pangs at being deprived of his favour. For all his faults and reputation, he had never been promiscuous, had been particular in his choice of *chère amies*, and had never indulged in more than one lover at a time, demanding fidelity in return.

Lexie, he brooded, was proving a provoking creature to ensnare. Of course the Duchess was right; he could not risk damaging her reputation beyond repair. Unsubstantiated gossip was one thing, certain knowledge of indiscretion quite another. He would have to conduct this affair with the utmost discretion. He was quite prepared for that.

After another dance with the object of his desire he danced with Fanny, while Lexie danced with Felix, who had joined their party. After that the girls were claimed by a succession of partners, though Storm had insisted Lexie keep the waltzes for him.

The Czar, who loved dancing, arrived with his entourage and accompanied by his sister, the Grand Duchess, a fair-haired, vivacious widow whom Storm abhorred, for it was she who had turned the Czar against the Regent, whom she had taken in intense dislike. For some little while Storm found himself cornered by the Grand Duchess and it took all his resolution to maintain his languid, charming mask.

Extracting himself from the reach of her caustic and critical tongue, he returned to claim the hand of another fair-haired and vivacious widow, in whose company he would gladly spend the remainder of the evening if only convention would allow.

Mr Cresswell had turned up with his mama, the Viscountess, and dutifully asked Fanny to stand up with him, after which he requested the honour of standing up with Lady Amber.

'Mama is gettin' most insistent,' Oswald grumbled as they came together in the dance. 'Orders me to seek permission to pay my addresses. But Lady Fanny don't want to marry me any more than I want to marry her.'

'So you have said before,' murmured Lexie. The steps of the dance gave her a few moments to think before they met again. 'Why don't you approach Lord Stormaston?' she suggested. 'He is Fanny's guardian, you know. I fancy he might solve your problem for you by refusing permission.'

'You mean he don't like me, don't think me good enough,' muttered Oswald gloomily.

Lexie shook her head. Poor Oswald, he had little self-confidence. He was probably right, though. But if the Duchess pushed the match Storm would no doubt agree in the end.

'I did not say that, Mr Cresswell,' she told him firmly. 'But I doubt he thinks you would suit. And if he did give permission, Fanny has only to refuse, you know. He would not force her to wed against her will.'

Oswald brightened visibly at this. 'I sit at your feet in admiration, Lady Amber,' he declared as they made their bows at the end of the dance. 'You are divinely beautiful and extraordinary clever, too. You would not marry me yourself, I collect?'

Lexie smiled, a certain compassion in her gaze. He really was the nicest of young men, but not to her taste and too immature altogether. 'You do me great honour, Mr Cresswell, but no, I would not. We should not suit, either, I am far too rackety for you. Your mama would never agree.'

'I'll be out of leading strings in a couple of months, you know,' Oswald informed her. 'Mama won't be able to tell me what to do once I'm one and twenty.'

But she would still try, and Oswald, bless him, would not have the strength to resist. Lexie could see it all. However, all she said was, 'If you wish to please her, Mr Cresswell, do as I suggest. Once you have been refused she must give up.'

'She'll only pick on some other female I ain't interested in,' he prophesied dismally.

The next dance being a waltz, Lexie found herself taking the floor with Stormaston and afterwards, breathless from a number of causes, allowed him to lead her to the refreshment room.

He handed her a glass of lemonade. 'We should drink it outside,' he murmured. 'It would be cooler there.'

And darker, more private, thought Lexie, a thrill of excitement sending a shiver down her spine. But she could not risk such an expedition yet. She trusted the Marquess not one inch and herself little more, knowing the strange, dizzying effect his nearness had upon her. So she must hold him at arm's length for as long as it took to bring him to the declaration she desired.

'I would rather sit here,' she said, choosing a chair. 'Tongues are wagging quite enough already. Were I to disappear into the darkness outside with you, I tremble to think what would be said. And,' she added quickly, before he could challenge her on the point, 'although I do not object to being spoken of as unconventional or even as a flirt, I would dislike intensely being thought to play the whore.'

For an instant Storm frowned, as though he found her reasoning distasteful. But then he dropped into the seat beside hers, draping one arm across its back as he faced her with a lazy smile. 'You disappoint me, Lexie, my love. I thought you had more courage.'

'And I thought you a gentleman, my lord, despite your reputation! Never tell me I was wrong!'

He suddenly put his head back and laughed. '*Touché*, my love! Despite all appearances, I would not have your reputation sullied. I see I must bide my time and find a more suitable opportunity for dalliance.'

Lexie smiled. 'But I have never promised to dally with you, Storm. Merely to accept your escort to certain events and occasions. Do not read more into my offer of friendship than is there.'

'But you still owe me a kiss.'

This time Lexie, prepared, was able to meet his words with equanimity. 'You may consider it so, but I do not.'

He smiled that lazy, devastating, knowing smile. 'We shall see.'

Over the next weeks they appeared everywhere together. In the end the gossip waned for lack of further fuel. The couple behaved with the utmost propriety apart from dancing together rather more than was acceptable and spending more time sitting together when in company than did most married couples. Lexie enjoyed it all hugely.

Storm was a charming, amusing and knowledgable companion. They talked about everything under the sun. He was certainly not the idle fop he appeared. He spoke with enthusiasm about his country house in Wiltshire, Stormaston Park, his extensive estates and the modern farming methods with which he was experimenting.

'You would like Stormaston, Lexie,' he told her as they chatted quietly waiting for a concert to begin. Caro, who had accompanied them since she was fond of music, had found a place near the front, sitting with the chaperons. 'You must visit there with me when the Season ends.'

'I planned on going to Brighton for July,' said Lexie, hiding her jubilation at the invitation although she would not go, of course, unless it was to join a house party. 'And then back to Merryfield. My estate needs my personal attention if I am to introduce all the reforms you suggest. Although I have an excellent steward, he is set in the old ways and will need persuading to change.'

'Perhaps we should exchange visits,' murmured his lordship. 'I should be happy to assist you in any way within my power.'

'You are kind, Storm. Perhaps we should. But I promise nothing.'

Storm, who found his companion more enchanting by the day, hid his frustration in some lazy rejoinder. The minx was teasing him to distraction, giving freely of her company yet granting him no chance to deepen their relationship except upon the most austerely friendly terms. Even in his own coach, with Lexie chaperoned by her maid or by her cousin, who, on occasion, could be tempted out by a visit to the theatre or to hear a musical concert, he must sit properly in his corner.

Despite her fluttery ways he liked Mrs Baldwin, who amused him by regarding him with rather suspicious awe. Beneath her ineffectual manner she was, he had discovered, perfectly capable of ordering Lexie's household and helping to organise an entertainment to which most of the *haut ton* had been invited.

It was to take place on the thirteenth of July and the Duke of Wellington, who would be in London by then, had promised to attend. The Sovereigns had departed on the twenty third day of June and London was enjoying a slightly less frenetic few days before the Duke's arrival. Because of this they had met only twice in the last week and Storm found he missed seeing Lexie more than he was quite ready to admit.

Hermione had been dismissed and his discreet flat lay empty. Perhaps, he thought vaguely, his opportunity would come when they joined a party to visit Vauxhall. That was not for two weeks yet, a couple of days after Lexie's soirée. But they would all wear masks and the possibilities of luring a female into dark, lonely paths was one of the main attractions of the place. He cared little for the amusements laid on or the firework displays either, but such things pleased the ladies.

'The arrangements for your soirée are going well?' he enquired out of politeness. He did not expect to enjoy an occasion where Lexie would be a busy hostess while he languished on the sidelines. He would, he decided, make for the card room and spend the evening there.

'Excellently, I thank you. Cousin Caro is a wonder.' Suddenly Lexie smiled. 'You and she are alike, you know. You hide your true self behind a lamentably foppish mask while Caro's efficiency is concealed behind a vague, fluttery manner. I do not believe her deception is deliberate. But yours is.'

'A protection, merely,' drawled Storm.

'Oh dear,' muttered Lexie. 'Here comes Hugo.'

'Young puppy.'

Lazy amusement filled Storm's tone, yet Lexie knew he was not pleased. Hugo had been pursuing her for the last couple of weeks, and despite all her efforts to dissuade him he persisted in asking her to stand up with him, which she could not refuse to do without appearing to lack conduct.

Under normal circumstances he would not be seen dead at a musical evening. He was quite deliberately attempting to oust his brother in her affections; the very idea that he thought himself able made her want to laugh.

Hugo greeted them with one of his extravagant bows and demanded to know whether there was any way in which he might serve Lady Amber.

'Should Lady Amber require anythin' I am, despite my great age, quite able to render the service,' pointed out Storm agreeably.

'I lack for nothing, I thank you,' put in Lexie quickly, 'and I am certain you would find entertainment more to your liking in the card room, Lord Hugo.'

'Oh, I shall retire there once the music begins,' said Hugo. 'In fact, I may as well wander along now,' he added, seeing the musicians about to take their places. 'I shall look forward to seein' you again at supper, Lady Amber.'

'Does he annoy you?' asked Storm, watching the departure of his brother with narrowed eyes.

'Not really.' Lexie had no wish to stir up more animosity between the brothers. She sensed that there was quite enough already. 'But I do wish he could take a hint!'

'Hugo,' stated Storm grimly, 'never could.'

Hugo did not appear for supper after all. 'Deep in a game, no doubt,' observed Storm when Lexie remarked on his welcome absence.

Later, returning from a visit to the cloakroom, she heard Storm's unmistakable voice as she approached an open door on her way back to the salon. She was quite alone in the corridor and his words rose easily above a distant hum of conversation and the faint strains of instruments being tuned in the background.

She halted, not wishing to intrude, and realised he was speaking in a tone she had never heard him use before, authoritative and implacable, as he declined to meet Hugo's vast gaming losses.

'You'll not allow the name of Graham to be sunk in iniquity!' declared Hugo.'

'You think not?' came back the biting retort.

'I had thought better of even you, brother!'

'You repose too much faith in my determination to defend the honour of our name,' came Storm's cold response. 'I have bought you out of enough sad scrapes in the past, I will do so no more. If your allowance will not cover your expenses and losses, then I suggest you do not incur them. I have no intention of allowing you to squander any more of the Graham fortune. You will live within your generous allowance or find some honest way of supplementing it. Gaming is not the way, as you must by now be fully aware.'

'I was attemptin' to recover my fortunes at the tables tonight. But Lady Luck was against me.' Hugo sounded childish in his whining truculence.

'The war with France is over at last. You could do worse than join the army. Your life would no longer be at great risk. I doubt you would be posted to America to prosecute the war there, which in any case is likely to be over shortly.'

'You forget, I would have to purchase a commission. I cannot pay my debts so I could not do that, either.'

There was a moment's silence. 'Would you like to follow the colours, Hugo?' Storm sounded surprised.

Lexie could hear the shrug in Hugo's petulant voice. 'There is little to entertain me here if I cannot afford to gamble. To be a half-pay officer would suit me well, and there will be plenty of those commissions for sale now Napoleon is defeated.'

'I will buy you a commission—but only provided it carries a posting.'

A stunned silence followed. Then, 'Not in a line regiment,' came Hugo's slow answer.

'Very well. And, Hugo, once you are commissioned and posted, I will pay your current debts and gaming losses. Let me have a list tomorrow. But mark me well, this is the last time I shall come to your rescue. Officers are cashiered for accumulating debts they cannot meet, and often end up in prison.'

'You'd like that, wouldn't you?' ground out Hugo viciously. 'Sittin' on a fortune, refusin' to help, blackmailin' me into going into the army and takin' up what will probably be a dashed uncomfortable posting in some foetid hole—'

'No fortune is inexhaustible, my dear Hugo. I am responsible for husbanding that of our family for future generations. My own extravagances, whatever you may think, are not now excessive, whatever they may have been in the past. The Graham fortune is in truth greater now that when I inherited it. Not even you, my dear brother, will be allowed to undo all the work I have put in over the last few years to achieve that end.'

'Unless I inherit.'

'I do not intend to quit my lease just yet, even to please you, Hugo. And I expect one day to set up a nursery of my own. You are not Marquess of Stormaston yet.'

'I shall return to Grosvenor Square and prepare my statement. You shall have it in the morning,' said Hugo stiffly.

Lexie had been standing mesmerised by what she was hearing, seeing Storm for the first time as a man of power, of stature, of principles. She had glimpsed this man before, but not in such convincing guise.

She came to herself with a shock, realised the interview was at an end and wondered what to do. She could not retreat. There was only one thing for it: to pretend to be hurrying back to the salon. Picking up the train of her skirt she went swiftly forward, feigning complete surprise when she bumped into the retreating Hugo.

'Why, Lord Hugo! You must excuse me for being such a gawk,' she cried, 'but I was hurrying back and never expected to meet with anyone—'

Hugo had his hands on her arms as he sought to help her recover her balance while retaining his own. They were hot and trembling.

'Lady Amber! My deepest regrets. . .my fault entirely. . .please allow me—'

'I will attend Lady Amber.'

Storm stepped from the room and Lexie turned. 'Lord Stormaston! I had thought to rejoin you in the salon!'

'Indeed, I should have been there except that Hugo and I had some business to discuss.' He nodded at Hugo. 'I will expect you in the morning, brother.'

'My duty, Lady Amber,' muttered Hugo with a sketchy bow, and hurried away.

Lexie stared after him and then looked up at Storm's grim face. 'A family rift?'

His face softened as he smiled at her. 'Nothin' to worry your head about, m'dear. A little business matter to be taken care of. Hugo has decided to follow the drum. He requires me to purchase him a commission.'

Lexie could not help her frown. 'Will the life suit him?'

'I doubt it, but it may do him a service. Forget Hugo.' He muttered something she could not quite catch. It sounded suspiciously like 'Lucky young dog,' but she could not be certain. And then he was drawling, 'Let us go and enjoy the remainder of this entertainin' concert.'

But Lexie was seeing her companion with new eyes and found it extremely difficult to concentrate on the music.

* * *

The days sped by. The Duke of Wellington arrived in London to be greeted by ecstatic crowds. The dinners, the balls, the parades began all over again. This was the man who had commanded the British army to victory in the Peninsula, who had chased the French out of Spain and back into France and taken Toulouse on the tenth of April, at great cost of dead and wounded, not knowing that Napoleon had abdicated over a week earlier.

And then, despite the peace, the Governor of Bayonne decided to fight on, causing the slaughter of several hundred troops on both sides in a useless sortie from the besieged town.

But Wellington was not to blame for that. He had restored British pride in her army and returned a hero. His arrival at Lexie's soirée caused such a stir that everything came to a halt; men left the card tables to come to greet him, the musical trio ceased to play, the ladies to chatter.

He came dressed in the field-marshal's uniform designed for him by the Regent, the scarlet coat embroidered on collar, cuffs, down the front and at the seams. A flock of aides-de-camp followed at his heels and he had soon collected a bevy of lovely, adoring women around him.

As the evening resumed its course Lexie smiled indulgently to where the Duke, an indifferent conversationalist, nodded, smiled modestly and murmured 'Yes, yes,' to whatever was said to him and paid laboured compliments to the ladies.

Lexie, aware with every fibre of her being of Stormaston's approach, was not surprised to hear his voice in her ear.

'You find the Field Marshal attractive?'

His voice held a tone she could not quite interpret. It seemed to hold an undercurrent of anger laced with jealousy, yet somewhere regret lay hidden. Looking up, she could see the mixed emotions reflected in his face as he studied the Duke through his quizzing glass, an affectation he seldom used.

Lexie placed her hand on his arm, feeling the muscles tense as she did so. She suddenly felt extremely hot, but she kept her tone light as she said, 'Not at all, although he does exude a certain aura of power, which I suppose some women find engaging. But I do believe his authority to be more contrived, a product of his calling, than natural. On the whole, I find him agreeable, but he has not brought his wife to London to share in his triumph.'

The muscles under her hand relaxed and Storm dropped his glass, allowing it to hang upon its ribbon. 'Nevertheless, I would have counted it a privilege to serve under him.'

That answered another question she had been nursing in her mind. He envied Hugo. He had wanted to join the army. 'Then why did you not?' she asked gently.

'As Downshire's heir. . .' he shrugged, letting the gesture speak for him.

'I see. Well, I am glad you did not volunteer, for had you been killed I should have lacked an escort this Season.'

'Soon,' he rejoined, his blue eyes brilliant, 'I intend to be more than merely your escort.'

CHAPTER SIX

VAUXHALL Gardens blazed with the light of innumerable lamps as darkness fell. They had arrived to enjoy their big adventure as the midsummer sun dipped below the horizon: Lexie, Storm, Fanny, Felix, Oswald and several other young people of their acquaintance, accompanied by Oswald's mother, Lady Wighton, as chaperon.

To Lexie, Lord Stormaston was immediately recognisable despite his black cloak and mask. He had, of course, called for her in his carriage, so the chance to mistake him for another was nil, but in any case she would have picked him out from any throng. He possessed such an air. And she could never have mistaken his blue eyes, dancing at her through the slits of his mask.

In truth, she had little difficulty in recognising Lady Fanny, Lord Dexter or Mr Cresswell, despite the last's devilishly pointed creation encrusted with gold embroidery, though the identities of some of the others, with whom she was less well acquainted, did tease her at first. Once safe in the pavilion reserved for their use, they discarded their disguises amidst much laughter and teasing before partaking of the refreshment provided.

The young people were eager to explore. Lady Wighton, a plump woman of some five and forty years, had an aversion to exerting herself. She lacked the breath to walk far and, although she took her duties as chaperon seriously, she was not persuaded of the necessity to accompany the young people on a stroll of exploration.

'Lady Amber, I entrust the office of chaperon to you!' she declared with an arch smile, forcefully poking her son into offering Lady Fanny his arm. 'Do not forget to wear your masks! And do not wander far,' she enjoined their departing backs. 'I shall look for you to return within the hour!'

'Very well, Mama,' muttered Oswald from beneath the weight of his gold thread.

Lexie, wearing a light green spotted muslin gown and close-fitting head dress, masked like all the rest in a matching creation which suited her admirably—Vauxhall was not the place for any members of the *haut ton* to be seen officially—took Storm's arm.

'I believe Lady Wighton has instructed Oswald to further his suit with Lady Fanny,' she murmured, watching the pair strolling in front of them.

'I have already refused him my permission to address her,' declared Storm, stating a fact of which Oswald had already apprised Lexie. 'Fanny begged me not to allow it.'

Lexie squeezed his arm without thinking. 'I am so glad you did!' she exclaimed. 'I was certain you would! Neither of them want it, you know.'

Storm tried to steady the hammering in his veins occasioned by her intimate gesture and to control his body's response. 'I collect you enjoy Mr Cresswell's confidence and that it was you who inspired him to approach me?' he asked.

'I hope you did not mind!' Lexie had become

aware of the consequences of her intimate gesture, not only upon herself but upon the Marquess as well. She would have to control her spontaneity in future if she were to avoid provoking him into thinking her a tease. She therefore took care to keep her hand featherlight upon his arm as she went on, 'It seemed the easiest way to dissuade Lady Wighton from her purpose, but her ladyship is not easily deterred.'

Oswald, still with Fanny, turned into one of the many byways, already becoming shadowed where the coloured lamps did not reach. Felix followed, a young woman on either arm. Others of the party hesitated at the junction.

'Lord Dexter,' murmured Lexie, 'is scarcely qualified to act the chaperon. I think perhaps we should follow. The Viscountess did say. . .'

'But without meaning it,' said Storm firmly. 'We shall leave them all to their own devices. Little harm can come of it. I have other things in mind for us.'

Lexie's conscience smote her but her heart leapt. When she had accepted the invitation to join the party, she had guessed Storm would take advantage of the surroundings, the occasion, to claim a kiss. And she had encouraged him by her unthinking, grateful squeeze of his arm!

Vauxhall was known to be the place for forbidden assignations, for the carrying out of plots to waylay and abduct the unwary. Lexie feared being alone with him, not because she anticipated Storm to have any devilish designs on her but because she did not trust her own responses where he was concerned. But the others had all disappeared from view and Storm was leading her behind a booth containing a bearded lady into the dark, labyrinthine byways behind.

'Storm!' she protested, trying to tug him back to the main path and virtue.

'You do not fear me, Lexie, surely?' he asked softly.

'No, of course not, but I think—'

He placed a reassuring hand over the one now clutching desperately at his arm. 'Then do not. Let us enjoy these moments of seclusion. The rules which decide that a man and woman may not be alone together without causing scandal are stupid and archaic, except, perhaps, for the very young.'

'Reason tells me so, but—'

'But dire warnings have been instilled into your mind since childhood! I know, my dear, but I mean you no mischief and what harm can there possibly be in our spending a few moments apart from others in a public garden where you would have but to scream and the world would come to your rescue in an instant?'

'None at all,' agreed Lexie, who had only been protesting because she wanted to be with him so much it must be wrong. How she longed for his kiss! But to what might it lead? She knew it would be prudent to insist upon joining the others or returning to Lady Wighton immediately, but prudence lost out to anticipation as Storm drew her into a tiny glade just off the path and took her into his arms.

Music, shouts, laughter, all faded into the background as she felt the urgency of his hold, the hammering of his heart, his breath fanning her face as his mouth hovered over hers while he removed first his own and then her mask, dropping them to the ground.

Her own heart beat hard and fast, her limbs turned to warm, sweet, viscous wine as she dropped her reticule and flung her arms about his neck, abandoning all modesty as the need to be close to him swept over her. Ridiculous as it seemed, this was, she suddenly knew, where she belonged. In Lord Stormaston's arms.

'Lexie!' he murmured deeply before his mouth claimed hers.

Lexie had never known such sweeping desire as possessed her in the next few moments. His kiss, deep and penetrating, tasting her and giving her a taste of him, lasted until it dragged a groan from her throat. Had her arms not been clasped tightly about his neck she would have fallen, so limp had her muscles become. Her body did not belong to her and neither did her mind, which whirled kaleidoscopically from sensation to sensation, drowning fear, responsibility, time itself.

His lips moved from her mouth to her eyes, the tilted tip of her nose, the fluttering pulse in her throat, and all the time he murmured words of endearment. Lexie's fingers tangled in his hair, quite destroying the careful arrangement his man had achieved.

He shifted his hold to turn her slightly so that his hand could cup one of her breasts, his thumb finding its peak through the thin muslin of her gown and chemise. Lexie gasped as new sensation lanced through her body.

'I want you, Lexie,' he said strongly; although his

heart beat like a hammer, his breathing came harsh, his voice trembled slightly and she could feel the urgency of his desire, he was in complete control of his actions. He went on, 'I know you want me, too. My love, I own a flat where we could meet discreetly. You need have no fear for your reputation, I shall guard it well. Will you come to me there?'

Abruptly, the rosy euphoria deserted Lexie. Disappointment surged through her. Sounds, harsh, jangling sounds, bestial, drunken laughter filled her ears. But she had known he wanted her for his mistress, not his wife. She should not feel so mortified.

She struggled to escape his hold. 'Are you offering me a *carte blanche*?' she demanded, her voice quivering uncontrollably.

At her tone he lifted surprised eyebrows. 'Naturally, my little tease. What else did you think I had in mind?'

She could not possibly mention marriage. She had known he did not intend that and apparently all her wiles had not changed his mind. She drew a breath.

'Friendship. Flirtation, maybe even dalliance. As tonight. But no more. You must have known that I could never accept such an offer, my lord. I may flout certain conventions, but I consider myself a respectable widow. You would have me become a whore.'

'I would have you become my lover, Lexie. There is the world of difference—'

'Not to me!' she raged, to cover her distress. 'How dare you. . .?' Words failed her as tears of frustration and anger filled her eyes. She dashed them away and pushed past him to regain the path. 'I would be much obliged if you would escort me back to our pavilion,' she managed on a choking sob.

Storm bent down to retrieve her reticule and their masks. He did not argue further, knowing it to be fruitless in the face of her real distress. Painful frustration expressed itself in his grim expression. His eyes, warm, holding fire a moment ago, became chips of blue ice. All his patience had been worthless. He had thought her merely playing hard to get, been confident that in the end she would capitulate as had so many others in the past.

But she had not. He deliberately encouraged wrath to replace rejection. He had seldom—never!—had his well-rehearsed advances refused before. Lady Amber, an amusing, stimulating companion, had encouraged his friendship. She was far from indifferent to him and should have fallen into his arms with cries of joy. She was, he decided, exactly what he had jokingly called her, a tease. There was nothing he hated more than a tease. She deserved a sharp lesson. A very sharp lesson indeed.

Lexie, glancing up to thank him for returning her mask and reticule, saw the harshness in his face, saw the white line of his scar shift as he clenched his jaw, and a tremor of fear added desperation to her already disturbed emotions. She had led him on, but in her mind towards marriage, a respectable union. But surely he was gentleman enough not to seek revenge?

Storm allowed nothing of his thoughts to show in his face or manner as he delivered her back to the chaperonage of the Viscountess, behaving as though nothing untoward had happened. Lexie, he noted, was trying to do the same and succeeding to all intents. Only he would notice the strain in her eyes, the slightly higher pitch to her voice, the tendency to distraction in her manner.

While Lexie, acting a part as she had never acted before, noted the disappearance of that dangerous expression and began to relax again.

At more or less the same moment as they had approached the pavilion Fanny had appeared at some distance walking between Mr Cresswell and Lord Dexter, with a group of their friends following on behind. By unspoken consent they had waited for the others and met up amidst great exclamations and enthusiasm over the pleasures of the gardens.

Despite the fact that he knew Fanny had been perfectly safe with Mr Cresswell, Storm felt uneasy. The Viscountess had proved a most dilatory chaperon. Could it be that she had planned to trick him into being compelled to allow a match between the two young people? He had not regarded that possibility earlier and had neglected his duty to Fanny while pursuing his own dalliance.

But it seemed that all was well. Despite all her arch questions to the young people, no hint of impropriety on Fanny's part emerged. Fanny and Oswald had kept with the others and his own laxity had been of no consequence.

Fanny, looking flushed and pretty, had arrived back at the pavilion as she had left it, on Oswald's arm. But behind her mask her shining eyes kept straying to the elegant form of Lord Dexter. Lexie wondered what had given the child such an air of hidden exaltation, but under the circumstances nothing untoward could have occurred. It was, after all, Fanny's first experience of Vauxhall and its wonders and no doubt this accounted for her excitement.

As the fireworks began to light up the sky with red, blue, silver and golden stars, Lexie dismissed a vague uneasiness in favour of living again those delicious, stolen moments spent in Stormaston's arms. If only he could be brought to propose marriage! She would be the happiest of creatures. But the evening had proved him proof against all her lures.

Having arrived in Stormaston's crested coach, Lexie had little choice but to return in it and that evening, for various reasons, neither Caro nor Chalker had accompanied her. Acutely aware of his presence inches away, Lexie pressed herself against the side of the carriage and gazed steadfastly from the window as they traversed the streets back to Mayfair.

Despite the hour they met plenty of traffic. After the fresh airiness of Vauxhall Gardens the coach seemed stuffy but the narrow, odoriferous streets rendered opening a window unwise. The weather really was too hot to remain much longer in Town. She would have retired to the country except that she would miss too many of the extraordinary entertainments planned for that summer.

She did not want to miss the centenary of the Hanoverian succession on the first day of August, when the Regent's grand jubilee celebrations would take place and all the royal parks be thrown open to the people.

Clinging to such thoughts in an effort to take her mind from the awful possibility that Storm would use their isolation to attempt another attack on her determination to resist him, Lexie did not speak. Storm, immobile beside her, travelled in equal silence and the tension flowed between them like a web of silken thread, strong, elastic, not easily broken. He had been confounded and angered by her refusal to accept his *carte blanche*. What would he do now?

She had grown used to his company. Without it, events to which she had been looking forward with pleasure would no longer appeal. She did not like to admit how much she had come to rely on his presence beside her. For one thing, it kept a host of unwanted, importunate suitors at bay.

A small sigh escaped her. Her soliciting of his escort for her own ends had rebounded with a vengeance. She should have seen long ago that an attempt to lure a gentleman possessed of the Marquess's rakish reputation into matrimony was doomed to failure. And in the failing she had lost even his friendship.

Her cogitations brought no comfort, simply gloom to add to her mortification. For if *he* would not wed her, she would remain a widow. She would consider no one else as a husband after the joy she had found in his arms that evening. She need not be lonely. She could buy companionship. Only weeks ago she had viewed such a prospect with equanimity, if not pleasure. But that had been before. . .

Such was her despondency that, when they arrived in Bruton Street and the Marquess saw her to her door, bowed and asked at what time he should wait upon her the following evening, Lexie was taken aback.

She quickly gathered her wits and named an hour. He bent formally over her hand in farewell and departed, watched by an astounded Lexie. Instead of quickly mounting the stairs to her bedroom, she stood rooted to the spot, watching his cloak swirl about his tall, commanding figure as the door closed behind him.

Slowly, it dawned upon her that he had not given up his pursuit. He anticipated that in the end he would emerge victorious.

So she would not accept defeat, either! Her hold on him was tenuous, but it did exist, for her attempts to bring him to a declaration had in truth succeeded. Because he still shied at the idea of committing himself to marriage, he had offered her the status he accorded all his women.

But she was not just one of his women! One day he would accept the inevitable. Dear Lord! he must, for in truth she doubted she could live without him as her mate, however unsatisfactory he might turn out to be as a husband. Of the alternatives, to become his mistress was impossible for her and to lose him from her life inconceivable.

She must think of something.

And so the next morning when, not at all to her surprise, Storm met her in the Park as usual, she behaved as charmingly as she knew how, totally ignoring the contretemps of the previous evening. It must be within her power to fascinate Lord Stormaston into a proposal—of marriage. He must now realise that, if he wanted to enjoy intimate relations with her, he had no other choice. And her life would be blighted for ever if she did not succeed.

Storm, chagrined by the rejection of the previous evening, had become more determined than ever to lure Alexia Hamilton to his bed. Of one thing he was now certain beyond all doubt. Her lightly flirtatious ways, her air of intrinsic innocence, hid a passionate nature which he had begun to stir into life. He doubted whether she knew the depth of the well of passion within her and he took secret satisfaction at the prospect of plumbing its depths.

For losing one battle did not mean that he had lost the war. The challenge of Alexia Hamilton excited him. There would be another day, another occasion. She *must* succumb! No woman's virtue was inviolable, he had proved that many times, and a few amorous encounters with him could do her no possible harm. On past experience, once he had possessed her his urgent need would die.

Not that he had ever felt quite the same compulsion to possess any other woman, but his desire could only be a matter of degree. It might take him a little longer to slake his thirst with her but. . . But first he had to achieve the seduction.

He therefore rode out the next morning determined to use every ounce of the charm he knew so exactly how to wield. And did not know whether to laugh or fume when he discovered her to be employing a similar weapon. What did the little tease expect to achieve? Did she think to render him so addle-witted that he would propose marriage? She would soon learn that he had no intention of being enticed into parson's mousetrap just yet!

If he begot an heir at around the age of forty, he should still live long enough to train the child and to see him achieve his majority. And a young girl, absorbed in her duties as wife and mother, would not interfere with his pursuit of his own life. Lexie, he knew, was bright enough and interested enough to want to share his interests: she would demand more from him than he was willing to give.

His grandmother's voice echoed in his ears but he refused to listen. Lexie wanted marriage, but had given him no reason to suppose that she held him in anything but critical regard. She did not, at bottom, approve of his manners or behaviour. Why should she? Like everyone else she believed him a rake, beyond redemption. Why should she even attempt to look behind the façade he chose to present?

He did not want her to. Or anyone else for that matter, apart from his grandmother who knew him too well. But why, then, did Lexie wish to become Marchioness of Stormaston? For the same reasons as all the other hopefuls he had discarded over the years, in order to become a Duchess one day and to become wife to one of the richest men in the country. Had she shown any sign of affection or tenderness he might, just, have heeded the Duchess's words. But she had not.

He smiled at her, a devilish smile that let her know he had guessed her purpose. She really was looking remarkably attractive, flushed and eager, full of life and vigour, up to anything.

Except allowing him to have his way with her. The

smile spread even as desire made him shift in his saddle. His resolve deepened. In a young girl such reticence was only to be expected. A widow should not be so stiff-necked in her attitude to an *affaire* outside marriage. She probably wouldn't be, he thought grimly, if it weren't for his title and his money.

Lexie, seeing the dangerous glint in his eye, almost panicked, but her inherent courage quickly reasserted itself. Whatever he liked to pretend, the Marquess was not an evil man. He would do her no true harm. Although, of course, he would not consider discreet seduction to be in any way grievous.

And she had to admit that, shocking as she found his offer of a *carte blanche*, all she would lose in the event would be her own integrity. A private pain that would not otherwise affect her life in any essential way. So she had no great reason to fear the worst Stormaston could contrive, although his intention remained unchanged. He would not, she was certain, force himself upon her. But he might easily seduce her were she not constantly on guard.

In this spirit of armed truce they continued their association much as before. Lexie took even greater care to have someone else in the carriage with them and never to be beguiled out to dark terraces or into empty rooms. Not that Storm tried excessively hard—he was behaving with the utmost propriety. He appeared to be biding his time.

Meanwhile, their discussions covered all manner of subjects of which Lexie knew a great deal, having devoured the contents of the Amber library during her exile at Porthewan and she eagerly absorbed any information he had to offer. Storm teased her over what he termed her magpie mind, which picked up snippets of information to store for future airing.

They enjoyed visiting exhibitions, the theatre, the opera and musical evenings together and discussed their merits afterwards. Despite the tension running beneath the surface of their relationship, Lexie had never been happier. And by the way Storm sometimes smiled at her she thought him to be enjoying himself, too. Even his grandmother remarked.

'I do declare,' she said one evening while she and Lexie were alone. 'James has lost much of his air of boredom recently. Your company is proving good for him, my dear Lady Alexia. And he has dismissed that actress creature from his flat, I hear. I never could approve his choice of *chère amies*—flighty, dimwitted chits I have always considered them.'

Lexie blushed, but laughed at the Duchess's outspoken words. 'I am certain you are not supposed to know of their existence, dear ma'am!'

'When the entire *ton* knows of his *affaires*, it would be difficult to keep the information from me, don't you think? Don't approve of the boy's behaviour, never did, but he was not allowed to join the army, so he had to find another outlet for his high spirits.'

'They have to sow their wild oats,' murmured Lexie with a wry grimace, remembering the conversation she had overheard between Storm and Hugo. Storm had lost no time in purchasing one of the many commissions now up for sale and Hugo was preparing to join his regiment, stationed somewhere in the north. 'Men are fortunate to be allowed such licence.'

'Women are allowed a certain amount, too, after the heir is born. That's what all this charade is about, y'know. Young girls put on show to catch a prize but sheltered and chaperoned so that there can be no doubt as to the paternity of the heir. Blood lines are important, d'y'see.'

Her gaze settled on Fanny, swinging down the centre of a set with a youthful partner. 'I'd like to see my granddaughter settled,' went on the Duchess with a sigh. 'Pity she don't like young Cresswell. Shan't force her, of course.'

'Unwise to do so, ma'am. It could lead to great unhappiness on both sides. He has no wish to form an alliance with your granddaughter. He is merely following his mother's orders.'

'Fancies himself in love with you, don't he?'

Lexie laughed. 'Fancies is the word. He is poetically in love with love and I am a safe object of adoration. He has no wish to shackle himself in marriage.'

'No more do most young men, more's the pity. James patronisin' the card tables tonight?' demanded the Duchess with a sharp glance from her old eyes.

'I believe so.'

'Devilish lucky at cards. There are those who will be sorry to see him there. Pleased to see him dancin' attendance on you these last weeks. They say you're his mistress, but I don't believe 'em. Hasn't he declared himself yet?'

Now Lexie's face positively flamed. 'He has made it most plain that he has no thought of marriage,' she informed his grandmother tartly. 'We remain friends, nothing more.'

'Humph,' said the Duchess, snapping shut her fan. 'D'y'think I'm blind, young woman? He's after you and you're holding him off, although I'd wager you're not indifferent. Holdin' out for marriage, though. Aren't I right?'

Lexie drew a deep breath. 'He does not intend marriage,' she informed Storm's grandmother with rather more bitterness in her tone than she realised.

'Don't he, now?' muttered the old lady. 'Young fool.'

But she said no more. She had discovered all she wished to know, thought Lexie resentfully, and much good might it do her.

Some days later, following a habit equally as reprehensible as riding alone in Hyde Park, Lexie took her usual afternoon stroll round Berkeley Square. She found the solitary walk relaxing after a morning spent calling, receiving or shopping, and spent the hour before changing for dinner taking the air. The open, leafy Square, inhabited by friends and acquaintances, was an oasis of comparative calm amidst the crowded streets and mews surrounding it.

She felt quite safe walking beneath the trees and saw no reason to ask Chalker or a footman to accompany her, however correct such company would be. After the freedom Amber had allowed her in Cornwall, she resented the necessity to have someone shadow her all the time. The servants had more useful things to do than to walk behind a woman quite able to take care of herself.

It had been raining earlier and everything sparkled, fresh and clean, in the sunlight as Lexie left the shade of the trees to return to her house. Caro had gone to visit her friend and Lexie had no evening engagement that day so she had dismissed Chalker, telling her maid to take the evening off, and informed cook that she would send down for a tray as and when she became hungry. So there was no hurry and she had loitered rather longer than usual.

Someone was throwing a dinner party at an establishment at one end of the Square and carriages were rumbling up to the door as Lexie strolled back towards Bruton Street. When a coach clattered to a halt beside her, she barely looked up until a voice hailed her.

'Lady Amber? His lordship is asking for you, my lady. Pray come at once!'

Lexie looked at the coach, expensive but plain, no crest on the door to identify the owner.

'His lordship?' she demanded of the man—a servant, evidently—who had accosted her.

The man bowed with perfect deference. 'The Marquess of Stormaston, my lady. I am Marlow, his lordship's valet. He sent me with a most urgent request—'

'Is he ill?' demanded Lexie, sudden anxiety in her voice. She did not know what to make of this sudden, most unusual and rather improper request. A lady did not visit a gentleman's rooms unaccompanied, for whatever reason.

'He was most insistent in his orders to me, my lady,' urged Marlow without directly answering her question. 'He instructed me to bring you to him without delay. He has been in low spirits recently, ma'am,' went on Marlow less formally. 'I quite despair of bringing him about without your help.'

Storm in low spirits indeed! He had seemed abstracted and subdued at the theatre last evening, but she had thought his mood due to the indifference of the acting. Even if this duel between them was affecting him as much as it was her, she could see no purpose in rushing to his succour. Only one thing would cure him of his megrim, and she had no intention of supplying it.

Undecided, Lexie eyed the valet. She saw a man of medium height and middle age, impeccably attired and very correct in his manner. Storm often mentioned his man, Marlow. And, when she looked more closely, she recognised the Marquess's coachman mounted on the box. The man acknowledged her by smiling and touching his hat with his whip.

They would probably do whatever the Marquess told them. But the coachman's presence was reassuring. 'Very well,' she told Marlow. 'I will return to inform my staff of my absence and find a footman to accompany me.'

She turned towards Bruton Street, but Marlow's voice stopped her. He placed a strong but deferential hand on her arm. 'There is no need, my lady. You will not be away long and his lordship was most particular that I take every care of you. Will you not allow me to help you into the coach?'

The thoughts raced round in Lexie's head. She knew this must be the Marquess's coach, however incognito, for these were indubitably his servants, though the horses harnessed to it were a lesser team that she did not recognise. He would not send his four famous matched bays if he did not wish to advertise the ownership of the coach—they were too well known. Why he should send for her she could not fathom, but he would not wish to put her reputation at risk by sending for her openly.

Her curiosity was aroused. He might truly need her presence for some reason but if it were some hoax he was perpetrating upon her, then she would simply enjoy the joke, walk out and take a hackney back to Bruton Street. St James's Street was not far away. Real uneasiness had left her with the realisation that these men really were Storm's servants. She still believed that he meant her no harm. She would be, in all essentials, perfectly safe with him. Besides, she wanted to know what he was at.

Coming to her decision, Lexie stepped towards the coach, wondering at the same time what Marlow would do if she refused. Would he force her inside? She did not feel disposed to put that question to the test. 'If his lordship truly needs my presence, for whatever mysterious reason, then I will come with you,' she told him, mounting the step.

Marlow shut the door, raised the step and joined the coachman on the box. The carriage, a comfortably sprung, beautifully upholstered vehicle, moved off. Lexie sank back into a corner, tense, nervous, excited and strangely exultant. Perhaps the weeks of tension and waiting were over at last. Storm was making his move.

What a tease he was! She could not believe he was ill. Marlow had not said so. This was part of his campaign to seduce her, of that she was becoming more certain every moment. And the moments were passing. They should have arrived by now.

Suddenly anxious, Lexie sat up and looked out of the window. The coach was moving fast, threading its way through the traffic with speed and expertise, for the coachman was excellent at his job. But they were not headed for St James's Street. She did not recognise the area at all at first and when she did, she did so with dismay. Covent Garden. Not far from Drury Lane. Where was she being taken?

She tried banging on the roof of the coach, but her urgent rapping brought no results. Perhaps they hadn't heard, she had only her knuckles and the roof was padded on the inside. But she doubted they would have stopped even if they had heard.

Not until they reached a respectable back street did the coach pull up, stopping outside a freshly painted door, which opened from the inside at their approach. Marlow jumped down, let down the step and opened the door for her.

'I will take you to his lordship, my lady. He is inside,' he informed her, his face completely inscrutable.

Lexie, trying to look as though she had known all along where they were bringing her, nodded and stepped with dignity towards the open door.

'Thank you, Marlow,' she said as she entered what could only be the flat where the Marquess kept his mistresses.

CHAPTER SEVEN

WHOEVER had opened the door had disappeared by the time Lexie entered. Marlow led her up a narrow staircase to a flat which must be over the draper's shop beside the front door. A small vestibule led through to a large, well appointed room containing an upholstered settee, several chairs of varying design, a *chaise-longue*, a collection of small tables holding various objects, a glass-fronted cupboard displaying pieces of ornamental china, a whatnot, and a writing table upon which sat a dainty pen and inkstand filled with quills and ink. Expensive rugs covered the floor and striped drapes dressed the windows.

Altogether a charming, feminine apartment, thought Lexie, cosy in winter when the fire was lit, but quite lacking in any trace of masculine occupation. Storm could not spend much time here. He must simply make brief visits to an available woman.

Gall rose in her throat. How dared he bring her to this place? For there could be no doubt that this was the flat so recently occupied by that Hermione woman, the actress he had been keeping as his mistress.

And where was he? She turned to ask Marlow, but he had withdrawn. She was about to investigate further when, beneath the window, she heard the rattle of carriage wheels, the clatter of horses' hooves on the cobbles. She looked out and drew a quite audible breath of distress, for she saw the carriage which had brought her disappearing round the nearest corner.

She heard a deep chuckle behind her. 'So you came. I thought you would be unable to resist the challenge, my dear,' came the familiar drawling voice.

Lexie spun round.

'The carriage!' was all she could gasp as she looked into devilish blue eyes sparkling with mischief and something more, which seemed to wrap her in heat.

'Do not disturb yourself, my love.' His voice came soothing, gentle. 'Grimshaw will return to convey you home when called.'

Lexie met the flare in those eyes, the eyes of the rake she knew him to be, and called upon all her strength to resist him.

'Why did you send for me? Why bring me here?' she demanded fiercely—for anger was her only defence—before noticing that his lordship's bare legs could be glimpsed beneath a long dressing robe of maroon satin with black lapels and girdle. Despite her resolution, her voice faltered as doubt crept into her mind. 'Are you unwell, as Marlow implied? Have you been confined to bed?'

'By no means,' said Storm with a predatory smile.

Lexie swallowed. They might well have been back in Vauxhall except that here she felt completely vulnerable. If only the correct, teasing yet perfect gentleman who had squired her to so many functions recently would reappear! This devilish male creature she did not trust an inch.

'He said you needed me,' she said faintly. He was coming nearer, his intention more plain with every step he took. She backed away, exclaiming, 'I suspected the summons was a ruse! How dared you send for me in that underhand way, sir!'

'Yet you came!' His grin was wolfish. 'And I do need you, my lady,' he returned plaintively. 'I have needed you in my bed this age. And you, and I mistake not,' he went on seductively, 'entertain a desire to be there.'

Lexie, his heat suffusing her body, longing to throw herself into his arms, clenched her fingers into fists. She must resist him! 'You are impertinent, sir!'

His dark brows lifted above those all-seeing, flaring blue eyes. 'Is it now impertinent to speak the truth? Lexie, my love, stop prevaricating. You are no green girl but an experienced woman. We want each other. What is to stop us indulging our desire?'

'I am not your love!' gulped Lexie.

'Through no fault of mine,' he pointed out reasonably.

Lexie ploughed on, ignoring his words. 'A matter of right and wrong must stop us, sir! I possess morals, even if you do not!' She began to tremble as he reached out to pull her towards him. 'We are not wed! Any union between us would be a sin!'

His voice caressed her as his fingers kneaded her shoulders in a soothing rhythm. 'You believe it would take a few words intoned over us by a parson to make expressing the feelings between us legal?'

'The Church and Society—' began Lexie desperately.

'May pronounce disapproval, but cannot make the

deed wrong. Any more than they can, in my opinion, make the compelled union of two completely incompatible persons right. What of a bride forced to endure the attentions of a man she loathes? Do the parson's words make that morally right?'

'They have been married before God,' uttered Lexie faintly, resting her hands, partly in protest, partly in surrender, against his broad chest, for at last he held her close and was busy removing her bonnet. 'A husband has rights his wife cannot deny.'

Storm smothered an expletive. 'There lies your sin! No woman should be coerced into a marriage where such a possibility exists,' he opined forcefully. 'Married before God or not, the joining of a man and a woman should be a matter of desire between them.'

In her heart, Lexie knew he was right. She should never have had to endure the attentions of Amber, kind and considerate as he had been. It had been like going to bed with her grandfather. She shuddered at the memory and felt Storm's arms tighten about her. Yet she could not have refused her husband, he had had the legal right to use her body as he willed. And, in fairness, she had, however reluctantly, chosen to wed him. No one had thrashed or starved her into submission.

'What is it, my dear?'

The gentle concern in his voice told her he had not mistaken her shudder for either desire or revulsion. He was experienced enough to recognise desire and of one thing at least he could be certain: he did not repulse her!

'Nothing,' she lied. 'But, Storm, I cannot agree to what you wish.'

'Can you not?' he murmured in teasing tones as he swept her into his arms.

His movements had loosened the girdle about his waist and the silk of his robe slipped apart. Lexie's breath caught at sight of the muscles revealed, the dusting of dark hair giving him an appearance of virility Amber had lacked. His sparse hair had been grey. She had had no desire to explore his old body but he had taught her where he liked to be touched and, to please him, she had complied.

Of its own volition her hand reached out to feel the roughness of Storm's body hair; her finger sought the nipple it only partly concealed.

At her touch, Storm sucked in his breath as he carried her through to the bedchamber. She heard the heart beneath her ear begin to hammer and snatched her hand away. This would would never do!

As he set her on her feet again, she vaguely took in a vast bed hung with creamy silken drapes, a large kidney-shaped dressing table with triple mirrors and matching hangings, frilly curtains and a full-length cheval mirror. Then Storm's fingers began to remove her gown with the expertise of someone quite used to undressing a woman.

She should stop him but her will had fled with the strength in her limbs. Dear God, why did his touch have such a devastating effect upon her? He hadn't even kissed her yet and she was like clay in his hands!

Her gown dropped to the floor and Storm flung off his robe to reveal the full glory of his strong, beautiful, roused body. After that she had eyes for nothing else but him as he followed her down on the bed and began to loosen the ties of her chemise.

When he was like this, tender, teasing, yet betraying controlled passion, she could deny him nothing! Her body opened, rose instinctively to meet his. But even as he lifted himself above her she caught a breath of unfamiliar perfume still lingering in the drapes of the bed.

That woman's!

What was she thinking of! She could not, simply could not make love with Storm in this bed, in the flat where he had entertained his other women!

'No!' she gasped, pushing at his chest, struggling to release herself from beneath him. 'No, Storm! I am not one of your lightskirts, to be taken in your love-nest like some cheap actress! Do not force me!'

For an instant Storm did not move, held still while he controlled his breathing. Then he lifted himself from her and, back turned, flung on his discarded robe.

'I have never yet had need to force a woman, madam,' he informed her icily, frustration clipping his words in a totally unfamiliar way. 'I am persuaded that I shall survive well enough without the gift of your valuable favours.'

In her distress Lexie fumbled to fasten her chemise, bent to rescue her gown, tried to find the opening, the sleeves, to pull it over her head. It was so long since she had dressed herself! His words brought her efforts to a trembling halt.

She had lost him now! 'Oh,' she cried. 'Are you so without feeling that you cannot understand, Storm?

Or are your desires the only things that matter to you? Your morals the only ones you can comprehend?'

The tears began to stream down her face unheeded as she at last managed to insert her arms into her gown and attempted to reach the fastenings down the back.

'I certainly cannot—'

'You have no finer feelings at all! To mortify me so by bringing me here, to this place where you have kept your cheap women!'

Storm frowned and, for the first time, looked slightly less than self-assured. 'Most were far from cheap,' he muttered wryly, then added, 'My dear Lexie, I merely sought to preserve your reputation. Here, you are unlikely to be recognised. I considered it a safe place for our tryst.'

'Tryst!' almost screamed Lexie, scrubbing at the tears she had previously ignored. How could she be so weak as to let him see how much he had hurt her! 'This was no tryst! Abduction would be a better description of the means you used to lure me here! I had not agreed to meet you! But Marlow was persuasive, I thought he was escorting me to St James's—'

'Had he done so your reputation would have been in shreds!' pointed out Storm coldly. 'No lady walks or drives down that street with impunity! Did you think me so shabby as to lay you open to abuse by every gabble-grinder in London?'

'I did not think,' admitted Lexie more calmly. 'But that does not excuse you for bringing me here and attempting to seduce me when I have rejected your *carte blanche*! And now, if you please, call Grimshaw to return me to my home!'

Storm had pulled on pantaloons beneath his gown. Now he removed it to don a shirt, which he tucked in at the waist but left unfastened. No doubt Marlow would dress him properly before he departed. Lexie only hoped that she looked respectable enough not to cause undue comment when she reached Bruton Street. She still had not fastened her bodice, and her hair must look a terrible mess.

Unexpectedly, Storm smiled, and led the way through to the sitting-room. Lexie, glad to escape the close proximity of that bed, quickly followed. Storm handed her her bonnet.

'Since I was so remiss as to remove your gown, allow me to fasten it for you, madam.'

His nimble fingers at her back shook Lexie to the core. Oh, why could he not woo her respectably?

Storm noted her quick breathing, the fluttering pulse in her neck, the feverish light in her eyes, and cursed her scruples. He could not resist the gentle kiss he placed in the sweet curve of her neck but regretted his impulse the moment he felt her whole body stiffen.

Secretly he honoured her for her principles. Society was loose in its morality, few members of the *ton* being quite the whited sepulchres they pretended. From the Prince Regent down, men and women indulged in numerous *affaires*; few behaved in private with the decorum they enjoined in public. Those noted Patronesses of Almack's, Lady Jersey and Lady Cowper, both had lovers. But then, like so many others, they had been married to men they did not love for dynastic and financial reasons.

He had, following his own code, always avoided such a marriage. He would demand faithfulness in a wife. Whether he would be able to return the compliment he rather doubted. He could not imagine the woman able to satisfy him for the remainder of his life.

He finished his task, lifted Lexie's chin with gentle fingers and brushed her lips with his own. And then startled both himself and her by saying, 'I apologise for my treatment of you, Lexie, my dear. I should have realised how sincerely you meant your refusal at Vauxhall. But please do not run away so soon. Marlow is an excellent cook and is preparing our repast. Will you not remain and enjoy it?'

Seeing her shaken, almost fearful look, hand on heart he added hastily and sincerely, 'I promise to behave!' And smiled his most wicked, teasing smile.

An apology and an olive branch. Lexie's heart melted. He could be both wicked and generous. That must be how he managed to seduce so many women to his bidding. Instinctively, she had known he would never truly harm her, never force her against her will. Otherwise she would not have entered his coach.

Surely she could be as generous, accept his apology and forgive his treatment of her? Apart from her own inclination to fall into his arms and forget scruples, the world, and every responsibility, she would be safe. And she was quite capable of resisting her own emotions. She had already proved that.

So, 'Very well,' she accepted. 'I must confess to

being sharp set and whatever it is that Marlow is preparing smells delicious. Thank you, Storm. I will stay a while, although I could never feel truly comfortable here in this place. But I must be back before Caro and Chalker return, so that I am not missed.'

He nodded and moved to pour her a glass of sherry. As he handed it to her he said, 'I intended to return you in good time.'

Lexie accepted the glass while giving him a fleeting, suspicious glance before hurriedly averting her eyes. She did not trust herself to look too long on the magnificent physique displayed beneath that open shirt without weakening. His garb was quite indecent but so alluring. She suppressed a smile. Rakish, in fact. 'You knew they would both be absent this evening?'

'And that you had no engagement. That you often walked in Berkeley Square before dressing for dinner, I already knew. Cousin Caro informed me of hers and your maid's plans while I was waiting for you yesterday. The opportunity to lure you here seemed too good to miss. I fell into temptation,' he confessed with a wry smile, a lift of one dark brow, and overdone contrition.

Lexie thought the best thing to do was to laugh. 'You almost made me fall, too, my lord!' She drank some of the wine, which seemed to loosen her tongue. 'I would not have come had I not trusted you, in the end, to behave as a gentleman should.'

'I am flattered. You do not, then, entirely believe in my reputation as a rakehell?'

Lexie smiled. 'I believe that in public you hide

behind a mask, my lord. In private, I have often glimpsed the essential gentleman concealed beneath. Besides, your grandmother would not be so fond of you were you as bad as you are sometimes painted.'

He regarded her quizzically. 'And that is why you consented to my escort, despite the gossip our constant appearances in public together has generated?' She nodded and he went on, 'Were my intentions known to be honourable, we would already be as good as betrothed. Since they are extremely suspect, you must, in their opinion, undoubtedly be my mistress.'

'I know, but gossip without foundation has little sting. Were it to be known that I had been here, even though nothing dishonourable has actually happened, I would be branded a harlot.' She met his eyes boldly. 'My chances of contracting a felicitous marriage to an honourable gentleman would be quite gone.'

'Do you wish for marriage again?' asked Storm interestedly.

Lexie drank the last of her sherry and then studied the glass in her hand with a slight frown. 'Yes,' she answered honestly. 'But only wed to a man who can be lover, companion and friend. I should like,' she added wistfully, 'to fall in love. If I do not find such a creature, then I shall be content to remain a widow. I have my freedom and sufficient means. I will not surrender those precious things merely in order to satisfy my longing for a family.'

She had, she realised too late, opened her heart to him. And he had made no reply. She risked a quick glance and saw that his brow was now marred by a slight frown. His lazy lids covered his eyes and his studied air of casual, indolent ease had been replaced by one of concentration. She wondered what he could be thinking.

He was wondering, in truth, why he did not propose matrimony there and then. And knew it was because he could not risk hurting such a jewel as Alexia Hamilton by the transgressions he would undoubtedly perpetrate at some later date. She would expect, nay, demand, fidelity, which he could not offer. So he would offer nothing.

He was saved the trouble of answering her by the timely entry of Marlow to announce that dinner was ready to be served.

'Bring it in!' ordered Storm, relaxing again. 'Lady Alexia, will you sit here?'

As Lexie took her place at the small, intimate table laid for two, she thought how wonderful it would be if only they could live like this, without ceremony, sharing the intimacy of companionship, friendship—and love.

But Storm had not reacted to her indiscretion save by that slight frown of concentration. And as the meal progressed and the atmosphere became easy she forgot everything else in the joy of sharing the company of so entertaining, considerate a companion.

With Storm on his very best behaviour—apart from the occasional glance from desirous eyes—she even managed to forget the real reason for her being there and the past history of the cosy flat. Only when, the platters empty, Storm called Marlow to summon the carriage, was the true nature of her presence brought home to her again.

Then she could not leave fast enough. But, it seemed, he was still escorting her to the theatre the following evening.

'We must not feed the gabble-grinders more grist to their mill,' he remarked calmly. 'I shall continue to escort you to those functions you choose to attend.'

Nothing had changed. Except that everything had changed.

She was hopelessly in love and did not know how she was to bear his constant attendance on her without giving herself away.

Lexie thought and thought. Somehow, the deadlock between them must be broken. It was, after all, mostly convention that coloured her morality and prevented her from casting prudence to the winds and agreeing to his offered *carte blanche*. That and an instinctive desire to know the man she loved would be hers for life. A mistress could be cast off at any moment. A wife could not so easily be set aside.

She saw rather less of Storm over the next week, since she chose to accept fewer invitations. When he did escort her he behaved with punctilious correctness, his languid manner and drawling speech never more in evidence. He had withdrawn behind his mask. Lexie ached to penetrate it again.

But Prinny's festivities were a must and Storm was taking her in his curricle, with his tiger up behind to act as chaperon. Caro, frightened of crowds, refused to be cajoled into accompanying them.

'It is high time his lordship declared himself,' she grumbled, fluttering her fan, for the weather was sultry. 'You have allowed him to make a spectacle of you all the Season, Alexia,' she went on querulously, 'and soon, no doubt he will retire to his estates and forget all about you! You have not made the most of your chances, my dear.' Caro, who had been quite won over by the Marquess's charm, added, with a languishing sigh, 'I always mistrusted the wisdom of your association with that rake.'

Lexie spread her hands, mischief lighting her features despite her broken heart. 'Confess, you have always wished you were in my shoes, Caro! He is not so very bad a rake, after all. He is too much of a gentleman.'

'But he has compromised you without being honourable enough to offer for you, it seems! Despite his reputation, he would make you a fine husband, Alexia. Can you do nothing to bring him to the point?'

Assiduously studying a slightly ragged nail, 'It seems not, Cousin,' said Lexie. 'Always assuming I have tried.'

'You are no more than a foolish chit if you have not! Your reputation is almost in shreds. . .'

Caro's indignant censure amused rather than offended Lexie. She looked up and grinned. 'Do not concern yourself over me. We are still received in the most austere of drawing-rooms!'

'But if his lordship casts you off—'

'Stop prating, Cousin! I am used to being the object of the latest *on dits*. We shall be retiring to Merryfield next week and people will soon forget the scandals of the Season. My present aberrations will be history by next year.'

'Unless you return to London and continue with your rackety ways. Then the gossip will start all over again,' wailed Caro.

'It scarcely affects you, Cousin, so do not refine over it,' said Lexie tartly. Caro's lamentations were chafing her raw nerves. 'Think of Merryfield and how much we shall enjoy the fresh country air!'

Thinking of Merryfield, an idea entered her head, so bold and outrageous that for a moment it stopped her breath. She had been recalling the pleasure of driving Pitch and Tar around the estate roads, racing them as she had been used to do in Cornwall. And an audacious plan formed in her mind.

'The Duke of Wellington is leaving Town soon, to take up his post as Ambassador in Paris. Once he has gone, London will empty. We will hold a house party of our own,' she declared with sudden decision. 'In fact, Caro, it would be most beneficial if you were to go on ahead to consult with Mrs Panning, open up the house and prepare it for the guests. Mrs Walker and Mr Dymock will accompany me down, and as many of the staff as you think necessary.'

The plan had an added advantage. She could well do without Cousin Caro's fussing and refining over her while she remained in Town herself.

'How many guests did you have in mind?' asked Caro, her eyes beginning to gleam, all cares forgotten in anticipation of this new enterprise. She would be in her element at Merryfield planning a house party.

'I don't know,' admitted Lexie slowly. 'I must make a list of those I wish to invite and then send out the invitations. As soon as possible, I should think, so that our guests may travel straight down.'

'Will they not have already planned to go to Brighton or Eastbourne for sea bathing or to Bath to take the waters?' objected Caro anxiously.

'Not those I would wish to invite, I think,' said Lexie thoughtfully. She had heard no mention of the Duchess doing anything other than returning straight to her husband and the Downshire estates in Kent, taking Fanny with her.

Storm, she knew, would make speedy tracks for Stormaston House, his favourite residence, which he spoke of with real affection but which she had yet to see. An invitation for her to go there would give her so much delight. . . But he would never be so foolish as to invite her to his home unless. . .

She cut her daydreams short as a waste of time and emotional energy. Her own plans had to be laid.

For propriety's sake, she would have to include a few others, of course, the Duke for one, whom she had never met, though she doubted he would be persuaded to come. Storm's friend, Felix St Clare, who had become her own dear friend must be asked, for Fanny's sake, if for no other, for Lexie was quite certain they were fond of each other.

Oswald Cresswell, too, whom she rather liked and felt sorry for. His boyish devotion acted as an antidote to Storm's aggressive, sexual pursuit. She could bask in the young man's adoration without fear of any untoward consequences. But what about his mother?

She did not, for Fanny's sake, want the Viscountess there to bully her son into pursuing a lost cause.

Lady Wighton might allow her son to come alone. She would try to arrange it, for his sake. He needed to escape his mother's leading strings.

There was a girl, one of those who had been at Vauxhall, what was her name? Melissa Daventry, that was it. Miss Daventry cherished a *tendre* for Oswald and would gladly come if she knew he was to be there. She would bring her duenna, of course. They would all bring servants. Merryfield would be full of life and laughter for the first time since she had inherited it.

Excitement surged through Lexie. She would make her list but she would not issue the invitations until after the Centenary celebrations. For it was during those that she intended to make her bid to engage the Marquess of Stormaston, that acknowledged gamester, who would bet on the most ridiculous of things if challenged, in a wager that would settle the matter of her future status in his life.

She could not allow things to go on as they were. She would end up a diminished wreck. Her gowns were already hanging loosely upon her. She must settle matters once and for all and then set about living contentedly, whatever the result.

She dressed carefully for the great day, choosing a becoming outfit in the latest fashion comprising a sky blue petticoat with braces, worn over a white spencer—ideal for walking in the summer heat. A large bonnet with matching ribbons tied under her chin covered most of her golden curls. Half-boots completed her toilet, for the ground was bound to be somewhat damp and she anticipated leaving the curricle to enjoy the promised spectacles.

'You look a perfect picture!' exclaimed Caro as Lexie presented herself for inspection, flourishing a matching parasol. 'But isn't the waist of your gown a little low?'

'Waistlines have been dropping for several years, Cousin. You,' teased Lexie, eyeing her companion's sprigged muslin and accompanying drapes affectionately, 'are old fashioned!'

'I am too old to change my style now,' fluttered Caro anxiously. 'Do you think I should?'

'Not at all,' assured Lexie. 'You have no one but yourself to please.'

'Thank goodness the morning rain has stopped. Do have a nice time, dear,' said Caro. 'I am so glad you have the protection of a gentleman. You will need it amongst all those crowds.'

Lexie, remembering a previous time when she had ventured alone into the crowds and been rescued by Storm, could do nothing but agree. It was so infinitely reassuring to be able to rely upon his strength. But today, win or lose, her dice must be thrown. He would agree to her proposition or he would not. If he did, Caro could be despatched to Merryfield on the morrow and there, she herself would have one final chance to fulfil her dearest wish, to win him as her husband.

He knew now that she would not respond to any illicit advances on his part and so she felt secure in accepting only his tiger, Bill Trappin, as chaperon. Of course, the tiger's presence would be a mere gesture toward the proprieties, but that no longer concerned her. They were to join friends by the Serpentine and her entire day would be coloured by finding the right opportunity to lay down her wager.

Storm was dressed as though for riding, in buff pantaloons and shining hessians topped by a snuff-coloured jacket. A large, reassuring umbrella reposed behind the seat of the curricle with the basket of food she had anticipated, for they did not intend to return before darkness fell.

'In case the rain returns,' explained Storm with a grin.

'I do hope it does not! Just think of all these crowds getting soaked!' said Lexie, eyeing the orderly throng spreading over the grass of Hyde Park as they entered the gates, having avoided the congestion in Piccadilly and elsewhere.

Storm was forced to drive slowly and carefully, threading his way through the crowds of pedestrians as well as other carriages and the many equestrians. People milled everywhere: eating their food, climbing trees, patronising the many gaming, drinking and other entertainment booths erected on the grass.

Lexie eyed his matched, almost pure white greys with a critical eye. She could not fault them. Mettlesome, reputedly prime goers, Storm had won a number of curricle races with them put to. But Pitch and Tar were equally fine cattle. She knew how fast they could travel, knew her own ability to drive them to an inch. Yes, win or lose, it would be worth the risk.

Before long they had to abandon the curricle.

'I fear we must walk from here,' apologised Storm, swinging himself to the ground. Trappin ran to the horses' heads and Storm assisted Lexie to descend.

His hands on her waist were firm and warm. She shivered. 'Trappin,' went on Storm, 'I trust you to return my cattle safely to their stables. After that, you may take the rest of the day off.'

'But your hamper, my lord!' cried Trappin, scandalised at the idea of his master demeaning himself by carrying it himself.

'I'm sure this boy will be only too pleased to carry it and the umbrella down to the Serpentine,' said Storm, picking up his silver-mounted stick and beckoning the child towards him. 'Will you not, my lad?'

'Do anyfink fer a tanner, yer lordship!' grinned the cheeky youngster.

'A tanner it shall be.'

Lexie saw the boy's grin, a response to Storm's easy manner. Most of the nobility assumed a lofty air when dealing with inferiors. But not Storm.

When they finally reached the water's edge and found their friends, Storm paid off the lad, leaving the impedimenta with the others' servants.

While he was engaged in making these arrangements, Lexie, having greeted the other members of their party, stared wide-eyed at the display on the water. The Serpentine had become an ocean on which sailed a fleet of miniature ships of the line, from three-deckers with up to seventy guns protruding from their ports, to lightly armed, graceful, fast-sailing frigates, all fully rigged.

'Just one of the Regent's grand flights of fancy. A representation of the battle of the Nile. An awesome sight were they real and not ships' barges dressed up!' came Storm's comment from her side.

'I saw such a fleet once, off Cornwall. Distant, of

course, sailing for Plymouth or Portsmouth, I suppose. But at the time it appeared a reassuring sight.'

'Returning from blockade duty off Brest, I dare say,' said Storm, offering his sleeve. 'Shall we stroll along the bank?'

'Oh, yes, do let us!' cried Fanny, overhearing. 'Come, Lord Dexter, Mr Cresswell! Do join us!'

Unable to evade the unwelcome company, Storm accepted the situation with grace.

'Miss Daventry!' called Lexie. 'Will you not walk with us?'

Melissa Daventry accepted with confused alacrity.

Lexie found herself walking with Felix while Storm, swinging his stick, escorted Melissa, leaving Fanny and Oswald to accompany each other. But conversation was general and partners quickly changed, more than once. Lexie had no opportunity for private converse with Storm.

The afternoon progressed. They ate their refreshments sitting on horse blankets on the damp ground before walking through to St James's Park, hung even by day with coloured lanterns, to find a band playing so that the populace could dance. A huge Chinese bridge and a pagoda, seven storeys high, lit by gas, caused astonished interest and admiration.

After a while, 'You are, I collect, able to walk back?' asked Storm of the company in general. He had, with natural authority, assumed command of the expedition. 'The sun has already almost set. We should make our way through to Green Park if we want to see the climax to the day's events. It is there that the Regent has really excelled himself.'

The rather large party had, before its arrival

before Buckingham House, split into several smaller groups, each attended by chaperons and servants. Storm and his immediate party arrived in time to see a hot-air balloon ascend from the platform especially built for it. The Regent and his guests were watching from the Royal Pavilion erected for the purpose but, 'We can see better from here!' cried Lexie.

Up the balloon majestically soared, dropping coloured parachutes, weighted at the bottom, which floated down amongst the happy, cheering throng. The balloon drifted off and was presently lost to sight.

'It will land safely, won't it?' asked Fanny anxiously.

'One can only hope so,' said Felix, giving her arm a reassuring squeeze, which brought a blush to Fanny's cheeks.

'But look!' cried Lexie. 'Just look at that castle!'

'I am told it is one hundred and thirty feet high,' said Storm dryly. 'It is symbolic, you know, a Castle of Discord and a Temple of Peace. The Prince designed most of it himself.'

'I am quite looking forward to the staging of the storming of Badajoz!'

'You sound quite bloodthirsty for a poet,' Lexie teased Oswald. His mother had not come. This seemed to be one of those rare occasions when the young people were allowed to play without much attempt to chaperon them. Fanny's maid and Melissa's duenna had accompanied them, ready to intervene but otherwise keeping well in the background.

'Poems have been written about it!' protested Oswald, affronted.

'I wonder what His Grace the Duke of Wellington will think,' ventured Melissa shyly. 'I can see him sitting in the pavilion with the Prince.'

'He will consider the whole show to be in bad taste, I should imagine,' remarked Storm.

'Why?' demanded Lexie. 'The representation is put on in his honour!'

'But so many of the ordinary men who were the real heroes, those who survived, are now reduced to begging in the streets. Just like the veterans of the Nile. We do not treat our soldiers and sailors well once the need for their services is over.'

A momentary silence descended on the party. Not one of them had escaped the sight of poor, maimed wretches with their begging bowls. Even those discharged fit were often reduced to begging or crime to keep body and soul together. And Chelsea was full of still others waiting demobilisation, lounging about the streets reeling with drink or squatting on the steps of the public houses.

'Nelson tried to do something and Wellington will, too,' said Felix seriously. 'But remember, most of the ordinary soldiers and seamen were recruited from the gutter. It will be no change for them to return to it.'

'But after serving their country—' began Lexie, frowning, only to be cut off short by Fanny.

'Today is a day of rejoicing! Do not let us refine over problems we can do nothing about!'

'Well said, little sister,' drawled Storm. 'Leave such problems to those who have the power.'

Yet Lexie could detect an undercurrent of anger in his languid voice. She looked at him quickly and saw the emotion reflected in his eyes. 'You have a seat in the House of Lords,' she reminded him softly.

'But no wish to engage in national politics,' he returned, equally quietly. 'Running my estates efficiently and seeing to the welfare of my people is more than enough to keep me occupied.'

'They are starting!' cried Fanny excitedly.

A battery of Congreve's rockets fired into the air, lighting the sky before descending in sheets of fire. Maroons went off, mines exploded. Redcoats, their faces blackened, crept through the fast descending darkness with bayonets glinting. Men dressed as Frenchmen stood waving their arms on the battlements of the Castle of Discord. Over in Hyde Park four of the Nile ships burnt with vivid flame and black smoke, while the swans screeched in protest.

The show went on for an age and the party wondered what more the Regent could possibly offer, but the entertainment was designed to go on until midnight. As the hour arrived, a deafening explosion made everyone jump.

The canvas walls of the Castle of Discord lifted to reveal the Temple of Peace, with its mock columns, rainbows, vestal virgins and pictures painted on transparent silk depicting the Golden Age Restored. Coloured lamps lit the scene, water flowed from the mouths of mock lions while fireworks shot skywards and guardsmen held aloft the Royal Standard where, earlier, the mock French soldiers had been seen. Peace had triumphed over war and destruction.

'A worthy sentiment,' murmured Storm.

'Oh, look! cried Melissa. 'Whatever can be causing that great blaze?'

Despite the distance, it was clear to see that something other than the ships on the Serpentine had caught fire. A sort of rumble rippled over the crowd, bringing the news that the Chinese Pagoda had gone up in flames. Most people seemed to think it was all part of the Regent's planned spectacular but Storm shook his head.

'I doubt it. I imagine the gas lamps have set it ablaze. But come, it is time we all returned home. Mr Cresswell, you will no doubt see that Lady Fanny, her maid and the Duchess's servants reach Downshire House safely. Felix, I leave the escorting of Miss Daventry and her chaperon to you.'

Murmurs of assent followed, though both Fanny and Melissa looked disappointed.

'I'm glad the Regent put on such a splendid show!' said Lexie stoutly as she and Storm detached themselves from the others in order to thread their way through the streets back to her residence. 'London has never known such a celebration! The crowds have enjoyed every minute of the day!'

'You have, I collect,' murmured Storm with an indulgent grin.

'Yes,' admitted Lexie. She had, in the end, quite forgotten her need for a private word with Storm. 'Did you not enjoy it, too?'

'This kind of entertainment is not normal fare for rakes like Felix and me,' explained Storm.

'Then why did you agree to come?'

'Ah, now that is an excellent question. I came to offer you my escort. It is, after all, what I have been doing these past weeks. Felix, I believe, came to lend me his support. Normally, wild horses would not have dragged us to an extravaganza of this sort.'

'I do not believe you!' protested Lexie, seeing the twitch of his mobile mouth. 'You are bamming me! No one wished to miss the occasion!'

'Ah, but most of Society saw fit to watch from the comfort of a pavilion. To think,' he added self-righteously, 'that I could have been enjoying the sights from the Royal Pavilion but for my promise to you!'

'Would you have gone?'

Storm shook his head, grinning ruefully. 'No. I have little liking for being confined on such an occasion.'

'You were strolling the streets when the Allied Sovereigns arrived,' remembered Lexie.

'So I was. At least we have that much in common. A sense of wishing to escape the confines of our milieu once in a while.'

'We have more than that in common,' said Lexie slowly. Now, surely, was her moment. She stopped, drawing him to a halt beside her. They had reached Piccadilly and one of the new gas lamps lit her earnest features as she gazed up into Storm's face. 'We both enjoy a challenge. I have a wager to offer you.'

CHAPTER EIGHT

'A WAGER?'

Storm's brows rose in surprise, as well they might, thought Lexie, almost losing her courage.

'Yes.'

Carriages rattled along the road, people swarmed past on foot, homeward bound. Hardly an appropriate place to hold the discussion yet, essentially, they were alone for the first time that day. Noises, odour, the presence of others, faded into the background as Lexie waited apprehensively for Storm's response.

'And what would the subject of this wager be?' Storm's tone was as languid as she had ever heard it and her heart sank still further in the direction of her half-boots.

'A curricle race.' Lexie dropped her hand from his arm. Why was she having so much difficulty in saying what she had to say, she wondered despairingly. What had seemed such a good idea in theory had become the least clever notion ever to enter her head.

'Between whom, may I ask?'

Lexie swallowed. 'Us.'

She watched a slow smile spread itself across Storm's face and inwardly cringed.

'You are challenging me to race my curricle against yours? Driven by yourself?'

Lexie's voice failed her. She nodded.

Storm leant negligently upon his stick. 'Indeed.' The smile became a grin. 'You little hoyden. Do you seriously believe that you could beat me?'

'I would not suggest the wager if I did not,' protested Lexie hoarsely.

'Hmm. My accepting your challenge depends largely upon the stake. What did you have in mind?'

She was forced to clear her throat before she spoke. Her hands were damp with sweat. 'If you win, you win my outfit. My blacks and the curricle.'

'And if you should beat me?' He regarded her musingly. 'Since you have not mentioned them, I collect that you have no use for my match pair?'.

'No.' Another swallow. 'No particular use.'

'Then what is it that I am to put at risk?'

Storm's bored tone did not match the intent expression in his eyes. Some emotions his mask was unable to hide. He was deeply interested in her reply.

'If I win, you agree to marry me.'

There, it was out. Lexie waited for him to burst into ribald laughter.

He did not. But the intentness in his gaze gave way to pained affront.

'You lose your horses and carriage or I lose my freedom, is that it?' At Lexie's timorous nod, he pursed his lips, stood up straight and swung his cane. 'That scarcely seems a fair wager to me. I have no more need of your horses than you have of mine.'

'Then I will stake their worth,' said Lexie desperately.

He shrugged a negligent shoulder. 'But I have no particular need of money, either.'

'Oh.' Lexie drooped. Her voice dripped disappointment. 'Then you do not accept the bet?'

'I have not yet decided.' Storm shifted his stance and waited for a crowd of merrymakers to pass. 'Tell me more. Where, for instance, is this proposed race to be run?'

'Around the estate paths at Merryfield.'

'Ah! You allow yourself an advantage, I collect.' *His* voice dripped cynicism.

Lexie fiddled nervously with the strings of her reticule. 'You could arrive several days before the race and familiarise yourself with the route.'

'What?' Storm swung his stick, leant against the lamp standard and infused his voice with shock. His eyes, however, held sheer, devilish hilarity. 'Reside with you at Merryfield? What would people say?'

Although Lexie knew he was only bamming her, she felt obliged to answer. 'There would be others there. Invited particularly to watch the race.'

'And to be privy to the nature of the wager?' enquired Storm interestedly.

'Well, no. They would think us racing for cash stakes.'

'You seem determined to have me leg-shackled, my dear.' He straightened up, reached out and flicked her chin with one long finger. 'I wonder why?'

Lexie clutched her reticule and parasol tightly with her sticky, gloved hands. He must not see them shaking. Or guess what was now the truth, that she loved him and longed for him to make love to her. So she admitted only her original reason for wishing to wed him. 'I should like a family and you need an heir. We deal well together. The match would be suitable.'

At this he took on a haughty demeanour. 'And you would become a Duchess in due course. And find yourself wed to a man of considerable wealth and influence. From your point of view I can well see the advantages, my love,' he asserted arrogantly. 'But for myself, they appear, forgive me for saying so, rather less obvious.'

'You say you want me,' uttered Lexie almost inaudibly, blushing a furious red which she hoped would not be noticed in the glare of the lamp. 'And I cannot come to you outside wedlock.'

But the gaslight which she hoped would conceal her blush sparked devilish fires in Storm's eyes.

'Rakes,' he informed her, still arrogant, 'do not *wed* the ladies they desire. They have no need. They wed a suitable young dimwit to bear them an heir.'

He sounded as though he found the idea distasteful. Lexie smiled grimly. 'And endure a lifetime of boredom.'

He settled himself back against the lamp standard, long legs crossed, a thoughtful expression replacing his former hauteur. 'Not necessarily. He need not endure much of her company. But you give me an idea,' he declared lazily. 'I offer you an alternative wager. If you should beat me, I will marry you.'

Lexie gasped, scarcely able to believe he had accepted such a stake until he went on, softly, mockingly, 'But should I win—an outcome which, I should warn you, I confidently expect—then you overcome your scruples and consent to become my mistress.'

Dead silence greeted his words. The bottom

seemed to have fallen out of Lexie's stomach. Why, oh why, had she embarked upon this nonsensical plan? She might have guessed the Marquess would turn it to his own advantage! Now it had come down to his liberty against her virtue.

And she had no guarantee of winning, although she did know a thing or two about the tracks at Merryfield which he did not. She had driven along them at reckless speed during her lengthy sojourn there while waiting out her period of mourning and Pitch and Tar knew every rise, dip and turn.

But he was a noted whip, a nonpareil. She must have been mad to think she stood any chance against him! It had not mattered so desperately when all she stood to lose was her precious pair of blacks. But pride would not allow her to back out now.

'Very well,' she said, as firmly as she could make herself.

Storm grinned, reached into his pocket and brought forth a slim notebook and pencil.

'I always record my wagers and the stakes,' he announced, Lexie thought insultingly smugly, as he wrote down the terms. 'Time and route to be agreed later,' he murmured, signing with a flourish. 'Now if you will append your mark, Lady Amber. . .'

'My mark!' muttered Lexie scathingly as she accepted the book. She scrutinised what he had written and signed her name, deliberately and clearly, despite trembling fingers and a renewed sense of doom.

Storm inspected her signature, grinned wickedly as he observed, 'You write an excellent hand, my dear,' tucked the book away and courteously offered his arm. 'Shall we walk on? People will begin to notice us if we remain idling here too long.'

Lexie put her fingers on his sleeve, glad of the support offered. But the deed was done. All that remained now was to sort out the details. And run the race. And pay the price if she lost.

But that was something she preferred not to contemplate. It stirred too many mixed emotions. How deep did her convictions really run?

The rain and unprecedented traffic had conspired to mire Piccadilly's carriageway with a noxious sludge. They waited while a ragged lad swept a clear path for them to cross. Storm tossed him a penny and they proceeded towards Bruton Street.

'Did you have a date in mind for this event? he enquired. 'I cannot delay my return to Stormaston Park much longer. There is much to be done there.'

'I thought the house party should be gathered as soon as possible, so that people who accept may travel straight to Hertfordshire before returning to their own estates.'

Storm nodded. 'An excellent notion. And who, exactly, did you have it in mind to invite?'

'Your grandmother and sister and the Duke, too, if he will come. Lord Dexter, Mr Cresswell, and Miss Melissa Daventry will form the core. More or less our set. Merryfield is not a large house. I could not accommodate many more.'

'They should prove witnesses enough to the fairness of the race. Were I you I should not invite others, even if I had room to spare. Few ladies of breeding have in the past dared to embark upon such a scandalous enterprise as you contemplate. Curricle racing is the dangerous preserve of gentlemen. If knowledge of the wager becomes widely spread, your reputation will suffer another blow. It would be best not to invite any who would be likely to censure the endeavour.'

'The Duchess might, I suppose,' said Lexie uncertainly. 'But I do so want her to come.'

'Why?' demanded that lady's grandson with interest.

'Because she has been kind to me and I value her opinion,' explained Lexie, leaving out the fact that the Duchess's presence tended to moderate the Marquess's more extravagant behaviour and that she enjoyed observing the affection in which they obviously held each other.

'I would not like her to think I was behaving in a havey-cavey manner, hiding my intention from her. And the Duke must receive an invitation out of courtesy. I have never met him, you know.'

'Grandmama,' said Storm with a chuckle, 'will be much diverted at the prospect of such a race. Wild horses will not stop her from accepting your invitation.'

'You think so? Then I shall send it tomorrow!'

'But I doubt those same wild horses would drag my grandfather from the Downshire estates,' added the Marquess crushingly.

'I shall still invite him. Or would you rather he were not present to watch your defeat?' speculated Lexie mischievously.

'Outrageous wench!' uttered Storm, unable to suppress a chuckle at her audacity.

'The party will be invited to gather a week today,

the eighth,' went on Lexie, unperturbed. 'And the race can be run on the tenth. The social calendar is fairly empty now that the victory celebrations and the centenary jubilee are in the past.'

The discussion had brought them to Bruton Street, where Storm escorted her up the steps of her town house. Luckily there were few about in this comparative backwater to observe the indecorum of Lady Amber arriving home at two in the morning, on foot, and quite alone apart from the dubious escort of the Marquess of Stormaston. Or to witness the speaking kiss he planted on her willing lips before he lifted the knocker and the door swung open.

As she lay sleepless in bed later that night Lexie again wondered why she had ever imagined Storm would accept such a one-sided wager.

She came to the conclusion that she had suppressed any doubts in her eagerness to find a way to bring him to an honourable declaration.

But if he won, he would surely not keep her to her side of the bargain. No gentleman would.

But Storm relished his role as a self-declared rake. If he did not forgive her her debt, she would have to overcome her scruples and honour it.

She dropped off to sleep with a smile curving the soft line of the lips he had so recently kissed.

The arrangements went smoothly. Caro was dispatched in the curricle with Pascoe, who received the news of the race with his usual dispassion.

'If you want the cattle in racing trim, my lady, I'll see that they have never been in better fettle. A week is not long to prepare them, but they are already fit and the journey into Hertfordshire will help with their endurance.'

'I stand to lose a substantial stake if I do not win, Jethro. If I fail because of my own lack of skill I shall not complain but to be let down by out-of-condition horses would appear inexcusable. Providing they can be brought up to prime condition in time, my pair should be able to hold their own against his lordship's, I think you'll agree?'

'His lordship's greys are fast, larger animals and heavier, but Pitch and Tar are fine little beasts, nimble and quick, sound in wind and limb. Round the estate tracks at Merryfield they should prove the most manageable.'

'And they are familiar with the terrain. Yes, Jethro, a win must be possible,' said Lexie, trying to convince herself as much as Jethro.

'I shall do my best to ensure it, my lady, you may rely on that.'

Lexie smiled affectionately. 'I know it, Jethro.' She often called her chief groom and coachman Jethro when they were alone, just as she called her maid Florence. 'And if I do win it will be thanks to your teaching me to drive, as well as your skill in training the horses. There will be a bonus for you, win or lose.'

Pascoe touched his forehead. 'Thank you, my lady. I hope the weather holds, for Mrs Baldwin will not like to get wet in the curricle.'

'If it rains she will have to ride in the old chaise, surrounded by her portmanteaux and bandboxes!'

'Travel in the curricle!' exclaimed Caro, upon

learning her fate. 'I do declare, I never heard of such a thing!'

'On a fine day there can be no better way of travelling such a short distance! But if you wish, you may ride in the old coach with your luggage. . .'

Lexie left the threat of an uncomfortable, unsprung journey hanging, amused by Cousin Caro's horror at travelling in an open carriage. She herself much preferred it. She considered Caro privileged to be driven by Pascoe behind the blacks.

She would herself travel down to Merryfield at the weekend in her travelling chaise, her only carriage remaining in Town, which was why she could not spare it to transport Caro. Storm would be driving himself down in his curricle on the Sunday in order to have three clear days in which to familiarise himself with the route. Felix St Clare intended to accompany him on horseback. She must be there to receive them.

The acceptances arrived by messenger the following day. Only one snag arose concerning the arrangements. The Viscountess proved intransigent over allowing poor Oswald out of her sight for more than a few hours. She therefore had to be invited to join the party.

Lexie had only one evening engagement that week, a visit to the theatre with Storm, who had been asked by friends to share their box. She had been included in the party because of her known association with him, she supposed, for she did not know her hosts well.

The ladies sat in the front of the box with the gentlemen behind. Storm maintained an unusual silence throughout. In the intervals he appeared abstracted rather than languid. The play was not particularly enlivening and Lexie wondered why her hosts had chosen to patronise that particular theatre. The explanation came right at the end.

The leading lady, a dark beauty with flashing eyes whose appearance had been the only alleviation of an otherwise drab production, stepped forward, stared up into their box, sought out the figure of the Marquess sitting behind Lexie, gave him an elaborate curtsy and blew a kiss in his direction.

The lady next to Lexie began to titter.

'Your former doxy does not forget you, Stormaston!' chuckled their host.

'His women never do,' murmured another of the party.

Lexie sat frozen. Dignity and self-respect demanded that she give no sign of discomfort. She pinned a smile on her lips and stared down on the still bowing and curtsying figure.

So this was the woman who had been Storm's mistress! She possessed a faultless figure, an entrancing face and a captivating manner that Lexie knew she could never hope to equal. Yet Storm had dismissed the actress apparently without regret while he concentrated on his pursuit of her, Lexie.

He must tire of his women easily. He was a hunter. The chase was all. He would become bored with her once he had secured her as his prey.

'She would do well to behave with more dignity,' observed Storm lazily, adding, 'How could she have known that I was here?'

No one bothered to speculate. Lexie could feel the

anger vibrating through Storm's body and her own growing suspicion was confirmed. They had been lured into a trap. She was supposed to create a scene. Storm was supposed to lose his self-possession. The summer would end on a highly entertaining note of scandal.

She turned to her hostess as the final curtain fell and the torches and candles blazed.

'Thank you for a pleasant evening, my lady,' she said, smiling thinly. 'Despite the poor production, I managed to enjoy the performance. I thank you for inviting me to join your party, but I fear I shall not be able to remain for supper. I have developed such a headache. Perhaps due to the putrid acting. Lord Stormaston, may we please leave now?'

Cries of shock and concern greeted her words although no one was taken in by her excuse. She gave Storm her most brilliant smile as she prepared to take his arm.

Storm made his formal devoirs, every inch the cool aristocrat. He expressed no thanks to his supposed friends for their hospitality, merely remarked that the evening had proved extraordinarily interesting.

Now that the die had been cast, the race arranged and the outcome, one way or the other, decided, they had managed to relax in each other's company again. In the privacy—for their final engagement in Town Lexie had dispensed with the services of a chaperon—and darkness of the coach his voice came to her.

'My most humble apologies, my lady. My mortification is such that I dare scarcely ask your forgiveness for exposing you to such an unpleasant episode.

Even when I recognised Hermione Green on stage I did not imagine. . . The thing was arranged, of course, for the titillation of those I had considered my friends. Hermione had been bribed, I have no doubt. Left to herself she would not have thought. . . She needed no revenge. She left me possessed of a substantial settlement.'

This quietly desperate, abject gentleman was not the Storm she knew! Impulsively, Lexie turned to him and laid a hand on his sleeve.

'It was not your fault, my dear. How could you have supposed anyone would stoop—?'

Despite his humiliation, Storm's heart leapt at the endearment. She had not taken offence. There must be a chance to win her willing surrender, whatever the outcome of that damned race. He hurried to interrupt. 'I should know the *ton* by now. God knows, I have had enough experience. I should have checked the playbill before accepting the invitation. Had I known Hermione Green was in the play I would not have accepted.'

'Storm—'

'You were perfect in your dignified behaviour, my dear.' He had taken both her hands into his own and drawn her closer. 'You gave them no cause to gossip over the affair. Anything they may say will be quickly forgotten.'

'Storm—'

In his agitation he cut her off again. 'For myself, I do not care. But that they could treat you so shabbily—'

'Perhaps, by indulging in rash behaviour I asked for such treatment,' said Lexie honestly. 'My dear

Storm, we are both used to being the subject of gossip. There is nothing for me to forgive.'

He drew a shuddering breath and pulled her to him. In an instant she was in his arms, his mouth had found hers and she lost all sense of time. The sound of the coachman's voice addressing the horses, the screech of the brake, the jerk as the carriage came to rest, brought them both back to reality.

'Now I have something else to apologise for,' muttered Storm.

Lexie withdrew from his arms reluctantly. 'Apologise? You, my dear?' She laughed, albeit a little shakily. 'No rake apologises for kissing a woman, given the opportunity.'

Footmen carrying flambeaux hurried down the steps to open the door. Lexie saw the wry smile which accompanied his response. 'Neither does he, my dear. God's blessings until Sunday, at Merryfield.'

'Until Sunday,' echoed Lexie as she left the coach. She did not question the cause of his not accompanying her indoors. After that kiss, any further exchange between them could only prove an anticlimax.

Merryfield Manor nestled in the Hertfordshire countryside, the colour of its slate roof and mellow brick walls ever changing as the clouds scudded overhead. The original manor house had been built in Tudor times and beams still laced the brickwork in the oldest parts. The wings, added on over several later ages, reflected the times in which they had been built yet managed to tie in together to present a harmonious whole.

Lexie loved it. This was home as she had never

known it before, her domain to order as she willed, to enjoy at leisure. Residence in her town house in Bruton Street could not give her the same contented pleasure.

One of Merryfield's attractions for her, having so long been buried first in Ireland and then in Cornwall, was its proximity to London, which could be reached easily within a day, the estate lying not far from the turnpike to St Albans.

Arriving on the Saturday, to be greeted by a flustered, bustling Caro with a buxom and smiling Mrs Panning bobbing behind her, Lexie sighed inwardly. At that moment, after the traumas of the past week and a long day's travel, she would have appreciated Merryfield's normal serenity; but the cause of the upset was all her own, so she could scarcely complain at the furious activity taking place all around her.

'We are almost ready to receive the guests,' reported Caro breathlessly. 'Mr and Mrs Panning have kept the house and grounds in excellent condition during your absence.'

Lexie gave the middle-aged caretaker, neat and comfortable-looking in her grey gown and snowy apron, an approving smile. 'So I notice.'

Mrs Panning bobbed again. 'I hopes as how you'll be pleased, my lady.'

'I'm sure that if Mrs Baldwin is satisfied, I shall be, too.'

'The Marquess's rooms are prepared, and we have put Lord Dexter in the adjoining suite, with Mr Cresswell beyond him. The ladies will occupy rooms in the other wing, the Duke and Duchess of

Downshire occupying the main guest suite. I trust that meets with your approval, Alexia?'

'Splendid, Cousin.' To her surprise, the Duke had been prevailed upon to travel to Merryfield, from where he would be able to escort his wife back to their estates without setting foot in his detested London. 'That means that we—' she grinned '—will occupy the middle ground between. I'll go straight up and change.'

Chalker had already gone upstairs and footmen were humping her luggage in. Lexie mounted the stairs to her suite on the upper floor, which looked out over the sweep of the gravel drive to a fine view over the countryside, much of which she owned. She looked out of the window, glanced up at the sky and smiled.

'Thank you for all this and so much more, dear Amber,' she murmured. 'I know you would approve of this race. You loved to watch me drive. And you would not object to Lord Stormaston taking your place. I believe you would like and trust him.'

'You were saying something, my lady?' asked Chalker, hurrying into the bedroom from the adjoining dressing room. 'Your boxes have been brought up. I was just unpacking them.'

'I was talking to myself, Florence. A bad habit. Just help me out of my travelling gown and into something cooler, nothing formal. We have no guests for dinner tonight.'

'A good night's sleep is just what you need, my lady,' said Chalker. 'You've had too many late nights over the past months, in my opinion.'

'Which I do not remember asking for! But I have

kept you out late, too, on many an occasion, for which I apologise, Florence. Once this race is run, we can settle down to a quiet sojourn in the country.'

'It's not London I object to, my lady, it's my home. But you've been overdoing things. Mrs Baldwin has been most concerned. . .'

'Quite unnecessarily,' said Lexie, irritated by what was fast becoming Chalker's familiarity. But she knew that it was born of genuine regard and so did not berate her loyal maid.

The Marquess of Stormaston and Viscount Dexter arrived in time for dinner. Lexie smiled when she saw his groom leading Brutus, for it meant that his lordship intended to ride horseback as well as drive while he was at Merryfield. All her horses had been brought from London and so she anticipated being able to ride out in the morning on Danny, accompanied by both gentlemen.

Dinner proved a cheerful occasion, everyone in splendid spirits. Lexie's excitement was mounting hourly. Both Stormaston and Dexter, while maintaining their natural air of breeding and conduct, nevertheless shed much of their Town bronze now they were in the country and appeared perfectly at home.

They did not linger over their port and brandy but quickly joined the ladies. It did not take Storm long to suggest that they should take a walk in the grounds, since the evening was both warm and bright.

The old building glowed in the declining sun. Storm turned to study it.

'You possess a fine dowry, my lady,' he said approvingly. 'Some gentleman will surely be happy to wed you to obtain control of the estate.'

'That,' said Lexie with a sidelong glance, 'is my one regret whenever I contemplate marriage. I wonder whether it is me or Merryfield which is the object of my suitor's desire. Besides, I know I shall lose control of it if I accept.' She gave a heartfelt sigh. 'Sometimes I am tempted never to wed again.'

Storm's eyes mocked her. 'Really? That is not the impression I had gained.'

'Yet you must know that I have rejected several gentlemen over the last months,' Lexie returned.

'You would have to trust the man you married to administer it well,' put in Felix, looking with interest and barely concealed amusement from one to the other.

He was not privy to the exact terms of the wager but it would have taken a complete dimwit not to sense some undercurrent of hidden meaning lying beneath the surface of their banter. Lexie smiled at him.

'Indeed, administration of the estate has been much in my thoughts recently.'

'The fields we passed through—I imagine they belonged to the estate—looked productive enough,' mused Storm, 'but from what you have told me, Lady Alexia, I believe their yield could be improved. You have not, I conclude, had a chance to consult with your steward yet?'

'I arrived only yesterday, but I shall put your suggestions to him, my lord. Perhaps you would consent to be present at the interview? I am certain your word would carry more weight than mine in such matters, and you would explain in terms he could understand and pass on to the tenants.'

Storm, his face inscrutable, bowed. 'I shall be delighted to be of service in any way I am able, my lady, once this plaguey wager is behind us.'

Lexie caught his *double entendre* and fought down her blush. '"Plaguey", is it, my lord? Yet you seemed willing enough to accept my challenge when it was made!'

She knew he was teasing her. Just as she was teasing him. Merryfield would make an excellent addition to the Stormaston estates just as he would make an excellent master. If she won the race.

If not. . .

Lord Dexter, unable to properly interpret the hidden meanings behind their words, remarked, 'I, for one, am anticipating your contest with keen anticipation. The Duchess and Lady Fanny arrive tomorrow, I collect?'

'Indeed, as do the remainder of the party. I do hope Lady Wighton does not irritate everyone to distraction!'

'I believe,' said Felix quietly, 'that both her son and Lady Fanny are clever enough to pull the wool over her eyes and keep her temper sweet.'

'You do, do you?' murmured Storm with a sideways look. 'Just as long as they do not engage in some deceit which puts my sister in a compromising situation. Since she is so against the match, I should dislike having to play the heavy-handed guardian and insist upon a marriage neither party wishes.'

'I am convinced they will make every endeavour to avoid that possibility.'

'So I should hope!' exclaimed Lexie, wondering that Storm did not seem to have noticed his friend's interest in Lady Fanny. Though perhaps he had, and approved the budding romance.

But that seemed unlikely. Fanny was young and innocent, Felix older and a confirmed rake, like Storm himself. Were Felix ready to reform, however, she for one would thoroughly approve the match.

She thought the strong-minded woman, so speedily emerging from the chrysalis of the uncertain young Fanny who had arrived in Town six months ago, might well tame Felix. The regard in which they held each other appeared to be mutual. But Felix would have to tread warily. Storm, so disreputable himself, would require respectability in the man he allowed Fanny to wed. If Felix persisted in his discreet pursuit of Fanny, Lexie could see a rough passage ahead.

Storm, she thought ruefully, was unlikely to be tamed by anyone. But should he choose to mend his ways, for whatever reason, he would make the most satisfactory of husbands. But—her nerves tensed—if she won the race he would wed her under duress. Such a forced match would be unlikely to inspire him to reform. It might have quite the opposite effect.

Something else she had not foreseen when she conceived her stupid idea, she thought miserably. Did she really want to win, when the felicity of her reward was so uncertain?

Yes! For a wife must necessarily exert more influence than a mistress—how she hated that term! And feared the consequences of being forced into becoming Storm's! But she would never give up hope of winning not only his hand, but his love as well.

'How long is the course we are to run?' asked the object of her thoughts, bringing her back to the realities of the situation.

'Pascoe says it is about three miles. I will ride out with you tomorrow morning and take you round the route.'

'My thanks.' Storm's smile had a certain cynicism about it. 'I shall spend the remainder of my time familiarising myself and my team with the terrain. That, I conceive, is only fair.'

'Perfectly fair, my lord. But the evening grows chilly and Cousin Caro will be anxious. Shall we return to the house?'

They had both ridden round the route, which groundsmen, under Pascoe's direction, had marked out with whitewash.

'I hope it does not rain!' had said Storm.

'If it does, they will do it again,' had returned Lexie.

This had left Lexie with little time the following day to watch Storm taking his team gingerly around the twisting tracks, making the sharp turns required both in the woods and out in the fields, and negotiating the narrow, humped bridge across a stream which meandered through the estate or to traverse it herself.

She took Pitch and Tar around the route once, an hour or so after breakfast, Storm following at a respectable distance. Naturally, she did not drive as fast as she usually did, for she had no intention of showing off her prowess to her adversary.

But Storm kept the same distance behind her all the way, apparently finding little difficulty in negotiating the difficult corners. He had only driven round it once before. He and his team learnt fast. But the ease with which he was mastering the course only confirmed her in what she already knew: Storm was a formidable opponent. But. . . Well, she would simply have to use all her skill and knowledge and leave the outcome to Fate. And accept the result.

Storm, with Felix riding with him as advisor, continued to study the route until dinner, which was taken early in the country, driving his team around for a third time after consuming a light nuncheon. Lexie noted that he was careful not to overtire his cattle. He had all the next day to continue his preparations, as did she. Tomorrow, her other guests would be settled in and able to amuse themselves while she took her blacks round the course.

The Duke of Downshire arrived just before dinner in a chaise driven by postilions who trumpeted his arrival, escorted by outriders and with a coach following behind with his servant and luggage. The Duchess and Fanny had earlier travelled in similar style. That they had condescended to visit so small an estate as Merryfield still caused Lexie some surprise.

As Lexie greeted the Duke and made her curtsy, she studied his face, seeing the resemblance Storm bore to his grandfather. He had his grandmother's eyes and something of her looks but his grandfather's nose and chin.

'Well, m'dear,' he greeted his wife, 'here I am.'

'Did you have a good journey?' enquired Lexie courteously.

'Damned uncomfortable.' The old face suddenly creased into a mischievous smile so like his grandson's that Lexie almost gasped. 'But worth it to make your acquaintance, Lady Amber. Where's that scapegrace grandson of mine?'

'Still out with his team,' Lexie told him rather breathlessly. That the Duchess had persuaded her husband to accept her invitation she did not doubt. And he had come especially to meet her.

As Fanny greeted her grandparent and he was introduced to those he did not already know, Lexie considered. Could the Duchess possibly suspect. . .?

More to the point, was it possible that she was trying to promote a match between her and her grandson?

Lexie gave her head a tiny shake. Such a notion must surely come purely from her own desire.

CHAPTER NINE

RAIN on Tuesday afternoon sent all those guests who had been out watching the practice runs scurrying for the house.

'Some of the going will be heavy after this,' observed Pascoe quietly when Lexie returned her team to the stables as it began.

'I suppose so,' muttered Lexie, wondering whether the conditions would favour a heavier or a lighter outfit. 'Pitch and Tar are used to the conditions here so I hope it will be an advantage. I shall need every assistance I can find. Do not forget to have the groundsmen mark the course again in the morning.'

'No, my lady.'

Pascoe's dry tone made Lexie realise she had succumbed to unnecessary fussing in her anxiety. As though Jethro was likely to forget!

That evening, although she joined in the general conversation, listened to Lady Fanny's rendering of 'Greensleeves' with apparent appreciation, watched the glances exchanged between Fanny and Felix with some misgiving and noted Miss Daventry's attempts to monopolise the attention of Mr Cresswell, despite Lady Wighton's forbidding frown, her mind refused to focus on any of these things.

While Storm, apparently completely relaxed and unconcerned, played a hand of piquet with his grandmother, she could feel her own nerves tightening in anticipation of the morrow.

Of one thing she could be certain, Storm would no more injure his cattle than would she. Neither would risk foundering their animals: they were far too valuable to be ruined, quite apart from any question of sentiment. So she would go only as fast as seemed safe. On certain paths, where overtaking was impossible, the one in front would set the pace. On more open, wider stretches the other would then try to overtake.

They must make the main circuit twice, but at the end would race up the drive to the finish, a line drawn across the sweep outside the main entrance to the house. There would be room along the drive for them to race neck and neck if necessary and, the ground being drained and level, they could risk going all out.

If she could keep in touch until that point her sprightly, game pair could surely overtake Storm's greys. Better still, if she could manage to be in front, then Storm would never manage to overtake her, for the course should take more out of the greys.

But what use speculating? Storm would have his plan worked out. He would not easily be beaten. Nor, she imagined, would he take defeat kindly. Although normally, as a sporting gentleman, he took his losses philosophically, this was no ordinary wager.

To be beaten by a woman and to lose his precious freedom—it would be too much. Whatever the outcome, Lexie knew that by dinner tomorrow her life would have become fraught with difficulty. She could see little chance of happiness in either outcome.

The temptation to withdraw was almost overwhelming. She could feign an illness. . .but that would only put off the moment. Storm would expect her to renew the challenge the instant she recovered. Even if he believed her truly indisposed.

Pride came to her rescue again. What she had started, she would finish.

Thanks to a posset administered by Chalker, Lexie slept better than she had anticipated. She woke with a slight headache which disappeared as soon as she had drunk her morning chocolate.

She went out to the stables to inspect her team long before breakfast, to find Storm already there.

'You slept well?' he enquired after greeting her with a formal bow.

'Perfectly well, I thank you,' returned Lexie, noting the excellence of his green coat, the fit of his buckskin breeches, the perfection of his shining boots. 'Your greys are on form?'

'So Coltby and Trappin inform me. And your team?'

'I am just about to find out. Excuse me.'

She swept across the yard, the skirts of her blue velvet carriage dress lifted to escape the mire. She really could not stand exchanging pleasantries with him, she was far too nervous.

Jethro Pascoe greeted her with a wide grin. 'They've had their feed and enough water, but not too much,' he reported. 'Couldn't be in better condition, my lady. They'll take a bit of handling to start with, mind. Eager and lively as young colts!'

'They'll behave for me. Won't you, my loves?' she

asked the horses as she allowed them to nuzzle her hands and find the lumps of sugar held in her palms. Although she trusted Storm to be honest, she wondered about Trappin. But she could not ask Pascoe to guard her pair against the supposedly kindly act of offering them a bucket of water just before the start. So, 'Look after them,' was all she said as she prepared to return for her own breakfast.

'I'll do that, my lady, never you fear,' answered Pascoe. 'No one but me or Jeffs shall enter their stable, that I promise you. Nor will any of us be allowed near his lordship's cattle. 'Tis best that way.'

Reassured, Lexie returned to partake of several cups of coffee but little else, pecking at a freshly baked roll spread with butter from her own dairy. His lordship, of course, ate a substantial breakfast of eggs, kidneys and ham, together with several rolls.

Most of her other guests drifted in to eat while she was there. Felix entered, dressed ready for walking in the country, for he, Marlow, Coltby and Trappin were to join Pascoe, Jeffs, the caretaker Panning, and several other grooms and groundsmen in lining the route at intervals in order to be on hand should there be an accident and, at the same time, to ensure that neither outfit deviated from the route.

'I trust both contestants are fit and ready?' he drawled as he took his place at the table by his friend. 'The day looks set fair. We should all avoid a soaking.'

'We shall walk over to the copse,' said Fanny, indicating Oswald and Melissa. 'It is the nearest point on the circuit to the house and once you have both passed there for the second time we shall come back here for the finish.'

'A convenient point from which to watch, as you discovered yesterday morning,' grinned Storm. 'Do not exert yourselves too much, ladies, or catch cold. The temperature is much lower after the rain. You will need extra clothing if you are to stand about in the open.'

The race was due to start at midday. Lexie returned to the stables to oversee the harnessing of her team, unable to relax enough to let Pascoe deal with it on his own. He seemed to understand and put up with her restless interventions stoically until Pitch and Tar began to sidle and sweat.

'You are upsetting your horses, my lady,' he pointed out. 'May I suggest that you take a short walk while I finish preparing the outfit?'

'I'm sorry. You are quite right. If I do not relax, neither will the horses.'

Chastened, Lexie walked from the yard towards the designated start, some hundred yards distant. She heard a tread behind her and turned to see Storm striding out to catch up with her.

He swept her a lavish bow. 'You are determined on this?' he asked, eyeing her flushed face critically.

'Of course!' Lexie, setting the pin in her driving hat to fix it more firmly on her head—for she had felt it shift as she inclined her head in greeting—met his gaze defiantly. 'I will not pretend not to be nervous. Unlike your lordship, I have never engaged in such an enterprise before. But that does not mean that I shall drive any less well!'

'Good girl!' He smiled suddenly, an admiring,

encouraging smile that did more to make her nervous—in a different way—than any anticipation had so far achieved. But it was an agitation which, surprisingly, settled her nerves as far as the race was concerned. For she knew that, whatever the outcome, Storm would accept the result in good spirit. Both their futures would be settled by a combination of skill and chance.

Her hands stopped trembling as she lowered them from her hat. The stable clock chimed the hour and the grooms led the outfits from the yard as the group of spectators came into view, led by Lady Fanny.

'Too late to back out now,' grinned Storm, holding out his strong, lean hand.

Lexie looked at it in astonishment. He was treating her as an equal. With a quick smile she took it and shook it, her own small fist quite engulfed by his, in a friendly gesture before the serious competition began.

'Good luck,' she said.

'And to you, my lady. You'll need it,' he warned.

They parted to mount their respective curricles. Lexie paused to fondle the muzzles of Pitch and Tar as she passed, glad to see that Pascoe had managed to settle them down again, though, their spirits being high, the groom was having a job to hold them.

Storm's greys were restive, too, full of running. He slapped their necks in passing and was up in his seat first. Lexie gathered her ribbons, flicked her whip and walked her pair to the start line. Storm brought his carriage alongside and grooms held both teams to steady them.

'Ready?' cried, Oswald, hat held high.

He had agreed to be the official starter. He had opened a book and had his money on Stormaston. The ladies had backed Lady Alexia. The staff all had money on one or the other or both of them. How each one had bet was Oswald's secret. Lexie felt the pressure of wanting to win so as not to let her supporters down more than that of winning for herself. Her own fate she had come to view largely as a matter of providence. Resignation had taken the place of apprehension.

Both contestants nodded.

'Then *go*!' shouted Oswald, dropping his hat with a flourish.

The grooms jumped back. Lexie gave her pair the office and set them to a modest canter. The first stretch, like the last, was comparatively straight and wide. She hoped that Storm would take the lead. Her plan was to overtake him here the second time around and make use of her better knowledge of the twists and turns of the route to get far enough ahead for him not to be able to pass her on the straight before the finish.

But Storm did not oblige. Doggedly, he remained almost abreast, his greys' heads level with her horses' withers. Either he would shoot ahead before the track narrowed or would fall behind and follow her lead through the looming wood. To force him ahead, she would have to pull her horses, make them lose their stride and rhythm.

She waited until the last moment. As the greys' heads began to slip backwards, Lexie reined the blacks in hard, making them snort and shake their heads in protest, but they dropped to a trot so abruptly that Storm was past before he could do anything but take the lead.

As his outfit plunged into the comparative darkness beneath the trees he gave a great whoop of laughter and waved his whip in acknowledgement of the success of Lexie's tactic.

Lexie, loving the feel of the ribbons in her small, capable hands and the responsiveness of her horses to her slightest command, urging them to pick up speed again as quickly as possible, laughed herself, exhilarated not only by her triumph but by the mere fact of driving in competition with so worthy an opponent. She had lacked such a challenge before. However well and fast she had driven, she had had nothing to tell her whether she was as skilled as Amber and Pascoe assured her she was.

Storm negotiated the remainder of the first circuit with care but fast, giving the path his undivided concentration, avoiding roots and potholes, mired patches and puddles with uncanny skill, taking the narrow bridge at a brisk pace, his wheel hubs always a safe inch from the stone parapets.

His curricle swayed dangerously only once, when a wheel found a root on a sharp bend. Groans from Felix and a groundsman greeted this potential disaster and scattered cheers followed their progress, especially when they came to the copse, but neither driver spared a thought for their audience.

Lexie had no difficulty in keeping close behind. In fact she knew she could have driven her horses faster. Her hopes began to mount. Pitch and Tar, straining at their bits, could surely pass their opponents on the straight!

She kept her place along most of its length, giving Storm no indication that she intended to pass him. Then, with room for manoeuvre running out, she flicked her whip and gave her pair their heads.

Storm did nothing to prevent her passing him. In fact he gave her a cheery wave as she sped by. He thought she had played into his hands, did he? Lexie smiled grimly as she set herself to show him just how speedily she was capable of setting her horses to cover the difficult ground.

They were, naturally, not as fresh as they had been on the first circuit, but she knew they still had a good turn of speed in their legs. She must reserve that for the chase along the drive. The track, too, had suffered from their first passage. Hooves and wheels had churned the surface, hiding many of the hazards.

Should she become stuck with Storm trapped behind her, she would have to allow him past as soon as the groundsmen and grooms had extricated her from the mire. So although she negotiated bends, bridges and rough ground at a faster pace than Storm had done, and the high-sprung vehicle swayed alarmingly once or twice, she drove within her limits. And tried to conserve her horses' energy for the final sprint.

Storm disappointed her by keeping up, too close behind for her comfort. She had expected to gain a hundred yards or more over the second circuit but she gained only a length. As both curricles burst out on to the drive his horses were snorting at her heels.

But the drive was smooth, well gravelled, safe. She leant forward to urge Pitch and Tar to give of their utmost. Gallantly, the small blacks took up the challenge of the larger greys thundering along behind. Lexie glanced over her shoulder. Inch by inch, Storm was gaining on her. But did he have time to overtake?

Looking forward again she simply concentrated on getting the utmost speed from her horses, ignoring as far as possible the threatening drumming and rattling which told her Storm was gaining even more ground, coming up fast. She could have used blocking tactics, but it did not even occur to her. This was a race, personal between her and Storm.

While tricks had seemed allowable in its first stages, now it had come down to who could cover the last straight in the least time. The greys' heads appeared at her shoulder. Another hundred yards to go! Grimly she hung on but, with a tremendous surge of power, the greys shot forward at the last moment and their heads were well ahead as both curricles crossed the finishing line to the sound of enthusiastic cheers.

Quite a crowd had gathered to watch the finish. Most of the ground staff and all the others scattered about the course had raced back to view the outcome. A few returning from steward's duties at the further reaches were still straggling in, the result being shouted at them as they panted up.

Storm, triumphant, appeared magnanimous in victory.

'My dear Lady Alexia, I confess myself surprised! I have never driven against a more worthy opponent,' he declared, springing down from his seat and stretching out a hand to assist Lexie to dismount.

The sheerly wicked look in those blue eyes, the

devilish curve to his lips as she looked down into his lean face and saw the livid scar standing out from his tanned skin, increased the weight of the lump of undigested suet pudding which seemed to have settled in Lexie's stomach.

His hands closed about her waist as he lifted her down. His touch had never seemed more intimate. Colour flamed in Lexie's cheeks. She felt light-headed.

'Thank you, my lord,' she managed to say. 'Congratulations on a splendid race. Your greys are nonpareil.'

He grinned again. 'I did warn you.'

Lexie turned to their audience. Her stomach might be churning, she might feel exhausted by the sheer mental and physical effort of controlling her horses and bringing her outfit safely home, but she managed to maintain a cheerful if rather wry countenance.

'I can only apologise to those who have lost money on my performance. I did my best but lost to a better team—which includes the driver!'

A chorus of disclaimers greeted this, all the ladies protesting that it did not matter in the least, but nevertheless their disappointment showed.

'No, our disquiet is not in that we lost money on you, Lady Alexia,' Fanny hastened to inform her, 'but that you could not win against my arrogant brother! He has too high an opinion of himself and it would have been so satisfactory to see him beaten for once!'

'Wretch!' chided Storm.

'No more than you deserve, James!' declared his grandmother, leaning heavily on the stick she used when her joints stiffened and became painful. The overnight rain had quickly had its effect.

The Duke joined in the congratulations being showered on Storm's head. 'Well done, Stormaston!' He chuckled. 'I trust your winnings are handsome?'

'Handsome indeed, sir,' acknowledged Storm, not looking at Lexie, for which she silently thanked him.

'And you, young lady, I take it you can afford your losses?'

'I would not have staked something I was unable to deliver.'

The Duke chuckled and offered her his arm. 'Allow me to escort such a gallant loser back to the house. I am certain my grandson can find his own way.'

Lexie took the offered arm and had her mind taken off the future consequences of her loss in answering the questions put to her by the old man, knowledgeable about land management as only the owner of vast estates could be, who wanted to know all about the house and gardens, for which he professed a great admiration.

He was nice, Lexie decided, glad he had been able to come. She would not enjoy deceiving him or the Duchess, but she would do it to protect her name and keep their regard. The Duchess appeared to ignore the rumours circulating about her and Storm. Maybe the Duke had not yet been regaled with them. She liked them both far to much to want to cause them any hurt.

Back at the house, Oswald set about paying out the winnings. Any profit was to be divided amongst the servants.

'I will settle my debt to his lordship later,' murmured Lexie, preparing to escape to her room to change.

'Make sure she doesn't renege, Storm,' grinned Felix.

'You may be sure of that,' murmured Storm, bowing over her hand with perfect elegance. 'But I do not anticipate any such possibility. Lady Alexia is above all things an honourable lady.'

Only Lexie could see the questioning, challenging look in those blue eyes.

'I always pay my debts,' she retorted tartly, 'however reluctantly.'

'So I should hope!' cried Oswald's mother, the only guest not to venture out to watch the race.

Cousin Caro, following inclination and her duty as surrogate hostess, had remained indoors with Lady Wighton but had watched the finish from a window. She sprang to her young cousin's defence.

'Of course she will! Alexia is the most principled of creatures! How can you doubt it?'

'I cannot feel able to rely upon Lady Amber's doing anything any lady of sense and breeding would think proper,' retorted Lady Wighton spitefully. 'To think of her racing her curricle against a gentleman! I have never heard of such an outrageous thing!'

'Really, Mama—'

Oswald's brave protest was lost in a chorus of indignant dissent. Only the Duchess's voice could be distinguished above the rest.

'I believe you owe Lady Amber an apology, Lady Wighton! To so insult a fellow peeress in her own house!'

Lady Wighton bridled. Before she could respond Storm intervened.

'I, personally, shall count it a grave disservice if I ever hear any hint of disapproval of Lady Amber circulating. If I discover you to be the source, madam, then I should most certainly be forced to terminate our acquaintance.'

A murmur of assent greeted his words. Such a refusal to acknowledge her would amount to social disaster. Lady Wighton smiled, if thinly.

'My dear Stormaston, I shall, as always, keep my opinions to myself. As long as you are satisfied that the debt will be met I have no more to say.'

'I should think not!' muttered Oswald furiously.

For Lexie the remainder of the day passed in a kind of limbo. She performed all her duties as hostess, entertained her guests, laughed with them, chatted on inconsequential matters. But her mind had run on to the night ahead. Would the Marquess claim his winnings straight away? Here, at Merryfield?

He could do so with a certain amount of security. Chalker slept in a room some distance from her suite and Caro's rooms, although leading from the same landing, were entirely separate. Were he to leave his room to visit her no one would be any the wiser.

When the time came she dismissed Chalker, telling her to leave a branch of candles burning, for she wished to read.

'Sleep well, then, my lady,' said Chalker as she left the room. 'You must be worn out after that race this morning.'

'I hope you did not lose too much money on me, Florence,' said Lexie ruefully. 'I did my best to win.'

'I knew you would my lady and I placed some money on you.' The maid coloured as she stood with her hand on the door to the dressing room, where she would tidy up before going to her own bed. 'But his lordship has a formidable reputation. I put money on him, as well. So I didn't lose anything in the end.'

'Well, I'm glad of that,' said Lexie, wondering how she could have been so naïve as to think anyone would have backed her to win without hedging their bet.

'By the way, Florence, after this house party you may take a holiday,' she promised. She could not be sure of the Marquess's intentions but having her as his mistress seemed to imply more than a single night spent in her bed and she wanted to be free to please herself—and him.

Not that she did not trust Chalker's discretion, but to Lexie, keeping the affair secret was all-important. If the liaison could be kept entirely hidden from others, she would not feel quite so bad about it.

'I can manage without you for at least a week. Say two. Make what arrangements you like.'

Chalker's face lit up. 'You mean it, my lady? Then I'll send a message to my mother. She'll be glad to see me. She hasn't been too grand lately, by all accounts. I can travel by stage from the posting inn in St Albans.'

Lexie nodded. 'And you may sort out a couple of my old gowns to take with you. Do it tomorrow and let me know which ones you would like.'

'Very well, my lady. And thank you.'

With Chalker's departure nervousness started the butterflies fluttering in Lexie's stomach. Storm had said nothing, but the expression in his eyes as he had bidden her good night led her to expect him. The memory of the fire in his gaze sent frissons of anticipation down her spine. She shivered, despite the warmth of the night, and pulled her dressing wrap close about her.

She could not bring herself to get into bed to wait for him—that would be too embarrassing—so she sat in her chair with a book open on her lap, listening to the sounds in the house gradually die away. If he was coming, it would be soon.

The candles guttered and she sprang up to take a taper to light others to replace them. The activity took away some of her nervousness and she was so concentrating on her task that at first she failed to hear the soft sound of her door opening.

When Storm came in, she was standing with a freshly-lighted branch of candles in her hand. The glow from their flames fell upon her luxuriant hair, cascading like molten gold from beneath her lacy cap. Colour flooded her face and then fled, leaving her skin alabaster white apart from the freckles sprinkled across her nose. Her hand began to shake, the flames to waver.

Storm turned the key in the lock before striding forward to take the candelabra from her grasp.

'You'll drop it,' he chided, putting it down in place of the others, which he carried over to a distant table where he proceeded, quite calmly, to extinguish the flames.

'I did not know whether to expect you or not,' gulped Lexie.

'Did you think I would not claim my winnings?' His eyebrows lifted quizzically as he came back to her.

'A gentleman would not,' uttered Lexie.

'No?' The eyebrows approached his hairline. 'But then, you knew I was no gentleman when you accepted the wager.' His hand came out and his fingers lifted her chin so that their eyes met. Wide, anxious green met teasing blue in which the fires of passion burnt, but well banked down. 'Would you have let me off, had you won, my lady?'

Lexie gulped. 'I might have done. Had you appeared too greatly displeased at the idea of marrying me.'

'If I had threatened, by my behaviour, to make your future life a misery?' He laughed, none too pleasantly. 'But had I accepted my debt in good spirit, then you would have claimed your reward. Is that not so?'

Dumb, Lexie nodded.

'And are you, by your behaviour, going to make me wish that I had not won today?' he demanded softly.

Lexie shook her head.

'I thought not.' His fingers stroked the line of her cheekbone, ran down to her firm chin. His thumb lifted to smooth across her full lips and Lexie's limbs melted. 'We both want this too much. But, my dear, if I thought lying with me would harm you in any way, then I should withdraw. But I believe the opposite. And I cannot conceive that, to one as unconventional as yourself, indulging in an *affaire* with me will cause undue distress.'

'Provided no one knows,' managed Lexie hoarsely. 'My conscience is bad enough as it is. If I thought people—the servants, for example—were sniggering behind my back I should not be able to hold my head up.'

'No one will know. No one saw me come.'

'The sheets. . .'

He pursed his lips, his head on one side. The candles lit his dark hair, painted his face with shadows. 'You could come with me to my room. The servants would think nothing of finding soiled sheets on my bed.'

He was not serious. His eyes were dancing. But he should not laugh at her scruples.

'You are a beast!' she accused, pushing him away.

'Not at all.' He refused to retreat and was, suddenly, in deadly earnest. 'If the problem troubles you, then I suggest spreading a towel, which I undertake to smuggle into the linen basket for you. Will that serve?'

'You think me a fool,' muttered Lexie. 'But I could not bear for the servants to gossip.'

'No, I do not, dearest Lexie. I think you absolutely adorable but a little naïve. They will already be gossiping. What harm can their speculations do you?'

'Speculation, none. But the stating of a proven fact. . .that would be different.'

'I suppose it would. So now, if you will point me towards a convenient towel. . .'

'The washstand is in the dressing room.' Lexie indicated the door.

Without further ado Storm went through to return with the necessary item, carefully locking that door after him, too.

'Now we cannot be disturbed,' he announced, turning back the bedclothes and spreading his trophy over the sheet. 'Come, my lady. Allow me to relieve you of your wrap.'

CHAPTER TEN

HE REMOVED her garments, each operation a caress, lifted her up and laid her on the bed. Lexie, her senses heightened to an almost unbearable pitch, watched as the gown concealing his nakedness followed her nightgown to the floor. She remembered the first time she had seen him unclothed, when she had come to her senses just in time and, for an instant, panic almost overcame her.

What was she doing, waiting for a man who was not her husband to join her in her bed? But the dismay had no time to bite, for his weight shifted the mattress beneath her and she felt the warm, entrancing silkiness of his skin against hers as he pulled the light covers up. Then she was in his embrace. After that, nothing mattered except that she was where she belonged, cradled in his arms. This was truly coming home.

As she relaxed against him, she realised with astonishment that he was trembling. Somehow, that gave Lexie the courage to touch the scar on his cheek, to whisper, 'I am glad you gave me no choice, Storm. My conscience has been such a trouble to me.'

'To you!' He pulled her closer. 'I have never known such a stubborn woman!'

'Then perhaps the experience has taught you a lesson, my lord,' she teased, poking admonishingly at his chin. 'Some females do value their virtue. You cannot assume all of us will fall into your arms as easily as you might expect!'

'I have only previously come across the other sort. You, my dear, provided a new experience.' He chuckled, kissing her curving nose. His tone deepened. 'Oh, Lexie, my adorable one, how I have burned for you!'

'And I for you,' she confessed shyly.

'Have you truly? Then the strength of your will is greater than I had supposed.' He shifted, leaning his weight on one elbow as he leant over her, smoothing the golden mass of hair spread over the pillow. 'But let us not waste time on post-mortems when all joy lies ahead. Come, my dear, allow me to worship your body.'

Oh! the exquisite sensations he roused as his hands and lips travelled from her hair to her toes. Bed with Amber had never been like this! Then, having exhausted new places to explore, Storm's caresses returned to her breasts, moulding them to his touch, taking each peak in turn into his warm, moist mouth, teasing, suckling, sending exquisite pain to the depths of Lexie's being. Eventually, as her hips moved instinctively, seeking release from the almost unbearable ecstasy, his fingers probed the source of her demand.

'How long. . .?'

He had no need to finish his murmured question. 'Five years,' muttered Lexie, ashamed to have to admit it.

'Then I will be careful, my love.'

My love! Did he mean it? Or did he use the

endearment to all his mistresses? Lexie did not, at that moment, care.

'Please, James! Hurry!'

In her passion, Lexie did not notice that she had called him by his name for the first time. But Storm did. His already thundering heart gave a great leap as he moved to cover her awakening body. That one word coming from her lips was worth more than a thousand other endearments! He had, at last, truly broken through the barrier of her resistance.

Despite the urgency this knowledge added to his own need, he managed to control his entry, to test her readiness before plunging deeper into her velvety depths.

Once there he paused to regain control. Lexie moaned and he groaned as he began to move. Her arms clasped his shoulders, her hips thrust upwards in perfect rhythm with his, her beautiful legs—having kissed and caressed them he could envisage every strong, perfect inch of them—tangled with his. He stopped again, fighting against the consummation of his own passion.

Lexie clasped him anxiously to her, strained upwards to take him deeper inside her, shifted her legs to embrace his hips. Why had he stopped? Amber had simply gone on and on, wearing away at her patience as she waited for it to end. But with James she did not want it to end.

'James?' she whispered.

His voice came, ragged, breathless. 'One moment, my love. Otherwise I shall come too soon and I want to make this last.'

'Oh.' Her hands wandered over the muscles of his back. 'But I want. . . Please?'

A sort of gasping laugh greeted her plea. 'How can I refuse?'

And then he was moving again, raising the tempo, filling her senses until she lost them completely in a wave of such purely breathtaking sensation that she seemed to come out of her skin to hover over her own limp, exhausted body.

For long moments she was unaware of anything but sheer joy. Then she discovered Storm collapsed on top of her, shuddering his own abandoned pleasure. She lay still, waiting for him to recover, moving only to kiss his neck, his shoulder, in awe-struck gratitude.

Eventually he lifted himself up on his elbows and looked down into her flushed, drowning face. Unable to resist, he kissed the passionate mouth which had been sending messages to his groin even as he recovered.

He gave a rueful, triumphant laugh. 'Truly a diamond of the first water,' he murmured, kissing her again, giving new meaning to a hackneyed expression. 'Even without recent practice,' he added wickedly. 'I cannot imagine what your response will be like after a little more application.'

'You have had plenty of experience,' retorted Lexie pertly. 'Such expertise! But oh, James, it was wonderful! Thank you!'

'You are calling me James,' he murmured. 'Do you remember my asking you to?' She nodded. 'And you said it sounded too familiar. Can I presume that no longer applies?'

'Not in private. But in public I must continue to address you as I have always done.'

He sighed. 'I suppose so. To do otherwise now would certainly cause speculation.'

Lexie was slowly coming down to earth. She landed with a bump.

'As would your absence from your bed were it to be discovered!'

'Marlow is the only one even remotely likely to venture into my room, and he has no reason. And in any case I would trust him not to mention the matter, even to me!'

'But you must go!' urged Lexie, wishing with all her heart that he had the right to remain. 'Supposing we fall asleep and the maid comes in with my morning chocolate only to find us together!'

Through an exaggerated yawn, 'I feel more like repeating our experiment than sleeping,' Storm informed her.

'Again? Is that possible?' Amber had only ever performed once at a time. It had taken him a day to recover.

'Give me a few more minutes and I will show you. Meanwhile, there are certain areas of your delectable body I have yet to explore.'

He proceeded to do so and Lexie found her hands wandering over his hard form, discovering the splendid muscles hidden beneath the smooth surface of his skin.

'No fat,' she murmured, pinching his ribs playfully.

He sucked in his breath as the ticklish shock shook him. 'Riding, boxing, fencing, all keep me in as fine a fettle as my cattle,' he gasped. 'Lexie, stop it! You'll have me helpless. . .'

'That will never do,' she murmured provocatively. 'Can you not manage just a little—?'

He gasped as she pinched him again. 'Witch! It seems I can excel even my own past performances with you! Come here!'

She was under him again, experiencing the same sublime sensations, finding her own exquisite release even as Storm subsided in his.

She could, thought Lexie contentedly, become addicted to the attentions of James Graham, Marquess of Stormaston.

He left shortly afterwards, taking the towel with him. But Lexie could still detect his scent, that indefinable odour which was James Graham, in the bed. It was something, but not enough. She wanted him there, sleeping beside her. Until death did them part.

Anyone looking perceptively at Lexie the next day might have guessed that something monumental had happened to her during the night. And anyone that perceptive would have been in no doubt as to the cause of her inner glow. Or the identity of the person responsible.

Lexie, cocooned in her euphoric dreams of the past night and of those to come, for she had little doubt that Storm would be back, bubbled with new energy and happiness, keeping all her guests occupied and entertained like the able hostess she was.

Whenever she thought of what she had done she almost blushed. She still felt like a scarlet woman, but was too happy to care. She wanted to ride out with the men, to be with Storm, but dutifully remained behind with the ladies, picking up some needlepoint she had started during the winter and taking the frame and her silks out into the garden where the others were enjoying the shade of an arbour built at the end of the formal gardens.

'Why gentlemen must always be taking exercise I do not know,' lamented Miranda, for Oswald, taking his example from Storm and Felix, had decided that an excursion on horseback would not come amiss.

'I have never liked horseback riding,' Fanny remarked.

'I used to be a great horsewoman in my youth,' said the Duchess. 'Could have given you a run for your money, Lady Alexia!'

'Indeed, ma'am, so your grandson has informed me.'

'Used to ride all over our estates with me,' said the Duke with a fond smile. 'Until she started breeding, of course.'

'That do put a restriction on a female's activities,' agreed his wife. 'But once I stopped breedin' I took it up again. Nothing like it.'

'Oswald has never shown any inclination to like horses until now,' lamented his mother, throwing Lexie a louring glance.

Oswald, enjoying the close company of two extremely experienced gentlemen, had begun to develop his own brand of independence. He tended to disregard his mother's wishes rather more than that lady liked.

Lexie wondered that no one else seemed aware of

the undercurrents flowing between the young people. Perhaps, being in love herself had made her more sensitive to atmosphere, for to outward appearances Felix divided his attention equally between the two young ladies who were his fellow guests.

Oswald did likewise, although he did also contrive to attend Lexie as often as he could. Unfortunately, his *tendre* for her had not yet died. Lexie felt sorry for Melissa but there was no more she could do to help her cause.

The servants plied them with refreshing drinks and the afternoon passed pleasantly enough. But Lexie's eyes kept straying in the direction of the stables. The men must return soon! Her steward and home farm manager, John Lyme, had ridden out with them as guide. She wanted to know what he and the Marquess had discussed.

Storm spoke so confidently of the advantages of the new ways of farming. She hoped Mr Lyme would be receptive to his ideas, for only he could persuade her tenants. She must fix a time for the meeting they had discussed.

The men returned. The Marquess and John Lyme appeared to be on the best of terms and the steward presented himself before her to request an interview to discuss the estate's affairs. Lexie, at a nod of approval from Storm, fixed the meeting for noon the following day.

When she went up to her room to change for dinner, Lexie discovered an unpalatable fact. Her monthly indisposition was upon her. She would be unable to receive Storm for several days. Certainly not before the planned end of the house party on

Monday. Perhaps—devastating thought—last night would be the only night of love she was ever to know.

'Devil take it,' she muttered to herself as she applied bandages. Disappointment sent her spirits plunging. And what would Storm think? Although he must be familiar with women's fertility cycles, she thought cynically.

She tried to warn him of her indisposition during the evening but the opportunity never presented itself. She gave him a speaking look and a tiny shake of her head as she said good night, but he simply raised his brows in interrogation, not understanding the message she was trying to impart.

So his arrival was not unexpected. Again, she was not in bed but sitting in her chair. She had thought it best to greet him in a less suggestive pose. His ardour would need dampening, not inflaming.

Nevertheless, at his stealthy entry, her heart leapt and rosy colour flooded her cheeks. He did want her again! He could not have found bedding her too disappointing.

That fact was evident in the way he looked at her as he advanced, carrying a towel over his arm like a waiter, and with two glasses filled with blood-red wine balanced in one hand.

He handed her one of the glasses with a flourish and bent to kiss her lips.

'You seemed a little doubtful as to whether you wished to receive me earlier,' he murmured. 'I therefore thought it prudent to bring a little stimulant to our enjoyment. Let us toast each other.' He raised his goblet. 'To us, my dear Lady Amber.'

All colour fled from Lexie's face. She sat down on the chair abruptly, shaking her head. Storm eyed her ashen cheeks and his own expectant expression chilled.

'Do you intend to reject me?' he drawled.

Lexie shook her head as she struggled for words. 'No, believe me, James, but it is the wrong time of the month for me. I am indisposed.'

He relaxed, quite visibly. 'Is that all, my love? Then drink up! We can still have a night of loving ahead, for there is no reason why we should not cuddle each other, is there? Here's to us, and confound our critics!' He watched her as he drank.

Her face returned to its normal colour and a look of radiant delight took the place of apprehension. 'To us,' she whispered, lifted the wine to her lips and gulped down a large mouthful.

He took the glass from her and raised her to her feet. 'We shall be fully together again, never fear. But tonight,' he murmured, 'I shall give you pleasure and teach you how to release me from my frustration. Unless you already know?'

'I have an idea,' she admitted. 'Amber—'

'Do not let us speak of him! I have no wish to be reminded of any man who had you before me. I—' he laughed ruefully '—who have never yet despoiled a virgin and have therefore always followed others in tasting the delights of feminine charms, discover that I am capable of sexual jealousy! An emotion new to me. I find this difficult to explain, even to myself.'

As she slipped out of her garments and took her place in the bed, Lexie's spirits lifted. If he felt like that then perhaps she could hope that he might come to love her as she loved him. The likelihood appeared remote but it was a hope she must cling to. Nothing else could keep at bay the chilling prospect of rejection when he tired of her. As he had tired of all his women before her.

At least, she consoled herself, he found her a new experience. Her pride would have suffered sorely had he simply classed her with all the rest. She could not have borne to be simply one of his women, no different in his eyes to all the others.

Once the house party broke up he planned to take her to stay with his old nurse, in whose eyes, apparently, Master James could do no wrong, who would have no objection to their sharing a bedroom, and whom he could trust never to mention their visit to a soul.

'She wished to retire to the sea,' he had explained before leaving her, 'and I set her up in a house in a tiny resort on the Essex coast called Frinton. Neither of us is known there, although I have visited Nanny Dean once or twice—on my own,' he hastened to reassure her.

'We may stay with her completely incognito. Marlow can put up at the local inn. I shall need him with me to fetch and carry and generally make himself useful to us both. I would trust my life to his discretion. What do you say, my love?'

'Yes,' responded Lexie, after only the slightest hesitation. Desperate as she was to spend time with Storm, she could not rid herself of the idea that to do so was a sin. But her conscience had caused her to hesitate for too long already. She would take what happiness he offered and suffer the consequences later, if she must.

Which reminded her of another unpalatable fact she had ignored until now. Clearly, their single act of union had not resulted in any unwanted child. Unwanted only because she was unwed, of course. Wanted most desperately, if only she were Storm's wife. But facts were facts and faced with them she could not contemplate giving birth to a bastard.

On past performance Storm would not care, though he would take care of the child financially—but what of her? If she did not suffer her confinement in secret and abandon the child immediately afterwards, but brought it up herself, which she would most certainly wish to do, she would be branded a harlot and ostracised from Society. More to the point, the child would bear the brand of bastardy all its life.

She could decide to wed another suitor in haste to obtain a name for the infant, but that would not be honest or to her taste. Storm might offer marriage—but he had never felt under any obligation to do so in the past, so why should he now? And she would never ask him to marry her again. So it would be best to avoid any such complication.

In Cornwall Lexie had visited the local wise woman several times in her capacity as the lady of the manor. Desperate over not conceiving Amber's heir, she had sought her advice.

''Ee can try this potion, my dear, but 'e be too gone in years, to my way of thinking,' old Demelza had told her. 'Find yersel' a young man and 'ee'll start breeding soon enough. Then, like as not, 'ee'll want to know as how to stop being brought to childbed too often.'

Lexie, from curiosity, had asked her how this could be achieved and been regaled with details of many devices to prevent conception and some proven ways to abort an unwanted baby. She could not remember them all, and would never get rid of a baby once conceived, but she did remember something of what the old woman had said. And decided to acquire a sponge and a supply of vinegar before leaving for Essex.

Foresight had already dealt with the question of Chalker. Her only remaining problem would be getting to the Saracen's Head at Chelmsford, where she was to meet Storm. But even that was solved by the end of the house party. On Storm's suggestion she announced her intention to make a very private visit to an old—fictitious—school friend she had discovered to be living in St Albans.

In her own unorthodox way, Lexie would insist on riding there without escort, stable Danny in the city, and from there make her way to Chelmsford. An adventure! She had a choice, she could go by post chaise, but preferred to take the stage coach, a new experience which she did not expect to be pleasant, but if Chalker could do it, so could she.

On his way back to his room one night, Storm almost bumped into Felix. Both men looked put out until the comedy of the situation shook them both with laughter. Felix, Storm thought, looked decidedly sheepish and he wondered into whose bed his friend had strayed.

Felix might well guess where he had been, but Storm could rely absolutely on his discretion. As Felix could rely on his. That two confirmed rakes should meet in a dark corridor after each had visited an obliging female caused neither of them undue surprise.

'Go and get some sleep, my dear fellow,' chuckled Storm.

'You too, my friend. It would not do for either of us to appear exhausted tomorrow.'

'What would my grandmother say?' agreed Storm lightly. He had refused to allow her presence to inhibit his actions. Lexie, he suspected, might have invited his grandparents with that hope in mind.

'Or our delightful hostess. I wish you a good night—what is left of it!'

Felix did guess, thought Storm ruefully. For himself he did not mind, but he hoped Lexie need never discover that Felix had guessed their secret.

Lexie would take only what would fit into a couple of saddlebags and a pack strapped behind her saddle. Chalker, due to leave for London at any moment, had insisted on helping her mistress, murmuring all the while, 'However will you manage, my lady, with only these few things?'

When Cousin Caro joined in Chalker's lament, Lexie lost her temper.

'Excellently well, I believe. Now, stop your lamentations, if you please! I am quite capable of looking after myself for a week or so, and if I find I lack for anything I can always visit a shop! Really, Caro,' she went on, when Chalker had been persuaded to go down to the gig waiting to take her into St Albans. 'Such a fuss! You know how I dislike being trammelled by convention! I am taking an opportunity to escape! A real holiday! Do not deny me these few days of freedom!'

Caro pursed her lips and fluttered a hand. 'If I could believe that was all it was. You could easily have arranged to travel into St Albans with Chalker. But you will please yourself, as always, Alexia.' She sighed, and her voice wavered. 'Why you bother to have me live with you as your companion and chaperon I cannot conceive!'

'Because you add respectability to what are considered to be my rackety ways, Cousin!'

'Which you promptly squander on some new exploit! As though racing your curricle against a gentleman for money were not enough! Now you are off, the dear Lord knows where, all on your own, without even Chalker or Jeffs to keep you company! I do declare, you will be the death of me, Alexia!'

'Nonsense!' Lexie spoke bracingly. 'I am not some poor thing who needs cossetting every moment of her life! I am going to visit a friend!'

Childishly, she crossed her fingers behind her back. Lies did not come easily to her but on this occasion some were unavoidable. Although this one had an element of truth in it.

'She will have a servant to look after me. Now, I trust you to see to things in the house in my absence. Mr Lyme has the estate in hand; I am so glad he is enthusiastic about the changes Lord Stormaston suggested.'

'Anyone might think,' said Caro in a resigned tone, 'that his lordship owned the place, the way he was laying down the law!'

Lexie, remembering the authority Storm had brought to bear on poor John Lyme, secretly agreed. 'But he achieved his ends—which were mine,' she pointed out. 'I asked him to persuade Mr Lyme. He did it for me.'

'It seems to me he would do almost anything for you, Alexia. He certainly behaved as though he had every right. . . I wonder he has not declared himself yet.'

'Oh, he will never marry,' said Lexie airily, ignoring the pain the assertion gave her.

'Hmm.' Caro eyed her pink face suspiciously. 'It seemed to me— But there. . .' She cut herself off with another resigned sigh. 'He flirts with every woman he meets, even the Duchess. He cannot help it. So I suppose there was really nothing particular in the way he looked at you.'

Lexie caught her breath. 'Of course there was not,' she maintained.

'But by the way you look at him, my love, you declare your feelings for all to see. You will have to be more careful when we return to London, or gossip will be fuelled anew. And although you are my benefactor and I have no authority over you, Alexia, I do consider myself to have a responsibility towards you. I feel I must warn you.'

'Of course you must, but you are imagining things,

Cousin Caro! I look upon his lordship as I would on any gentleman friend!'

'I,' remarked Caro with a shrug, 'have never seen you look at anyone in quite the way you look at his lordship.'

Dear Lord, were her feelings plain for all to see? She had thought herself circumspect in her dealings with Storm. Yet Caro— But Caro had had a clue, had known her to be interested in marriage to the Marquess. So she had imagined the rest.

At least, Lexie hoped so. It would be too mortifying for words were all her acquaintance to realise that she had fallen in love with the most notorious rake in Town.

Aiming to be in St Albans before nine o'clock, Lexie left early the following day, riding a frisky Danny. But, bowing to the anxiety and outrage of Jethro Pascoe, she had agreed to allow Jeffs to accompany her to the outskirts of the city. And had been persuaded to hire a man to ride back with her at the end of her visit.

''Tis not safe for a young woman like yourself to undertake such a journey alone,' he had scolded. 'What be you thinking of, my lady? Get away from everything if you must, but do be sensible and take precautions against being set upon by thieves and vagabonds!'

So Jeffs rode at Danny's rump and Lexie was not sorry for the company. It would have been a long, anxious ride had she been alone, with all kinds of travellers on the road and many a thicket near enough to conceal footpads and robbers.

'There is no need for you to come further than that inn just along the road, Jeffs,' she said as they came upon the first houses. 'You may assure Mr Pascoe that I arrived quite safely. Refresh yourself in the inn before you return.'

She handed Jeffs a coin; he touched his hat and dismounted at the door of the Weary Traveller protesting his gratitude.

Free of his company, Lexie made haste to find her way to the coaching inn where she was to pick up the stage. She did not know the town well and had to ask her way more than once. She arrived with a sense of relief and pride in achievement. She was perfectly able to survive on her own!

Dismounting in the yard, she handed Danny over to an ostler, asking that her packs be removed and the animal stabled and cared for until she returned to claim him. She was about to conclude the arrangements with the man pointed out as in charge when she caught sight of a familiar figure striding purposefully towards her.

Clad in country clothes, twill breeches and stout leather boots, a rough woollen coat and low brown beaver hat, his appearance still managed to stop her heart.

'Did you really imagine I would allow you to travel alone?' he asked, as he nodded a greeting. Formal bows and curtsies would not have been in place, but his eyes, warm and smiling, told her he was pleased to see her. And hers—hers probably revealed her overwhelming joy at the sight of him.

Marlow appeared at his shoulder, dressed simply and wearing a disapproving look. Used as he was to his master's adventures, he still did not have to approve all the cloak-and-dagger intrigue which was accompanying this *affaire*.

'Marlow will deal with the stabling of your horse, you may trust him to see it done right, and he will see your bags put into my carriage,' Storm went on, as Lexie, overwhelmed by his sudden appearance, seemed lost for words. 'We will go inside and partake of some refreshment.' He turned to Marlow. 'Take some yourself when you have made the arrangements,' he instructed.

'Yes, sir,' said Marlow, emphasising the last word.

'He objects,' murmured Storm, as he took Lexie's arm and ushered her towards the inn door, 'to having to call me "sir" instead of "my lord". He considers it *infra dignitatem*.'

'Poor Marlow,' said Lexie, recovering her voice, though it quivered with emotion. 'How our servants do disapprove of our ruses and foibles! Chalker was almost in tears over the few clothes I was proposing to bring and Jethro talked me into allowing Jeffs to escort me to the edge of the town!'

'Sensible fellow, Pascoe. I like him. I believe you could have taken him into your confidence. But thanks to him or not, you have arrived safely and I swear we shall not be parted again until we must return to our separate establishments.'

'You could not promise anything which would content me more,' she assured him.

Having partaken of light refreshments in a rather crowded inn parlour, where the Marquess, despite his unremarkable clothes, was accorded instant attention, his quality being unmistakable, Storm led her out to his waiting equipage. Lexie eyed it with amusement.

'Where on earth did you find that old chariot?' she demanded.

'At the back of the coach house at Stormaston. And the hired horseflesh is scarcely of the standard I normally use. However, one must keep up appearances. If we are to behave as an ordinary couple for a while, we must look the part.'

Trust Storm to enter into the spirit of the enterprise and to do things thoroughly, thought Lexie fondly.

The chariot, although elderly, was well sprung and comfortably cushioned inside. Lexie did not long lament her lost opportunity to take the stage, especially when she saw it arrive already laden with passengers and luggage. She would have found no room inside and been condemned to a seat on top.

'No,' said Storm, handing her into the chariot and nodding meaningfully towards the crowded coach. 'I could not allow you to travel in such discomfort! And knowing you, my dear Lexie, I guessed you would chose to travel that way rather than by post chaise.'

'Post chaises can be dirty and smelly,' Lexie reminded him. 'I thought the stage would be an experience.'

'One you would do well to avoid unless in an extremity! The mail coach would be preferable.'

'Is Marlow to drive?' asked Lexie as Storm followed her into the chariot's interior.

'He is taking the first stage, then we shall drive turn and turn about, all night if necessary. But we should arrive before midnight unless anything untoward happens. The journey should not take much more than ten hours.'

Ten hours, half of them spent in close proximity to Storm in the confines of the coach, the other half spent watching his broad shoulders through the front window as he shared the box with Marlow when he took the ribbons. Definitely better than travelling by the stage.

In fact, for the last part of the journey Marlow did all the driving while Lexie dozed, her head cradled on Storm's shoulder.

They arrived in darkness. Marlow drew the horses up before a neat cottage on the outskirts of the small resort nestling on the shore.

'In daylight you can see the sea,' Storm told her as she staggered out, to be caught fast in his arms.

Lexie yawned, moving to ease her cramped muscles. 'Like Cornwall,' she murmured.

'I doubt it! The coast is quite different here. No cliffs. Flat as a pancake.'

At that moment the door was flung open, revealing a small figure holding a candle high, while behind her more candles and a lamp threw out a welcoming glow.

'Master James!' cried his old nurse. 'I thought I heard you arrive! Do bring the poor young lady in at once!'

'Martha!' Storm moved forward, his arm about Lexie's shoulders. 'This is Mistress Lexie.'

'Any friend of Master James is welcome here,' said Martha, eyeing Lexie approvingly and bobbing a small curtsy.

'Thank you, Mrs Dean.'

'Do call me Martha, my dear. Master James always does.'

No further explanations were necessary. Storm had laid the foundations for the visit with great care. Martha took them up to a large, airy room on the first floor, decorated in cream with cheerful floral drapes and covers, cotton rather than silk, but none the worse for that. A washstand stood in one corner with an ewer of water in the basin and towels hung on a rail.

'You'll want to wash the dirt of the journey off yourselves,' remarked Martha. 'I'll fetch a kettle of hot water, there's one simmering on the stove.'

'I'll go,' said Storm. 'I'll not have you fetching and carrying for us, Martha. Where's Daisy, your help?'

'She's been abed this last hour or more. She'll bring a kettle up in the morning, empty your slops and the like.'

'I won't be long,' promised Storm, dropping a light kiss on Lexie's lips as he passed on his way to follow Martha downstairs.

'I shall probably be asleep,' yawned Lexie.

'Then I shall have to wake you up.'

His eyes laughed into hers. But he meant it.

CHAPTER ELEVEN

SHE had no time to do more than remove her pelisse and bonnet before Storm returned with a huge ewer of hot water.

'We must share this, I fear,' he told her, smiling wickedly. 'Just as we must share everything else while we are here. Do you need help to undress?'

Lexie laughed softly and turned her back. 'Chalker normally undoes the fastenings of my gown. If you would not mind?'

'A privilege, *madame*. Just a moment while I fill the basin and deposit this jug. Now, let me see. . .'

His skilled fingers soon unhooked the back of her gown, which he smoothed forward over her shoulders, brushing the enticing swell of her breasts as it fell to her feet. Lexie stepped out of the crumpled tan serge, an old but sturdy gown doing duty as a summer travelling dress. She bent forward to pick it up, but Storm's arms prevented her. His mouth nuzzled the curve where creamy shoulder met slender neck while his hands cupped her thrusting breasts. 'I haven't finished,' he murmured thickly. 'The ties of your chemise. . .'

Lexie gave a shuddering sigh. 'Stop it, James, or we shall never finish undressing and washing!'

'Do you really want me to?' he asked, mock indignation warring with laughter in his voice.

'No, but—'

'Then I shall not.' His teeth nipped her ear but one of his hands left its erotic fondling to tug at the bows of her garment.

'Do be sensible,' protested Lexie, whose legs were beginning to lose their strength. 'I really must wash the dirt of the journey off before we go to bed.'

Storm sighed. 'Cleanliness before sinfulness, I do declare!'

'Oh, Storm! Do not remind me!'

'My regrets, sweet Lexie, I was only joking. A jest in bad taste, I acknowledge. Pray do not let it spoil things for you.'

His voice held real contrition as he turned her to him and dropped a gentle kiss on her parted lips. His eyes, blue as a summer sky, gazed down into the clouded green depths of hers. 'I will make you forget,' he promised.

Lexie gave herself a mental shake. She had been so delightfully relaxed and happy it would be a crime to allow a careless word to ruin their time together. She had taken the decision to come. She could not allow conscience to intrude now.

Her eyes cleared. 'I was being idiotish,' she admitted.

'Only very slightly. The greater stupidity was mine. And I shall suffer for it,' he announced in resigned tones.

Lexie frowned. 'You, suffer? How?'

'I have appointed myself your lady's maid. I shall undress and wash you and put you to bed. But I have no one to do a similar service for me.'

'Oh, no?' Lexie grinned, all qualms forgotten. 'If your lordship would deign to instruct me in the art, I am perfectly willing to undertake the duties of your man.'

'You are?' He sounded delighted. 'Oh what joy! We shall tend each other like delicate blossoms—'

'Don't be a fool, James!'

But Lexie was laughing, revelling in this new, teasing, light-hearted facet of the man she loved.

Tend her he did, washing her from her forehead to the soles of her feet, drying her with rough, abrasive strokes that set the blood coursing through her veins. When she reached for her nightgown he stayed her hand.

'You do not need that, my love.'

Lexie nodded and, feeling excessively wicked, undressed him and bathed him while herself remaining quite naked.

By the time they tumbled into bed they could not wait. The fusion of their bodies came almost instantaneously. But, tired as she had thought herself, Lexie did not sleep but responded to Storm's love-making as often as he was able to revive his own resources. Daylight was streaking round the curtains before they dropped at last into the sleep of utter exhaustion.

The days passed in quick succession, golden days of early autumn as August faded into September. They walked, rode hired horses, lazed on the beach and even made use of the single bathing machine the little resort boasted. But above all they made love. The week they had promised themselves flew by, turned into two and then ran into a third. Lexie wanted their time together never to end.

Storm, surprised that his initial passion seemed not

one whit abated by more than two whole weeks of Lexie's exclusive company and the innumerable occasions upon which he had possessed her, began to assess the possibilities for carrying on the affair once they resumed normal life.

'I really must return to Wiltshire,' he sighed. 'I may not neglect my duties any longer.'

'Duty!' lamented Lexie. 'How I wish we could live like this for ever, simply, our needs small, able to exist on a competence!'

'How bored we should both become without some kind of occupation!'

'You can say that, when you idle about Town for the most part of the year?'

'There, dear Lexie, I must beg to differ! I normally spend far more time at Stormaston Park and travelling around my other estates than I do in Town!'

'So you may. I apologise! But for myself, I could find plenty to do, even in a place like this.'

Looking after our children, she dreamed but did not say.

'But what of the challenges you so much enjoy, the social round you craved when isolated far from Town? No, my love, you would soon tire of playing the milkmaid, just as you tired of Cornwall! Administering my estates takes time and skills which I enjoy deploying. And I should sadly miss experimenting in my laboratory were it taken from me! I am on the very point of completing the design of an engine to work the water pump!'

He had told her of his interest in steam engines, his self-imposed task of discovering how they worked and how best to utilise their power, and Lexie shook her head. Such an interest did not sit well with his reputation, but she was fast discovering that the man she loved was far from the idle rake he appeared to be. 'You will blow yourself up one day!'

'Do not fear for me! But I have been thinking. We need to plan how to go on once we return to the world. I think it best if I find a convenient house or flat in London where we can meet as often as we like. If we are discreet—'

'No!'

Lexie's flat denial cut him off short. He studied her angry face in astonishment.

'But I thought you would want to continue—'

'I denied my conscience to pay my debt.' Disappointment that he could propose nothing more than the continuation of a casual *affaire* after the rapturous time they had spent together roused Lexie's anger. She would not carry on as his mistress. She had far too much pride. If he could not see that his precious freedom meant nothing in the face of what they shared together, then he could enjoy it without her help.

'The length of time I should submit to being your mistress was never mentioned. I am now saying that leaving here marks the end.'

His clipped response made Lexie shiver. 'Very well. If that is your wish. Our liaison ends here.'

Storm was angry, too. Knowing he still wanted her, the creature was no doubt hoping to force him into offering her more. He would not be blackmailed into marriage, the idea of which he both disliked and feared. All his years of adolescence had been circumscribed, his behaviour dictated by others. His freedom was too precious to be surrendered for the sake of mere carnal delight. There were plenty of willing women in the world.

The anguish in Lexie's eyes almost undid him; but her bitter words served to strengthen his resolve.

'I am unused to the courtesies normally observed in a situation like this and bow to your superior knowledge, but if you are expecting me to wait until you tire of me and decide to dispense with my services, then you are sadly mistaken, my lord. I will not be cast aside like soiled linen!'

'Then it is certainly best that we part as soon as possible,' he bit back. 'But we cannot depart now, it is too late. We must wait until tomorrow. Neither can I conveniently vacate your bed. I do not wish to distress Martha. So—' His manner changed as he reached for her hands and smiled his most rakish smile. The smile that ravaged her senses. 'One last night together, eh?' he suggested.

Lexie swallowed. He was attempting to manipulate her and she knew it. She was sorely tempted to accept one last night of Heaven before she need contemplate the bleak future. She had, after all, suspected that he would not offer marriage even had she become pregnant. So nothing had actually changed.

But even as she thought of it her senses rebelled. She could not stand to have him touch her under the circumstances. She shook her head. 'We will share the bed if we must, but I cannot agree to anything more. I will go up now and pack.'

Storm hid his triumph. Tonight he would have a last chance to slake the raging desire the woman roused in him, for she would not be able to resist his skilled wooing. Then, after they parted next day, he would put her from his mind.

It did not quite work out that way. He had forgotten Lexie's will, her ability to deny her own desires. He should have remembered that occasion in the flat.

At his first overture, Lexie stiffened.

'No, Storm. You will have to force me.'

'I think not, my dear. You may not wish to continue the relationship, but your craving for me is not yet dead.'

She did not deny his charge. 'But my willingness to indulge it is! Our intimate relationship is over. It should never have been. Leave me alone, Storm, or I shall have to seek refuge with Martha.'

How long she could have withstood the searing demands of her body Lexie did not know. But her threat sobered him and he desisted.

'You are a fool, Lexie,' he gritted. 'But I am not an animal, whatever you may think. I shall not attempt to force you against your will. I wish you a good night.'

He turned his back, grappling with his need. Lexie's breathing became steady behind him. How easily she had fallen asleep! Had he really failed to stir her?

He lay for a long time contemplating a future without the warmth of her near him and did not like it. But he would recover.

He almost got up to walk off his frustration, but before he had quite decided on that course he fell asleep. Only as he edged into oblivion did his mind register that the things he valued most about her, her courage and pride, her determination, her principles, even her refusal to be entirely restricted by convention, remained intact. And had defeated his rash assumption that she would be willing to countenance anything he might desire.

He should have been more circumspect. He would try a more subtle approach in the morning.

But when he woke he found her side of the bed empty.

At first he did not worry. She had woken early and gone for a walk. Or gone down to make herself a drink in the kitchen, something she had taken to doing whenever either of them felt thirsty, for she enjoyed a cose with Martha, with whom she got on famously.

But when he rose and went downstairs there was no sign of her.

'Has Mistress Lexie gone out?' he asked Daisy, who was busy clearing the grate preparatory to boiling up water for washing.

'I haven't seen her, sir,' said Daisy, her rosy face beaming up at the handsome gentleman.

Martha was still abed. Storm returned to the room they had shared and only then did he notice that all Lexie's things had gone.

'The Devil! She has walked out on me!'

Nothing remotely like it had ever happened to him before. He had always been the one to end an *affaire*. Rejection tasted bitter.

But then he shrugged. What did it matter? They were to part today in any case. The end of an *affaire*.

Nothing new in that. And perhaps she had merely woken early and gone to wake Marlow to have him prepare the chariot for the journey. That must be it.

But why take all her things?

Frowning, Storm descended the stairs again. 'I am going to the inn to speak to Marlow,' he informed Daisy, who was by now scrubbing the floor.

The small place boasted only the one stables and post house, which were attached to the inn. The stables showed signs of life, but Marlow was nowhere to be seen.

'Not down yet, sir,' a pot boy told him upon enquiry.

'Have you seen the lady who normally accompanies me?'

'I seen her, sir. Hired the post chaise an hour ago. Had to wake the post boy. Grumpy, he were, at being roused so early from his bed.'

Storm cursed under his breath. He could probably catch her up, but why trouble? She wanted to go and should be safe enough in a hired chaise. He would knock Marlow up, tell him they were returning to Stormaston Park forthwith, and after submitting to Marlow's razor, go back for breakfast and bid Martha farewell.

Lady Amber would soon be forgotten once he returned to his estates, his duties and his experiments.

Lexie scarcely noticed the discomfort and poor state of the series of chaises which carried her to St Albans. Forced to change carriages at every stage, she was glad to have only scanty luggage with her.

She arrived, after hours spent dully watching the rise and fall of a succession of postilions' bottoms, with just enough time to make the journey to Merryfield before dark. Or—should she take accommodation for the night and ride back tomorrow, at a respectable hour?

She decided on the latter course. She had slept scarcely a wink last night, though she had pretended to while the hot tears ran silently down to soak her pillow. Storm, she knew, had lain awake, too, though she sensed immediately when at last his breathing changed to the steady rhythm that told her he was asleep.

As the first streaks of dawn lit the sky she had slipped out of bed, silently donned her travelling gown, fearful of waking him with every rustle, picked up her bags and crept from the house. She regretted not being able to say goodbye to Martha but the old lady already knew how grateful she was for her hospitality. She would write her thanks the moment she reached home.

Now she needed time to recover her composure, to rehearse the story she would tell, to garner enough courage to smile, smile, smile, when she wanted to hide away and cry her heartache away.

Told who she was and having been shown several gold coins, the innkeeper discovered that he did have a small, private room the lady could have for the night. The head ostler would be pleased to allow her to inspect her animal and he could arrange for one of his stable hands to ride out to Merryfield with her the next day.

If the story spread that Lady Amber had slept at

the Post House alone and unaccompanied, she would think of some explanation. A sudden emergency at her friend's—anything would do. She was, at that time, past caring what anyone thought. Except that she must hide her hurt. She could not bear to be looked upon with pity.

So she rode into the stable yard at Merryfield, paid off the man who had accompanied her, and returned Jethro's greeting with every appearance of cheerful good humour. Danny did not seem to have suffered unduly from his period in stables, though Jethro looked askance at his rough coat and slightly tangled mane.

'We'll soon have him trimmed and gleaming again,' he promised. 'I trust you enjoyed your visit, my lady?'

'Very much, thank you,' answered Lexie, truthfully. She would always have those golden days to remember as she drifted into elderly widowhood.

But as she settled back into the routine at Merryfield she found the unadulterated company of her cousin somewhat tedious. It certainly did nothing to relieve her misery. Caro's presence had been fine in London, when she was out most of the time and entertaining for much of the remainder, with Caro organising her household. She had scarcely noticed Caro's incessant chatter about trifling matters.

The truth was, she was missing Storm. His company had made all else bearable. Without it, life had become a wasteland.

She could not allow herself to drift into an uncaring decline. She did not need to marry, yet she had gone to London wanting to, for life was not pleasant or easy for a woman alone, however well situated. She had not looked for love before she met Storm. Just affection and compatibility. Having fallen disastrously in love, she had thought she could never marry anyone else, but. . .

If only there were some decent gentleman of suitable rank able to fill the empty places in her life, he might manage to change her mind. She needed children to love, to take away the ache the loss of Storm had left in her heart. Every time she had used her sponge and vinegar, she had had to grit her teeth.

It had been effective, for her monthly show had arrived spot on time almost as soon as she returned to Merryfield, relieving her of anxiety in that quarter, yet bringing a new cause for grief. Storm had passed no comment on her precautions. She wondered whether he had noticed. But having his child outside wedlock would not have been the answer.

Perhaps there would be different gentlemen in London looking for wives during the Little Season before Christmas. From what he had said, she did not think Storm would be returning to Town before the New Year, except for short business visits. He had no plan to circulate in Society. So she could take up residence in Bruton Street without fear of running into him at every turn.

'We are returning to London,' she told Caro that evening. 'I need to do some shopping.'

To her surprise, Caro beamed. 'I shall not be sorry, Alexia. Life here seems rather dull, does it not?'

'I did not think you would find it so!'

'I enjoy running the household here, of course,

but—' Caro gave Lexie a guilty look '—I do miss a comfortable cose with Mrs Seacombe.'

'So you must! Well, I am glad we are agreed. Shall we leave at the end of next week?'

'I will go ahead and make certain that all is in readiness to receive you!'

'That will scarcely be necessary, Cousin. A note to Mr Dymock should be sufficient. Mrs Walker is quite capable of catering for us without supervision. We may travel together in the coach. Pascoe can arrange for my horses and curricle to follow.'

'You'll be dashing about in that again, I collect. Will you never change, Alexia?'

'Not if I can help it,' said Lexie grimly, envisioning some future husband frowning at her capers and forbidding them. She would have to be very sure of her man before she consented to relinquish her freedom.

For the first time, she appreciated Storm's reluctance to abandon his. But surely he knew that she would not attempt to restrict him? At least, not in ways unconnected with women! Just as she was certain he would not seek to restrain her?

Resolutely, she put such thought from her mind. She would forget. One day, as she watched her children grow up, she would wonder why she had allowed herself to be made so unhappy.

But tears gathered in her eyes as she acknowledged that they would not be James's children.

Once back in Bruton Street Lexie set about visiting acquaintances who were in residence and leaving her card. To her surprise, the Downshires were back in Grosvenor Square.

'My dear,' said the Duchess, eyeing Lexie critically. 'How delightful to see you again so soon. I did not expect you to return to Town until the main Season next year.'

'Neither did I,' admitted Lexie. 'But the estate does not need my attention and I missed the social life to be found here. A number of acquaintances seem to have either remained or returned to Town. My diary will soon be full! I trust I shall see both you and Fanny at many of the functions.'

'Probably not,' said the Duchess, her expression sobering. 'We are here to enable the Duke to consult a heart specialist. He is bein' forced to adhere to a strict regime, which I am certain he would soon abandon should we return to Downshire. He declares that he is not ready to quit his lease just yet, but we are all most concerned over his health. James has returned to Town to be on hand should his presence be required.'

'Oh, how sorry I am!' cried Lexie. 'I did so enjoy entertaining His Grace at Merryfield. He is one of the few gentlemen who would not condemn me for racing my curricle against his grandson!'

'Considers you a rare plucked 'un. Don't censure James for allowin' the wager, either. There are those who think it most reprehensible of my grandson to take money from a lady as a result of winnin'. But he is well used to weatherin' such criticism. He seems to court it. How are you, my dear? You do not look in plump currant at the moment.'

The Duchess's sudden change of topic took Lexie

by surprise. She had been sleeping badly and eating little. She knew she looked tired and drawn and mention of James had almost overset her. But she turned to Fanny with a laugh. 'Just because I have grown thin everyone thinks I am ill!'

Fanny nodded. 'I seem to be adding flesh and everyone tells me how well I look. As though weight had anything to do with it!'

'Do call again, my dear,' pressed the Duchess as Lexie took her leave. 'You know we shall always be pleased to receive you.'

To Lexie's relief, Storm appeared to be retired from Society for the moment. As far as she could gather, he spent most of his time at White's. A much improved Hugo appeared at Grosvenor Square, splendid in his uniform. He had been granted compassionate leave to visit his grandfather.

'Best thing I ever did,' he informed Lexie when they met. 'Havin' a splendid time in the army, enjoyin' the life immensely. Fine crowd of fellows in my mess, don't you know. We get up to all kinds of larks.'

'Innocent ones, I trust?' murmured Lexie sweetly, seething that he had put it forward as his idea to purchase a pair of colours and anxious that the good name of Graham should not suffer by his pranks.

'Oh, no harm in it, no harm at all. We hunt every day, ride like fury. Tally ho!'

He did seem pleased with himself and with life, which must be a relief to Storm. And to his grandparents.

'He is much changed,' the Duchess confided in the privacy of her boudoir, to which, some weeks later,

Lexie had been invited. 'We was becomin' worried over him. Threatened to become frivolous, vain and spiteful. The discipline seems to be knockin' those unfortunate traits out of him. James bought his commission, y'know. Wanted to join the army himself years ago, but Downshire and I managed to persuade him against. Have you seen him lately?'

Lexie's heart continued to hammer, as it always did when Storm was mentioned. She clasped her hands in her lap, then plucked at the wool and silk mixture of her soft violet morning gown. 'No, ma'am. He is not attending many functions. We have not met since my return to London.'

'Hmm.' The knotted fingers arranged her grey skirts more comfortably as the Duchess lay back on her *chaise longue*. 'Just as well, the mood he is in. Never known him so morose. Nothing right.' She raised her lorgnette. 'Have you quarrelled?'

Lexie flushed. 'We are no longer on the best of terms.'

'Won't ask why.' She dropped the glasses to her lap. 'Reprobate won't wed you, I collect. Do him good not to get his own way in everythin'.'

'He did not get it over joining the army,' Lexie reminded the Duchess quietly.

'No, but there ain't been many things he's been denied since he came of age. Especially women. Runs through 'em like smoke.'

Lexie winced.

'But there don't seem to be anyone at the moment,' went on the Duchess disingenuously. 'Treat him kindly when you meet. You can never tell, with James. He don't give in easily, but when he does, he does it handsomely.'

Unable to stand any more of the Duchess's hints, Lexie turned the subject. 'Has Fanny any new suitors?'

'One or two. But she don't take any notice of 'em. She's like James in that. Won't do what she don't want to. But she's young. I've heard that Cranley is after you. What do you think of him, eh?'

Lexie chose her words carefully. 'He seems a kind, decent sort of gentleman. Pleasant enough.' But wildly boring.

'Will never set the Thames on fire, but he's well placed. You could do worse than consider him if James refuses to come up to scratch. Cranley is turned forty. He won't wait much longer to find himself a wife.'

'No.'

The Duchess took the hint and the conversation turned to fashion for the winter ahead. It was already chilly and damp, with fogs rising off the Thames. Fanny came in and joined the conversation. She was looking particularly wan, in Lexie's opinion, despite her rounded figure. She wondered how much she was seeing of Lord Dexter, for Felix was in Town.

A couple of days later she was surprised to be told that Lady Fanny Graham was below, asking if her ladyship would receive her.

'Alone?' asked Lexie in surprise. Fanny usually came with the Duchess.

'Apart from her servant, my lady.'

'Send her up immediately!'

Lexie had no other callers that morning and

received Fanny in the morning-room, where she had been sitting at her writing table composing letters to her mother in Ireland and John Lyme at Merryfield.

'Fanny!' she greeted her friend. 'How nice to see you! Do sit down.'

She indicated a comfortable winged armchair and Fanny perched on the edge of the seat, clearly in a considerable state of agitation.

'Oh, Lexie!' she exclaimed. 'I do hope you may be able to help us!'

Lexie lifted enquiring golden eyebrows. 'Us?'

'Felix and me.' Fanny swallowed. 'I am pregnant.'

Lexie, who had subsided into the depths of her comfortable chair, sat up straight.

'By Felix?' As though she needed to ask! The rake!

'Yes, but it is not what you think! I begged him to make love to me. We were desperate, you see. We love each other so, but we both knew from things James has said that he would never approve the match. He has as good as warned Felix off. Yet Felix has changed, he does not even look at other women and would abandon everything for me! But I will not allow that.'

Now that the flood-gates had opened, Fanny seemed unable to stop her rush of words. Her hands were twisting together in her lap. 'We could elope but just think of the scandal! And I believe that once he is faced with the fact of my condition, James will have to permit our marriage. That is why I did it,' she finished on a gulp.

'I cannot deny that you astonish me, Fanny! When did you conceive this desperate plan?'

'At Merryfield. Felix came to me there. It was easy. And I began increasing immediately. I wasn't certain at first, I have never been very regular, you know, but I am quite sure now. I must be three months on and I shall begin to show soon. We must act immediately. Oh! Lexie, could you tell James and persuade him to let us marry? He respects your judgment. Please, Lexie!'

'Your condition explains your added pounds,' said Lexie wryly. Ask James? How could she? 'Do your grandparents know?' she asked, to gain more time.

Fanny shook her head. 'I would rather they need not. I have no wish to hurt them. But James is my guardian. I must have his permission if I am not to elope. Do say you'll break the news to him, Lexie!'

'They can count, Fanny. They will guess when your baby is born so very early.'

'Well, we shall go on a tour abroad. We can, now Napoleon is defeated. No one will know exactly when the infant is born.'

'You would lie about his birthday? Celebrate the wrong date?'

'What would it matter?'

'Not much, I suppose. But Fanny, I have to tell you that Storm and I are no longer so friendly as we were. I have not seem him this age.'

'Oh.' Fanny's countenance fell. 'I did wonder, for he has stopped circulating in Society while you have not. But I am certain he still holds you in high regard! He always mentions you when he comes to visit Grandfather.'

Lexie sighed. No doubt he was covering up his discomfiture over being abandoned in Essex. He would never admit to what he would see as her rejection. She could understand that.

She spoke of him to his grandmother, for the Duchess related all the latest gossip. Much good it did her to hear it, for he seemed to be behaving with remarkable restraint despite his reported ill-temper, and that made her love him all the more; but just to speak of him seemed some kind of comfort, even though it caused immense agitation of the spirit. Dared she hope he felt the same?

No, that would be foolish. He had never loved her, simply desired her. Perhaps he wished to hear that she was in a fit of the dismals so that he could know the satisfaction of thinking that it served her right. Or to ascertain whether her unhappiness was liable to throw her back into his arms. Or whether desperation to wed would result in her accepting some dullard like Cranley. She hoped that, if she did, he would be a little upset.

But Fanny was waiting eagerly for her response. How could she refuse to try to help? She did not really know how Storm now felt about her. Her intervention might set him further against the match rather than influence him towards it, but she felt compelled to try. She had grown fond of Fanny, she liked Felix enormously, she liked and respected the Duke and Duchess and would save them from hurt if she could.

In the end she reached out and took one of Fanny's restless hands in hers. 'I will speak to him, Fanny, but do not rely too heavily on my proving successful.'

Fanny departed full of profuse thanks. Lexie

resumed her seat at her writing table and embarked upon the difficult task of sending Storm a note asking him to call the following morning to discuss a delicate but important matter.

When she was satisfied with the wording she sent a footman round to his rooms to deliver the note. Storm was out and so she had to wait in some trepidation for either an answer or for his advent the next day.

She wished that the prospect of seeing him again did not cause her so much agitation. He might refuse to come. In that case she would have done her best, her conscience would be clear.

But her heart would feel heavier than ever.

CHAPTER TWELVE

LEXIE dressed with especial care the next morning. A note had arrived early to say that his lordship would call at eleven o'clock and she did not want him to think her pining.

'There, my lady,' said Chalker. 'You are looking splendid, this morning. It is a long time since his lordship called, is it not? Will he be your escort again next Season?'

Lexie suspected that Chalker had her own ideas as to what had happened while she was on holiday. But Lexie had not confided in either her or Caro. Better to keep her secret locked in her heart.

'I do not expect so,' she responded. She smiled. 'Lord Cranley would be certain to object.'

Chalker looked disapproving. 'Oh, him.'

'What is it, Florence? Do you not like Lord Cranley?'

'He's not for you, my lady,' burst out Chalker, then blushed a furious red. 'Forgive me, my lady! I should not have said that.'

'No,' agreed Lexie repressively, 'you should not. However, I incline to agree with you.'

'You do? I'm that glad, your ladyship! Couldn't bear the thought of you marrying that dull stick of a gentleman! You and Lord Stormaston were meant for each other!'

'The Marquess does not think so,' said Lexie drily.

She did not reprove her maid further. She had given Chalker the opening and, in truth, was glad to have her own opinion confirmed. She would have to discourage the man or he would gain the wrong impression. Unlike Storm he was serious in his intentions. Perhaps if she did something really outrageous. . .

The hint of a smile played at the corners of Lexie's mouth. Her green eyes sparkled back at her from the mirror. Yes, she looked in fine fettle, thank goodness! If only she were not so nervous! But the heat generated by her tension had put a healthy-looking flush on her cheeks. She hoped he would be punctual. He usually was.

Dymock announced his arrival as the clock on the mantelpiece in the morning-room struck the hour. Lexie remained seated as he made his bow.

Against all propriety, Caro was not present to act as chaperon and Lexie gestured to Dymock to close the door of the morning-room behind him.

Storm did not take the proffered seat and had a faint sneer on his face as he spoke.

'If you hope to compromise me by conducting this interview in seclusion, ma'am, you will fail.'

Lexie gasped and the faint colour in her cheeks fled, leaving her looking pinched. 'You are unkind! I had no such idea in mind, my lord! I merely wished for privacy. I would not like others to overhear our conversation this morning.'

'No? I must admit you surprise me. If you are to tell me you are pregnant despite all your care, an audience would appear an advantage.'

He was, she sensed, in a towering temper, which

he was unleashing on her, although his quite unwarranted scorn seemed to hold an element of hurt in it, too. But she had no time to search out the reason for this. She composed herself to face his anger, his contempt, without quailing. For Fanny's sake.

'I am not pregnant,' she informed him steadily, her knuckles white on the hands clasped in her lap. 'I would not have requested an interview on my own behalf. I wished to speak with you about your sister, Lady Fanny.'

'Fanny!'

The explosive exclamation illuminated Lexie's understanding. He already knew! And thought she was about to attempt a similar form of blackmail! She heaved a sigh, partly of relief, partly to bolster her courage.

'She came to see me yesterday in great distress. She and Felix—'

Storm interrupted her with a smothered curse. 'Have behaved in the most scandalous manner!' he finished her sentence for her in his own words. 'And Felix has the gall to tell me that he wishes to wed the chit! No doubt some would regard this as an honourable intention, but I know better! He seduced an innocent girl for his own ends. I will not have it. I have called him out. My seconds are meeting his today.'

'James! You cannot mean it! They are so in love! Are you blind, that you have not noticed how they adore each other? But they knew you would not approve the match and so Fanny begged—yes—' as Storm gave a snort of disbelief '—Fanny begged Felix to lie with her! I had it from her own mouth!'

'Fanny would never—'

'Have you spoken to her, James? Does her happiness mean nothing to you? Oh, I know Felix has a bad reputation with women, but any man can change. Fanny is convinced he is devoted to her. And if you deny them the chance to wed, what becomes of the child she is to bear?'

'It will be taken care of.'

'Poor little soul!' Then, 'Did Felix speak to you?' wondered Lexie again. 'Fanny pleaded with me to intercede—'

'I cannot imagine what good she imagined you might achieve.'

'She did not know of the extent of our estrangement. I told her you probably would not listen to me, but she still pleaded with me to approach you. Did Felix. . .?' She left her repeated question trailing.

'No, he did not have that much nerve! I had to discover the truth from Hugo.'

'Hugo! Is he in Town again?' And up to his old tricks? 'How did he find out?'

'Put two and two together and made four, I collect. He is her brother, they are more of an age and he knows her better than I do.' Storm sounded resentful rather than regretful. 'His conclusions were confirmed by a weeping Fanny and he took the greatest of pleasure in informing me, coming straight round last evening to my rooms to suggest that I was to blame for introducing her to my disreputable friends. I suppose I am, but I thought she had more sense!'

'Love,' pronounced Lexie sadly, 'takes no account of common sense. So you tackled Felix, who admitted the offence, and you called him out!'

'Exactly.'

'And what good will that do, except to prove who is the better shot? Or is it to be swords? Really, Storm, I thought you had better judgement! They will make a well-matched pair—'

'Fanny is well dowered, Felix lacks funds. So much for your so-called love!'

'I do not believe that to be his motive. From what I have observed, he is truly enamoured of your sister. And why not? She is a fine young woman.'

'Hugo told me you encouraged the match!' Hurt and anger mingled in his voice as he made the accusation. 'That was why you brought them together at Merryfield, no doubt—to give them the chance to misbehave. I saw Felix returning to his room one night and thought he had been with the parlour maid!'

'You, my lord, sound like the pot calling the kettle black! Where had you been?'

'That was an entirely different matter! You are a widow, not a green girl scarcely out of the schoolroom!'

'To you, perhaps it is. Not to others, should they learn of it. But why don't you speak with Fanny? Let her plead her cause?'

Storm threw back his head and regarded Lexie down his aristocratic nose. 'The matter will be settled between Dexter and myself.'

Lexie found it impossible to remain seated a moment longer. She sprang to her feet.

'Is Fanny to have no say in the matter? Is her opinion to be treated as of no account? Really, Lord

Stormaston, I thought you more enlightened than to behave like a despot!'

'I will not argue with you, Lady Amber. I will bid you good day.'

He bowed and, without waiting for the butler to show him out, marched from the house. Lexie watched his retreating form, the stiff set of his shoulders and wept for Fanny. And for herself.

Where was the James Graham she had come to know over those wonderful weeks by the sea? If the Marquess did not watch his behaviour, he would soon become as dry a stick as Lord Cranley.

Storm, striding back to his rooms, felt all the bitterness of defeat.

Unable to bear the thought of his life without her, he had been on the point of abandoning his resolve, lowering his pride and declaring himself to Lexie, asking her to marry him. And then Hugo had come along to trample on his hopes.

Fanny and Dexter had deceived him. This alone he could have borne. But for Lexie, his high-spirited, green-eyed, golden nymph, to conspire in their deceit, had hurt him more than he would care to acknowledge.

He had thought her eminently honest and open. But all females were the same. Every one of them would betray a man at the drop of a hat. Just when he thought he had at last found a woman he could both love and trust, the creature had to prove otherwise.

But it simply confirmed him in his earlier opinion. He must make a marriage of convenience to beget an heir, but not until he could no longer put off the evil moment. That was all he had left to hope for in the way of domestic felicity. The woman whose company he craved had proved false.

Upon his return, Marlow greeted him dourly.

'Lord Hugo called to tell you that the duel is arranged for just after dawn tomorrow. That is, at six-thirty of the clock. I have cleaned your pistols.'

'What is it, man? You look as though you had just lost a fortune.'

'Never having had one to lose, I wouldn't know what that was like, begging your pardon, my lord. But what I do know is that this affair is foolish. Lord Dexter is your friend. He is a lively young man, but there is no real vice in him. If Lady Fanny—'

'Remember your place, Marlow!' barked Storm. 'Are you daring to question my actions?'

'No, sir.' Marlow failed to look abashed. 'Only your sense. You cannot fight your best friend, sir!'

'You think not? We shall see!'

Storm's displeasure with Fanny and Felix had cooled somewhat overnight. He knew the temptation desire could put in a man's way, and in a woman's, too, if they were only allowed to admit it. But the pair should have confided in him earlier.

Felix should have requested his permission to address Fanny. That he would probably have refused did not signify. He might, in the end, have been persuaded, for Felix had been his companion in sin for many years and he knew perfectly well that, like his own, Felix's behaviour was not as disgraceful as many thought.

He himself had been contemplating marrying a

modest young woman he had seduced by a trick, against her will. His conscience smote him at the thought, but he quickly pushed it aside, telling himself again that she had, after all, agreed to the wager, as he followed his line of reasoning. If he had considered himself a suitable husband for Lexie, why should not Felix make Fanny a desirable spouse?

He had acted from outrage and pique, anger against the erring couple, and disgust and disappointment over Lexie's betrayal, all fuelled by her note, which he had immediately taken to be another attempt to blackmail him into a course of action he would never choose. Or rather, that Lexie believed he would never choose.

But that had not been so. He could not doubt the sincerity of her denial. At least he had that comfort. If comfort it was.

But, death and hell, he had committed himself to a confounded duel and could not back out now! He had no desire to either kill or injure Felix. He was the better shot, but Felix was pretty accurate and could not be relied upon to miss. It seemed likely that one or the other or both would end up with a bullet in him. He hoped Hugo had engaged a competent surgeon.

Hugo was relishing this. The army had made him somewhat bloodthirsty. But on the whole his behaviour had been greatly improved by the discipline, everyone had remarked upon it. And most of the time he was away, swept from under the feet of his family, unable to cause embarrassment.

It was as well he had been home yesterday. Otherwise Lexie might have pulled the wool over his eyes, might have pleaded Fanny's cause without his ever knowing the despicable part she had played in the drama.

That, he considered, was quite the most hurtful aspect of the entire affair. Even a bullet in the shoulder would not occasion him so much pain.

Fanny came tearing round to Bruton Street quite unable to restrain her tears, even in public.

'Oh, Lexie!' she cried. 'Hugo guessed! He made me confess and went straight round to inform James, and James went to see Felix and they are to fight a duel! Felix will be killed, I know it, for he is not as accurate a shot as James, although he is better with a pistol than a sword, which is why he chose it—'

'I know, my dear,' said Lexie, the moment she could get a word in edgeways. 'Lord Stormaston came round here in a towering rage. He accused me of conspiring with you to arrange a suitable venue for your fornication!' she added grimly.

'Oh, how could he! I must see him, but he is keeping out of the way, he has not been to Grosvenor Square today. Why will he not listen to what I have to say?'

'Because he is arrogant and pig-headed. But do not despair. Felix may fire a lucky shot. James may be killed.'

Her voice shook but Fanny, wrapped up in her own grief, did not notice.

'Oh, do not say so! I could not bear that, either! How could I marry the man who had killed my brother?'

'An impasse, I agree,' said Lexie drily. How could

she still wish to wed a man who considered her a liar and a cheat? 'But I cannot conceive of any way to stop this foolishness. We do not even know where the duel is to be fought, or the time that has been fixed. Although Hugo probably knows. Could you winkle the information from him?'

Fanny shook her head. 'I have not seen him since yesterday, either. Now he is in the army he is staying at the Guards' Club with fellow officers, as guest of a friend in the Foot Guards. I cannot visit him there.'

'Neither can I. But you could send a note asking him to call.'

'Which, knowing Hugo, he would ignore, guessing I would want to drag the details of the meeting from him.'

'So we must wait in ignorance, the lot of women down the ages, it seems to me. But you know, Fanny, I do not think either man will attempt to kill his opponent. They have been too close.'

'I do pray you are right! And there is another thing. Grandmama is beginning to suspect that there is something wrong. I dread her quizzing me when I return!'

'It would take a moron not to notice that something is upsetting you, Fanny! Of course your grandmother can see something is wrong! I think you should make a clean breast of the entire thing. She may be able to influence your brother where I cannot. He does listen to her.'

'Only when he wants to,' said Fanny gloomily. But her tears had dried up. 'It would be a comfort to tell her everything. But she will be so upset!'

'Perhaps not as much as you might expect. She is

an unusual lady, my dear Fanny. And, you know, she favours Lord Dexter.'

'You think she does?' Fanny responded eagerly.

'I am certain she has a fondness for him. Whether that extends to approving a match between you I could not say. But do not despair, Fanny. Things may not be as black as you believe them to be.'

Lexie sent Fanny on her way in a more sanguine state of mind than when she had arrived. As for herself, she could only pray that neither Storm nor Felix would wish to seriously harm the other.

But she could not sit about waiting for news to be brought to her! Had she been in Fanny's shoes she would have defied convention, scandalised Society and charged round to the Guards' Club to demand to see Hugo. However, the duel was not to be fought over her; she had no official reason to be concerned in the affair. So her involvement must be discreet, secret.

Somehow, she must contrive to be present. She would not be able to prevent the exchange of fire, but she had to know the worst the instant it happened. For if Storm were badly injured she would indeed defy convention once more and rush to his side. That should prove outrageous enough to deter Cranley, she thought, enjoying a momentary gleam of humour. And should Felix be the victim she would like to be in a position to carry the news to Fanny.

Her thoughts were much occupied for the remainder of the day. By evening she had formed a plan.

Chalker was used to her irregular ways and evinced little surprise at being asked to call her mistress at five and dress her for riding. The yawning stable boy saddled Danny without demur. And Lexie set off alone just before dawn broke to loiter in the shadows at the end of St James's Street, hoping that Storm and his seconds had not already left for the rendezvous.

She saw Hugo and another man arrive and relaxed. She watched them leave shortly afterwards with Storm, followed by Marlow carrying his master's gun case. All four travelled inside the unidentifiable coach Storm had used to abduct her.

It was easy enough to follow them to Hampstead Heath. Felix and his party arrived almost simultaneously and another carriage drove up shortly afterwards, apparently carrying the surgeon and umpire.

Lexie, dismounted, holding Danny's headstall, and watched from the shelter of nearby bushes. If only she could do something to stop the madness! But the men would never allow a woman to intervene, to prevent them carrying out an idiotic ritual which a misguided sense of honour demanded they enact. They would simply set her to one side and carry on.

So she waited, silent, tense, her mind offering up unformed prayers for some intervention from the Almighty, while the seconds went through the motions of arranging the details of the duel to everyone's satisfaction.

Storm stood ready, remembering that first duel he had fought with rapiers, his sense of utter disillusion when he had discovered his defence of the lady's honour to have been ill-advised. He had vowed never to love another woman, false creatures that they were, and had treated Lexie badly because of his bitterness but, despite his vow, had allowed himself to be drawn into its meshes again. He had, against all his principles and wishes, fallen in love with Lexie. And she, too, had proved false.

And now he was about to fight his best friend for deflowering his sister. He did not want to believe that Fanny had been the instigator of the affair. She was no wanton, while Felix was a proven rake. He must be the guilty party. But women were unreliable creatures. He should have tackled Fanny. But it was a delicate matter and he had not managed to steel himself for the task.

Honour demanded he seek satisfaction from Felix, who had wronged his sister, his ward. But his heart was not in it. Storm stood back to back with his friend, who looked haggard and anxious—as well he might, since he was by far the worse shot, proved time after time in Manton's shooting gallery.

The umpire began to count. His mind clear as crystal, his hand perfectly steady, Storm strode forward the fifteen paces demanded, turned and fired. He heard Felix's almost simultaneous shot and waited for the jolt and the pain as the round tore into his flesh. Or for oblivion.

Lexie watched, holding her breath, as they strode apart, turned and fired. Incredulous, she saw puffs of dust rise a yard or so in front of Storm and a yard to one side of Felix. Choked by overwhelming relief, she saw them come together and shake hands. Then she was on Danny's back, riding like fury to Grosvenor

Square in order to give Fanny the news of both men's safety.

When she arrived at Downshire House and asked to see Lady Fanny, she was shown into the Duchess's bedchamber. The elderly lady was still in bed, propped up against a mound of pillows, with Fanny sitting beside her. Her Grace sat very still. The old eyes, slightly watery, fixed themselves on Lexie's face.

Lexie made a quick curtsy and while she did so, without preamble, she announced, 'They are both unharmed.'

She saw the stiffly held shoulders of the Duchess relax. Fanny gave a gasp of surprise and pleasure and threw herself at Lexie, clasping her so tightly in her exuberant relief that Lexie, laughing, protested.

'I pray you will not strangle me, Fanny!'

'But how did you find out?' demanded the cause of all the trouble breathlessly.

'I followed the Marquess to the meeting place and watched. Both gentlemen aimed their shots at the ground.'

A snort from the bed brought Lexie's attention back to the Duchess. Her lace-covered head had subsided against the pillows but her eyes held a new alertness.

'What a sad roil you made of this, Fanny! Why could you not have spoken to me earlier? I would have made James see sense. All these dramatics were quite unnecessary!'

Fanny, abashed, hung her head. 'I told you, Grandmama, at first I believed that you would side with James. You did wish me to wed Oswald

Cresswell, did you not?' The question was rhetorical and, ignoring the Duchess's impatient grunt, Fanny rushed on.

'Then, later, when I discovered my condition, I did not wish to upset you or Grandpapa. Lexie said you liked Felix and had influence with James, but I was afraid to test the truth of it in case I caused a quarrel between you. Even now,' she added gloomily, 'I suppose James will oppose the match.'

'Probably,' agreed her grandparent. 'But he will allow it. And as for you, young woman,' turning to Lexie, 'we owe you a debt of gratitude. You have saved us from hours of lowerin' suspense, for I doubt if either participant will make haste to present himself here.'

'I could not bear to wait idly for news and knew you would be equally anxious.'

'And so, being the enterprisin' creature you are, you took matters into your own hands! Did it by yourself, no doubt, eh? Didn't take a groom with you, I'll wager!'

Lexie made a regretful face. 'No, ma'am.'

'You must take breakfast with us. They are sendin' up trays. Then I'll instruct one of my grooms to ride back with you, after you've paid your respects to Downshire. Might as well make some show of behavin' with proper decorum.'

'Yes, ma'am,' said Lexie meekly, her eyes dancing as they met those of the Duchess.

'Did James know you were present?' demanded that lady.

Lexie shook her head. 'I took care not to be seen. Since they were engaged in an affair of honour, I did not wish either gentleman to think me an interfering female.'

'Hmm. So he will not realise that we know what transpired. Excellent. Fanny, you will not admit to knowing the result of this farce, d'you hear me?'

'Very well, Grandmama.'

The Duchess greeted the appearance of the breakfast trays with a smug expression on her lined face. All three set about demolishing their contents with good appetite. An hour ago Lexie would not have thought herself capable of eating a bite. As for Fanny. 'I'm eating for two,' she giggled.

That giggle was a sign of her relief. Lexie felt like joining her in senseless merriment. James was safe. But she wondered what kind of reception he could expect when he presented himself later, as he must, to tackle the problem of Fanny's future.

Storm had not yet given Felix permission to marry his ward. He had not killed him or even maimed him for daring to aspire to winning Fanny's hand, or for robbing her of her virginity. Yet Felix had felt equally unable to try to further his cause by killing or maiming the man who stood in the way of his ambition.

'I will think about it,' was all Storm would promise as they parted after shaking hands. 'And you will not communicate with my sister until after I have seen her and you have my permission. Is that understood?

Felix had looked about to argue, but seeing the steely glint in his friend's eyes, had compressed his lips and desisted. 'She will wish to hear from me,' was all he had said.

Storm had heard the sound of hoofbeats retreating at a gallop and looked up to glimpse a shadowy figure on a chestnut horse, its coat shining copper in the first of the sun's rays, and his heart had lurched.

It could not have been Lexie. She could not have known where the meeting was to be held. And even she would surely not venture out alone to attend a duel. Yet the impression persisted as he made his way back to St James's. Had she, somehow, discovered the venue and come to watch?

Was her conscience troubling her, that tender conscience which had caused him such frustration over the last months? Despite her denials, she must have encouraged the pair, have contributed to the situation which had led to the meeting. No doubt she wanted to witness the result of her intrigues. Would she have been troubled had it resulted in death or injury? To either man?

His uneasy ruminations did not prevent his eating a hearty breakfast and, thereafter, he took over an hour to dress in full fig in preparation for an interview with Fanny and the Duchess. He had no doubt at all that his grandmother was by now privy to all that had transpired and of his challenge to Felix. And if that had been Lexie galloping off, then she probably already knew he was safe and sound, too.

So let her wait while he donned the togs of the consummate man about Town. Weston's tailoring was superb, he admitted, inspecting the fit of his black superfine coat with satisfaction, the hang of his fashionable trousers with approval. Pantaloons were going out and he did not regret the change. He knew he looked the epitome of restrained elegance as he later made his way, at a leisurely stroll, to Grosvenor Square.

He needed no announcement in what would one day be his own domain. He deposited his hat and stick, nodded dismissively to the butler, who had informed him that Her Grace and Lady Fanny were in the morning-room while His Grace was resting in bed, and made his way upstairs.

At sight of him Fanny jumped to her feet and flew across the room.

'James!' she cried, flinging herself into his arms. 'You are safe! Oh, I am so glad!'

Fanny was not a good actress. Her surprise and pleasure at seeing him safe were obviously feigned. She had not asked about Felix's fate. Storm grinned with false amiability.

'I collect that Lady Amber has already conveyed the news of Lord Dexter's survival,' he remarked drily, and noted the look of frustrated annoyance which crossed his grandparent's face.

His mood lightened. The Duchess had been about to pretend she knew nothing of the outcome of the affair. No doubt she would have made dragging the details from him an embarrassing business. He was almost grateful to Lexie for forestalling him.

'And now, if you please, I would wish to speak with my ward in private. Come, Fanny. Let us retire to the library.'

The Duchess tapped her stick on the floor, a single, loud, authoritative thump. 'You will conduct the interview here, James. I will not have Fanny intimidated or upset by your prejudices!'

'You agree to the match, I collect, ma'am. I have

to inform you that, although I have no dislike for Lord Dexter and find him an agreeable companion, I do not consider him a suitable husband for my sister. He is, to put it bluntly, a confirmed womaniser and reckless gambler. Fanny would soon discover her mistake when she had to suffer the humiliation of countless infidelities and discovered that all her dower had been frittered away.'

'He would not—' began Fanny, only to be interrupted by the Duchess.

'Fustian, James! I am surprised at you! Ain't you noticed a change in Dexter's behaviour this Season? Even my old eyes could see how attached he and Fanny have become!'

'Your eyes are sharp enough when you wish, Grandmama.'

'And they ain't quite so concentrated on my own affairs and misdeeds as yours, my boy!'

'So,' said Storm, dropping languidly into a chair, since it seemed he must conduct his interview with Fanny in the presence of his grandparent, 'do I collect that you approve of Fanny's misconduct?'

The Duchess snorted. 'Foolish child! Of course I do not! But it was your attitude which drove her to it, James. Told her, should have asked me. But there you are, young people these days will go their own way. You can't fight this, James. There's the baby to consider. This great-grandchild—' she shot a withering glance at her grandson '—won't have it born a bastard. So get Dexter along here immediately. Settle the matter. Make the child happy.'

'I want nothing more than Fanny's happiness,

believe me. I just cannot conceive that marriage to Dexter will bring it.'

'Just as no mama can imagine their daughter finding happiness with you. Yet you have it in you to make an excellent husband. If you wed the right woman.'

Storm made an impatient gesture. 'Leave me out of this! It is Fanny's future happiness we are discussing! As her guardian, I cannot approve the match.'

'Oh, James!' wailed Fanny. 'Must you be so difficult? Felix and I love each other! We must marry!'

'You have made it imperative and left me small room for manoeuvre, that I concede. I cannot give the match my absolute blessing: however, neither can I prevent it.'

'Oh, I knew you could not be so hard-hearted! Thank you, oh! thank you, James!'

'Had you chosen to marry Mr Cresswell—'

'But we neither of us wanted the match! Why, he helped Felix and me! We would all go off together and he would leave us alone somewhere and then escort us back again!'

'Oswald Cresswell did that?

The incredulous note in Storm's voice made Fanny giggle. 'Oswald is so sweet! And not nearly as much under his mama's thumb as you might imagine!'

'But it was Lady Amber who encouraged you to lie together to enable you to blackmail me!'

'No, she didn't know a thing about that. Lexie is far too scrupulous to do anything to encourage impropriety!' The blank stare Storm gave her could not stop Fanny now she had begun her confession. 'It was entirely my idea, James, and I had to threaten

Felix that I would abide by your wishes and wed Oswald if he wouldn't compromise me!'

Storm's eyes sharpened. 'You gave me to understand Cresswell had no wish to marry you!'

'Neither had he! Felix didn't really believe I was serious, but it made him realise how determined I was. Oswald cherishes a *tendre* for Lexie, you know, although he knows it is hopeless. But I believe he is growing fond of Miss Daventry. Once Lexie is wed—'

Storm crossed his long legs and fiddled with the set of his trousers. 'Lady Amber is considerin' marryin' again, is she?'

'Lord Cranley, if she has any sense,' interrupted the Duchess. 'I am confident he is on the point of offerin' for her.' Ignoring Storm's sudden frown, quite at odds with the studied nonchalance of his manner, she waved an imperious hand. 'There is a pen and paper on the table. Send a note to Lord Dexter this moment! Put the poor creature out of his misery. Had I been he, I'd have winged you, James, for bein' such a numbskull.'

Storm was left wondering in which direction the Duchess thought he had been foolish. Or whether she considered his every action had been that of a dolt. He was beginning to doubt his acumen himself.

'Fanny,' said the Duchess when the note had been dispatched, 'go and make yourself tidy for when Felix arrives. You will not wish to greet your betrothed looking all of a scramble. And I wish to exchange a few private words with your brother.'

CHAPTER THIRTEEN

STORM'S, heart sank at his grandmother's words. He could guess what was coming and had no wish to discuss his own affairs until he had sorted out his feelings.

Lexie had not been culpable. He had accused her wrongly. She might refuse to forgive him, and he could not blame her if she did.

But more to the point, he had a large bone to pick with his dearly beloved brother. Without doubt, Hugo had been up to his tricks again, sowing distrust and discord in his elder brother's path. Would the fool never learn that jealousy such as his could sour his entire life? He had been given the chance to make something of himself and on the surface had profited from the experience.

But the heart beneath that red jacket with the blue facings and gold lace had not changed. Hugo's resentment at being born the younger son still lived and he would seek to damage his brother in any way he could.

A lesson Storm would not soon forget. He should have realised that Hugo was not to be trusted. Hugo had sold him a pack of lies about Lexie.

'Forgive me, Grandmama, but I really must leave,' he said, rising as Fanny left the room. 'I have to see Hugo. Make sure everythin' is settled, no loose ends left after the affair this mornin'.'

'Of course everything is settled, James! You shook hands with Felix, neither of you was hurt and if the doctor has not been paid he will send in his account! Oblige me by sittin' down.'

With a resigned shrug, Storm did as bidden. When his grandparent was in this mood, there could be no gainsaying her without being discourteous.

'Hugo,' pronounced his discerning relative, 'doubtless engineered the duel. Thought the boy was gettin' over his resentment and envy of you, but it seems he still bears a grudge. Told you about Fanny and Dexter in such a way as to put you out of temper, I'd wager.'

Storm had to admit that the Duchess was right.

'I believe he told you lies about Lady Alexia, as well. Poor child, your lack of trust upset her dreadfully.'

Storm was not going to admit, even to the old lady giving him a well-deserved set-down, that he had also accused Lexie of an intention to use a similar excuse to blackmail him into marriage. He remained silent.

'How could you believe Hugo's version without question?' went on his inexorable critic. 'You've known the boy as long as the rest of us! Fond as I am of him—for he is, after all, my grandson—I have never blinded myself to his faults. If he can hurt you, James, he will. Never forget it.'

'I have excellent reason to remember, ma'am.'

'You have behaved like a pot-head, James. There was no need for all this pother, let alone the farce this mornin'.' She glared at him, pointing at his cheek. 'I thought you'd had enough of duels to last you a lifetime!'

Storm lifted his brows and gave a slight, deprecating smile. 'I have fought others. Surely you knew?'

The Duchess glared down her nose and sniffed. 'I heard. You were not hurt. Gentlemen indulgin' in sword fights or shootin' each other's heads off over a stupid point of honour don't concern me.'

Storm's brows quirked and his eyes laughed in wicked contradiction.

'Even when you are involved,' continued the Duchess repressively, 'know you can take care of yourself and it's usually all over by the time I hear. Besides, you're not likely to kill or be killed, the penalty is too harsh. Even if you escaped with your life you'd be condemned to live abroad, have to forfeit your estates and inheritance. Too much sense for that, thank God. And so have your likely opponents. But when Fanny is involved, then I do consider it my business. Hurt Dexter and she'd be devastated. And Society would be flooded with gossip and innuendo. She would have been ruined. She may well be now, if the affair becomes broadcast.'

Slowly, Storm sat up straight. He looked his grandmother in the eye, his expression horrified. 'Can you believe, Grandmama, that that consequence never entered my head?'

'Easily! Nothin' sensible has entered your head for months!' declared the Duchess. She shook her head in disgust, setting the ribbons and lace of her cap fluttering.

'Would never have believed a son of mine could have reared such a witless brood. Hugo doin' his best to ruin himself and take you with him, Fanny goin' off at half cock because she thinks she won't get her own way, and you, my boy, have offered over the past months as prime an example of dimwitted behaviour as I ever hope to witness!'

Storm lifted his eye-glass and eyed his grandparent through it in his most arrogant manner. 'In what way exactly, may I ask?'

'No need to glare at me through that thing! Don't signify with me! Why haven't you offered for Alexia Hamilton?'

Storm's fingers tightened about the slender handle of the glass. His grandmother heard the snap of the delicate silver stem. She gave a wolfish grin.

'That came near the bone, eh? There's been somethin' goin' on between you for months. She refused to warm your bed for you, and so she should, a respectable widow like the Countess of Amber. So what did you do? Give up? Or continue to pester her? And what was that curricle race at Merryfield really about? Who suggested it?'

'Lady Amber herself.' Storm had recovered himself. He spoke with a careless shrug of his impeccably tailored shoulders. 'She wished to prove her skill at drivin' to be superior to mine. Unfortunately, she couldn't and lost the wager.'

'And looked uncommonly disconcerted at doin' so. Until the followin' day. I'd swear she'd lost a lot of sleep during the night, but to me she looked like a woman who had been comprehensively ravished.'

'She did?' murmured Storm lazily, still attempting to avoid admitting the true terms of the bet, but immodestly conceding the truth of the Duchess's words. They had, however, brought back to vivid memory the satisfaction, the delight of shared passion during those hours spent in Lexie's bed. He crossed his legs. The old lady's eyes were still sharp.

'I gather,' said that lady with another wolfish grin, 'that you took your reward in her bed. No one else is likely to have been responsible. So you won all round, did you not?'

'I do not usually lose, Grandmama.'

'Ha! So you admit it! I knew as much. And when my agent could not reach you at Stormaston and Chalker told my girl that her mistress had given her a couple of weeks off because she wouldn't be needin' her services, I concluded you'd gone off somewhere together. I trust you had an agreeable time.'

'Capital, I thank you.'

'Where'd you go?'

The disclosure was inevitable. Storm grinned, daring his grandmother to disapprove. 'To stay with Nanny Dean in Frinton.'

'Of course. She always indulged you dreadfully, James. So why are the two of you at odds now?'

Reluctantly, Storm admitted, 'Because Lexie would not continue our *affaire* once we returned.' Unconsciously, his voice took on a bitter tone. 'She had paid her debt and, for her, that was the end of it.'

'She wasn't happy indulgin' in love outside marriage, I collect. You should have wed her, James.'

'You have informed me of your opinion before, ma'am. But I have no wish to wed.'

Which was still essentially true. He did not relish the idea of surrendering his freedom; yet, living with Lexie, even for so short a time, had made his present existence seem peculiarly unsatisfactory. Even

Stormaston and his laboratory had not been able to lift him from the dark mood her rejection had plunged him into.

'So you have been goin' around like a bear with a sore head because she has withdrawn her favours, and she's been pinin' because she can't square her conscience. And you refuse to wed her.'

'She did not look as though she was pining to me.' Still bitter.

The Duchess's snort could have been heard outside the door. And at that moment a footman entered to announce that Lord Dexter had called and to ask whether Her Grace would receive him.

In fact, since he had been summoned, Felix had followed hard on the fellow's heels. The Duchess saw him hovering beyond the door and called out to him to come in.

Felix did so and then, seeing Storm, who had risen to his feet, halted just inside the room. The men eyed one another, still not back on the old, easy terms.

'Come in, come here, Dexter! James has somethin' to say to you.'

The imperious tones of the Duchess cut through the uneasy atmosphere. Storm gave a slight shrug and made his bow. Felix made his devoirs to them both and looked questioningly at Storm.

Storm eyed his friend of so many years and saw what Fanny and the Duchess had seen, a personable young man with an engaging manner, upon whose handsome features his so-called vices had left no mark. They'd both rattled about Town, raised hell on occasion, drunk too much, gambled too deeply, known too many women. But Felix was an honourable man, well-liked, without a vicious bone in his body. And one day would inherit an earldom. If Fanny loved him, well, Storm supposed that could be the making of him.

'Have you mentioned your aspiration to my sister's hand to St Clare?' Storm demanded.

Felix looked surprised at the question. 'Of course.'

'Then why in damnation—' he cut off, bowed to his grandmother '—my apologies! Why did not one of you approach me? Am I so d— so unapproachable as you make me appear?'

Felix faced up to him with a wry smile. 'On some matters, yes. You made my unacceptability as a suitor for Fanny's hand abundantly clear on several occasions.'

'I am still not entirely happy with the match. However, since Fanny's happiness apparently depends upon it and the Duchess approves, I must allow it.'

Felix bowed gravely. 'I can assure you of my most earnest intention to make her happy.'

Suddenly, Storm relaxed, and laughed, if a trifle ruefully. 'My friend, the trouble is I know you too well. We have caroused together too often for me to feel entirely convinced of your ability to do so for long. Yet if you can reform, then I must believe that there is hope for me yet! Go along to the library. Fanny will join you there. My solicitors will meet with yours as soon as can be arranged.'

Felix laughed, too, and once more held out his hand. 'I thank you from the bottom of my heart, brother! The wedding must be soon, as you will appreciate.'

'But don't arrange some hole-and-corner affair.' The Duchess spoke up again, holding out her hand for Felix to take. 'Welcome to the family, Felix,' she murmured as he kissed it, then went on. 'That would not be sensible. Fanny's reputation must be guarded at all costs. If you go abroad immediately afterwards, the ceremony may be delayed for as much as a month, I think. That will give us and the lawyers time to make all the necessary arrangements.'

'We do not wish for a grand affair, Your Grace,' said Felix. 'A simple ceremony with close family and friends present would suit us both excellently.'

'You've discussed the matter and have it all arranged, I collect,' interjected Storm. He sighed. 'I really was fighting a losing battle, was I not?' he remarked in a histrionically resigned voice.

'I fear we were ready to elope had you not come round,' Felix told him with an apologetic smile. 'But for everyone's sake, and especially Fanny's, I was reluctant. I had no wish to begin our life together with such a cloud hanging over us.'

'Very sensible of you, my boy,' said the Duchess. 'And now, run along. I have not finished what I have to say to my grandson.'

As he passed, Felix clapped Storm on the back. 'No hard feelings, I trust?' he asked.

'None, brother,' responded Storm, and meant it.

'And now,' said the Duchess when once again they were alone together, 'what of Alexia? You love the child, do you not?'

Storm, who had been about to sink down into his chair, straightened up again.

'I have no wish to discuss Lady Amber.'

'But I have. It is time you wed, I've told you so before.'

'Many times,' interjected Storm in a bored tone.

The Duchess ignored him. 'You'll never find a more fittin' bride. You suit each other admirably. I cannot conceive what is stoppin' you from askin' her.'

'A constitutional objection to the state of matrimony, Grandmama.'

'Then you are more idiotish than I thought you, James. Look about you, boy! Do you see every marriage in terms of those famous examples of failure to which the Regent subscribes? What of my marriage? What of your parents'? Reasonably felicitous marriages outnumber bad ones, even amongst those that are arranged. And you need an heir.'

'As you have informed me *ad nauseum*. But either I shall marry where mutual love exists, or I shall make a marriage of convenience when it is no longer avoidable.'

'Then what in Hades are you waitin' for, boy? You love her and she loves you. Get on with it!'

'Really, Grandmama, your language sometimes requires moderating!'

'Fiddlesticks! You are prevaricatin'. Go and beg the girl to marry you and thank Providence for sendin' her your way!'

Slowly, Storm sat down, elegant as ever, but with an abstracted air. 'Lexie does not love me.'

'Nonsense! Of course she does! Anyone but a fool could see she's head over heels in love with you by the way she looks at you. It is just as obvious that she is in love with you as it is that you are besotted with her. Why else has she been in the dismals ever since she returned to Town?'

Storm glared at his relative. He did not like being told he was besotted. He was not. 'Simply because she failed to manoeuvre me into Parson's mousetrap?' he enquired cynically.

'Not Lady Alexia.' The Duchess defended her protégée firmly. 'She would put you behind her and concentrate on findin' someone else to marry.'

'Which she appears to have done,' pointed out Storm dryly. 'Lord Cranley, I understand, is on the point of offerin' for her.'

'But, mark my words, she'll never accept him. Might think she could, but when it comes to the point she'll not bring herself to do it.'

'Our desire may be mutual—you see, I am being honest—but I doubt she loves me. She wishes to wed me for more worldly reasons. Cranley is heir to a marquessate and is very rich. He will do her very well.'

'Ask her,' suggested his grandmother.

Storm left Downshire House with his emotions in turmoil. Could he believe his grandparent's word? Did Lexie love him? She had behaved as though she did, but then, so had plenty of other women. Before all this furore he had intended to seek her hand. But. . .

Lexie had, only half an hour earlier, proved the Duchess right. Lord Cranley had presented himself requesting a private interview with Lady Amber. Although feeling far from ready to cope with what she guessed he had come to say, Lexie could not refuse to see him. She had left it too late to remedy the false impression she must have given.

He had, he said, having greeted her with elaborate courtesy, naturally heard that the Countess had appeared attached to Another during the summer, but since she had not recently been seen in His Lordship's company and had accepted his own attentions, Lord Cranley ventured to hope that she might welcome his suit. He had come to request her agreement to his approaching her father, the Earl of Webley, to seek permission to address her with a view to uniting their lives to their mutual advantage.

Lexie, her feelings of guilt almost overcome by the inclination to fall into a strong fit of hysterics at the form of his declaration, had managed to command herself sufficiently to send the slightly-corpulent gentleman away with his pride and temper intact. She had apologised profusely for any wrong impression she had given but, highly as she regarded him, she did not love him, and therefore could not marry him.

More protestations had followed but Lexie had, in the end, managed to extricate herself from a difficult situation and, on his departure, breathed a sigh of relief. At least that problem was now solved.

She hoped Fanny's dilemma had been resolved to mutual satisfaction all round: that Storm had given in graciously and was no longer at odds with Fanny and Felix. She longed for news, but knew she would have to wait until she saw Fanny again to learn the outcome.

She did not have long to fret. A radiant Fanny,

escorted by an equally happy Felix, called the following morning.

'And we are to be wed on the first day of December,' Fanny told her. 'You will come, will you not, Lexie? Be my Matron of Honour?'

This compliment Lexie graciously declined. Storm, she gathered, was to support Felix—when he gave in, he did so handsomely, as the Duchess had said—and she could not bear the thought of being so intimately involved with him at the wedding. It was to be a modest, quiet affair, and this she made her excuse.

Fanny was disappointed, but not downcast. Melissa Daventry would almost certainly agree to support her. And in the excitement of discussing the forthcoming wedding, no mention was made of Lord Cranley's proposal and Lexie's refusal of his suit.

Over the next few days Lexie tried to behave as normally as possible. She could not hide herself away from the criticism she knew would greet the news that she had refused Cranley. She had behaved badly, she could not deny it. But it seemed a small offence to live down compared to some of the others she had committed.

News of the engagement spread and Fanny and Felix received so many invitations they could not possibly accept even half of them. However, they did appear together at a musical soiré with Lexie, improbably, acting as Fanny's chaperon. The Duchess did not wish to leave her husband's side, for although his condition had improved she was still concerned for his health.

'Angina don't often kill accordin' to the doctor,'

she had said, 'but it is a distressin' complaint. If Downshire is goin' to have an attack, I want to be there.'

It was at this social occasion that Fanny and Felix heard of Lexie's shocking treatment of poor Lord Cranley, who had gone off to his estates to digest his disappointment. And when Felix saw Storm a couple of days after that, Storm, who had not even visited his club in the meanwhile—he had been paying a flying visit to Wiltshire, certain business matters at Stormaston having demanded his immediate attention—was also made aware of the facts.

The information crystallised in his mind the decision he had already subconsciously taken.

'You're all goin' to the ball tomorrow evenin', you say? I received my invitation and declined to attend, but I'm certain Lady Castlereagh will not object if I change my mind. I shall look to see you there.'

Lexie did not know of Storm's intention to attend the ball, one of the few to be held in the last month before people returned to their estates and Christmas house parties. She had been invited to spend the festive season with the Duke and Duchess of Downshire but had so far avoided giving a definite answer.

Fanny would not be there but Storm and Hugo probably would. If she heard that Storm intended spending Christmas elsewhere, then she might consider travelling to Kent with them. Provided the Duke was fit enough to travel. Otherwise the Duchess planned to remain in London.

Lexie had already danced several times when a stir at the door made her glance across. Storm's dark head shone in the light thrown by thousands of candles in chandelier and sconce. His unexpected arrival had created an excitement akin to that normally occasioned by the presence of the Regent. Lexie's heart thumped its way to her throat. She had not expected to see him and the shock made her stumble.

'Ouch!' exclaimed Oswald in an ungentlemanly manner. 'That was my toe, Lady Alexia!'

No poetic superlatives from the young man tonight, Lexie noted, amused despite her distraction. He had matured beyond measure since his visit to Merryfield and his calf-love was fast turning into genuine, friendly affection. Miss Daventry appeared to be waging a successful campaign to win his heart, which pleased Lexie. They made a suitable pair.

'Oh,' said Oswald when next they came together, oblivious of the cause of Lexie's earlier clumsiness. 'There's Stormaston! Ain't seen him in weeks! Alone, too. Ain't gone back to his crowd of cronies now he ain't escortin' you.'

'Felix St Clare is here,' Lexie observed.

'But he don't mix with 'em any more either, since he fell in love with Lady Fanny.'

The set ended and Oswald escorted Lexie back to join Fanny and Felix. Storm had already sought out his sister.

'Grandmama has remained at home with Grandpapa,' Fanny was explaining as Lexie came up. 'Lexie! See who is here!'

'Greetings, Storm,' said Lexie evenly, as she curtsied in response to his bow. 'We had become resigned to your continued absence from Society. To what do we owe the honour of your company this evening?'

'Why, Lady Alexia, what else but the pleasure of dancing with you again?'

Lexie's gay laugh held only the faintest of false rings. 'La, sir! What flattery! Was it not that you had become bored with your retired life?'

Storm ignored this. 'They are striking up for a waltz. Shall we take to the floor?'

He crooked his arm and offered it. Lexie, more flustered than she would have liked to admit, glanced down at her card. 'But this dance is taken—'

'I will deal with the disappointed gentleman. Who is it?'

'The Duke of Clarence.'

'Ah!'

He turned as the Sailor Duke barged his way towards Lexie, and made him an elegant, deferential leg. 'Your Grace, I am convinced you will not object to my claimin' the Countess for this dance. It has been so long since we have had occasion to waltz together.'

The Duke, good-humoured as ever, gave a guffaw of laughter.

'Back in circulation again, eh, Stormaston? How's the Duke?'

'I am happy to report that my grandfather's condition is greatly improved. We anticipate his being able to return to Kent for Christmas.'

'Be able to attend little Fanny's wedding, eh? Sly dog, Dexter! Congratulations. Heard you'd become engaged.'

'Thank you, Your Grace.'

Felix and Fanny made their devoirs and Storm took the opportunity to steer Lexie out onto the floor, where the waltz had just begun.

'Such impudence! How can you treat the Duke so disrespectfully!'

His arm came about her waist. 'My dear Lexie, I would brave worse fates than the displeasure of a Royal Duke in order to dance again with you.'

Lexie moved into his arms like one in a dream. A dream come true. But before she could believe that she must discover exactly what were his lordship's intentions toward her.

But dancing a waltz with him was not the best moment to inquire. Her mind was spinning in time with her feet. She danced in blissful, if dubious, silence.

At the end, Storm escorted her back to her friends. He had not spoken, either. He bowed.

'I shall give myself the pleasure of calling upon you tomorrow morning, Lexie. I trust you will be able to receive me?'

Lexie had intended to go calling herself. But she nodded.

'I shall be at home all the morning,' she told him.

'Then you may expect me at midday.'

He left her then. And shortly afterwards he departed the ball. It was evident that he had come only to speak with her. Lexie, her heart aflutter, slept very little that night.

CHAPTER FOURTEEN

LEXIE could stomach no breakfast next day, but drank several cups of chocolate. Waiting alone in the morning-room in a demure but becoming gown of damask rose and with Caro banished to the small parlour, her eyes kept straying to the clock on the mantel. Its ornate hands seemed to move at a snail's pace, the pendulum's tick-tock to become slower and slower. However, the quarters did chime, the hours struck and eventually the hands met in upright triumph over the twelve.

And Dymock himself announced the Marquess of Stormaston as the last stroke faded into the silence.

Lexie did not rise—her legs did not feel strong enough—or speak. She waited until Storm stood in front of her and then offered her hand.

He bowed over it before, gently, kissing the knuckles. Instead of releasing her he turned the hand palm upward and touched it again with his lips.

Lexie's breathing quickened in time with her pulse. He was playing the suitor. But what was the nature of his suit?

'Do sit down,' she managed to say, remembering her duties as a hostess. 'May I offer you a drink?'

Storm, equally tense, but determined not to show it, sank lazily into the indicated chair and said, 'A glass of Madeira would not be unwelcome.'

'Dymock?' The butler had not yet left the room. 'A decanter and two glasses, if you please.'

He brought the tray holding the requisite items from a cupboard and placed it on the table near Storm before pouring the wine and handing each a glass.

'Thank you.' Lexie accepted hers. 'Shut the door as you leave.'

Dymock bowed. 'Yes, my lady.'

They drank in silence. Storm's glass was soon empty. 'Excellent vintage,' he remarked.

'Help yourself to another,' invited Lexie.

'And you?'

'I have enough, I thank you.

She needed to have her morale boosted, but not to have her mind fuddled. It was quite confused enough as it was.

He poured his second glass and sat holding the dark tawny liquid to the light. He was, realised Lexie, exhibiting an unusual degree of reluctance to come to the point. His lordly self-assurance normally carried him through any difficulty without any sign of uncertainty. He had not hesitated a moment before attempting to seduce her.

'Why did you wish to see me?' she asked at last. Incredibly, he seemed to require help in coming to the point.

'I've missed you,' he said simply.

'Indeed?' Lexie congratulated herself on the coolness of her tone.

Storm swallowed a mouthful of wine before he went on, frowning. The love of his life appeared remarkably cool, which made his task the more difficult. 'You should not have walked out, Lexie. I intended to apologise for my conceit in taking it for granted that you would wish to continue our liaison. But, since I believed you enjoyed our love-making, I did not think to question it.'

'I did enjoy it.'

'But not enough to want it to continue.'

'More than enough, Storm. But not under those circumstances.'

'Quite.' The silence echoed for a long moment. Then Storm said, harshly for him, 'For reasons known only to yourself, you wished to trap me into marriage.'

Lexie shook her head. 'Not trap. Persuade. There were many excellent reasons for us to form an alliance.'

He swirled the remaining Madeira round in his glass and inhaled the bouquet. 'Whatever your reason may have been for suggesting it, I have been considerin' that race. It was a close run thing. Had your drive been twenty yards shorter you would have emerged the victor.'

'But it was not and you beat me by a head.'

'Almost a dead heat,' mused Storm. 'And I took my winnings, as you so pointedly remarked before you left Frinton. But—I think you are entitled to claim yours, too.'

'Mine?' Lexie had calmed down now. This was a game of cat and mouse. He was not going to admit to wanting to wed her. She hid a smile. 'But I won nothing.'

'True. But a dead heat would have proved a fair

result. We would both have won. What would we have done had that occurred?'

Lexie looked at him, wide-eyed. 'You tell me.'

He grinned, suddenly sure of himself again. 'I would have warmed your bed immediately, but at the same time we would have announced our engagement.'

'So,' said Lexie calmly. 'What are you suggesting?'

'Why, that we treat the result as a draw. We both win. In other words, Lexie, I will marry you, despite the fact that you have no true love for me and do not relish bearing me an heir. But in the event of our marriage that would become your duty.'

'Duty?' Lexie coloured hotly. Not love him! But he had not admitted to loving her. She would let that go. 'What makes you think that I would consider it a duty?'

'All those elaborate precautions you took during our time together to avoid conceiving my child. Did you think me so green that I did not realise?'

'I hoped you had not. I did not wish to offend you.' Lexie clenched her fists in her lap and drew a deep breath. 'Shall I tell you exactly why I took care not to become pregnant? I would have borne a bastard, labelled for life as such whatever his or her upbringing. A boy child would have had no claim on your inheritance. He would have been in a worse situation than Hugo, who at least has the right to use the family name and to expect help and support from his relations.'

Storm looked taken aback by this tirade. The arrogance returned as he met her challenge. 'I have always seen my children well cared for. Surprising as it may seem to you, my dear, I take an interest in their welfare.'

Lexie could accept without rancour the fact of his having already sired children. In that respect he was no different to a widower with an existing family. 'But you would not contemplate making one of them your heir, I collect.'

'Their mothers' quality would scarcely support such a notion.'

'I see. And would mine have made a scrap of difference? I think not. And what of me, Storm? Look at the furore over Fanny's conceiving a child out of wedlock! Imagine the sensation if the outrageous Countess of Amber were to appear with a bastard in leading-strings!'

'You would have had no need—'

Lexie cut him off. 'No need to keep it. I agree. But I am not made like that, my lord. I should have wanted to nurture the child, to bring it up myself. Which would have meant complete retirement from Society. And the chance of making a decent second marriage would have been gone for ever.'

Storm regarded her broodingly. 'Did it never occur to you that, had you conceived, I would have married you?'

'I could not depend upon it, my lord. You have never felt the necessity before. Besides, I did not want to pressure you once my venture with the wager failed. I accepted defeat.'

Storm was, suddenly, kneeling by her side, both her hands clasped in his. 'My dear girl, I had no idea you would feel like that. My masculine mind could not conceive. . . My former mistresses, the two who each bore me a child, accepted the situation without regret. It meant they would be kept in comfortable circumstances for life, that their child would never want. I had forgot that your outlook would be different.'

Lexie had begun to tremble. Reaction, his nearness, a myriad of emotions jostled for predominance. The one that won was love.

She released one of her hands from his grasp and ran her fingers through a stray lock that had fallen over his forehead, smoothing it back, and looked deeply into blue eyes which, for the first time that she could recall, were limpid, clear of all pretence or artifice.

'Do not imagine I did not long to bear your child, my dear James. It was simply more practical to ensure that I did not.'

'You mean it would not be a mere duty to carry my heir?'

She shook her head. At last she felt free to say it. 'I love you, James. I have done so for a long time. Only at the very first did I want you because of other things, and they were not money or title, but compatibility, pleasure in your company. By the time I suggested the wager, it was in order to win my heart's desire.'

Storm sat back on his heels, studying her captivating face. Rosy now to match her gown, her golden curls escaping from her little cap to frame it. And her eyes, greener than he had ever seen them before, were regarding him with such a look in them that his heart begun to thud.

'Grandmama said you loved me,' he said with a breathless laugh. 'I did not dare to believe her.'

'She is perceptive and wise. I find her quite delightful.'

'She also informed me that I was besotted with you,' he went on wryly. 'I would not admit it, even to myself, but she was right, as usual. Lexie, my dearest love, I declare myself your slave for life. Dare I hope that you will marry me?'

Lexie's eyes closed as a sweep of relief stopped her breath. Then her face broke into a radiant smile.

'Oh, yes, James!'

He lifted both her hands to his lips and then looked up, all the old, mocking laughter back in his eyes. Only this time it was self-mocking.

'I never anticipated that I would find myself declaring my love on my knees, despite a regrettable expectation among most green girls that no suitor could mean it unless he did!' With which he lifted her to her feet the better to take her in his arms and kiss her until she had no choice but to cling to him for support.

'When will you marry me?' he demanded at last, seating her on the sofa and dropping beside her to take her back into his arms. 'It must be soon. I am impatient to have you back in my bed.'

'You think we should wait?' murmured Lexie naughtily.

'Most certainly. I am determined upon observing the utmost propriety.' His hand found her breast and cupped it, his thumb teasing through the layers of cloth.

'Really?' murmured Lexie, revelling in the thrill of

his touch. 'I believe you are behaving in a most forward manner, my lord!'

He chuckled. 'Allow my hands a little licence, do not starve me entirely. But I shall not make the mistake of seducing you again before our wedding. You were not designed for such intrigues, my darling.'

They were still engaged in savouring their new-found happiness, mostly without the aid of words, when Dymock rapped on the door and coughed discreetly before entering.

Storm kept Lexie firmly in his arms.

'Yes, Dymock? What is it?'

Dymock coughed. 'May I be the first to congratulate you, my lord? And to wish you happy, my lady?'

Reluctantly, Lexie extricated herself from Storm's embrace.

'I suppose finding us like this could have but one explanation,' she admitted. 'Thank you, Dymock. See that there is plenty of ale in the servants' quarters this evening with which to drink our health.'

'With pleasure, my lady. I came to inform you that Lord Dexter and Lady Fanny Graham are below. Are you at home?'

'Send them up!'

As Dymock bowed and withdrew, Storm stood, too.

'They will be surprised to hear our news.'

'Perhaps. But pleased, too. You will put an announcement in the papers?'

'That an engagement has been entered into, yes. And the date of the ceremony, if we can agree it.'

'I am so thankful that you did not come merely to

ask permission to approach my father, like Lord Cranley! I am no longer dependent upon his approval for anything I do!'

At that moment Fanny came into the room, closely followed by Felix.

'James!' she cried in surprise. 'I did not expect to discover you here!'

'Did you not, my love?' wondered Felix. 'I cannot say I am surprised, after your appearance at the ball last evening, Storm. Are we to congratulate you?'

'Indeed you may! Lady Alexia has agreed to marry me.'

'Oh, James!' Fanny rushed over to kiss him and then Lexie. 'Grandmama will be so pleased! She positively dotes on Lexie!'

'So,' observed the Marquess, 'does the Duke. Lexie won his admiration during his stay at Merryfield. He has not stopped singing her praises since.'

Lexie walked over and put her hand through Storm's arm. 'Poor James! When you were trying so hard to put me out of your thoughts!'

'An impossible task, my love.'

'When are you to wed?' demanded Fanny. 'Is it decided?'

'Not yet. Give us a chance, dear sister! We only agreed on it half an hour ago!'

'Then we are the first to know! How enchanting! Felix, my love, I have an idea! How amusing to have a double wedding!'

'A charming idea, my love. Storm, what do you say? You and your sister wed on the same day! That should give the gabble-grinders something to speculate about!'

'But I am supposed to be supporting you, my friend.'

'I can easily find someone else to fill that role.'

Storm looked at Lexie. 'What do you say, my love? Could you be ready in time?'

'What do I need but a new gown? And if we harry the solicitors. . . But the notice may be too short to allow of my parents travelling.'

'Does that concern you?'

Lexie shook her head. 'They abandoned me to Amber, caring little whether I was happy or not. We correspond only occasionally and I do not pine to see them again. But we must inform Cousin Caro!' She pulled the bell cord and when Dymock appeared told him to inform Mrs Baldwin that she was wanted in the morning-room.

Caro was predictably effusive in her congratulations and excited at the prospect of a double wedding. But Lexie noticed a look of concern on the older woman's face when she thought no one was looking.

'You will remain with me, of course, Cousin,' she hastened to reassure her. 'I shall be in need of someone to take care of both this establishment and Merryfield when we take up residence at Stormaston Park. Would that responsibility suit you?'

Caro's face immediately cleared. 'I am honoured that you should trust me with it, dearest Alexia,' she fluttered.

And talk returned to the forthcoming nuptials.

* * *

In the event the double wedding became the highlight of the Little Season. Every effort was made to keep the ceremony simple, the attendance restricted, but this proved impossible, despite the shortage of time left to make the arrangements.

The days passed in a whirl of activity, of planning, not only for the wedding but for life afterwards.

'Come to the Continent with us!' suggested Fanny one day as she and Lexie were discussing the wedding. 'You surely do not wish to spend your honeymoon at Stormaston Park! And if you do not, I shall have no companion but my husband after we are wed!'

'My dear Fanny,' laughed Lexie, to whom this wholly unattractive proposition had been put. 'I am more than happy to go to Stormaston Park—remember, I have not yet seen my new home! And you will need no other companion but Felix! You will have your maid and his man with you. You will not wish to travel with a larger party.'

Fanny appeared uncertain. 'But it is usual for new brides to take a companion on honeymoon.'

'Green girls who scarcely know the man they have married! Who have no notion of what goes on in the bedroom! You have no need of the missish misgivings which bedevil those poor creatures. You know Felix in every way. You may trust him to see that you want for nothing while you are away.'

'But the baby,' murmured Fanny. 'Supposing something goes wrong?'

'Your maid is an experienced woman of the world. And if you are truly in trouble later on, you may always send for help. But I do not think either James or Felix would approve your plan. And I confess, Fanny, I would rather have James to myself during the first weeks of our marriage.'

'Well, of course, I would prefer to be alone with Felix. But. . .'

'But you are suffering from bridal nerves! Bear up, Fanny! You have no need to be nervous. You will return in a years' time with a bonny infant to bring your nursery to life.'

Fanny went away reassured, leaving Lexie with her own worries. When Storm next called, which he did daily, she confided them to him.

'James, I wonder whether I am doing right in marrying you,' she began as he released her from his embrace.

His expression of outrage almost overset her composure. His words did.

'Right? My dear girl, who was it who urged the match from the beginning of our re-acquaintance? It is a little late to begin to have doubts now! Unless, of course, you have discovered that you do not love me after all?'

Considering the ardour with which she had returned his kiss, he could not truthfully believe that! 'Don't be silly, James!' Her voice trembled, but whether with laughter or apprehension even she did not know. 'Of course I still love you! And it is because I love you so much that this thing has been worrying me recently.'

James, collecting his patience and wondering what worm was eating his beloved now, asked, 'What thing, my love?'

'I failed to provide Amber with an heir,' she

whispered miserably. 'Old Demelza in Cornwall said it was because my husband was too old. But supposing she was wrong? Supposing I prove barren?'

He gathered her into his arms again and pressed her hot face into his shoulder.

'That would be unfortunate. But not reason enough for me to regret marrying you. There is always Hugo and his progeny to fall back on. Or even,' he added, half-mischievously, 'one of my by-blows.'

'You truly would not hate me for not being fruitful?'

The anxious expression on her face brought a tender smile to James's, a soft light to his eyes. 'I should regret the circumstance, but I should still love you, my Lexie. Depend upon it, the old woman was right. You need have no fear.'

'You are such a comfort,' sighed Lexie, kissing the scar on his cheek. 'Do you know, Fanny wanted us to join them on the Continent to share our honeymoons?'

James's horrified expression confirmed Lexie's view of what his reaction would be. 'You did not agree?'

'I did not! Felix would probably have a fit, not to mention you! She is simply suffering from pre-nuptial nerves!'

'And so are you, my love. In a year's time you will both be contented matrons visiting your offspring in the nursery and neglecting your poor husbands!'

'Never!' Lexie gave a happy laugh, her doubts laid to rest, for the moment at least. 'Oh, James, I can hardly wait for the great day!'

'Nor I. But I am glad we are. Only a week more and I can take you with God's and the world's blessing. And you will have no dark cloud on your conscience to interfere with your pleasure. You know, I never felt you were truly mine.'

'I never felt entirely comfortable,' Lexie admitted.

'But there will be no limitations on our love once we reach Stormaston Park. I am eager for you to see the estate. I love it, and I hope you will, too.'

Lexie did, on sight, despite the lateness of the hour of their arrival. The windows of the house blazed with light to greet its new mistress. The staff lined up and were introduced. So many of them! Lexie wondered whether she would ever remember all their names! But, it appeared, James knew each one by name, knew their position in the household, whether they were married, how many children they had and what ailments they suffered, right down to the yawning boot boy.

She would explore the rest of the house next day. Meanwhile, she discovered that the master suite contained a huge tester bed in which generations of Grahams had been born.

Lexie submitted to Chalker's ministration while Marlow assisted Storm to disrobe. They both took a bath, necessary after the heat of the reception room and the long journey which followed.

'God's blessings on you both, my lady,' offered Chalker as she prepared to leave for her own bed.

'Thank you, Florence. I hope you will be happy here.'

Chalker smiled. 'I can see no reason why not, my

lady. Such a household! And you'll be visiting London at least once a year. Don't worry yourself over me.'

Caro had returned to Bruton Street, preening herself on being left in charge. Lexie knew her cousin would keep the place in perfect trim. Merryfield, too, for she had been left with a coach and horses to take her there whenever she felt it necessary.

All in all, things had worked out well. For Oswald Cresswell and Melissa Daventry, too. Melissa had won her campaign to captivate Oswald and had even managed to overcome the opposition of his mama. They were to be wed the following autumn.

But although such thoughts ran along the surface of Lexie's mind as she lay waiting in the bed, her ears were strained for the sound of her husband coming to her from the adjoining dressing room.

He did not take long over his ablutions. As he slipped in beside her, the unhappy intervening months dropped away and it seemed like only yesterday that they had been together. Yet although their voyage of discovery of each other followed a familiar pattern, their emotions were heightened not only by long abstinence, but also by declared love and the new awareness of being joined together in matrimony until death.

The cloud had disappeared from Lexie's mind. And Storm, discovering in himself the capacity to actually enjoy being leg-shackled to his new Marchioness, exceeded even his previous achievements in the matter of expert wooing, combining this with such tenderness that Lexie ended up in tears of supreme joy.

They spent Christmas with the Duke and Duchess in Kent, but returned thankfully to Stormaston Park as soon they decently could.

Lexie had never enquired as to what had transpired between the brothers after Storm had discovered the truth after the duel, but Hugo had returned to his regiment nursing a sore chin and a black eye. They saw nothing of him, although he did visit his grandparents from time to time.

'To extract money to pay his debts, no doubt,' Storm remarked cynically. 'He knows there is no point in applying to me.'

In May news reached them that Fanny had been delivered, without trouble, of a boy, in Italy. Napoleon, who had escaped from Elba, was back in Paris and an army, led by the Duke of Wellington, was gathering near Brussels to confront him. Viscount Dexter and his Viscountess would perforce remain in Italy until the autumn before attempting the journey home. They had named the boy Peter and the family could announce the birth in late August.

The last of Lexie's fears were laid to rest when she became pregnant some two months after the wedding. The child was born in November. The Honourable Peter St Clare, who had been brought home a week earlier, was, of course, obviously older and much bigger than his diminutive cousin.

With the defeat of Napoleon at Waterloo, where Hugo had unexpectedly distinguished himself, the Dexters had been able to journey home through France. No one outside the family had seen the baby yet. Fanny intended keeping him incommunicado on a remote St Clare estate.

'In a year or so's time no one will notice the difference,' she proclaimed cheerfully when she came to visit Lexie after her confinement.

Felix had poked his head round the door and the couple appeared radiantly happy, which, for Lexie, was all that mattered.

Alone with James, she sighed. 'Perhaps it is as well our baby is a girl. No one will expect her to be so big as Peter. But I am sorry I could not manage you an heir, my darling.'

'I am already deeply in love with Lady Elizabeth,' James told her, touching the baby's silky, golden hair where it had escaped from its cap. 'And I'll wager that our next will be a boy.

'What do you have in mind as a stake?' demanded Lexie.

Storm grinned. 'Nothing too dramatic or exhausting. Fifty guineas?'

'Done!'

He won the wager, naturally. Lexie parted with her money in a glow of delighted achievement.

And received it and more back again in the form of an exquisite heart-shaped brooch, presented with her husband's constant and abiding love.

DEVIL-MAY-DARE

by

Mary Nichols

Dear Reader

It was after I had written two or three 'ordinary' historical romances that I thought it might be fun to try my hand at a Regency. The period has always fascinated me and many of my novels have been set in the early nineteenth century, so the background research was not too difficult. But the Regency romance is different. It is such a light, 'bubbly' genre, a little outrageous, highly improbable, full of mannerisms and conventions which the hero and heroine often scandalously flout, it is a joy to write. I am almost sorry when the ramifications of the plot bring it to an end. I enjoy creating the characters for you, making them come to life and setting them on the road to true love. If, along the way, I make you smile, or even shed a tear on their behalf, then I will have achieved my aim. I hope you enjoy re-reading *Devil-May-Dare*.

Mary Nichols

Born in Singapore, **Mary Nichols** came to England when she was three, and has spent most of her life in different parts of East Anglia. She has been a radiographer, school secretary, information officer and industrial editor, as well as a writer. She has three grown up children, and four grandchildren.

Other titles by the same author:

In Love and War
The Heart of the Lion
Dear Rebel
The Danbury Scandals
The Price of Honour
A Dangerous Undertaking
To Win the Day
Last Gamble
The Ruby Pendant
Dear Deceiver

CHAPTER ONE

LORD WENTHORPE paused on the top stair with his hand on the polished wood balustrade, wondering what had put the notion into his head to go up to the old schoolroom floor; he had not been there in an age, not since Lydia and Tom were knee-high to a grasshopper. He had only ventured into this wing of his considerable mansion then because Nanette had upbraided him for not taking an interest in his off-spring's education. Dearest Nanette—who would have thought that the darling of the Parisian stage would make such a splendid mama? He stopped to remember and then wished he had not. The memories were painful, laughter and tears, happiness and unending sorrow. But life was like that. He sighed and turned to retrace his steps; let the memories stay locked away.

The sound of merriment came from a door along the corridor which was not quite closed. Tom, down from Cambridge with his friend, Frank Burford; they were no doubt playing some prank on Lydia. Would they never grow up? He had glimpsed Lydia from his bedchamber that morning, long before most ladies would have dreamed of rising, galloping across the park with poor Scrivens so far behind her as to be useless to help if she took a tumble. Not that she would, he was confident of her horsemanship, but he could have sworn she was riding astride. He could ask the groom of course, but Scrivens was loyal to his mistress and he would not put him in the position of having to tattle on her. When would she learn to behave like the lady she purported to be? Eighteen—no, he corrected himself, nineteen, and still behaving like a schoolroom miss, and that in spite of acting as his housekeeper for the last six years. There were plenty of young ladies of her age already married. He ought to be thinking of getting her a husband. She was not wanting in sense and had no difficulty making decisions and giving instructions to the indoor staff; she would make some young blade a fine wife, so long as she managed to quell her tendency to mischief.

It was his fault, of course; he had let her grow wild with only her brother for company, while he mourned the passing of their mother. If his darling Nanette had still been alive, Lydia would not now be something close to a hoyden. He had prevaricated too long. Resolutely he moved towards the schoolroom and pushed the door open.

Lydia, in pink satin breeches, yellow stockings, brightly striped waistcoat topped by an old-fashioned coat with huge patch pockets and enough silver lace to bedeck a field marshal, not to mention a hugely knotted neckcloth, was mincing up and down in front of the two young men, who sat on the schoolroom chairs watching her. She stopped in front of them to make an elegant leg which made the white powdered wig she wore slip sideways over one ear to reveal her own dark hair. She righted it and then put up the quizzing glass which dangled from a ribbon round her neck and peered short-sightedly through it.

'Demme,' she said, affecting the voice of a pink of the *ton*. 'Demme, if I don't teach you young pups some *manners*.'

The young men hooted with laughter.

'Miss Wenthorpe, if you don't make a most fetching dandy, I'll consume my best beaver!' cried Frank.

Lydia took another turn up and down, stopping to twirl the quizzing glass, then added, 'You think I am *man* enough for you, sir?'

'I've got it!' cried Tom triumphantly. 'Manners maketh man.'

Lydia dropped her pose and laughed. 'You'd never have guessed if I hadn't given you a hint.' She looked up and saw her father in the doorway. His frown told her she was in for a scolding, but she was by no means subdued; her papa's scoldings were only ever of the mildest and nothing to be afraid of. 'Papa, we were playing charades.'

'So I perceive.' She did, indeed, make a very passable male. She was tall for a woman, long-limbed and slim-waisted. She had high cheekbones and strong, dark brows and her violet eyes, so like her mother's, gazed back at him without the least sign of being cowed. 'Go and change out of that frippery into something more becoming a daughter of mine, and come to me in the bookroom,' he said gruffly, disappointed not so much in her as in himself. He turned to the young men who were scrambling to their feet. 'Could you not think of something more manly to do? A gallop perhaps.'

'Sir, it has been raining, all day,' protested Tom.

'The rain has ceased. A brisk walk to curb your high spirits before dinner, I think.'

The young men exchanged meaningful looks and left the room with alacrity, leaving Lydia to face her father. 'In ten minutes, miss, in the bookroom,' he said and turned on his heel.

Lydia, indignant that he should be so up in the boughs over something so innocent, marched off to her room to remove the offending garments. Charades was a game they had played ever since they had left the cradle. Had not Mama encouraged them in it? Had she not kept a huge basket full of costumes for that very purpose and showed them how to use stage make-up to produce almost any face they desired? Mama herself had often played a male when there were not enough men to take all the parts in the little plays they produced. Papa had always been indulgent, so what had put him into such an ill humour now?

Within the stipulated ten minutes she presented herself at the library door and knocked. Her father's voice bade her enter and she crossed the threshold to stand before him, hands clasped in front of her blue cambric skirt and her head, now neatly arranged in classic-style ringlets, downcast so that all she could see of him was his shining top boots and well-fitting buckskins.

'Sit down,' he said, indicating a straight-backed chair on one side of the hearth.

She obeyed and lifted her eyes to his. 'It was only charades, Papa.'

His craggy features softened; he could not remain out of humour with his daughter for long. 'I know, and though you may see no harm in it and I own I would not have done so myself a few years ago, we must remember you are no longer a child and must begin behaving like a lady and not a hoyden.'

'Yes, Papa.'

'It is not as if you and Tom were alone; young Burford was a witness. . .'

'But I have known him since he was in leading-strings and his mama used to bring him to play with us in the nursery.'

'Nevertheless, he is a young man, a personable, lusty young man, and you must be aware of that.'

'I was not—I did not think. . .'

'No?' he smiled. 'But the time has come for you to learn how to go on in Society. You must come out and start looking for a husband. . .'

'But, Papa, I have met no one I like well enough.'

'Nor will you if you remain in Suffolk.'

'Leave Raventrees! Oh, Papa, I don't think I could bear it. . .'

'You will do as I say.'

'But you have not left the country for years, ever since. . .' She stopped, not wishing to hurt him by reminding him of the reason he had lived in seclusion for so long.

'Nor do I intend to. I have been thinking. Your aunt Agatha can bring you out.'

'Aunt Aggie!' she exclaimed. 'But she is. . .'

He smiled briefly. 'She is old and somewhat eccentric, but she is acquainted with everyone of any importance and she knows how to go on. Besides, I can think of no other who would do it.'

'Am I that bad?' Lydia whispered.

He chuckled. 'Not so incorrigible that you cannot be taught correct behaviour and how to display to best advantage. And that,' he added severely, 'is not in dressing up like a popinjay. You are a beautiful young lady, Lydia, a trifle on the tall side, but there must be some eligible bachelors who are taller. . .'

'Is that all that matters?' she cried. 'That he should be tall?'

'And have a decent background, with a good title and a fortune to match yours. I would not wish him to be too old, either, nor too free and easy with the ladies, for your sake. . .'

'That seems to me to be something of a high order,' she said. 'Supposing Aunt Aggie finds such a one and I say we will not suit?'

'You will not be coerced, my dear, you have my word, but I beg you to consider carefully before you reject a promising suitor. Marriage is a far better state than spinsterhood, I can assure you.'

'Has Aunt Aggie agreed?'

'Not yet, because I have only now thought of it. I shall write to her tonight. As soon as I have her reply, I will order Wenthorpe House to be opened and Tom can escort you to London. It won't do him any harm to acquire a little town bronze.'

Lydia was downcast, not only because she was to leave her beloved home, but that she was to be parted from her over-indulgent papa, but no amount of arguing would make him change his mind, and two weeks later she found herself being driven post-chaise with Tom and her maid for company, while everything she held most dear receded further and further behind her.

The heavy rains of the previous few days had left the roads in a shocking state and they were thrown from side to side as their coachman and postilion negotiated the potholes. By the afternoon of the second day Betty, who always travelled badly, was sitting in the corner looking whey-faced and Tom was wishing he had chosen to ride alongside. 'I'll be relieved when we stop for the night,' Lydia said, righting herself after having been thrown across the carriage almost into her brother's lap. 'I shall be black and blue at this rate. Why could we not have waited until the roads improved? It is still very early in the Season.'

He smiled. 'You know Papa; when he gets an idea into his head, nothing will serve but it must be attended to without delay.'

'I have never known him so impervious to reason. All over a simple game.'

'Oh, it was not the charades so much as his own conscience which smote him. You know, it really is time you were taken in hand. . .'

'Not you, too,' she said. 'I would have thought you would have understood.'

'Most assuredly I do, but I also realise that my little sister. . .'

'Not so little,' she said with a wry smile.

'Very well, my not-so-little sister must grow up and, if she does not, spinsterhood is not a state to be envied.'

Her protests were lost in a great swaying and creaking of springs, followed by a terrifying sound of rending wood accompanied by the shouts of their coachman and the screaming of the frightened horses. She was catapulted on to the opposite seat and then the whole carriage slid over sideways and she found herself sitting on one of the doors with Betty, screaming at the full extent of her not inconsiderable voice, on top of her. Tom found the door which was immediately above their heads and hauled himself out.

Lydia extricated herself and stood up. 'Are you hurt, Betty?'

The maid's shrieking subsided to sobs as she endeavoured to right herself. 'Oh, we should never have come; we should have stayed at 'ome where it's safe.'

'You said you wanted to come,' Lydia said, concluding from this that her maid was unhurt. 'I gave you a chance to stay at Raventrees.'

'What, and leave you to the mercies of a new maid who don't know your ways? I ain't so unfeeling.'

Lydia smiled. 'Then don't look so dismal. At least you are not now being rocked to death and we shall have to stay somewhere hereabouts until the carriage is repaired and that will give you time to recover.' As she spoke she put her head out of the door.

The carriage lay on its side with one of the uppermost wheels still spinning; their boxes had been thrown from the roof on to the muddy road and one of them had sprung its straps and deposited lace-trimmed garments into the water-filled hole which had overturned them. One of the horses had freed itself from the traces and was galloping across a field while Tom endeavoured to free the others who struggled against their harness. Watkins, the coachman, bent over the inert form of Scrivens who had been riding postilion. She looked forward and then back the way they had come but the road, which divided fields of newly sprouting corn, was empty; there was not a building or another traveller in sight.

'Bend over!' she commanded Betty. 'I must get out and see to Scrivens.'

Reluctantly her maid complied, and with a great heaving and a shocking display of petticoats Lydia stood on her maid's bent back, hauled herself out of the carriage and jumped down on to the road, leaving Betty wailing, 'What about me?'

She ran to where Scrivens lay in the ditch beside the road and knelt beside him in the wet mud. 'Is he badly hurt?'

'I don't think so, Miss Lydia, he's got a rare hard head on 'im,' said the coachman, who was feeling over the inert body for broken bones. 'See, he's coming round.' A groan and a fluttering of eyelids from the unfortunate servant seemed to bear this statement out. 'Now, miss, if we was to help him up. . .'

Betty, who had somehow managed to scramble out of the coach, came running across the road, trying to hold her skirts clear of the mud, which was more than her mistress had attempted to do. 'Oh, is he hurt?'

Scrivens, by this time, was in a sitting position and shaking his dazed head, but appeared not to be badly injured. Lydia left him in the care of her maid and returned to her brother, while Watkins set off across the field to catch the runaway horse. Tom had freed the remaining three and was looking down at the broken wheel and splintered axle of the coach, scratching his dark head.

'What's to be done?' she asked him.

He looked up at her. 'I shall have to ride one of the horses to fetch help.' Adjuring her to watch over their belongings, he flung himself on the postilion's mount and set off for the nearest village, where he hoped to procure a conveyance to bring them on and to arrange lodgings, for assuredly the coach could not be mended before nightfall. Watkins returned leading the errant horse and Lydia and Betty began gathering up their belongings and pushing them back into the broken trunk.

'They are ruined, that's what they are,' Betty grumbled, holding up a pair of frilly nether garments. 'They'll never come clean.'

'At least no one was badly hurt,' Lydia said, snatching them from her and bundling them in with the rest before the two men could see them. 'We could have all been killed. I wonder how long Tom will be? It will be dusk soon and I do not fancy being set upon by highwaymen. I wish I had asked him for his pistol.'

'Oh, miss, you don't think. . .' The sudden sound of an owl hooting in the trees beside the road made Betty fling herself behind her mistress with a cry of alarm.

'Don't be a little goose,' Lydia said. 'There's no one there.' She stopped speaking as the sound of horses and crunching wheels came to their ears, and this was followed by the sight of a travelling chaise coming round the bend behind them at a spanking pace. It was drawn by a perfectly matched pair of bays and Lydia stood and watched its approach with a gleam of admiration in an eye accustomed to evaluating horseflesh. When the equipage drew to a halt beside them, it became obvious that, although the horses were of the highest order, the coach was even older than their own and certainly more ramshackle. She was wondering what ninny could bear to harness such prime beasts to such a vehicle when its occupant flung open the door and jumped into the road. He was very tall indeed, something she almost always noticed first in a man, being so tall herself, and what with that and his long, aquiline nose it seemed as if he was looking down on them with a loftiness which was belied, however, by the twitch at the corners of his firm mouth. He swept off his tall beaver, revealing brown curls cut short in the latest style, and bowed over a leg encased in mustard-coloured pantaloons and polished hessians. 'Your servant, ma'am.' He looked about him for her escort, but, perceiving none but the servants, turned back to her. 'May I offer you assistance?'

Lydia hesitated, for what assistance could he offer except to take them up, and she was reluctant to agree to that, not knowing him from Adam. He might be a highwayman, a ne'er-do-well, a thatchgallows of the worst sort—anything. 'Sir. . .' she began, uncomfortably aware of her muddied skirts and that her bonnet had slipped down her back on its ribbons and her hair had come unpinned. 'Sir, I do not know you.'

'As there is no one else to do it, let me introduce myself,' he said, taking her right hand in his and raising it to his lips, without taking his glance from her face. To her consternation, she found herself looking straight into his eyes. They were nut-brown and had a depth which seemed to draw her down into them, like a whirlpool pulling a fallen leaf into its vortex, powerless to resist. They seemed to say, Here I am; escape me if you will. Disconcerted, she tried to pull her hand away, but he held it fast. Then he smiled and the extraordinary sensation faded. 'I am Jack Bellingham,' he said, releasing her. 'Marquis of Longham, second son of the Duke of Sutton. . .'

'How can you be a marquis if you are only a second son?' she put in, still feeling weak.

He gave a ghost of a smile. 'Because, ma'am, my elder brother died a month back on the hunting field.'

'Oh, I am sorry.'

'And now you are assured of my credentials, will you allow me to help you?'

'Assured?' she queried, her common sense returning. 'Just on your say-so, that is poor assurance. You could have said you were the Prince Regent and I none the wiser.'

He laughed. 'Have you ever met the heir to the throne?'

'No.'

'Then I forgive you.'

'For what?'

'For the insult. His Highness is somewhat older and a great deal fatter than I.' He paused to walk round their overturned coach and inspected the broken wheel, while she endeavoured to set her bonnet to rights and brush the mud from her clothing with a kid-gloved hand. 'I doubt you will ride further in this vehicle this side of a se'enight, certainly not tonight. . .'

'My brother, the Honourable Thomas Wenthorpe,

has ridden one of the horses to fetch help,' she said with as much dignity as she could muster. 'He will be back directly.'

'How long since he left?'

'Half an hour, perhaps a little longer.'

'Then he cannot possibly be back before dark; the next village is ten miles away and I doubt he will be able to hire a conveyance immediately, certainly not one to take all that.' And he pointed at the two large trunks, one of which would no longer shut and revealed rather more of her most intimate apparel than she liked. She felt herself colour, but he appeared not to notice and went on, 'Of course, if you prefer to take the greater risk of being left by the roadside, I will continue on my way. I am in a great deal of haste.'

'Then you had best go on, my lord. I have servants with me.'

'Damn your scruples, girl,' he said. 'I cannot leave you. Get in and cease your protests.'

She opened her mouth to tell him just what she thought of his top-lofty attitude but changed her mind when Betty seized her hand. 'Please, Miss Lydia, don't let him leave us here; it will be dark soon and I'm afeared. . .'

'I fancy I am the lesser of two evils, Miss Wenthorpe,' he said with a smile which infuriated her. 'And I promise to keep my baser urges in check.'

'I am afraid one of my servants has been hurt. . .'

'Badly?'

'I do not think so, my lord, but I do not like to leave him.'

He looked across at Scrivens and, perceiving that

he was now on his feet and dusting himself down, said, 'He can ride with my driver. Now, are you coming or not?'

Lydia looked along the road for signs of Tom returning and then across the darkening fields, where the hedges and trees were beginning to throw sinister shadows, and decided he was right. 'I did not mean to be ungrateful,' she said. 'I should be most obliged to you if you would take us up. . .'

'Certainly I will, but not your luggage; there will be no room for it and, besides, I do not wish my chaise to go the way of yours.'

'Watkins will stay by our belongings and wait for Tom, if you will be so kind as to convey me and my maid and Scrivens to the next posting inn. No doubt we will come upon my brother on the way,' she said, too polite to make a reference to the incongruity of the magnificent bays and the scuffed old coach, though her curiosity was almost overwhelming. 'I have a small overnight bag, if that is not too much trouble.'

While Scrivens, who would not for the world have complained that his head ached and his shoulder was so painful he did not know how to haul himself up there, took his place beside the driver, their rescuer leaned into the overturned vehicle, pulled out her bag and marched off to his own carriage with it. He put it in the boot and turned to hand Lydia up. Afraid of sensations she did not understand, she was reluctant to give him her hand again, but it would have been churlish to refuse, so she allowed him to help her into the carriage. As soon as Betty had seated herself beside her mistress, he took the facing seat and called to his driver to proceed.

When they had safely negotiated the blockage in the road and were once more on their way, Lydia sought to express her gratitude for his help and began an explanation of how they came to be on the road and why their coach was not as roadworthy as it should have been. 'It has not been out of Suffolk for years,' she said. 'And our coachman knows the roads around our home so well there has never been the least chance we should fall into a hole.' If she had hoped that this statement might persaude him to similar explanations, she was wrong; he appeared not to wish for conversation. He had obviously discharged his duty as he saw it but that was as far as he was prepared to go; polite exchanges and confidences were no part of it. Very well, if he wanted to be a stiff-neck, so be it; they would soon be off his hands.

She turned to watch out of the window for Tom, but mile succeeded mile and they met no one. Surely they could not have missed each other on the way? 'Do you know the road well, my lord?' she asked.

He came out of a brown study to answer her. 'Tolerably well.'

'Then how much further is it to the posting inn?'

He smiled suddenly and his grim expression lightened so that she became aware of the humour behind his hazel eyes. 'I am poor company, Miss Wenthorpe, I realise that, but be assured I am as anxious to arrive at my destination as you are.'

'And what is your destination?'

'Ultimately London, but for tonight a good bed and a change of horses.'

'Have these already been bespoken, my lord?'

'Indeed yes, my man came on ahead. And you?'

'Arrangements were made before we left home, though I collect we were meant to go a little further before nightfall, but what with the bad roads and the accident. . .' She paused for another look out of the window for her brother. 'I do hope Tom has been able to find somewhere for us to stay while the carriage is fetched and repaired.'

'Ah, your brother. . .'

The tone of his voice brought her up sharply. Surely he did not think she was travelling unescorted and had invented a brother? Or did he think Tom was not her brother, but her lover? If he thought that of her, what else was he thinking? Oh, how she wished she had braved the darkness and waited by the damaged coach. 'I do hope he has not encountered some difficulty,' she said, trying to remain calm.

'You will soon see; we will be at the King's Head in a matter of minutes.'

And if Tom is not there, she thought, what then? What would she do? What would the Marquis do? She glanced sideways at him beneath the brim of her silk-ruched bonnet while pretending to be looking out of the window. He looked decidedly uncomfortable trying to keep his long legs tucked out of the way of her skirts, but apart from that he seemed entirely composed. His well-fitting coat of blue superfine seemed not to need padding at the shoulders and his waist had no need of stays. She supposed him to be about thirty, though it was difficult to tell because his features were tanned and there were tiny lines running from the corners of his eyes, as if he had spent long hours out of doors screwing up his face against the sun, but he was certainly old enough to be married and have a brood of offspring. She fell to wondering what kind of a husband and father he made—probably very cool and distant, except when roused to anger. She did not think she would care for his anger, though perhaps it would not be any worse than his present indifference. He had resumed his thoughtful expression with his chin resting on the folds of his impeccable neckcloth between the points of his collar, almost as if he had forgotten she was there. What was he thinking of, apart from what a devilish inconvenience she was to him?

It was not so much the inconvenience of having unexpected passengers which had put Jack in a browse but the notion that fate had taken a hand in his affairs and was conspiring to prevent him reaching his destination. His own travelling carriage had overturned the first day out from home and, though his horses had not been injured, thank God, he had been obliged to buy this antiquated coach to continue his journey. And now to find himself not alone in this particular misfortune was the outside of enough. He only hoped the vehicle was sturdier than it looked and would convey them all safely to the next posting inn and even more sincerely trusted that his passenger was telling the truth and there really was a brother to take charge of her; he had enough on his hands as it was.

As Captain Jack Bellingham, he had returned

from service with Wellington's army at the end of the war, expecting some respite from continual fighting, only to be faced with another kind of conflict at home. In the six or seven years he had been out of the country his father had grown prematurely old and even more inclined than before to take refuge in the bottle. He had let the estate go to ruin. And his heir, Jack's elder brother, far from helping to set matters to rights, had made them worse by drinking, womanising and gambling. His death on the hunting field when in his cups had left Jack, who had never regarded himself as a future duke, as heir not only to extensive land and property but to all the debts and problems as well.

One of these latter was a neighbour called Ernest Grimshaw who had taken advantage of the general neglect and encroached on woodland which most certainly belonged to the Longham domain. He had cut down any number of fine trees and sold the timber so that, where before the war there had been a fine stand of oaks, larch and elm, there was now nothing but an ugly scar of stumps and bracken, and, what was worse, the game had naturally disappeared with the trees. The man had had the temerity to show him some ancient map on which the wood was clearly marked but the devil of it was that it was not shown inside the Longham boundary. He had defied his lordship to turn him off or deprive him of the not inconsiderable revenue the timber provided. Jack was on his way to meet the lawyers, but he had a feeling in his bones that he was going to need all his wits about him to win through. It would have been easier and certainly a great deal cheaper to have let the fellow get away with it and concentrated on the rest of the estate, but that was not Jack's way; he would be blowed if he would let some land-thieving cit get the better of him.

It was not that he was particularly in want of funds; his personal fortune, inherited on the distaff side, was more than adequate, even setting aside the fortune in gold and jewels he had brought out of France with him. It was plunder, of course, but, since he had found it in a French sergeant's knapsack after the battle of Toulouse and it had obviously been plundered by him in the first place, the finding of its original owner, so his one-time batman and now his valet had told him, would be well-nigh impossible, even if he or she were still alive. He ought to be grateful to the unknown Johnny Blue-coat and lose no sleep over something which, in Tewkes's opinion, was a stroke of good luck. Jack intended to make a push to discover the true owner of the cache, but that would have to wait upon the business with Grimshaw being satisfactorily concluded.

He had said nothing of it to his father, who would, he was sure, take the same view as Tewkes, that anything acquired on a battlefield was a fair prize and meant to be used. His father, who had never cared a straw for his younger son, was, now that he was the heir, insisting on him marrying and continuing the line. Jack had had little time and even less inclination to marry while he was a serving soldier; following the colours was not something he would subject any wife to and leaving her at home seemed to defeat the object of the exercise. He had seen too many marriages fail because of long separations to take the risk. He was home now and, while he owned he ought to be thinking about marriage, to do so simply to produce an heir went against the grain. He would not stand in line, fawning over eager débutantes, just to please his profligate father. He grinned as the old coach jolted over a particularly bad rut; arriving in town in this dilapidated conveyance would certainly not endear him to the fortune hunters. He smiled to himself; if he were to allow the gossipers to think his pockets were to let, he might gain the breathing space he needed.

He lifted his head to find Lydia surveying him with wide violet eyes and a tiny twitch to the corners of her mouth which might have been the beginnings of a smile. In his experience young ladies usually fell into a swoon or burst into floods of tears when confronted with a mishap of this magnitude; that she could smile made him feel a deal more comfortable. 'We are slowing down,' she said. 'You will soon be rid of us.'

Chastised, he said, 'I apologise, Miss Wenthorpe, I am afraid I am poor company. Please forgive me.'

'Oh, it is I who need forgiving for the intrusion.' They were pulling up in the yard of an inn and the driver was shouting to one of the ostlers who had run out to meet them. 'If we can find my brother, I am sure he will add his thanks to mine.'

But Tom was nowhere to be seen. On enquiring after him, she was told that he had been there but as there were no spare horses or carriages of any sort he had gone to a farm along the road in the hope of borrowing a cart.

'A *cart*?' She could hardly believe it and she knew

that the Marquis, who stood immediately behind her, was laughing at the picture thus created in his mind of her and her maid sitting atop their luggage on a farm cart! 'Whatever was he thinking of?'

'Better than walking,' the innkeeper said, with a shrug. 'And he could bring on your luggage, not to mention the broken wheel to be repaired.'

'Eminently sensible,' commented the Marquis. 'But we did not meet him on the road, so where is he?'

'The horse he rode was lame and he had to walk to the farm—all of two miles further on, it be—and if the farmer were not at home or the cart loaded and needing to be unloaded it would take time. Ten to one he's still there.'

'Could you not have lent him a horse?' Lydia asked.

'Ma'am, we have no spares, as I told the young gentleman.'

'I thought I saw two looking over their stalls in the stables when we came into the yard.'

'They are bespoke for his lordship.'

'Oh.' She turned to the Marquis. 'You have taken the last two horses. How are we to go on?'

If this was a hint to relinquish the animals to her, he did not take the bait. 'I'll lay odds your carriage wheel will not be ready by tomorrow,' he said. 'And by the day after your own horses will have been rested.'

'One of them is lame; you heard the landlord say so. What about the ones you brought today?'

'They go back to Longham,' he snapped. 'I do not

leave prime cattle like that for any Tom, Dick or Harry to spoil.'

'But we must go on—my aunt is expecting us tomorrow evening at the latest; she will be very worried if we do not arrive.'

He did not see that it need be any concern of his but he could no more abandon her now than he could when he'd first come upon the overturned coach, especially as her brother, if he truly was her brother, seemed to have left her to manage on her own. Confound the pair of them! 'I will deem it a privilege to convey you and your brother on tomorrow,' he said, then, turning to the innkeeper, 'Have you a room for Miss Wenthorpe?'

It seemed the Marquis had also bespoken the only spare room but he gave it up with every appearance of cheerfulness, saying he would do very well on a settle in the parlour. By the time Tom arrived, it was quite dark and Lydia was being entertained by her rescuer to an excellent supper of fish in oyster sauce, boiled beef and apple flummery.

Tom was cold and wet and dismal and not inclined to be gracious when he discovered that Lydia had arrived in the village in comparative comfort, had washed and changed, and was sitting unchaperoned in the dining-room with a man to whom she had not been introduced. It really would not do, and he told her so in no uncertain terms when, at last, they left the dining-room to retire for the night and he was able to speak to her alone.

'What would you have had me do?' she retorted. 'Sit under the broken carriage and freeze to death while you took your time bringing a *farm cart*? His lordship has been kindness itself...' Kindness was not really the right word, she decided; he had been vastly entertaining, sarcastic and charming by turns, while remaining unfailingly polite. He had been solicitous for her comfort and sent the inn servants scurrying to please her, and then sat without speaking for several minutes watching her eat, as if he had never seen a woman with a hearty appetite before. Her concentration on her plate had not been so much hunger as a reluctance to raise her head and find those searching eyes on her.

'You need not have dined with him,' Tom said, unconvinced. 'It is hardly the thing. He is a stranger.'

'But he gave up his room for me, and a very fine room it is too; I could not be so ungrateful as to refuse his company, and we were not alone—the dining-room was full.'

'We should have gone on to Watford where our rooms were booked.'

'How?'

He had no answer and gave her none, but turned to grumbling that he had been obliged to dine on left-overs and was to sleep with Watkins and Scrivens above the stables and if he did not catch his death of a chill then he would be more than surprised. She made light of his catalogue of complaints, saying he would feel more the thing after a good night's sleep and, taking her leave, went up to her bedchamber where Betty was waiting to help her undress.

It was a squeeze for them all to pack into the Marquis's chaise the next morning, even though they left Watkins and Scrivens behind to see to the repairs of the coach and follow on when these had been completed and the horses rested. Tom, still sulking a little, sat beside his lordship facing Lydia and Betty and it seemed to Lydia that the Marquis was having even greater difficulty with his long legs. By the time they stopped for nuncheon they were all glad to get out and stretch their cramped limbs. The inn was the one where she and Tom would have stayed the previous night but for the accident, and their fresh horses were waiting for them; but now, of course, they had no carriage to harness them to. Tom was all for riding one of them but he would not leave Lydia alone in the carriage with the Marquis, especially as they were approaching London and might set the tongues wagging with unfavourable gossip about her before she had even set foot on its flags. It would not be a very auspicious start to her come-out. Jack, seeing and sympathising with his dilemma, decided he, too, would prefer to ride, even if the mounts were a couple of mediocre carriage horses and he was hardly dressed for it, and thus the calvalcade entered the metropolis and pulled up at the door of Wenthorpe House in Portman Square.

Mrs Agatha Wenthorpe, widow of Lord Wenthorpe's younger brother, had arrived from her own home in Edgware a few days previously and had immediately set about opening up the house, which had remained unoccupied, except for a handful of servants, for years. She had engaged more staff, ordered all the windows opened and fires lit in every room. The dust-covers had been removed, the carpets beaten, floors scrubbed, furniture polished and flowers brought in and arranged in vases on every table and ledge big enough to receive them so that overriding the lingering fusty smell of disused rooms was the scent of soap and beeswax, narcissi and pansies.

It was some years since Lydia had seen her aunt and in that time the lady had become even more eccentric in her appearance. She was sitting in one of the small downstair parlours with her feet on a footstool by the fire, reading one of Miss Austen's novels through a very thick quizzing glass, when they were announced, but rose quickly to greet them. She was a short, dumpy woman, made even broader by the caging she wore in her very old-fashioned gown of coffee-coloured brocade with its wide over-sleeves. Her face was heavily powdered and a patch on her cheek disguised an ugly pockmark. On her head she wore a startling red wig. Lydia had loved her as a child and she saw no reason now to change her opinion. She hurried forward and allowed herself to be embraced. 'Dear Aunt, such an adventure we have had,' she said, after Mrs Wenthorpe had released her and held her hand out for Tom to kiss, which he did, thankful that she could not see his smile at her extraordinary dress.

'Aunt, may I present the Marquis of Longham?' Lydia said, turning to Jack who had been prevailed upon to come in to meet Mrs Wenthorpe. 'He has been a prodigious help, for without him we would have been delayed for days and days.'

'Indeed? Then I must add my gratitude to my niece's,' she said, putting up the quizzing glass and eyeing him up and down with great candour. 'You will stay for supper?'

Jack, without a trace of discomfort, bowed low

over her plump, bejewelled hand. 'Alas, I have pressing business, ma'am.'

'Then you must call when you are not so pressed. We cannot let you go unthanked.'

'I have been sufficiently thanked, ma'am,' he said. 'And now that Miss Wenthorpe is safely in your hands, I must take my leave.' He bowed again to Mrs Wenthorpe and then to Lydia and, with a, 'Good evening, Wenthorpe,' to Tom, left the room.

'Well!' said Aunt Aggie, letting out her breath in a long sigh. 'There's a top-lofty male if ever I saw one. He could not get away fast enough. What have you done to him, Lydia?'

'I, Aunt? Why, nothing. I do believe that is his usual manner. I really think he did not want to rescue us and now he is glad to have us off his hands.'

'Why should he not wish to help? Is there something wrong with him?'

'I hardly know, Aunt, but his carriage was worse then ours. If it had not been drawn by the most beautiful pair of bays I have ever seen, I would have taken him for an impostor. And, you must admit, his manners leave much to be desired. . .'

'I expect he took a leaf out of your book,' Mrs Wenthorpe said in mild rebuke. 'But we can soon put a town polish on you and then you will have any number of offers. Tomorrow we must shop for clothes. . .' She stopped because Lydia had barely been able to conceal a smile at the thought of her outrageously dressed aunt Aggie selecting clothes for her. 'I do not pretend to be all the crack myself and I am too old to change my ways, but I know someone who will see that you are dressed properly. I shall take you to my great friend, Lavinia Davies. Tonight we will sup quietly and go to bed early, for we have a busy day ahead of us.' She turned to Tom. 'What had you planned, young man?'

'Oh, I shall amuse myself, never fear,' he said. 'A visit to Weston's for a new suit of clothes, a few hands of cards at White's, a ride perhaps. And don't you think we had better buy a new town carriage? Even supposing our travelling chaise can be repaired, it is as old as the ark. Not having ridden in it since before I went to Cambridge, I had not realised how old-fashioned and unsound it was. It is hardly suitable for town use; Lydia cannot go to balls and routs in it, nor to the park, and expect to be noticed by the *ton*—unless it be for being a frump.'

'I am not a frump!'

'I did not say you were, but I am sure that is what the Marquis thought when he saw you looking as though you had been tumbled in the hay. And as for our equipage. . .'

'Damn the Marquis!' his sister said with feeling. Was that why he had looked at her so hard and long?

'Lydia!' Mrs Wenthorpe was shocked into reaching for the glass of claret at her elbow. 'That is not the language of a lady.'

'I am sorry, Aunt, but if I have to weigh up every man I meet with nothing but marriage in mind, then I would as lief not marry at all.'

'But you must, child! That is what you are here for and why I am here, to make sure you come out in a manner fitting your station and wealth and to make sure you are not gulled by unsuitable offers.' She smiled and laid a hand over Lydia's. 'You will enjoy it, my dear, and I am sure you will find someone to suit before the Season is over.'

'And if I don't?'

'Then I will have failed your dear papa, and so will you.'

Lydia fell silent on the subject. It would do no good to argue and she would have to pretend to be enjoying herself, even flirt a little, but that did not mean she was committed. Unless, by some miracle, she fell in love, she would put off making a decision; that was—and she smiled to herself—if anyone offered for her, which was not at all a certainty. She was too tall and not especially beautiful and she was certainly outspoken, none of which would endear her to would-be husbands who, for the most part, only needed a breeding machine. It was not that she was against marriage and having children, but she had, in her growing up, had plenty of time to observe the disastrous marriages of her acquaintances and compare them with the loving relationship of her own parents, and nothing less than that would do.

CHAPTER TWO

THERE could not have been a greater contrast between Mrs Wenthorpe and the modishly attired Mrs Davies, but neither seemed to pay any heed to that, and after a cosy exchange of the latest *on-dit* they took Lydia to visit a dressmaker where Mrs Davies bespoke dresses for morning wear, for walking and for carriage rides, dresses for assemblies, for breakfasts, for the opera, for balls, and a dark blue velvet riding habit with a jacket frogged in the Polish style, to be worn over a white silk shirt with ruffles at throat and wrist. From there they went on to buy a tall beaver hat with a curly brim and a peacock feather to go with the riding habit, bonnets, caps and shawls, underlinen, mantles and muffs, shoes, dancing slippers and half-boots of crimson jean.

Lydia sincerely hoped the expense her father was being put to would be worth his while and was beginning to feel guilty that she had no intention of allowing herself to fall into the marriage net simply because he though it was time she was wed. If he wanted grandsons, let Tom produce them. The idea of Tom as a father was so amusing, she was still laughing when he joined them for luncheon at three o'clock, having taken a leaf from her book and decked himself out in the latest fashion.

'Why do you laugh?' he asked, affronted. 'These

pantaloons are the latest thing and I spent a devilish long time tying this neckcloth.'

'It isn't that,' she assured him. 'You look bang-up. I was wondering if you might enter the marriage stakes instead of me. After all, you are the one who has to produce Wenthorpe heirs, not I.'

'But you are the one Papa has fixed his mind on and you ought not to disappoint him. The whole thing must be costing him a prodigious amount.'

'And I wish that it did not,' she said. 'I do not like being groomed like some thoroughbred to be paraded in the selling ring.'

'Oh, my dear, it is not at all like that,' protested Aunt Aggie. 'You will enjoy it and I am persuaded you will be the belle of the Season and have any number of offers to choose from. It is the young gentlemen who are being paraded, not you.' She rose from the table and smiled at them both. 'Now, as I have not spent such a fatiguing morning in years, I shall go and lie down. Tom, you will look after your sister.'

'But Aunt, I am going to choose a new carriage.'

'I'll come too,' Lydia said, rising quickly. 'It won't take above a minute to fetch a bonnet and mantle.'

Since her aunt did not object to this, a footman was sent to bring a hackney to the door and brother and sister set off for Mount Street, where the coach-builders, Robinson and Cook, had their premises.

Tom was torn between ordering a barouche which would have been suitable for Lydia and her aunt, and a high-perch phaeton, a showy vehicle which had enormous wheels and high seating which was known to be unstable in inexpert hands. He wanted to show off his driving skill and Lydia, who considered herself a good whip, was also tempted, but she knew her aunt would disapprove on the grounds that young ladies who drove high-perch phaetons were considered fast. While they were thus debating, the Marquis of Longham arrived on the same errand.

He was wearing splendid riding breeches of soft buckskin and well-cut riding boots which emphasised his long, muscular legs. His corded coat with its high collar covered a yellow brocade waistcoat and a neckcloth of moderate dimensions; the whole effect was discreetly modish. Greeting them cheerfully, he bowed over Lydia's hand and then, with those hazel eyes twinkling with mischief, looked about him at the vehicles on display, some of which were only half complete, and enquired if it had not been possible to repair their carriage after all.

'Not at all, my lord,' Lydia said, affecting a haughtiness which was so unlike her that Tom turned to her in surprise. 'A travelling chaise is hardly the thing for town; even you must admit to that. We have come to bespeak a light carriage.'

'Surely not this one?' his lordship said, pointing at the high-perch phaeton Tom had been admiring.

'What is wrong with it?' Lydia demanded, annoyed that he should question their judgement. 'It looks a very handsome carriage to me.'

'Oh, no doubt of it,' he said calmly. 'But surely you were not intending to buy it for yourself, Miss Wenthorpe?' He looked her up and down as if measuring her up for the vehicle in question, though, in truth, he was thinking how attractive she looked and how the colour of her costume set off the deep colour of her eyes.

'Why not?' She was so stung by his attitude, she forgot her attempt at hauteur. 'I'll have you know I'm considered to have a sound pair of hands on the ribbons.'

'That I do not doubt,' he said, appraising her with one eyebrow lifted higher than the other, which made her think he was laughing at her. 'But have you considered your aunt's feelings? She will have to accompany you when you go out and I hardly think someone of her years would find it to her liking.' He did not add that he thought the worthy matron would find it extremely difficult even to climb into its seat without an undignified push from behind, nor what the gossips would say if Lydia were seen driving it.

'And I'll wager the truth is that you are determined to have the vehicle for yourself in order to cut a dash in Hyde Park,' she said, knowing he was right about her aunt and annoyed that he should have the effrontery to point it out to her. 'Let us not disappoint you. I dare say we can manage with a barouche.'

'Why not a park phaeton?' he suggested, without denying her accusation. 'It is light enough for you to drive, if that is what you have in mind, and not too dangerous if handled sensibly. If you wish, I'll undertake to teach you to drive it.'

If this was an effort to placate her, it had the opposite effect; she could drive as well as most men and not even Tom would presume to suggest she needed lessons. 'I am sure your lordship has more pressing business,' she murmured, stifling her inclination to tell him so. 'We would not wish to impose on you.'

Anyone but the Marquis of Longham, she told herself, would have recognised the put-down for what it was, but he simply smiled and said, 'Not at all.' Then, deciding he would get nowhere with her, he turned to Tom. 'How say you, Wenthorpe; will you consider this one? It is wide enough to seat three at a pinch and low enough slung not to turn over in a tight corner.'

Tom accepted the offer of help with alacrity and the two men began a long discussion about the merits of the carriage in question and the colours in which it should be finished, and, the deal being done, arrangements were made to collect it two days later.

'In the meantime,' his lordship said, 'may I offer to convey you home?'

Tom agreed at once without consulting Lydia, who had been silently watching the Marquis's handling of the transaction and secretly admitting to herself that Tom, left alone, would not have done half so well. Not until they were once more on the street did she realise that the conveyance was the self-same coach which had brought them to London. She had already been ungracious and could not compound that by refusing to get into it, and thus they arrived at Wenthorpe House in the same ramshackle way they had the day before.

The arrival of Tom and Lydia with the Marquis in attendance had not gone unnoticed the first time it had happened. It seemed incomprehensible to the ladies of Society that Miss Wenthorpe, who was so obviously in London looking for a husband, should turn up in that skimble-skamble state and should have for an escort a man whom no one knew. That he was handsome and dressed in the pink of fashion none disputed, but his mount! Did one ever see such a broken-backed mule? And as for the carriage, it was twenty years old if it was a day. Surely Wenthorpe was not that pinched in the pocket? If he was, the tattlers did not see how his daughter could be safely brought out. And to compound everything by driving about town in that self-same vehicle was enough to set the neighbourhood tongues wagging even more furiously.

Servants, tradesmen, not to mention candlestick-makers and chimney-sweeps, were sent far and wide to find out what they could. They returned with the intelligence that the horses had been hired and the carriage belonged to the Marquis of Longham, the only surviving son of the Duke of Sutton, who, like their present monarch, was as mad as a hatter. As for Lord Wenthorpe, as far as could be ascertained, there was nothing wrong with his credit and Miss Wenthorpe stood to come into a considerable portion on her marriage.

'That, of course, would account for Longham dancing attendance on her,' they said over the teacups, having heard accounts of the profligate ways of the Duke of Sutton and his elder son and assuming the younger was cast in the same mould. It was their duty to rescue her from this mountebank. And if their informants should be wrong and the Marquis was not a spongeing toadeater but a man of consequence, then all the more reason to detach him from Miss Wenthorpe and speedily attach him to their own daughters. They were prepared to expend any amount of time and energy on the project. And thus it was that so many invitations poured into Wenthorpe House, Lydia and her aunt were hard put to it to decide which to accept.

In spite of this, Mrs Wenthorpe held to her original view that Lydia ought to try her wings at small functions and not come out in a blaze of glory at a high-stepping affair, where one false move, one little slip could ruin all their plans. 'Besides,' she said, with a twinkle in her eye, 'keep 'em waiting, that's what I say. Make 'em dangle a little.'

Her aunt's choice of phrase did nothing to make Lydia feel any better about coldly setting out to catch a husband, but if she had to, then she would take her time. Accordingly, they accepted invitations to quiet little suppers and tea parties, drove in the park in the new phaeton, drawn by a pair of greys which, though not up to the Marquis's bays, were creditable enough to win admiring glances, made up a party to visit Vauxhall Gardens with Tom and Frank Burford as escorts, were seen at the theatre and the opera, were almost squeezed to death in the more popular routs and generally conducted themselves with genteel reserve. In the course of three weeks they had made the superficial acquaintance of almost everyone who was anyone, but no young man had been singled out, so that it became a kind of game to be noticed by the nubile Miss Wenthorpe.

Occasionally the Marquis of Longham was seen in Lydia's company, but always within a party, and his behaviour gave the tongue-waggers no cause to think he was making any progress with her if that was his intention. Indeed, Lydia herself was inclined to think him too high in the instep by far and, though always polite, she would not go out of her way to show him any favouritism. When he chose to unbend and make himself agreeable, then so might she, but until then she would keep him at a distance.

It was the only thing on which she and her aunt disagreed, for Mrs Wenthorpe had, on closer acquaintance, taken a shine to the young man and enjoyed his company, especially as he did not appear to think her dress anything out of the ordinary. In fact he had, on one occasion, complimented her on her looks. 'And he was not funning me,' she asserted over nuncheon one day. 'He is the very embodiment of good taste and sensitivity.'

'He's bought a bang-up rig—prime cattle and a spanking new curricle,' Tom said enthusiastically. 'He let me take the ribbons the other day and felicitated me on my handling of them.'

'You mean he did not go back and buy the high-perch phaeton after all?' Lydia asked, choosing to ignore the fact that the Marquis had not actually said he intended to buy it.

'Apparently not,'

'Then I was right. He pretended to want it only to prevent us from having it.'

'And glad I am he did,' Agatha put in with a twinkle in her myopic eyes. 'Can you imagine me riding as high as the house-tops in one of those?'

'Do you know his circumstances, Aunt?' Tom asked. He saw in the Marquis an entry to the *ton* and invitations to places that young ladies like his sister had no idea existed, or, if they did, spoke of them behind their fans with bated breath and a sense of daring. He liked the cut of Longham's jib, his self-assurance, his air of command and he had every intention of modelling himself on this aristocrat with the long nose and the haughty bearing. 'Has he taken you into his confidence?'

Mrs Wenthorpe smiled enigmatically. 'If he had, I would not break it to satisfy your curiosity, young man. All I know is that he is a soldier, or he was, and highly thought of by Wellington, so I suppose he must have been a good one, but since the peace he has been little seen in Society. His father, the Duke, is a buffle-head without a feather to fly with and his brother was a dissolute rake and he will have his work cut out to bring everything to rights.'

'Well, I take no note of the gabble-grinders,' Tom informed them cheerfully. 'He ain't one to shout the odds about his affairs, plays his cards close to his chest, but that don't mean he's dished up. But if he offered for Lydia. . .'

'That would be an entirely different matter,' his aunt said. 'Then it would be my duty to make enquiries. . .'

'But as he has made no such offer,' Lydia put in with some asperity, 'and I would not accept him if he did, we need not trouble ourselves about him.'

Her aunt sighed. 'He is not likely to offer when you give him so little encouragement.'

'I am not going to lick boots to find a husband, Aunt Aggie, and I am sure Papa would not expect me to.'

Mrs Wenthorpe smiled. 'No, but he might hope that you would make just a little push, my dear.' She smiled suddenly and her blue eyes lit with mischief. 'No matter, it is still early in the Season.' She paused to pick up a gilt-edged invitation card to a ball to be held at Thornton House, Park Lane on the following Friday week. 'Let us see what this brings forth, for everyone who is anyone will be there.' She tapped the card against her chin, pretending to think. 'Now, who shall be your escort? I think Longham, don't you?'

'Frank Burford has already asked me,' Lydia put in quickly.

'Frank?' Tom repeated. 'You haven't been such a ninny as to agree?'

'Why not?'

'Oh, Frank is a capital fellow, I'll allow,' he said. 'But you may as well have stayed at home and saved Papa a deal of blunt if you are going back to Raventrees on his arm. You've known him since he was in short coats.'

'I'm comfortable with him and, as he has been so good as to ask, I have accepted.'

'I hope you have not held out any false hopes, Lydia,' her aunt said, rising from the table. 'It would be most unfair of you.'

'Not in the least,' she said cheerfully, putting down her napkin and following her aunt from the room. 'I know he has a penchant for little Miss Thornton, but so far she has not deigned to notice him.'

'Miss Thornton!' exclaimed Tom, deciding that as there were no other men with whom to smoke and drink he might as well join his sister and their aunt in the withdrawing room, where they settled themselves to await the arrival of the tea tray. 'She's a little above his touch, don't you think? I cannot see her mama agreeing to that match.'

Lydia was inclined to agree with her brother when, ten days later, they took their turn in the long line of guests waiting to be received by Lord and Lady Thornton, and realised what a lavish affair it was. And all in the cause of marrying off their daughter.

The ballroom was filled to capacity and noisy enough to have been a battlefield. The orchestra which was tuning up on a dais at the far end of the room could hardly be heard above the din of people greeting acquaintances, being introduced and exchanging the latest *on-dit*. The heat from the gas lamps was already intense and ladies' fans were much in evidence, not only for cooling purposes, but for whispering behind.

'What a squeeze!' said Frank, resplendent in a yellow brocade coat and matching satin knee-breeches, tied above his white silk stockings with ribbon bows. He looked a little ridiculous, Lydia thought, but not for a minute would she have hurt him by letting him know her thoughts, any more than she would have wounded her aunt by commenting on her lavish rose satin *décolleté* ballgown with its wide panniers, a fashion at least a generation out of date.

Tom pushed his way through the crush and found a seat for his aunt before wandering off to find himself a partner for the cotillion which was then forming, and Frank led Lydia on to the floor. She was engaged for every dance after that by a multitude of young men, to all of whom she was charming, laughing and thoroughly at ease, aware that she looked her best in the cream silk gown Mrs Davies had helped her to choose. The very simplicity of its high waist and softly falling skirt displayed her slim figure to perfection and its not too low neckline and puffed sleeves set off pale shoulders and a throat encircled with nothing but a rope of beautifully matched pearls. Her hair was drawn back in a Grecian style with a top-knot and ringlets woven with more pearls. Nothing could have been a greater contrast to most of the other gaudily attired young ladies with their beads and feathers, rubies and emeralds.

It was late in the evening when she spied the Marquis of Longham, standing by himself just inside the door as if he had only then arrived. His pose was nonchalant, and Lydia, who was dancing a Chaîne Anglais with the Honourable Douglas Fincham, youngest son of the Earl of Boreton, was forced to admit to herself that his figure was made for tight jackets and close-fitting pantaloons. Not long before, these would not have been allowed at a ball, knee-breeches being the accepted dress, but now only Almack's stuck to the old ways, and here was a man for whom the new fashions must have been made. His long-tailed black evening coat was exquisitely cut to his broad shoulders and narrow waist, while his black pantaloons served to outline muscular thighs that drew a sigh of admiration from many a débutante. Lydia told herself severely, but not very honestly, that she was immune.

'For someone who don't have a feather to fly with, he's in prime twig,' commented her partner, who considered himself no end of a fine fellow. He was very young and extremely chubby, like a round young puppy. His shoulders were padded and his waist corseted and his collar points scratched his cheeks whenever he moved his head. His enormous cravat was tied into an intricate pattern of loops and folds, while across his pink and yellow striped waist-coat hung a multitide of chains and fobs. Beside the elegantly clad Marquis, he looked a veritable macaroni. 'But it don't signify,' he added. 'Everyone knows his father is batty and has lost his fortune.'

'Where did you hear that?' Lydia asked, forgetting her determination never to listen to gossip.

'It is common knowledge,' he said airily. 'His creditors will be hammering on his door before the Season is out, unless he can find himself an heiress.'

'And I think you would be wise to refrain from such scandal,' she said sharply, making him redden from the wilting points of his collar to the roots of his fair hair. 'He might call you out for it.'

'Why, I set no store by Canterbury tales,' he said, speedily recovering from this rebuke, having little imagination and an extraordinary idea of his own worth. If a young lady gave him a put-down, it only meant that he should try the harder to engage her attention.

Correctly judging his character, she set about teasing him so that by the time the dance ended and he returned her to her aunt he did not know whether to be elated or resentful. Aunt Aggie was in lively conversation with one of the dowagers who sat in regal splendour along the side of ballroom, making sweeping and quite scandalous statements about all and sundry, but she was attentive enough to look up at her niece with a humorous quirk of her brow and a flutter of her fan behind which she was heard to murmur, 'A veritable pea-goose, my dear. Do send him about his business or he will cling like a leech.'

Lydia stifled a giggle but she was saved having to take her aunt's advice because Douglas drifted off, and she joined Tom and Frank who stood near by waiting to claim their partners for the next dance. Frank had already stepped forward to stand before Miss Thornton, when Lady Thornton pushed herself between them and drew the Marquis towards her daughter.

'Well, of all the put-downs!' Lydia exclaimed, feeling very sorry for the dejected Frank, as he turned away to seek solace in the card-room while Amelia Thornton, pink of face, set off with the Marquis. 'Lady Thornton is making a fool of herself with her daughter besides, throwing her at every unmarried man in the room from old Lord Winters who is sixty if he is a day to Douglas Fincham who was only yesterday taken out of short coats; the only thing they have in common is a title—or the expectation of one—and a fortune. As for the Marquis of Longham, I thought he had more sense than to be used in that fashion.'

'He could hardly snub the poor girl by refusing,' Tom said, reasonably. 'That would have made matters worse.'

'I feel sorry for poor Miss Thornton, for she will not be allowed to make up her own mind,' Lydia went on, her own sense of justice making her admit Tom was right. 'I'll wager if I were to present myself as an eligible man, Lady Thornton would have me stand up with her.'

Tom turned to stare at her. 'I say, Lydia, you wouldn't dare,' he said, then added, as he saw the gleam in his sister's eye, 'You wouldn't, would you?'

'Why not?' The sight of the Marquis of Longham dancing a quadrille with Amelia Thornton and showing every sign of enjoying it made Lydia feel as if it was she and not Frank who had been snubbed, and filled her with an illogical desire to do something entirely reckless.

'You'd never pull it off,' he said. 'Lady Thornton will see through you and then you will be sent home to Raventrees in disgrace, and what will Papa do with you then? No, no, you cannot.'

'*Cannot*?' she queried, raising one arched brow. Ever since they had left the cradle, Tom only had to say she would not dare to do something than she needs must do it. 'Will you take a small wager that I cannot, Thomas? Shall we say twenty pounds?'

He stared at her for a moment and then laughed. 'You're on! Twenty pounds say you cannot hoodwink Lady Thornton into accepting you as a man and allowing you to dance with her daughter.' He paused. 'You'll have to gull Miss Thornton as well or she will kick up a fuss before you have taken half a turn about the room.'

'Naturally, everyone must believe it. I shall let Miss Thornton into the secret when the dance is ended.' She smiled, her boredom vanishing in this new challenge to her acting ability. 'I'll need a title and a name which is credible but not too easily discounted. It had better be French; their nobility is in such a tangle since the Revolution, no one will suspect.' She paused, then laughed. 'I know, we will use Mama's name. How does Comte Maurice de Clancy sound to you? I am the only son of a French *émigré* who came to England to escape the Terror when I was but a babe, which accounts for my being able to speak both languages perfectly. Oh, how glad I am that Mama insisted on speaking French to us! And if I assume an accent, it may help to disguise the fact that my voice is somewhat high.' She sighed. 'I am very much afraid I shall have to be a very effete suitor.'

'But you need a fortune, and how is that to be contrived? You can be sure Lady Thornton will want to know about that before her daughter is allowed to stand up with you.'

Lydia thought for a moment. 'Jewels smuggled out by my parents during the Revolution, caskets of the stuff, gold too, and none of it trusted to a bank. Given that piece of nonsense, the tattlers will do my work for me, then it will be enough if I give the appearance of being well-breeched. Her ladyship will never be able to disprove it before my wager is won.'

'When is this deception to take place?' her brother demanded. 'It must be done publicly, you know, and I must see it with my own eyes.'

She laughed, realising the occasion had to be right; she could not expect to deceive her aunt, however short-sighted she was, or Frank Burford, who had already seen her dressed as a man. 'I will tell you when I am ready.'

They were interrupted by the Marquis who, having returned Miss Thornton to her mama, was now bowing in front of Lydia and claiming the waltz. She smiled a mischievous little smile which both intrigued and alarmed him and allowed herself to be led on to the floor.

She had spent hours in the schoolroom learning the steps of the waltz with her brother and such friends who lived in the neighbourhood of Raventrees, though she had never danced it on a crowded ballroom floor, but she need not have worried, for her partner was expert and was so tall that he made her feel small and feminine, an unusual sensation for her. They moved as if moulded together and she hardly noticed that he was holding her closer than the regulation twelve inches.

'It is a refreshing change to dance with someone without being tickled under the chin by a feather head-dress,' he said, referring to the fact that her head was on a level with his shoulder and not the middle button of his waistcoat.

'And I to find I am not looking over my partner's head,' she responded quickly. 'You know, one of Papa's criteria for a husband for me is that he should be tall.'

He was slightly taken aback that she should be so outspoken about it but recovered himself quickly. 'What other requirements would a suitor need before he could approach the eligible Miss Wenthorpe?' he asked. 'A title, perhaps? And a fortune?'

She laughed, knowing he was bamming, but she was her brother's sister and if she had allowed a teasing to bother her she would have had a very unhappy childhood. 'Plain Mr is a title of sorts and a guinea might be a fortune to some poor beggar, so I suppose I could reasonably say yes to that.'

'And handsome?'

'Handsome is as handsome does.'

'And should he be head over heels in love with you?'

'Oh, that above everything,' she said, turning her head to laugh up into his face. He was regarding her with a slightly lop-sided smile and a light dancing in his eyes which disturbed her. It was as if he had thought of some jest but was unsure whether to share it with her. 'You do not agree with that, I see.'

'On the contrary,' he said. 'I concur whole heartedly. Do you think you will find such a one here?'

'Probably not,' she said. If her wager were to succeed it would have to be done when his lordship was absent, for he would, she was certain, see right through any disguise; he seemed to be able to look right into her heart and make it beat so fast she could hardly breathe. She was beginning to regret the impulse which had made her throw out such a challenge. It was madness. She smiled to herself. Mad and bad and heaven help her if she failed!

'A penny for your thoughts,' he offered, as they whirled round the floor in perfect unison, with his hand comfortably about her waist.

'Oh, no, my lord,' she said, colouring. 'Not even for a golden guinea.'

He laughed, so that the dowagers closest to them looked up with startled expressions and then began to whisper among themselves that Miss Wenthorpe was far too forward and it would be her just deserts if no one offered for her except that scapegrace

Longham, who would undoubtedly make her miserable. 'Then I must remain in ignorance, for I have no intention of bidding any higher.'

'I perceive, my lord, that you always consider carefully before you lay out your money.'

'Now, I wonder what you can mean by that observation?'

'I collect you were going to purchase a high-perch phaeton.'

'Was I? Then I changed my mind. It was an unnecessary extravagance.' He was enjoying the exchange, teasing her and titillating her curiosity. If she passed on what he had said to others, the town would soon believe he was mean-spirited as well as down on his uppers. Serve 'em right, he thought. He would not have his bride chosen for him by gossips or avaricious mamas, and if Ernest Grimshaw were to hear that he was without the blunt to pursue his case, then so much the better. 'Would you join me for a drive in the park one afternoon?'

'But how can I do that if you did not buy the phaeton?' she queried, lifting her eyebrows at him and proving that she, too, could tease. 'Surely you do not intend to drive me in that old coach of yours? I am still black and blue from my last outing in it.'

'It's that or nothing,' he said, trying in vain to keep a serious face. 'Do you dare?'

'My lord, you should know I never refuse a dare.'

'Then I will call for you the day after tomorrow. Shall we say at two?'

Oh, she should never have been so rash, she decided, as she lay sleepless in the early hours; it was almost as if the two glasses of champagne she had consumed had bemused her senses. Accepting the Marquis's dare was enough to put her beyond the pale, but the wager with her brother was almost criminal and certainly cruel. She began to wonder how she would feel if she were Amelia Thornton and such a prank were played on her. Mortified and humiliated were the words that came to mind. No, she could not do it and she would tell Tom so. If it cost her twenty pounds, then so be it.

But her brother was nowhere to be found when she rose towards noon and went in search of him. His bed, she discovered, had not been slept in and his valet vouchsafed the opinion that Mr Wenthorpe had gone on to play cards after escorting her and her aunt home after the ball; Barber had been told not to wait for him, so he could not be sure. Forced to wait for Tom's return, she decided to go for a ride and, ordering her horse to be saddled, she went to her room, changed into the blue velvet habit, perched the beaver on her curls and made her way to the stables, determined to gallop off her fit of the blue devils.

The day was fine, with a promise of spring, and Hyde Park was full of horses and carriages, barouches, phaetons, curricles, tilburys and gigs, each one containing its share of fashionable ladies, demi-reps and débutantes, together with their escorts, all wanting to be noticed, and the pace they were setting was slow, if not actually stationary. Riders were also out in great numbers on high-stepping thorough-breds, neat little cobs and hired hacks. She saw Lord Longham sitting astride a huge black stallion, engrossed in conversation with a modishly dressed lady in a barouche across the railing which divided the Row from the carriageway. They were laughing together, oblivious to others around them. Lydia reined in; she was in no mood to exchange polite nonsense when all she could think of was that foolish wager. He looked up and their glances met and held. Disconcerted, she wheeled her mount away and cantered off.

Finding herself in what might pass in the metropolis for open country, she set the horse to gallop with Scrivens vainly trying to keep up. 'It won't do, Miss Lydia,' he called after her. 'It won't do. At 'ome in Raventrees it don' matter, but in London. . .' When she returned home she was in a much better humour and even the scolding her aunt gave her for being late for nuncheon failed to dampen her spirits.

It was Tom who managed to do that. She met him on the stairs on her way to change out of her habit. His face was grey from lack of sleep, his hair was tousled and his cravat tied so carelessly it resembled nothing so much as a dishcloth. 'Tom, have you been up all night?' she demanded.

'Got caught up in a game at White's,' he said.

'Oh, Tom, you haven't lost a great deal of money, have you?' She looked directly into his face, but he could not meet her eye. 'Oh, you buffle-head! What will Papa say?'

He caught her hand and pulled her into his room, where he shut the door firmly. 'It ain't that much and he need never know.'

'How much?'

He hesitated, then mumbled, 'Five hundred.'

'Five hundred!' she squeaked, shocked to the core.

'How could you possibly have let it happen? Did you give them vowels?'

'Yes. I promised to pay by the end of the month.'

'How? Your allowance will never cover it.'

He smiled sheepishly. 'No, but I thought of a capital hum. I wagered five hundred that you would persuade Lady Thornton you were an eligible bachelor and would stand up with Miss Thornton at a ball.'

'You did what?' She sat down heavily on the bed, hardly able to believe her ears.

'You can do it, you know you can,' he went on, unperturbed. 'It's only like playing charades.'

She was almost angry enough to slap him. 'Who did you make this outrageous bet with?'

'Douglas Fincham. I have either to give him five hundred guineas by the end of the month or you have to become a man for an evening.'

She stared up at him. 'Oh, Tom, Tom, what have you done?'

'It was your idea in the first place, or I would never have thought of it.'

'It was a cork-brained idea. I changed my mind almost at once and decided to pay you the twenty pounds and forget the whole thing.'

'But Lydia, you can't,' he said in anguish. 'It will ruin me. I shall never hear the last of it. I shall be ostracised.'

'Serve you right.'

'Oh, Lydia, you can't mean that. I've got you out of any number of scrapes in the past. . .'

'Childish pranks,' she said with asperity. 'They were not like this at all.' She paused as the implication of what he had done came to her. How could she face everyone if it became public knowledge that she fancied herself as a man? She would lose what friends she had and the Marquis of Longham would be confirmed in his belief that she was the most outrageous hoyden in the country. She would never be able to look into those searching eyes again. 'Did you enter it in the betting book for all the world to see?'

'No, for it would not do for it to become public or Lady Thornton might hear of it. It was a private bet.' He stood looking down at her, unable to believe that she was prepared to renege on a wager; such a thing was unheard of, either for her or for him or anyone else who valued their reputation. 'That don't mean it don't have to be honoured,' he said. 'Besides, Fincham. . .'

'You could not have chosen a worse person to gamble with,' she put in sharply. 'He will never keep his tongue between his teeth if you do not pay up.'

'Do you think I don't know that?' he said miserably.

'We can't let it come to that.'

He brightened considerably. 'You'll do it?'

'I have only to deceive Lady Thornton?' she queried, her heart sinking. 'I may take Miss Thornton into my confidence?'

'No, you have to convince everyone and that includes Miss Thornton,' he said. 'And you have to complete the dance and leave undiscovered.'

'Supposing I cannot do it?'

'Oh, you can, you know you can. Oh, Lydia, do this for me, I beg you.'

'I don't see why I should make a fool of myself so that you may not make a fool of yourself,' she said. 'You must tell Papa.'

'Lydia, I'll die sooner than do that. Please. . .'

'How many other people know of this wager?'

'Only Frank Burford and a steward at the club.'

'Frank?' she queried. 'Is he in it too?'

'Well, you know old Frank. He must needs put his stake in.' He smiled suddenly. 'He has already seen you in disguise, don't forget.'

'In the schoolroom! That hardly counts and, besides, I had costumes and make-up there.'

'What costumes and make-up do you want? I'll undertake to obtain them for you. It would not do for you to be seen buying such things.'

'I don't know, I shall have to think about it. How am I to disguise curves I should not have and fill out those places where I am lacking. . .?'

'A tight waistcoat, padded shoulders and a little more fullness in the breeches. I am sure you can contrive.'

'Does it have to be a ball or will a small supper dance suffice?'

'It was not stipulated.'

'Then we will aim for a quiet evening where the lighting is likely to be more subdued than at a grand affair and the fashions need not be so up to the mark.'

'Then you will do it!' It was surprising how his weariness left him and his face came alight at the prospect of this burden being lifted from his shoulders. 'Oh, Sis, I knew you would. You've saved my bacon.'

'Only if I succeed.' It was madness to contemplate it, she knew, but if she could pull it off and the young Comte de Clancy was afterwards to disappear never to be seen again no harm would be done and Papa need never know what a young fool his son had been. 'I ought to have a rehearsal,' she said. 'Somewhere where we are not known.'

'I heard there is a fair on the Heath; what say you to that, two young men out for a lark?'

'Oh, very well,' she agreed, entering into the spirit of it now the die was cast. 'But how shall we get out of the house?'

In the event it was not difficult, because Mrs Wenthorpe decided to retire early after the exertions of the previous evening and as soon as she was safely in her room with a late-night drink of chocolate Lydia hurried to Tom's room, where she borrowed one of his suits of clothes and took it back to her own bedchamber.

There was very little difference in their height although he was broader than she was. A little padding in the shoulders of the frockcoat and a sash, half hidden by the waistcoat, to pull in the waist of the pantaloons soon put that right. That done, she surveyed herself in the long glass and then began on her face. Lampblack was used to emphasise her brows and make them thicker and the dregs from her coffee-cup used to darken her complexion. Pads of cotton stuffed into her cheeks made her face seem rounder and would also help to change her voice. Then she pushed her hair up under a wide-brimmed felt hat and decided she might do in a poor light, but in daylight or in the bright lights of a ballroom she would have to improve the make-up. She would not be able to change her hair colouring with dye, which she would have liked to do as an extra precaution against being recognised, because she would afterwards have to reappear as Lydia Wenthorpe, so she would have to wear a wig.

Tom called to her from the other side of her bedroom door and she ran to open it, standing before him, quizzing glass in hand. 'How do I look?'

'Bang-up,' he whispered in admiration. 'Not even Aunt Aggie would recognise you.'

'I hope she may not see me. Are you ready?'

'Yes. We'll hire a rumbler down the road.'

The night was dark and the gas lamps shed a poor light, which suited Lydia, and they took care not to linger when they came under their yellow glow. A hackney was found and in a very short time they were deposited on the outskirts of the fair and were soon swallowed up by the mêlée of people, old and young, male and female, gentry and artisan, who had come to enjoy themselves.

They attracted no attention as they wandered between stalls which offered a huge variety of goods from sweetmeats and mussels, to poems and broadsheets proclaiming the latest news. Prize-fighters, stripped to their waists, defied anyone to take them on, slack-rope walkers tottered precariously above their heads, barkers shouted for custom to view the bearded lady or the two-headed sheep. All around them were jugglers, fire-eaters, performing dogs and fortune-tellers.

'Shall you have your fortune told?' Tom asked. 'If

you can fool a fortune-teller, it would be a capital test.'

'Should I?' It had been so easy up to now and being lost in the crowds was certainly of little use as a test for her disguise. 'You'll wait close at hand?'

'I'll be right outside.'

Thus reassured, Lydia entered the tent where a gaudily dressed gypsy, all dangling earrings and bracelets, sat at a table. 'Sit ye down, young feller,' she said, indicating a chair opposite her and whipping the cover from a glass ball on the table. 'Which is it to be, the crystal or the palm?'

'The crystal.'

'Cross my palm with silver. A tanner will do but if you really want to know the future a fore-coachwheel would be the least of it.'

Lydia dug into her pocket and extracted a half-crown and put it into the gypsy's open palm.

'Ah, my lovely,' the old crone said. 'I do not need a crystal ball to tell me you are not what you seem.'

'Oh?' Lydia raised one blackened brow.

'You would have me think you are a young gentleman of fashion. . .'

'And I am not?' Lydia queried, keeping her voice huskily low.

'No, barely out of the schoolroom, you are. Your clothes are too big and no doubt belong to an older brother and your voice is scarce broken. Slipped your leash for a night, is that it? I do not think I care to take your money, for your future lies in a spanking from your papa and that needs no second sight.'

Lydia gave a low chuckle, determined not to let her pose lapse. If the old hag thought she was dealing with a boy, at least she was halfway to her goal. 'What can you tell me that does need a crystal ball?'

The gypsy put her hands around the glass and peered into its depths. 'That's strange,' she said. 'It is all misty, nothing is clear; it is as if someone were trying to deceive me. This I do not like.' She looked up with bright boot-button eyes. 'But this I do see—a fortune in gold and jewels, and a tall, dark man who is not pleased. Beware of trying to deceive him, young miss.'

'Miss?' she queried, taken aback.

'Thought you'd take me for a fool, did ye?' the old woman cackled. 'But it takes more than clothes and bootblacking to hoax a Romany princess. Do it for a wager, did ye?'

'Yes, yes,' Lydia said, afraid of the gleam in the woman's eye. 'I meant no harm. I can see you are, indeed, very clever and I will remember what you say about the tall, dark man.' With the gypsy's cracked laugh ringing in her ears, she ran from the tent and straight into the broad chest of the Marquis of Longham.

CHAPTER THREE

STARTLED, Lydia stifled the Oh! she had on her lips and changed it to a husky grunt, as he took a step backwards and looked down at her. 'Look where you're going, boy.'

'*Pardon, monsieur.*' Why had Tom not seen the Marquis and waylaid him, or tried to warn her? If it was his idea of a test for her disguise, then it was a very dangerous one. 'My fault entirely.'

The Marquis was regarding her in the same lop-sided way he had used at the ball and she was afraid he had penetrated her disguise. Oh, what a fool she had been to suppose she could get away with it! He was far too perceptive and if he recognised her now the whole masquerade would be at an end for she would never dare to repeat it in their own social circles. She was swamped by a feeling of relief at the thought of not having to do it, followed immediately by the dread of what Douglas Fincham would do. Tom was a fool and she was an even bigger one. And she would rather anyone but the Marquis know it.

'No harm done.' He touched the curly brim of his tall beaver and strode away to be lost in the crowds.

She let out a huge sigh and turned to look for Tom. He was standing on the edge of a knot of people watching a boxing match and had his back to her. She went to stand beside him and nudged his arm. 'Fine look-out you turned out to be.'

He turned and grinned. 'Oh, it's you.'

'Who did you think it was, Lord Longham?'

'No, why?'

'I just bumped into him.'

He seemed unconcerned, as he craned his neck to see the end of the bout. 'Did he recognise you?'

'If he did, he did not say so.'

'There you are, then!' He began pushing his way through the spectators to reach the front as the fight ended with the amateur challenger being carried off unconscious. The barker began haranguing the watchers for a new challenger. 'Who'll go a round with the champion?' he shouted. 'Who fancies themselves at the fisticuffs?' One round, that's all, one round and still standing and twenty yellow Georges will be yours. Come on, ain't there a fighter among ye?'

Tom pushed his way to the front and had his hand on the rope before Lydia realised what he intended. She pulled on his coat-tails. 'No, Tom, he'll kill you.'

While Tom turned to remonstrate with her, his opportunity was lost because another contender had climbed into the ring. 'Let's go home,' she said, more unnerved than she liked to admit by her encounter with the Marquis. 'I've had enough for one night.'

'After this bout,' he said, turning back to the ring and gasping with surprise because the man who was stripping off his coat and waistcoat was none other than Jack Bellingham. 'Oh, this will be a rum 'n and no mistake.'

He would not leave and they were so near the

front that Lydia could see every bruise the protagonists inflicted on each other and hear every grunt of pain; she found herself wincing and wishing she could look away, but she could not take her eyes from the two men, one huge and thick-set with cropped hair and a thick bull-neck which disappeared into massive shoulders, and the other, as tall as his adversary, but whose broad shoulders tapered to a slim waist and hips and whose long, supple legs were serving him well as he moved lithely about the ring. Jack Bellingham had boxed before, that much was evident, and he was giving as good as he got as they weaved and ducked and threw punches while the crowd yelled their support and Tom cried, 'Go to it, Jack! Send him to grass!'

The heavy pugilist, frustrated that he could not get the early knockout he was accustomed to, began to slow as the crashing punches with which he floored his less experienced challengers were, for the most part, knocked harmlessly aside. But the Marquis was not having it all his own way and Lydia winced and had to put her hand to her mouth to stop herself crying out whenever the fairground pugilist landed one of his ox-felling blows and Lord Longham's head rocked back with a sickening crunch. The round seemed never-ending and both boxers were visibly tiring when the crowd began to yell, 'The bell! Ring the bell, he's done it!'

But the barker was reluctant to do so, hoping his man could still floor the challenger and save him his twenty guineas. The fight went on, with both men becoming more and more exhausted until Lydia was sure they would fall together in a heap and neither be declared the winner, in which case the challenger would leave empty-handed. In the midst of her concern for him, she fell to wondering why he had gone into the ring in the first place. He was surely not short of twenty guineas, nor could he possibly enjoy being punched black and blue. And Tom had thought he would have a go! How glad she was that he had been prevented, but if the Marquis won her ninny of a brother might even now fancy his chances on the next bout. She pulled on his arm. 'Tom, let's go.'

He turned to her, grinning. 'What a mill! I ain't going before the end. Wait for me beside the gypsy's tent if you've no stomach for it.'

She turned and was trying to push her way out when the spectators, furious at the delay, began a concerted rush towards the barker, shouting again for him to ring the bell. Realising his danger, he complied and Lydia looked back to see Jack's hand raised in triumph. He was hoisted on to the shoulders of the nearest spectators, among whom her brother, grinning from ear to ear, was prominent. Tom was not in the least concerned about her, nor the fact that she was being buffeted about by the exultant mob. If he brought the Marquis over to her. . . Oh, how could he have forgotten their predicament? She felt herself go hot all over and was sure that sweat was trickling down her forehead and face, making tracks in her make-up. She could not face the Marquis a second time. She forced her way out of the crowd and found a hackney. Climbing in, she bade the driver wait and sat inside trying to compose herself while the spectators, knowing the entertainment was over for the night, dispersed in great good humour.

She sat on until Tom appeared with Lord Longham at his side and began to look about him for his 'cousin'. Shrinking back into the shadows of the hackney, she heard him say, 'I left him here somewhere, told him to wait, had to come and offer my felicitations before I left. What a mill! Where do you train? Oh, drat Maurice, where can he be?'

'Tired of kicking his heels and gone home perhaps?' The Marquis sounded weary, as well he might. The flickering light round the booth was poor, by Lydia was surprised to see no outward evidence that he had been in a gruelling fight, apart from a slight pinkness around his left eye and a cut on his right brow which sported a plaster. 'If it's all the same to you, Wenthorpe, I'll take this hackney and get off home myself.'

'What?' Tom sounded vague. 'Oh, yes, of course, take it; I shall have to stay and look for L... Maurice.'

Lydia could not let that happen. 'Tom!' She sat forward, glad the fairground lights were being snuffed out. '*Mon Dieu*, where 'ave you been 'iding?' She pretended a prodigious yawn. 'Do come 'ome; I am dead with *l'ennui*.'

Tom's face lit with relief and he grinned. 'Maurice! What a capital fellow you are to hold the last cab.' He turned to Jack. 'Will you join us?'

If she had hoped the Marquis would refuse, she was disappointed; he accepted cheerfully. She shrank to the opposite side of the carriage and pulled her hat down as Tom got in beside her and squeezed up to make room for the Marquis.

'My cousin, Maurice, Comte de Clancy,' Tom said, by way of introduction. 'Jack Bellingham, Marquis of Longham. You should have waited, Coz, for it was a capital fight and the Marquis stood up for the round and earned his twenty pounds. Had it not been the last bout, I would have made a challenge. . .'

'Poof,' she said, affecting the voice of the Comte. 'You Engleesh, I will never comprehend why you like so much the fighting.'

The Marquis laughed easily, though he must have been aching in every limb. 'That is why we win our wars.'

There was an uneasy silence until Tom said, 'My cousin has lately come from Canada; his father, my uncle, was French, you know. He took his family there at the beginning of the war to escape serving Bonaparte. He died there and so did his wife, but now the war is over Maurice has returned to claim his land and fortune. He came to England to see lawyers. . .'

'I hope he may have luck with the lawyers,' Jack said.

'You 'ave 'ad trouble with the law, *monsieur*?' Lydia put in, feeling she ought to make some contribution to the conversation.

'A trifling matter,' he said, then, to her consternation, added, 'I am sure we have met before.'

She was about to deny it, when Tom dug her in the ribs and muttered, 'Gypsy tent.'

'*Mais* I 'ave thought that also,' she drawled. 'I am not sure for there is not light enough to see.'

'It is your voice, I think,' Jack said, and Tom stifled a chuckle and turned it to a cough.

'Ah *je me souviens*,' she said. 'We—how do you say?—bumped outside the gypsy tent, *n'est-ce pas*?'

'Of course.' He seemed to accept that. 'And did you learn anything of value from the fortune-teller?'

She gave a low chuckle. 'If the 'ag speaks true, I will 'ave once more my fortune. She spoke of gold and jewels, and a dark man. I am to beware of 'im.'

'Did she say why?' Tom asked.

'*Non*. The crystal does not tell much for 'alf an Engleesh crown.'

Having said as much as she intended to on any subject, she lapsed into silence and Tom took up the conversation by asking where the Marquis lodged. On being told he had rooms at Albany, he ordered the driver to go there first, saying he would then drop his cousin off before going home himself. When the Marquis offered to share the cost of the hackney, Tom said it was his pleasure; after all, his lordship had furnished him with excellent entertainment and it was the least he could do.

As soon as Jack had been deposited on the steps of his apartments and they were on their way again, Lydia turned on her brother. 'Tom, how could you bring him to the cab? He of all people. . .'

Tom turned towards her. 'Of all people,' he repeated, grinning. 'Do you mean to say you have developed a *tendre* for the fellow. . .?'

'Of course not,' she said, so quickly that he was not in the least convinced. 'But we did travel to London in his coach. He has seen more of us than anyone. Why did you have to bring him out to me?'

'You would have left him to make his own way home, I suppose, after he had gone that gruelling round.'

'He did not have to go into the ring. I can't think why he did.'

Tom laughed. 'Like you, he is a devil-may-dare; he cannot refuse a challenge.'

'Then he must take the consequences.' It was not like Lydia to be unsympathetic to others' suffering and she felt more like ministering to his lordship's injuries than blaming him, but she was still shaking from the encounter and her narrow escape and her sharp tongue hid a multitude of tangled feelings she could not put into words, not the least of which was the sincere wish never to have set out on such a foolish escapade and never, never to have tried gulling the Marquis. If he ever found out, he would never speak to her again, and somehow the prospect of that filled her with melancholy. 'Oh, why did he have to be at that fair?'

'It was he who told me about it; said he might flex his muscles. . .'

'You knew he would be there! Tom, don't you care that he might have seen through my disguise?'

'You needed a good test, did you not? Besides, he saw me collecting my winnings; I could not have crept off without speaking to him.'

'Your winnings? Oh, Tom, you did not bet on the outcome?'

'Naturally, I did.'

'How much did you win?'

'A pony.' He smiled. 'Not enough to pay Fincham off if that is what you are thinking.'

'Oh,' she said, for that is exactly what she had been hoping. 'All the same, the more I think about this scheme of yours, the more worried I become. Someone, if not his lordship, is bound to see through my disguise and expose me. I shall never, never live it down. I think you should tell Papa. He will be angry but he will pay your debts.'

'Oh, sis, you are not turning traitor on me, are you? I cannot tell Papa. The last time he bailed me out, he gave me such a set-down, you've never heard the like—as if he had never lost a wager in his life!—and he said if it happened again he would cut off my allowance and make me live at home until I had repaid the whole.'

'He did not mean it.'

'Yes, he did. Rusticated by my own father; how could I endure that?'

'A great deal easier than I would live down passing myself off as the Comte de Clancy.' She paused, smiling in spite of herself. 'Why Canada?'

'If the Comte de Clancy had been in England since childhood, he would be known to someone, wouldn't he? No one as rich as he is supposed to be would be a stranger in Society. And he would have lost that dreadful accent you have saddled yourself with, so Canada it has to be.'

'And my fortune is still in France? Where exactly?'

'Oh, we shall think of somewhere. It is to the good that we met Longham. When others set the tale off, he will naturally affirm he has already heard it from the horse's mouth, so to speak.'

'Tom, I cannot do it.'

'You must.' He paused and seized her hand.

'Lydia, you cannot see me in such dire straits and do nothing to help me. I promise you it will never happen again, only do it, this once, please.'

The cab had drawn up at the door of Wenthorpe House. 'And is the Count lodging with you here?' she asked, making no move to get down.

'Yes.' He paused. 'Oh, lor', no, for if anyone were to call and ask for him. . .'

'Quite so. Now do you see what a spider's web we are weaving for ourselves? We shall be caught in our own trap.'

'A hotel.'

'A reputable hotel would deny the existence of a fictitious guest and a disreputable one would hardly endear the Count to Lady Thornton.'

'I know!' he said, eyes shining. 'The Count is lodging with Frank Burford. He can be trusted to make excuses for his not being at home if anyone should call.' He jumped down on to the flagway. 'I'll go in first and make sure the coast is clear.'

Tom had instructed his valet not to wait up for him and had ordered the door to be left unlocked against his return, so that there was no one in the hall as they crept indoors, lit the candles placed in readiness on the table and went up to bed.

'As soon as the whole dreadful sham is over, the Comte de Clancy will leave for France and will never be seen again,' she whispered. 'I want your word on that.'

'You have it,' he said, giving her a brotherly peck on the cheek as they reached her bedchamber. 'He can come to an untimely end, for all I care.'

Lydia slipped into her room without disturbing her

maid and made ready for bed, carefully hiding the male clothes in the back of her wardrobe so that Betty would not find them when she came to wake her, then she climbed between the sheets, blew out the candle and shut her eyes. But it was hopeless to expect to sleep; she tossed and turned, thinking of every kind of mishap which could reveal her deception to the whole world.

It would not have been so bad if the masquerade were to be enacted out of doors, simply to have some sport with Tom's contemporaries, but to deceive an innocent young lady and at a ball where knee-breeches or pantaloons had to be worn was the outside of enough. Quite apart from the clothes, she might forget herself and say or do something out of character; she might be taken ill or have an accident and a doctor sent, for who would know immediately that she was not what she pretended to be? Oh, there was no end to the dreadful possibilities; not least was the chance that someone would recognise her, particularly the Marquis of Longham, because he had a way of looking at her with eyes which seemed to see right into her soul. Just why she should feel that so keenly she could not fathom, unless Tom was right and she really was developing a *tendre* for the man. No, it could not be; she hardly knew him, and he had done nothing but look down his aristocratic nose at her ever since they met. The idea was unthinkable. Oh, she could cheerfully strangle her brother and that pimply Douglas Fincham, and Frank Burford too! But it was Frank who, in some measure, came to her rescue.

He arrived next day, long before the proper hour

for morning calls, and asked to see Tom. He refused to leave, even when told that Mr Wenthorpe was undoubtedly still asleep; he would, he said, wait for him. The footman, with a sigh which was meant to convey his disapproval of young men arriving on doorsteps before the streets were aired, went off to tell Tom's valet to rouse him. By the time the young man had put in a bleary-eyed appearance, Lydia had come downstairs and taken Frank into the breakfast-room.

'Frank Burford, I suppose you think I should make you welcome,' she said with an outspokenness which came of knowing him since they were both children. 'Let me tell you I am surprised at you encouraging Tom in this cork-brained idea and I have been thinking I will not do it.'

'You will ruin everything if you let us down now,' he said, looking pained. 'You can do it; you know you can.'

'I should have thought you had more care for Miss Thornton's feelings than to wish to humiliate her.'

'I do not want to humiliate her, only her stiff-rumped mama, and if that makes her think twice before throwing her daughter at every plump-pocketed dandy in town, then so much the better for my hopes. I have had a bang-up notion. . .'

She sighed. 'Not more, Frank, I beg of you.'

Tom came in at that point; his hair had been hastily combed and he looked only half awake. 'It's devilish early for morning calls, Frank,' he said and then, seeing his sister, 'And you are going too far to receive a gentleman alone. What will Aunt Aggie say?'

'Aunt Aggie never rises before noon, you know that, and as for Frank being a gentleman, I can think of other things to call him which are not so polite. . .'

'Children, children,' Frank said. 'Do stop your brangling and hear what I have come to suggest.'

'Have you had breakfast?' Tom asked him, helping himself to ham, eggs, oysters and muffins from the chafing-dishes on the sideboard. 'Take something and sit down. What about you, Lydia?'

'I'm not in the least hungry. I would rather hear what Frank has to say for himself, for I am heartily disgusted with him, and you too.'

Tom laughed. 'By the bye, Frank, did you know you had a Comte Maurice de Clancy lodging with you?'

'Who?'

'Comte Maurice de Clancy,' Tom repeated. 'He has lately come from Canada where his parents took him in '94. They have died and now the war is over he has come to England to see lawyers with a view to recovering his substantial lands and fortune in France.'

Frank looked puzzled. 'I have never heard of him, so how can he be lodging with me?'

'Oh, everyone will soon have heard of the charming young Comte,' Tom said airily. 'He is slight of stature and some might think effeminate, but, considering he has been brought up out of Society, he is the catch of the Season for some fortunate mama.'

The light dawned on Frank's features and he laughed aloud, slapping his thighs and saying, 'Oh, what a hum! What a Banbury!' Then, wiping his eyes with a lace-edged handkerchief plucked from his sleeve, he added, 'Now, do you want to hear my idea?'

'If we must, we must,' Lydia said with resignation.

'A costume ball. If the Comte is invited to a costume ball, then Lydia can wear something. . .' he paused, embarrassed '. . .something a little less. . .less tight than pantaloons or breeches.'

'Will that serve?' Lydia asked, as a ray of hope lightened the darkness of her foreboding.

'Nothing was said against it, so I don't see why not, as long as you are perceived as a man.'

'Who is to give such a ball?' Tom asked. 'And how can we be sure the Count will be invited?'

'I've already asked the doting parent,' Frank said, referring to his widowed mother. 'She has agreed, only stipulating it is not to be a squeeze. Fifty couples at the most, she said. I will invite the Comte and undertake to present him to Lady Thornton. What could be simpler?'

It was madness, all of it, and Lydia's head was in a spin, but she could see no way out of her dilemma without discrediting her brother and Frank, though she hated deceiving honest people, particularly Miss Thornton and Mrs Burford who must be led to believe she was entertaining a French count as a house guest. 'I suppose Miss Lydia Wenthorpe must develop the headache and cry off accompanying her brother to the ball,' she said waspishly. 'And then she must creep out of Wenthorpe House without a soul seeing her, make her way across to Park Street and then creep into Burford House, all ablaze with lights and surrounded by carriages with their grooms and drivers, and make her way up the stairs past everyone waiting to be greeted, in order to descend them again as the Count de Clancy, a young gentleman who has been his hostess's guess for at least a se'enight! I am persuaded nothing could be easier!'

'Oh, do not be such a cross-patch, Lydia,' said her brother. 'You will not be alone; Frank and I will be there.'

'And that odious Douglas Fincham too, doing his best to expose me.'

'Do you take us for a pair of widgeons? No, if he does that, the wager is off and he knows it. No interference from him, that was a condition.'

'It would serve better if Miss Wenthorpe came to the ball and became unwell after she arrived,' Frank said, his brow creased by unaccustomed thinking. 'She would then be found a bedchamber where she could rest and recover. Switching clothes and reappearing a little later as the Count would be easy.' He looked at her appealingly. 'When the deed is done, all you have to do is change back, return to the ballroom and say your headache has gone. The Count leaves for France, I collect my blunt and Tom his vowels, all right and tight.'

'And what do I do when I am denounced?' she demanded with some asperity.

'No one will denounce you,' Tom said. 'And you will have the satisfaction of knowing yourself to be the best actress in London, and earning my undying gratitude. I would do the same for you if the shoe were on the other foot.'

'Pretend to be a girl, you mean?' she queried, lifting one finely arched brow and smiling in spite of her annoyance with him.

'No, no,' he said quickly. 'I meant by coming to your rescue when you are in a scrape.'

This was so true, she immediately bit back the retort she had on her tongue and stood up, saying she meant to go out riding and they could do as they pleased for she had said and heard all she was going to hear and say on the subject of the Count for the rest of the day and the night too if she could contrive it.

The ride did nothing to ease her troubled thoughts and neither did the morning calls she subsequently made with her aunt. She felt even worse when she sat down to nuncheon and Mrs Wenthorpe looked at her in concern and asked her if there was anything troubling her. 'Only you do not look quite the thing,' she said. 'If you would rather not go to the opera tonight. . .'

'No, no, Aunt, I am perfectly well,' she said, wishing she could unburden herself but knowing she could not do anything of the kind. 'I have a little headache, that is all; it is nothing.'

'Then go and lie down, child. I shall go and visit Lady Courtney without you.'

'I think I would rather read in the garden. I fetched Caroline Lamb's *Glenarvon* from the library.'

If Mrs Wenthorpe thought that this was a strange way of curing a headache, she did not say so; her niece was perhaps in the throes of her first attachment and if that were so she hoped the object of it was the Marquis of Longham. She did not believe half the tales that were being circulated about him and he would be just right for her. She needed someone strong and as wilful and full of spirit as she was or she would be bored to death. Not that Mrs Wenthorpe would dream of interfering; she believed in letting nature take its course, just so long as the gentleman was suitable. Not in the least strait-laced, she would have smiled with satisfaction if she had been at home to witness the events of the afternoon.

Lydia was descending the stairs with her book in one hand and her parasol in the other when she heard the front doorbell jangle. She paused on the half-landing while a footman went to answer it and, though she could not see the caller, the voice she knew. 'I believe Miss Wenthorpe is expecting me.'

In all the business over the Comte de Clancy, she had forgotten the Marquis's challenge, but he evidently had not. He was being admitted now and having a tricorne hat taken from him. It was not just his hat which made Lydia open her eyes in surprise, but the rest of his clothes. He was dressed like a common coachman in a heavy brown overcoat which had at least five capes and huge flap pockets, and which was so long that its skirts fell below the tops of his boots. He was such a comical sight that she could not suppress a laugh, making him look up at her.

'Miss Wenthorpe, good afternoon.' He attempted to make a leg but the heavy coat impeded him, then, realising she was not dressed to go out, he added, 'You were expecting me?'

She walked slowly down the stairs towards him, gripping the banister rail while she fought to regain possession of her senses. Had he recognised her the night before? Why did the sight of him make her feel so guilty, so exposed, so utterly contemptible? 'I. . . I did not think you meant it. . .'

'Meant it! Surely you did not think me so wanting in conduct as to renege on an invitation?'

'No, of course not,' she said quickly, taking hold of herself. Who was he but a pocket-pinched ex-soldier, no one to fear at all. 'Why are you wearing that ridiculous coat, when the weather is already over-warm for the end of March?'

He grinned. 'I thought it would be just the touch.'

'And from that I may assume that the vehicle you have waiting outside is that monstrous travelling chaise and that you intend to drive it?'

'Of course,' he said, bowing again and smiling broadly. 'Had you forgot my challenge? I shall understand if you should wish to cry off.'

Lydia could well have backed out at this point but the little devil-may-dare inside her urged her on. 'Poof!' she said, wondering why this remark should make the Marquis suddenly look startled, as if she had uttered something profound. 'If you wait while I change into something more suitable I will show you whether the Wenthorpes do not dare!' She paused, looking thoughtful. 'My aunt is out; do you think my maid will suffice as a chaperon, seeing you will be on the box and not sitting inside with me?' Before he could answer she laughed softly. 'I am afraid the poor girl will hate it; she stands far higher on her dignity than ever I do.' Leaving Jack staring after her, she hurried upstairs to change.

Betty was in her mistress's room, busily putting away discarded clothes and making a heap of those needing to be cleaned. She readily abandoned her task when told she was going to accompany her mistress on a carriage ride in the park and helped her into a skirt of a plain blue weave and a caraco jacket frogged in silver. While Lydia put on her hat with its sweeping feather, the maid fetched her best pelisse and bonnet. It was not until she saw the Marquis and then the vehicle in question that she realised that this was some sort of hum. She hung back. 'Oh, Miss Lydia, you never mean to ride in that thing *again*!'

'Indeed I do. Now get in. If you sit back, no one will see you.'

But it was soon evident that Miss Wenthorpe herself had no such reservations. Might as well be hung for a sheep as a lamb, she told herself, sitting forward in her seat and smiling, her violet eyes brimming with mischief. They made their way towards Hyde Park with the Marquis sitting on the box, flicking his whip and weaving the coach in and out of the traffic just as if he had been driving the latest bang-up rig. Fully expecting to find herself in the daily parade of phaetons, curricles, landaulets and gigs to be found there, Lydia realised, after they had turned into the park, that this was not to be. They turned aside on to a quiet lane where there was no one to be seen except a couple of urchins chasing a mongrel and a single gentleman rider who reined in and looked at the carriage as if it had come from another age, which, indeed, it had. The lane became rather bumpy and, though the Marquis drove well, it took all his concentration to keep the coach on the road.

'Oh, miss, wherever is he taking us?' Betty wailed. 'I thought we were going to drive in the park.'

'We are in the park,' Lydia said sharply, not wanting to admit that she was also puzzled.

'He is carrying us off to have his evil way with you. Whatever shall we do?'

'Don't be a goose.' All the same Lydia put her head out of the window and called up to the box. 'My lord, do please stop.'

It was a minute before he could bring the coach to a standstill, but he managed it, to the admiration of the solitary rider, if no one else, and then turned to look down at her. 'My apologies, Miss Wenthorpe, I had not realised that this path was so rough.'

'Turn round at once and take us home.'

'It cannot be done,' he said with a hint of a smile. 'This old coach needs half an acre to come about and if we leave the path we may well overturn. If we go on to the trees ahead of us, we shall find oursevles at the end of the Ride and can turn there.'

'Then please do so.' Furious with him, she withdrew her head and they moved forward again. If he was trying to teach her some kind of lesson, she had no idea what it was, but it did occur to her that if he had really meant to humiliate her he would have driven the coach straight along the Ride where they would have been seen by all the occupants of the fashionable carriages who were daily to be seen there.

Two minutes later he pulled up in the shade of the copse of trees, where a spanking new curricle harnessed to a very fine pair of chestnut horses was standing empty. A servant, lolling against a tree, jumped to attention as soon as he saw them arrive. The Marquis sprang lightly from the box-seat and came to open the door and let down the step for Lydia to alight. 'I felicitate you on your courage, Miss Wenthorpe,' he said, smiling broadly and holding out his hand. 'And now you shall have your reward. Come.' He led her over to the curricle and handed her in before taking off the coachman's hat and coat and revealing himself in buff-coloured pantaloons, a magnificent coat of mulberry superfine, a striped silk waistcoat, and a cravat mathematically knotted around a high starched collar. Throwing the discarded coat and hat at his man, who caught them deftly, he picked up a tall beaver from the seat of the curricle and clapped it on his head. 'Tewkes, be so good as to escort Miss Wenthorpe's maid home and put the coach away.'

Ignoring Betty's protests, Tewkes climbed on the box of the coach and turned it back the way it had come while his lordship, smiling perversely, took his seat beside Lydia. 'Now, let us put matters to rights, shall we?' he said, picking up the ribbons and turning into the carriage ride.

'And how much did you wager that I should do it?' she enquired mildly, as they were bowled along, bowing this way and that at the other carriages with their illustrious and modish occupants.

'Wager, Miss Wenthorpe?' he asked innocently.

'Yes. Do not try and gull me into believing you had nothing on the outcome.'

He laughed. 'You know, Miss Wenthorpe, I never thought of it. When I made the dare I had meant only to drive a little way with the coach blinds drawn, just to show you that it does not do to take up rash challenges. . .' He turned his direct hazel eyes on her, making her shrink inside herself with guilt. Was he looking at her and seeing the Comte de Clancy? 'But I soon saw that would not serve, for never did I see anyone less mortified by the prospect.'

'Thank you, my lord,' she said, bowing to Lady Jersey who acknowledged her graciously. 'But a dare is a dare, after all.'

'And you would not have cared?'

'Did I look as though I did?'

'You do not mind being thought a trifle. . .' he paused, smiling '. . .eccentric?'

'Not in the least. It would not be the first time.' He could make of that what he liked, she thought, Comte de Clancy and all.

'Nevertheless, I could not parade you in front of the *ton* in that dilapidated vehicle, whatever the dare,' he said. 'So I hit on the idea of taking a roundabout way where we would not be seen until now.'

'It was kind of you, but unnecessary. And I am still lacking conduct, for you have sent my chaperon home.' She pretended to sigh, but could not suppress a smile. 'Aunt Aggie will wash her hands of me.'

'No, she won't, for if anyone should mention seeing you I shall own that it was entirely my fault because I hoaxed you.'

'But why should you do such a thing?'

'A wager, you said so yourself. Everyone gambles; it is the accepted thing. . .'

'But I collect you do not approve of gambling,' she said.

'I have seen many a good man ruined by it. And ladies, too. Do smile at Lady Hertford, my dear; she will think you in the suds because of something I have said. You are a gambler yourself, are you not?'

'Only for fun with Tom sometimes.' Oh, she was getting in deep and the more he said, the more worried she became. 'And not for money. Well,' she added truthfully, 'only a very little.'

'Then it must be for the joy of creating a mull.'

'Now, why should I do that?'

'From boredom, perhaps?' He touched his hat to Lady Sefton. 'I am persuaded there are times when you envy your brother.'

'Envy Tom? How, my lord, have you come to that conclusion?'

'Men have a much livelier time of it than ladies, do they not? They are not so bound by convention. They come and go as they please, they can gallop if they've a mind to and don't need chaperons.'

She decided to ignore his reference to having seen her galloping. 'But they have responsibilities, is that not so? They must protect and provide for their womenfolk and worry about managing their estates, and politics and waging war and coping with their labourers, who must be treated firmly but fairly. At least, that is what Papa would have me believe.'

'And do you?'

'Naturally I do.' She smiled mischievously. 'I am a dutiful daughter.'

'From that I may deduce you do not feel restricted and are enjoying your come-out Season?'

'Of course.'

'Then, knowing the risks, why did you not do the ladylike and refuse to drive out with me?'

'That would have been a dishonourable thing to do after accepting your challenge.'

'Exactly my point,' he said, with satisfaction.

She changed the subject hurriedly; he was getting too near the bone. 'Why have you kept that disreputable coach?'

'Oh, I might yet find a use for it,' he said airily. 'But I shall not ask you to ride in it again.'

He would never ask her to ride in anything with him again, she decided, if the coil she had got herself into ever came to light. She longed to confess, but wondered what he would say if she did. Would he laugh and think it a capital rig or would he condemn her forever for the hoyden she had protested she was not? She had a sinking feeling it would probably be the latter.

She looked up to see a yellow-painted landaulet with the hood down approaching them, bearing two ladies she knew very well. One was Frank Burford's mother, a lady of ample proportions dressed in a hideous purple mantle with wooden cherries nodding under the brim of her bonnet, and the other, severely dressed in grey jaconet, was her companion, Miss Whiting.

'Why, Miss Wenthorpe!' Mrs Burford called as the coaches drew level and stopped within two feet of each other. 'How are you?'

'I am well, thank you, Mrs Burford. Allow me to introduce the Marquis of Longham.'

'Longham,' she said, peering through her glass at

him. 'Know you, don't I? Son of the Duke of Sutton, if I'm not mistaken.'

The Marquis bowed and smiled. 'Yes, ma'am.'

'Knew you and your brother when you were both in short coats; how many years ago must it be? No, we will not go into that. I was sorry to hear of Edward's death; such a shock to the Duke, I imagine. Give my condolences when next you see His Grace. He was a friend of my late husband, don't you know? How is he keeping?'

'Tolerably well, ma'am, but afflicted with gout. It keeps him in the country. . .'

'It's gout, is it?' She had heard otherwise. 'To be sure, that's bad enough, and I'm sorry, but it's better than being touched in the attic, like the poor king.'

Lydia, aghast at the tactlessness of the woman, turned to look at her escort; his jaw had tightened and his smile had faded a little, but he gave no other sign that the barb had gone home. Mrs Burford prattled on, unaware of the tension she had created. 'It must be prodigious hard stepping into your brother's shoes so soon after returning from Waterloo and then to have to take over the estate from his grace, when by all accounts it has been sadly let go.' Hardly drawing breath, she continued. 'You will come to my costume ball, will you not? It is to be on the first day of April; such an appropriate day for dressing up, don't you think?'

'Indeed, yes, ma'am.' Jack's expression remained immobile.

'Give me your direction and I will see you are sent an invitation. It will be an intimate affair, just a few friends to whom we can introduce the Comte de

Clancy. The poor boy knows so few people in London. . .'

'The Comte de Clancy?' queried the Marquis, and Lydia knew with heart-stopping certainty that if he had been going to refuse the invitation on account of Mrs Burford's veiled insults he would not do so now. He would go simply to satisfy his curiosity. If he had not seen her mortified by the prospect of parading in the old coach, he could, if he chose to turn and look at her now, see exactly that; her cheeks were bright pink and there was a light in her eyes which was almost terror.

'Yes, do you know him?' asked Mrs Burford.

'I have made the young gentleman's acquaintance, ma'am.' He turned towards Lydia and again she received that penetrating look. 'I collect he is cousin of yours, Miss Wenthorpe.'

Her mouth was so dry and her heart pumping so furiously, it was an effort to speak, but she managed to murmur an affirmative.

'He is to be Frank's guest for a few days,' Mrs Burford went on. 'It is better than lodgings or a hotel, especially as all the best ones are beginning to fill up at this time of year, though why he cannot stay at Wenthorpe House I do not know.' She heaved a sigh which made her many chins wobble above her heaving bosom. 'Our family don't go in for these cork-brained family feuds, I'm glad to say. Agatha Wenthorpe ought to feel ashamed of herself for prolonging it. I am in two minds whether to invite her. Do you think they will bury the hatchet for one evening? I should hate to be the cause of any ill feeling for the boy; Agatha has a cutting tongue when she decides to use it.' She paused only long enough to draw breath. 'But she is Miss Wenthorpe's chaperon and I cannot leave her out without leaving Miss Wenthorpe out and Frank would never hear of that.'

Lydia felt she ought to make some reply to this, but her head was in a whirl and she could think of nothing which would not complicate matters even further. Frank had obviously returned home and regaled his mother with a much embroidered story of how the Count came to be in England, and until she saw him again she had no idea what it was. And now she had colluded in the whole charade by agreeing that the Count was a relative, and it had all gone beyond the point when she could back out.

She became aware that his lordship had taken a card from his cardcase and was handing it to Mrs Burford, who tucked it into her reticule. 'I shall look forward to seeing you at Burford House,' she told him with a smile.

The coaches drew apart to go their separate ways with Lydia so immersed in her troubles that she could barely bid the other ladies good-day. Frank and Tom had both promised her they would not invite the Marquis to the ball, but how were they to know Mrs Burford would do it for them? Oh, what had she let herself in for?

She stole a glance at her escort. He was looking severe, but whether it was because of Mrs Burford's insults to his family or because he knew the Comte de Clancy was not all he seemed she could not tell. She tried to close her eyes and her heart to the feelings which assailed her; pleasure in his company, for there was nothing dull or ordinary about him and he seemed to understand her—too well sometimes; and a wish, which she would not for the world have openly admitted, to be held high in his esteem. She suspected that beneath his outwardly haughty manner was a caring man who would always be loyal to his friends. On the other hand, she had no doubt that he would make a deadly enemy! She was reminded of the gypsy's warning to beware a tall, dark man and shivered a little.

He turned to smile at her, making her insides quiver like a blancmange. 'Are you cold?'

'Not at all.'

'Then what is wrong?'

'Wrong?' she queried, falsely bright. 'Why should anything be wrong?'

'I don't know,' he said, so gently that she felt like bursting into uncharacteristic tears. 'But something has upset you and I don't believe it has anything to do with riding in the old coach. You were perfectly at ease until we met Mrs Burford.'

'There is nothing wrong, my lord. I cannot think why you should say such a thing.'

He stopped the carriage and turned towards her. 'I say it because I feel it,' he said softly, taking her hands in his. 'And you are shaking. Are you afraid of me?'

She dared not look up into those limpid eyes or she would be lost to all reason; instead she stared down at his strong brown hands, holding hers so tenderly, and that was nearly as bad. 'No, my lord.'

'But you are troubled.' He paused, waiting for her

to answer, but when she did not he added, 'I wish you would tell me why.'

'I. . .' She stopped. If only she could confide in him, but that would only give him a disgust of her. He was one of those rare people who did not gamble and he preferred ladies who behaved like ladies. She took a deep breath and made herself look up to meet his gaze. 'There is nothing in the least troubling me and you are making people stare at us. Please drive on.'

'As you wish.' He picked up the reins and they continued on their way in silence, both feeling hurt and dejected and neither knowing the reason.

CHAPTER FOUR

Lord Longham was such an unconscionable time taking his leave after bringing her home that Lydia began to think he was delaying on purpose to discomfort her. He knew she was worried, he had said so, and he imagined it had something to do with Mrs Burford's remark about a family quarrel and he was curious, especially as he had met the Count out with Tom the evening before and there had been no evidence of a family quarrel then. She stood, bonnet and gloves in her hand, wishing he would go away instead of smiling and making himself agreeable to her aunt. And now Aunt Aggie was inviting him to stay and take some refreshment and if he accepted then the subject of the Comte de Clancy was sure to come up. She dared not look at him and held her breath for his reply.

'I regret, ma'am, that I have another engagement,' he said, with a smile which captivated Mrs Wenthorpe and filled her niece with apprehension. 'But give me leave to call again.'

'Any time, my lord, any time,' her aunt said, offering her hand, which he took and raised to his lips.

'Your servant, ma'am.' He turned to bow over Lydia's hand and the mocking smile he gave her seemed to say, I have not done with you yet; I shall ask you again and again until I am satisfied. Aloud he said, 'Miss Wenthorpe, your servant. May I have the pleasure of your company again soon?'

'I am much engaged,' she said, wishing he would leave so that she could go and find her brother. And that young man would know the length of her tongue when she did. 'Will you go to Mrs Burford's costume ball?'

'If you are going to be there, Miss Wenthorpe, then I would not miss it for worlds,' he said, and finally took his leave.

She ignored her aunt's scold at her coolness towards him when he had been nothing but amiable, and, murmuring that she was going up to change, she hurried from the room and tracked Tom down in the library, where he was lounging in one of the armchairs, reading the *Morning Post.*

'What family quarrel, pray?' she demanded, without preamble. 'What Mrs Burford thought of me I cannot think, for I sat in his lordship's curricle with my mouth open like a fish out of water when she said the Count was staying with her on account of some disagreement in the family.'

He looked up at her, standing in front of him with her eyes blazing and her cheeks pink with annoyance. 'Do come down from your high ropes, Lydia; you will surely alert Aunt Aggie that something is afoot if you go about in such a bubble. Sit down. What did you say to Mrs Burford?'

She refused to sit. 'There was nothing I could say, though she must have wondered at it. What Banbury tale have you told her, Tom?'

'I? Nothing at all. It was Frank. You see, when he asked if the Comte de Clancy might stay a few days, she naturally asked why he could not come to Wenthorpe House. The Count is supposed to be our cousin, after all. Frank could think of nothing but a quarrel between his parents and Aunt Aggie and Aunt Aggie's determination never to speak to any member of the de Clancy family again.'

'Oh, Tom, he ought not to have brought Aunt Aggie into it. What she will say when she finds out I shudder to think. A scolding will be the very least of it.' She sat down suddenly in the chair opposite him. 'Tom, we must forget the whole thing; we are getting in too deep. There will be more questions we cannot answer and more stories until we have got ourselves into such a bumblebath there will be no getting out of it.'

'Fustian! It is too late to back out now. Mrs Burford is expecting the Count, bag and baggage this afternoon.'

'No, Tom, no. It is over a week to the ball; I cannot stay there in disguise all that time and don't you think Aunt Aggie will notice my absence from here?'

'We have thought of that. The Count is in London on business, so he will spend a great deal of his time with lawyers and such like; he will hardly be at home at all.'

'And what about evenings and at breakfast?' she asked with some asperity.

'The Count is an early riser and will be out of the house long before his hostess makes an appearance, and he will be out most evenings. He is intent on seeing all the plays and operas, visiting Vauxhall Gardens, not to mention the gambling hells. Frank says his mother will not find it the least remarkable that she never sees her guest. And he will ruffle up the bed and leave linen for the wash to allay the servants' suspicions.'

'But Mrs Burford will meet the Count when he arrives. If she should recognise me straight off. . .'

'She won't. I have acquired a whole box full of clothes, stage make-up, wigs, beards, everything you need; so, you see, I have not been idle while you have been amusing yourself with Longham.'

'Amusing myself! I was never so discomfited in all my life.'

'Ah!' he said, knowingly. 'That is the nub of it. It is the Marquis of Longham who occupies your mind, not your poor brother.'

'Nothing of the sort!' she snapped. 'But he dropped more than a hint he knew I was up to something and then we met Mrs Burford. . .' She paused. 'What else has Frank told his mother?'

'Only enough to satisfy her curiosity. The Count has come to London to see lawyers about his fortune and his lands. He has not been in England long enough to set up his own establishment or acquire things like horses and carriages, and would not want to, not having decided if he will stay in this country.'

'It gets worse and worse,' she said, her heart sinking into the jean half-boots she wore. 'I can't do it.'

'Course you can. It ain't as if we are doing any harm. . .'

'No harm!' she squeaked. 'One falsehood after another, a veritable Canterbury tale becoming more and more involved. Hoist on our own petard, that's what we'll be. It will be on the lips of every tattle-monger in town and my reputation and prospects will be ruined.'

'I shall be ruined if you do not,' he said sharply. 'You don't suppose Fincham will keep his tongue between his teeth, do you?' He paused and when she did not answer went on, 'Come, dearest of sisters, you can do it on your head. 'Tis only a little charade, after all, and Frank and I will be on hand to protect you.'

She was not at all sure that either could be relied on to do that, but neither did she see how she could back out when Mrs Burford was expecting her guest that afternoon. 'I shall go with you to Park Street,' she said tersely. 'But if Mrs Burford shows the slightest suspicion, we will confess it all a prank and take our leave.'

He laughed with pleasure and, jumping to his feet, pulled her up and whirled her round. 'Oh, I knew I could count on you. The clothes and make-up are in the attic; thought it best not to leave it in your room. We'll have to carry it to Burford House ourselves; can't involve the servants. I've told Aunt Aggie we are dining with Mrs Burford and as she don't like Frank's mother above half she don't care a groat that she is not to come too. She says she will dine in her room.'

Lydia spent the remainder of the afternoon with her aunt but, as Mrs Wenthorpe liked to chatter, all that was required of her was to say 'yes' or 'no', or 'indeed' as she plied her embroidery needle. At five o'clock her aunt rose to go to her room and, once the door had safely closed on her, Lydia sped up to the attic and found the trunk Tom had left there. In less than an hour she crept out, dressed in a high-collared coat with rows of frogging, a blue and white striped satin waistcoat and voluminous Petersham cossacks which were so outlandish a new fashion that the sight of her sent Tom into gales of silent laughter. On her head she wore a wig of golden curls cut in the Windswept style. Her eyebrows had been thickened, her cheeks padded, her nose made larger and there was a slight shadow under her eyes which betokened lack of sleep.

'Oh, bang-up,' her brother whispered, as he picked up her portmanteau and carried it downstairs. 'You will take the town by storm.'

'I do not intend to do any such thing,' she hissed back as they reached the hall. 'Do be silent or you'll have the whole household out to see what the racket is.'

Tom had already brought a hackney to the side-entrance and they climbed into it with a sigh of relief. Not ten minutes later they were being admitted to Mrs Burford's drawing-room and the good lady was coming towards the Comte, chins wobbling under her smile, and holding out her hand. 'I am pleased to meet you, Count. Frank has told me all about you. Such a pity you should find no welcome at Wenthorpe House, but no matter, you are welcome here.'

'Your servant, *madame*,' the Count said languidly, bowing over her hand. 'We will not talk of things so un'appy, *non*? It is good that I 'ave a 'ome found 'ere.'

'One of the footmen will take your baggage to

your room,' Mrs Burford said, sitting down and indicating a chair beside her. 'We will have a comfortable coze until it is time to dress for dinner.' She cast an eye over the Count's cossacks as she spoke and suppressed a smile. 'Frank will be here directly and he will show you to your room. I collect you do not wish for a dresser, for I am sure we can find someone to help you if you do.'

'*Merci*, *madame*, but me, I like to dress myself.'

Frank arrived at this point and joined in the conversation, prompting Lydia with leading questions about her family and her life in Canada and regaling them at some length with all the latest *on-dit* and offers to take the Count out and about, until, at last, he suggested taking their guest to his room so that he could dress for dinner.

'You will stay, Tom, won't you?' Frank said. 'You do not subscribe to the feud, do you?'

'I cannot understand Agatha,' Mrs Burford said, as Tom accepted the invitation. 'It is not like her to bear a grudge.'

'Oh, it is something and nothing,' Tom said quickly. 'My aunt will be over it in a week, I'll wager.'

'I do hope so. I do not want any unpleasantness at my ball. . .'

'If *madame* wishes, I will not attend,' the Count said, earning startled looks from Tom and Frank.

'Not come! Why, the ball is in your honour, my dear Count!' Mrs Burford exclaimed. 'There can be no question but you will come.' She rose ponderously to her feet and the young men sprang to theirs. If

Lydia was a little slow to do likewise, Mrs Burford did not seem to notice it. 'Now I will go and change.'

As soon as she had gone, Tom and Frank clapped each other on the shoulders, congratulating themselves on the success of the ruse and calling Lydia poor-spirited when she demurred. Frank, in fine good humour, took her up to a guest room on the second floor and left her to change for dinner, saying his room was next door and to shout out if she needed anything. The only thing she needed, she told him tartly, was to wake up and find it had all been a dream. But as her wish was not to be granted she changed into dark pantaloons, grey waistcoat and an evening coat with well-padded shoulders, and went down to dinner.

It was an interminable evening and she found herself having to invent a history for the Count which sounded so false in her ears that she wondered at Mrs Burford's gullibility. Having invented a cache of gold and jewels, she was obliged to elaborate by saying it had been hidden on the de Clancy estate when the family fled and only on her father's deathbed had she learned the hiding place. She planned to go to France shortly to recover it.

'Oh, how romantical!' Mrs Burford cried, and Lydia knew with dreadful certainty that the story would be all over town the following day. 'I wish you may find it and return safely, for I declare France is not the place to be now, what with occupying armies and bands of brigands roaming the countryside.' She heaved herself to her feet. 'Now if you will excuse me I shall retire.'

The young men rose and Tom declared his intention of returning home. 'I promised Aunt Aggie I would not be late,' he said, leaving the room with Mrs Burford.

Lydia turned to Frank. 'Now what am I to do?'

'Do? Why, go to bed, Count.' He smiled suddenly. 'Change back into skirts and creep down as soon as you hear my mother's door shut. I will let you out of the house and Tom will be waiting with a cab.'

When she joined Tom half an hour later, she told him in no uncertain terms that she would not for the world go through an evening like that again and if he thought she would he was very much mistaken.

During the following week the Count, though never seen, became the subject of the latest gossip and Lydia tried, largely unsuccessfully, to put him from her mind and enjoy her Season. She visited the opera and attended a supper party given by one of Aunt Aggie's bosom bows, went to Vauxhall Gardens and for drives in Hyde Park, when Tom allowed her to take the ribbons of the phaeton, and generally was seen by everyone, including the Marquis of Longham, who kept his promise to call again and asked her to ride out with him.

Above all else, she loved to ride, and as Tom spent more time than was good for him at his club he could never be roused from his bed early enough to accompany her and she felt starved of her customary fresh air and exercise. Riding with the Marquis was a pleasure, particularly as he did not seem disposed to mention their last encounter. She supposed he had delivered his little lecture and had assumed, like most self-opinionated men, that she had taken it to heart and was now prepared to behave in the proper ladylike manner. It irked her a little that he should be so loftily presumptuous, but as she had no wish to reopen the discussion she let it go.

He seemed to know, without being told, that she would prefer to ride in Green Park rather than the more fashionable Hyde Park where gossip, rather than exercise, seemed to be the order of the day, and they turned in at the Bath Gate with the faithful Scrivens in attendance. After half an hour, in which the horses were put through their paces, they dismounted to walk and talk. Lydia had to admit that he was an amusing and knowledgeable conversationalist, that he had a sense of the ridiculous which was refreshing and that his smile, when it reached his eyes, transformed him from a haughty aristocrat to a gentleman of immense charm. If only the spectre of the Comte de Clancy did not loom between them!

His lordship did not seem interested in gossip, the scandalous behaviour of Caroline Lamb or the latest *on-dit* about Beau Brummel and Lord Byron, but, on being encouraged to do so, told her something of his experiences on the battlefields of Europe, carefully omitting the worst horrors. This led to a discussion of politics, the falling price of corn and his sympathy for the labourers. ''Tis little wonder they riot and break up machinery,' he said. 'Like those of us who should have known better, they expected peace to bring Utopia with it.'

'You do not think we could have a Revolution like they had in France?' she queried.

'There are those who fear it, but I do not think so,' he said with a wry smile. 'The guillotine is a French invention and I doubt the aristocracy of

England will be obliged to flee their homes in the way your cousin, de Clancy, did.'

She stiffened. Had he deliberately introduced that name in order to test her? If he had, he had ruined what had been a happy interlude. He was still playing his cat-and-mouse game with her and she would not endure it. 'Goodness, how late it is!' she exclaimed, beckoning to Scrivens to come and help her mount and puzzling Jack, who could so easily have offered his hand to throw her into the saddle. 'I must go; I have a costume-fitting in half an hour.'

Her abrupt ending of their outing must have confirmed his poor opinion of her, she realised afterwards, but she could not have continued their conversation with anything like an easy mind. He remained amiable and pretended not to notice her silence as they rode back to Wenthorpe House, where he politely refused her far from enthusiastic invitation to come in for refreshment. 'I shall see you at Mrs Burford's ball, I hope?' he said, dismounting and escorting her to the door.

'Yes, indeed,' she said, trying to hide her wretchedness behind a bright smile. 'I am looking forward to it.'

She was far from anticipating any pleasure at that function and, though she tried, she could not prevail on Tom to abandon the masquerade.

'If word gets out I cannot even pay a debt of honour, then I'll be dunned by every tradesman in town,' her brother said when she tried. 'We are in too deep to back out. Mrs Burford is convinced, so why not Lady Thornton?'

Lydia could see nothing for it but to choose a

costume for the Count which would help to hide her curves and have it delivered to Burford House in readiness for the ball. But that would not satisfy Tom; he insisted Lydia should go with him to pay a morning call on Mrs Burford the day before the ball and once again she found herself taking part in a farce which, in spite of her misgivings, made it difficult to keep a straight face.

Frank, who was expecting them, was sitting with his mother in the morning-room when they arrived. Once the usual greetings had been exchanged and Mrs Burford had told Lydia how comely she looked in her yellow and white striped silk gown, and how well she had managed to match the ribbons in her bonnet, Frank informed them the Count had been up half the night playing cards at White's and was still abed and he would go and wake him. Being nudged by Tom into a reply, Lydia said she had another engagement and could not wait. 'If you wish to stay,' she said to her brother, as she drew on her lemon kid gloves, 'I'll take a chair and leave the phaeton to you.'

A chair was procured and she took her leave while Frank went to rouse the Count. As soon as she had rounded the corner, Lydia dismissed the chairman and hurried back to the side-entrance of the house, where Frank was waiting to let her in. They crept up to the Count's room, where he left her to change while he went back to his mother and Tom. 'Maurice will be down directly,' he told them. 'He is trying on his costume for the ball.'

Lydia had chosen an eighteenth-century costume because its full coat would help to disguise her curves and it was a time when the lavish use of make-up was normal. Working rapidly, she stripped off her gown and sat down before the mirror to transform her face into that of the plump-cheeked, dark-browed Comte de Clancy, adding a liberal amount of white paint and powder and a patch beneath one eye. When she was satisfied with her face, she took the costume from her portmanteau and put on a silk shirt, white breeches and stockings and shoes with high red heels and silver buckles. Flinging back the lace which fell over her wrists, she tied a lace cravat about her neck and tucked it into a flowered satin waistcoat which came almost to her knees. The coat that went on over that was of pale rose with huge silver buttons and lavishly embroidered in silver. Then, settling a full powdered wig on her own curls and picking up a three-cornered hat, she returned to the drawing-room.

Now she was dressed, her nervousness faded and she began to feel like the actress her mother had been; she became the Count. Her voice deepened and her accent became even more pronounced as she paraded before them to show off the costume. The two young men silently marvelled at the way every movement and gesture proclaimed the man; there was very little that was feminine about the Comte de Clancy, unless it was his unblemished skin and delicate hands. 'It needs just a leetle tuck 'ere, *n'est-ce pas*?' she said, pulling in the waist of the coat.

'Oh, you will have all the young ladies by the ears,' Mrs Burford said. 'So handsome, you are, and such elegant address. I could wish myself twenty years younger.'

There was a great deal more and it took all Lydia's acting ability not to laugh aloud. She agreed that if she should find any of the young ladies to her liking she might very well think of marriage. Then she returned upstairs, re-made her face, changed into the cossacks again and rejoined Mrs Burford with her own clothes done up in the paper in which her costume had been delivered.

'Count, we could have had the tailor come and fetch the coat,' Mrs Burford said. 'There is no need for you to take it back yourself.'

'I 'ave to go out to see my lawyer,' the Count said, bowing over her hand. 'I pass the shop on the way.'

'I'll take you up,' Tom said, bidding goodbye to the Burfords and following the Count to the door. 'I'm going your way.'

They left together and climbed into the phaeton and, as soon as it turned the corner, collapsed into a heap, laughing so much that the horses nearly took fright. They were still laughing when they arrived in Portman Square and drew up at Wenthorpe House.

'Stay here, while I make sure Aunt Aggie is out,' Tom said, wiping tears from his eyes with a lace handkerchief plucked from his sleeve. 'I don't think she would entertain the Count, do you?' He jumped down and went to the door, leaving Lydia alone in the phaeton, in full view of anyone who might happen to be passing.

One of these was the Marquis of Longham, though his intention had not been to pass but to call. Something about the figure of the Count sitting alone in the carriage made him check his stride and then step smartly beind a tree in a neighbouring garden to watch events.

He had just come from seeing his lawyer, a young man who had been in the Peninsula with him and who had returned to take over the practice from his father. Charles Wilmott had confirmed that the land Ernest Grimshaw had appropriated had not been part of the original Longham domain. 'But I don't doubt it belongs legally to the Bellingham family,' he had said. 'There is a rumour that it was won in a wager but I have been unable to find any documents to support this. Without proof, His Grace will find it difficult to turn the man off.'

'I'll be damned if I let that Jack-at-warts make a cod's head of my father, just because His Grace is. . .' the Marquis had paused to find the word to describe his father's state of health '. . .not in plump currant and disinclined to make a push to claim his rights. I will return to Longham Towers and find the proof. In the meantime I have another small commission for you.' He had pulled a fob from his pocket and held it out on his palm, where it sparkled in the sunlight coming into the office through a rather grimy window. It was decorated with a shield-shaped crest in which a stag and falcon were picked out in precious stones. 'I need to find the owner of this.'

Charles had picked it up to examine it more closely. 'Whose insignia is this?'

'That's what I want to discover. It is French, or I think it is, and there is a great deal more—necklaces, armlets, tiaras, rings—a fortune, in fact. Some of it has a design similar to this, but this is the clearest and most easily identified.' He had gone on to tell his friend that he wished to return it to its true owner and received the same advice Tewkes had given him so freely—not to be a ninny and to be thankful for his good luck.

'I would not think myself lucky if I were in his shoes,' he had said, referring to the original owner of the haul. 'He must have been plucked clean and I would give him back his feathers.'

'Some feathers!' Charles had said laconically. 'I will do my best to trace the crest, but finding a living owner might be more difficult. He may have had a meeting with Madame Guillotine, or fled to America, or died on some European battlefield. If the cache was found in a soldier's knapsack, then I'll lay odds it was the latter.'

Jack had left Charles with the problem and decided to walk to Wenthorpe House to pay his respects to Miss Wenthorpe and tell her that he had been called out of town and would not, regretfully, have the pleasure of seeing her at Mrs Burford's ball.

Now, as he watched, Tom came out of the door, spoke to the Count and together they entered the house, and a minute later a servant came out and took the horses and phaeton round to the stables. The Comte de Clancy, if Mrs Burford was to be believed, was not welcome at Wenthorpe House, and yet here he was, going in with every appearance of belonging there. Jack was sure that if he were to knock and ask for the Count the young man could not be produced, not by Mrs Wenthorpe at all events. Tom Wenthorpe was a scapegrace but he was unwilling to believe that Miss Wenthorpe, in spite of the tomboy impression she had given him, was a party to intrigue. Crouching inelegantly behind a tree, watching Wenthorpe House for signs of the Count leaving, he fell to wondering what it was about Lydia Wenthorpe that put her so constantly in his thoughts. It could be the derogatory expression 'Poof!' she had used. It had sounded a warning chord somewhere in his memory and for the life of him he could not place it; as far as he knew he had never met her before that journey to London. He would have remembered if he had. She was memorable; classically handsome rather than pretty, she was just the right height for someone as tall as he was, though that was of less consequence than her zest for life, her energy, the sparkle in her deep eyes and the way her mouth twitched into a smile, as if life itself was a jest. Was this a jest? He was curious, curious enough to postpone his visit to Longham for a few days and remain in town. He extricated himself from behind the tree and, with a last look at the closed door of Wenthorpe House, turned on his heel and went back to his lodgings.

Lydia took a long time dressing the next evening. It was not that the simple gingham costume of a shepherdess was difficult to put on, for it laced down the front, but she was so nervous, she could not keep still and Betty found herself chasing her mistress all over the room to try and arrange a few flowers in her hair. But at last Lydia succumbed to Tom's entreaties from the other side of the door and, picking up her crook and a muff stuffed to look like a lamb, she joined him and their aunt for the carriage ride to Burford House, meekly enduring her aunt's scold for her tardiness.

Owing to the press of traffic, it was over an hour before they found themselves at the head of the line waiting to be greeted by Mrs Burford, and the dancing had already begun. Their ears were assailed by music from an enthusiastic orchestra, laughter and excited voices and, in a sudden stillness, a stentorious voice announcing, 'Mrs Wenthorpe, the Honourable Mr Thomas Wenthorpe and Miss Wenthorpe.'

Agatha, panniers swaying, sailed majestically into the room, followed by Lydia whose eyes were dazzled by the colourful scene. There were kings and queens, gods and goddesses, highwaymen, Roundheads, serving wenches, coachmen and harlequins, cossacks and soldiers of every nationality and hue, and dandies so exquisite one could believe them already in costume. In spite of the open windows and the flutter of a hundred fans, the air was made oppressive by a multitude of gasoliers. Since Mrs Burford's room was not over-large, it was, as her aunt had foretold, a squeeze. Even so, Lydia wished there were fewer to witness the masquerade and was almost relieved to note that neither the Marquis of Longham nor the Honourable Mr Douglas Fincham was to be seen.

Frank left his position at his mother's side to bow before Lydia. 'You are in looks tonight, Miss Wenthorpe,' he said, as he led her down the ranks of dancers in a country dance. 'And you have a sparkle in your eyes which betokens mischief.'

'Tis not mischief but terror,' she whispered, smiling to left and right. 'Where is Mr Fincham?'

They parted, she smiled and curtsied to her new partner and took a turn with him, then came to Frank again. 'I pray he will not come.'

He smiled. 'Oh, he will come.'

'I wish the whole thing could be gainsaid. Look at Lady Thorton now, casting her eye about like some predatory animal. She will tear me limb from limb.'

'But she cannot eat you.' He chuckled, bowing as they parted again, continuing when they met again as if there had been no break. 'I fancy you would be a little indigestible. Smile, do; I do not want a set-down from Mrs Wenthorpe for making you cast down.'

She smiled a little woodenly and then stiffened as she saw Douglas Fincham enter the room. He stood, dressed as a Cavalier, looking about him until his eye rested on her, then, as the dance ended and she left the floor on Frank's arm, moved forward to bow before her. There was nothing for it but to take the floor with him.

'You know, Miss Wenthorpe,' he said, leading her towards a set then forming, 'I am persuaded that someone with a countenance as beautiful and a figure as graceful as yours could never be transformed into a frog-eating *aristo*. I offered your brother terms so that you would not have to attempt it, but he is not so careful of your reputation as I am. He refused.'

'My reputation is in no danger, sir,' she said, stung to anger, 'but I feel a little unwell and would leave the floor.'

He did not believe her, but he escorted her back to Mrs Wenthorpe who was sitting on the sidelines talking to Mrs Burford and Lady Thornton. 'Miss Wenthorpe is feeling a trifle giddy,' he announced. 'Perhaps some hartshorn might steady her.'

Lydia glared at him and sank into a chair, fanning her face with the lamb muff. 'I think it is the heat, Aunt, though to own the truth I have felt out of curl all day.'

'Do you want to go home?' Mrs Wenthorpe asked, looking at her niece's flushed face and bright eyes. 'You do look a little ferverish.'

'No, I do not want to spoil your enjoyment. Nor Tom's.' She smiled wanly towards her brother who was flirting outrageously with a young lady dressed as Nell Gwyn. 'Perhaps if I could lie down for a spell. . .'

'Of course.' Mrs Burford beckoned to her companion. 'Jane shall take you to her room.'

Miss Whiting hurried forward and, putting her arm around her, helped her from the room. They moved slowly across the head of the stairs, just as the Marquis of Longham arrived, magnificent in the gold-braided green uniform of an officer of the Ninety-fifth, the elite Rifle Regiment. He handed his shako and sword-belt to a footmen and mounted the stairs. 'Why, Miss Wenthorpe,' he said when he saw she was being supported by Miss Whiting, 'Is something amiss?'

She glanced up at him and wished she had not. She felt the colour flood into her cheeks and for a fleeting moment his hazel eyes seemed to be looking right into her head and she thought she really would faint.

'Miss Wenthorpe felt unwell,' Miss Whiting said.

'Then allow me,' he said, and before she could protest had swept Lydia up into his arms. 'Lead the way, ma'm.'

Ignoring Lydia's feeble protests, he carried her up to the next floor behind Miss Whiting and gently deposited her on that lady's bed. 'Thank you,' Lydia murmured, wishing they would both go away, not so much because she had to make the transformation to the Count, but because their sympathy was so ill-deserved; and not only that, she had suddenly discovered how comfortable it was in his lordship's arms; she had not wanted him to put her down. 'I shall be right as ninepence as soon as I've rested.'

'Are you quite sure?' he asked. 'Shall I send for a physician?'

'No,' she said quickly and a trifle too sharply so that he looked down at her in surprise. 'Pray do not concern yourself, my lord. Go back to the ball.'

He looked as if he might like to stay but as Miss Whiting showed every sign of obeying the invalid's entreaty he had perforce to follow. 'If you make a recover before the evening is ended, I shall claim my reward,' he said with a smile which seemed to say he did not, for a moment, believe in her illness. 'A waltz.' Then, seeing Miss Whiting's disapproving look, he preceded her from the room.

It was guilt and nothing else which made her think he knew the truth, she decided, and now was definitely not the time to dwell on the last time they had waltzed. She listened to the murmur of their voices as they went downstairs; she must concentrate on what she had to do. She scrambled from the bed and crept to the door. The sound of music and lively chatter carried up to her but there was no one about and she made her way along the corridor to the Count's room, where she changed into the Count's costume and carefully made up her face. She took a last look at her reflection in the cheval-glass, decided it would do, and, taking her courage in her hands, went downstairs, where Frank met her at the door of the ballroom.

'Ah, there you are, Maurice,' he said, beaming at her and leading her to where Mrs Wenthorpe sat chatting to Lady Thornton and Mrs Burford. The latter was making some comment about the Count being late.

'He is a charming guest,' she was saying. 'I do hope you will be kind to him.' This last was addressed to Mrs Wenthorpe, who was obviously puzzled.

Frank stepped in quickly to make the introductions. The Count bent low over Lady Thornton's hand, murmuring, '*Vraiment*, it ees a *plaisir*, my lady,' and then looked up to find her aunt squinting short-sightedly at her. She knew a moment of panic and then her aunt said,

'If you will excuse me, I see Lady Melbourne. It is an age since I saw her.' And with that she swept away to have a comfortable gossip with her old friend.

'That was the cut direct,' Lady Thornton said and added with a sigh, 'But then Agatha Wenthorpe never did have any manners. It is to be hoped she does not give you a disgust for London Society, for we do not all behave so badly.'

'Pray, think no more of it,' Lydia said, noticing

that Frank had seized the opportunity afforded by her ladyship's momentary inattention to take her daughter off to dance. 'They are a 'andsome pair, *n'est-ce pas*?' she said, as Lady Thornton snapped her fan shut in annoyance.

'This is her come-out year, did you know?' her ladyship said, but before Lydia could frame a reply she added, 'She is so much in demand and so innocent that I have to watch that she is not taken in by every rake in town.'

'Monsieur Burford? A rake?' queried Lydia, trying not to smile at the idea.

'Well, perhaps not, but he is not suitable, not suitable at all.' She sighed. 'His mother is one of my oldest friends and so I cannot be blunt about it, but if he does not cease his dangling I shall have to swallow my sensibility and say something.'

'Dangle, what is dangle, my lady?' Lydia asked innocently. 'This word I know not.'

She smiled. 'I had forgot you were not English. It is a silly word meaning he would like to offer for Amelia.'

'Oh, this I comprehend. But Miss Thornton has, perhaps, many offers?'

'Indeed, yes. But her papa is particular whom she entertains; we are, after all, one of the oldest families in the kingdom.' She paused, then went on, 'You, I collect, also come from a very old family. I have heard your story from our hostess, so you need not be shy of telling me.'

'What 'as *madame* said?'

'Why, that you are going back to France to find your fortune.' She laughed in an embarrassed way.

'Not that you need it particularly, for I am told your papa did well in Canada.'

'There is no more to add,' Lydia said. 'You are well informed.'

This seemed to satisfy her ladyship and she smiled, holding out her hand to her daughter who was returning on Frank's arm at the end of the dance. 'Come, Amelia, and meet the Comte de Clancy.'

A moment later, Lydia was leading Amelia out on to the floor, praying that the next few minutes would soon be over and she could escape. She was acutely aware of the eyes of half London Society following her progress and none more than those of the Marquis of Longham, who stood languidly in the doorway, as if wondering whether it was worth his while to continue into the room. Her costume seemed to her to be transparent and her full wig doubly false. She watched him walk over to Lady Thornton and engage that lady in conversation and knew with certainty that the subject of their discourse was a certain Comte de Clancy.

'Such a beautiful couple, don't you think?' Lady Thornton murmured. 'And the young man has prospects, or he will have, once he has been to France to fetch a fortune in gold and jewels from a secret hiding place.'

'If they are still there,' Jack said laconically, regarding the young couple as the dance brought them nearer. 'It must be a long time since they were hid.'

'He is confident of success.' She bowed and smiled as the Count and her daughter went by. 'He is not wanting in conduct either, considering he is not an Englishman. A true gentleman, in fact.'

'Indeed, ma'am,' his lordship said in his lazy way. 'I find the young pup a trifle effeminate.'

'That is the sort of remark one would expect from a campaign soldier who had not been much in Society himself,' her ladyship retorted.

'Let us hope my taste improves with the Season.' He smiled. 'I think I will play a hand of faro.' With a last look at Lydia and a bow to her ladyship, he left the room, much to Lydia's relief when she saw him go.

Without the Marquis's eagle eye on her, Lydia found her taut muscles relaxing and looked down to find Miss Wenthorpe smiling up at her with corn-flower-blue eyes twinkling. 'Do not mind Mama,' she said. 'She will have me betrothed before the Season is out but you do not have to make an offer this very night.'

Lydia chuckled; Amelia was far from the insipid, biddable girl she had at first supposed and it made it doubly hard to continue the deception, but it was nearly over; two more minutes and the Count could take his leave. 'Your *maman* will first wish to be sure I 'ave my fortune recovered, *n'est-ce pas*?'

Amelia laughed. 'Something like that, and in the meantime I shall amuse myself and keep her and everyone else guessing.'

'I see *ma'm'selle* is a young lady of very great sense,' Lydia said, bowing to Amelia's curtsy as the dance ended. She offered her arm to promenade the floor and found herself looking into the amused eyes of Douglas Fincham. She flashed him a look of triumph as she returned her partner to her mother. She had done it! Tom's wager was safe and it was time for the shepherdess to reappear.

'You will join us for supper, Count?' her ladyship said. 'We make a small party at one of the tables.'

'I. . . I beg you will excuse me.' Everyone seemed to be looking at her and she could not wait to divest herself of the costume and with it her false identity. 'I 'ave to go to France early in the morning.'

'Leaving?' queried Mrs Burford, who stood within earshot. 'So soon?'

'*Je regrette*, I must. An urgent message.'

'How disappointing for everyone,' Lady Thornton said. 'But do promise to call on us the moment you return to England. We shall all be agog to hear of the success of your venture.'

'*Mais oui*. Your servant, my lady. Miss Thornton.' She bowed to Lady Thornton and her daughter and thanked Mrs Burford for her hospitality, and with their cries of '*Bon voyage*!' ringing in her ears hurried off in search of her brother.

She ran him to earth at last in one of the gaming-rooms, where he was about to sit down to a hand with Frank Burford, Lord Thornton—a jovial gentleman, though many said he lived under the cat's paw—and the Marquis of Longham. She acknowledged them briefly and turned to Tom. 'Cousin, I would 'ave a word before you begin.'

'Later, Maurice.' He began shuffling a pack of cards.

'*Maintenant, s'il vous plaît*.'

Reluctantly Tom put down the cards and followed

her to a corner. 'Will you never learn?' she whispered. 'What stakes are you playing for now?'

'Counters.' He grinned. 'No more than counters.'

She did not believe him for a minute, but she let it pass. 'As long as it has nothing to do with the Comte de Clancy, because he is about to disappear for good.'

He grinned like schoolboy. 'You've done it?'

'Yes. Witnessed by Mr Fincham, the Count has danced with Miss Thornton and reluctantly declined an invitation to join her and her mama for supper. Now I am going to make an end of the odious gentleman.'

'Odious! I thought him a devil of a fine fellow.' He was suddenly serious. 'Thank you, little sister.'

She turned to leave, only to find Lord Longham at her elbow. 'I'll not be above a minute,' he said to Tom. 'I want a word with the Count on a private matter.'

'*Moi*?' Just in time, Lydia remembered her role. 'I am much in 'aste, my lord.'

'I would like some conversation with you, Count, about your family. I have heard some talk of jewels. . .'

She turned startled eyes on him and for a split-second her guard dropped, but she recovered herself and smiled. 'Jewels, my lord?'

'They were lost in France, I believe?'

Just when she thought it was all over and she had come out of it unscathed, this tall, far too perceptive, far too handsome man had contrived to overset her. She knew her face betrayed her fear and yet a streak of obstinacy in her drove her to continue the charade. '*Mais oui.* Why do you ask?'

'I was there recently and...' He paused, watching her face.

'I go there myself tomorrow,' she said. 'Tonight I leave to catch the packe' for Calais.'

'Forgive me, but is that wise? Things are very bad there still and the old aristocracy are not welcome, especially if they go to reclaim their lands.'

'Poof!' she said, tilting her chin into the air. 'The Comte de Clancy 'as not the fear.'

He smiled slowly, his suspicions confirmed by that one word. 'No,' he said softly. 'I did not think you had.' What, in heaven's name, was she playing at? He looked closely at her. How had she managed to make that lovely face so plump and dissolute, like a man who spent all his nights at the card table and his days in bed? It was unbelievably clever. But it was the height of foolishness too. He felt tempted to tell her so; tempted, too, to put up a finger and trace the outline of her cheek and find the real Lydia underneath the paint, but that would certainly cause a stir. Already the gentlemen at the table were looking at them in curiosity. He turned to go back to them. 'I will await your return with some impatience.'

'You may have a very long wait,' she muttered to herself as she climbed the stairs and opened the door to the room the Count was supposed to have been occupying for the whole of the previous week. She hurried across to the bed where she had left the shepherdess costume behind the drawn curtains. It was over. Laughing softly to herself and unbuttoning her coat, she pulled the curtains back and gasped in surprise to find Douglas Fincham, lounging back against the pillows with her shepherdess costume and the lamb muff draped across his thighs. His supercilious smile sent her newly restored spirits diving into her red-heeled shoes.

'Felicitations might have been in order,' he said slowly, 'had you not cheated.'

CHPTER FIVE

'WHAT are you doing here?' she demanded, too angry to be afraid, though her knees were knocking and her hands shaking. 'Get out at once!'

'And if I don't, will you shout for help?' He dropped her dress and sat up in leisurely fashion. 'Dare you?'

One side of her brain was in a panic, the other side seemed to be coolly wondering what he intended to do, for he had not come simply to congratulate her and admit he had lost his wager. Seduction flitted across her mind, but he had nothing to gain from that. She could try making a bolt for Miss Whiting's room, but he was in possession of her dress and she needed it. 'I insist you leave this room,' she said, marvelling at the coolness of her voice. 'You have lost your wager; let it be an end of it.'

'I do not consider it lost,' he said smoothly, flicking a speck from his sleeve. 'A costume ball where everyone is dressed in ridiculous clothes is not a fair test. You have cheated and your brother's vowels will not be returned to him until the Count has appeared in modern dress.' His dark eyes glittered. 'In truth, I like you so much as the Comte de Clancy, I think you should maintain the impersonation at least until my parents give their own ball in May for the come-out of my sister.'

'If you think I will do that. . .'

'I should like to see Miss Amelia Thornton accept the Count as a genuine suitor,' he went on, as if she had not spoken. 'It should not be difficult; the young lady has astonishingly bad taste, don't you know?'

Lydia laughed suddenly. 'Oh, has she rejected you, sir? Are you jealous of the Count? Or perhaps someone with a little more substance? Who can it be?'

She knew she had gone too far when he scrambled off the bed and grabbed her shoulders, shaking her until her teeth rattled. 'You will do as I say, hoyden,' he muttered through clenched teeth. 'You will act the Count until I tell you to stop.'

'And if I don't?' She found her voice at last.

'The world will know the Comte de Clancy for an impostor.'

'I care nothing for that,' she snapped. 'I intend to tell Miss Thornton the truth this very night. You had not supposed I would leave her in ignorance?'

He grinned and released her. 'Neither Lady Thornton nor her daughter will openly admit they were gulled by a girl in men's clothes, but they will certainly be angry enough to confirm the story that the Count was a young nobody masquerading as a nobleman in order to deprive the real Comte de Clancy of his fortune. That is an indictable offence. You will be called to book and how will my Lord Wenthorpe view his progeny then?' He paused to let his words sink in. 'Add to that the fact that Tom Wenthorpe would rather anything than have the world know he has reneged on a wager. He will sacrifice his sister without a qualm.'

The near-truth of this bit into her anger and

weakened her determination to resist him; it was as much as she could do not to let him see it. 'There is no Comte de Clancy and you know it.'

'Do I?' His smile frightened her more than his anger. 'I should not be so sure, if I were you. If the true Count were to arrive on the scene. . .' He left the sentence unfinished and strode to the door, where he turned with his hand on the knob. 'For the pleasure of seeing Miss Thornton fall in love with one of her own sex, I shall make no effort to find him until after my parents' ball.'

The door shut on him and Lydia sank on to the bed. Blackmail! Oh, how foolish they had been to suppose that that odious creature would be content to accept defeat. Now what should she do? The whole charade must be stopped at once and she must find Tom and tell him so.

Fumbling in her haste, she stripped off her costume and put it in the Count's portmanteau, then washed the paint from her face and dressed once again as the shepherdess. With a quick look in the mirror to pat her own curls into place, she hurried downstairs in search of her brother. She could not find him in the card-room and had gone to look for him in the crowded ballroom when Mrs Burford spotted her. 'Miss Wenthorpe, you have made a recovery, I see.'

'Yes, thank you. I was looking for. . .'

'What a pity you missed the dear Count. He has been called away suddenly. News from France, I believe. Perhaps when he returns you will meet him. I do hope so, for he is so young and I do not like to think of him being obliged to sort out his affairs without family or friends to help him.'

'I am sure he has friends,' Lydia said distractedly. 'Have you seen Tom?'

'No. Should you have got up? You still do not look quite the thing.' She caught sight of her son dancing with Amelia a second time and gave a tut of annoyance. 'Look at Frank with Miss Thornton again. He will give the scandal-mongers something to stir in their broth besides sugar and Letty won't like it above half.' The dance ended and she beckoned her son to her. He returned Amelia to Lady Thornton's side and strolled over. 'What is it, Mama?'

'Should you have taken Miss Thornton on to the floor again, Frank? Her mama is already hinting that the Count will be offering for her very soon.'

Frank spluttered and hastily pretended to wipe his face with his handkerchief. 'Really, Mama?' he said, making an effort to suppress his mirth. 'And will she accept him, do you think?'

'Why you should find it amusing I do not know,' his mother said coldly. 'I am grieved to see a son of mine so wanting in conduct, but I will not give Letty the satisfaction of seeing me give you a scold in public. We shall speak of it later.' She paused and looked around her. 'Do you know where Mrs Wenthorpe is? Lydia is not feeling quite the thing and ought to go home.'

'No, no, I am perfectly recovered, Mrs Burford,' Lydia protested. 'And I want to enjoy the rest of the evening.'

Something in her voice made Frank realise something was seriously amiss. 'Then let us dance.'

She attempted to laugh. 'It will be the second time.'

'So it will. Let it not be said I am not equal-handed.' With that he bowed and led her on to the floor.

'What is it, Lydia?' His voice was full of concern.

'That hateful Douglas Fincham will not accept defeat. He was waiting for me when I went to change my costume. He is threatening to produce the real Comte de Clancy.'

'God! Oh, beg pardon, but is there such a person?'

'I did not think so, but what if there is? He also said he will put it abroad that Tom has turned his back on a debt of honour. Oh, Frank, what a coil we have got ourselves into.'

'We must tell Amelia—Miss Thornton,' he corrected himself hurriedly. 'There is no question of it now. And, whatever Fincham says, the Count must disappear.' He laughed lightly. 'I do not fancy him as a rival, anyway; he is too handsome by far.'

'But what about Mr Fincham?'

'Leave him to Tom and me. Now, you go and find Am. . . Miss Thornton and tell her all.'

'Will she understand?'

'Of course,' he said, drawing her away from the line of dancers and ignoring the cries which followed them that they had spoiled the set.

Lydia was not so sure of Amelia's forbearance and she dreaded the coming interview. How could she make it sound any less than the despicable, humiliating insult that it was? How could Tom have asked it of her? However could she have contemplated doing it?

She found Amelia sitting with her mother, sipping a cooling cordial, and was made to feel even more of a villain by the young lady's solicitude for her health.

'Oh, I am feeling much better, thank you, Miss Thornton,' Lydia answered, looking into her eyes in an effort to convey the urgency of her request. 'I was on my way to take a stroll on the terrace when it occurred to me you might like to accompany me.'

'Indeed yes, it is so hot in here.' She turned to Lady Thornton. 'May I?'

Her ladyship nodded and the two young ladies went, arm in arm, down to one of the lower salons which they knew led to the garden. Here Mrs Wenthorpe sat with her wig askew, playing loo with three other matrons. She looked up and enquired if Lydia was recovered and, being given an affirmative answer and the information that Lydia was going with Miss Thornton for some fresh air, turned again to her hand. 'Then mind you do not stay out too long and catch a chill,' she said as the girls passed out on to the terrace.

'Oh, this is better,' Amelia said, breathing deeply. 'I do not wonder at your feeling faint.'

They began pacing slowly along the terrace, which was lit unevenly by the light coming from the windows of the first-floor ballroom above it. Lydia was silent, unable to find the words to begin her confession, while her companion prattled on about the different costumes the guests had chosen, the fineness of the night and the brightness of the moon. There was nothing for it but to plunge right in.

'Did you like the Comte de Clancy, Miss Thornton?'

'Why, yes, I find him charming. Why do you ask?'

'I want to talk to you about him. . .'

'If you are going tell me about that silly family quarrel, I have no wish to hear about it,' Amelia said quickly. 'I will not hear a word against your cousin.'

'You have not developed a *tendre* for him already, have you?'

'No, of course not.' She stopped walking to turn towards Lydia. 'If you have come to warn me off him, you may save your breath.'

'But if he were not all he appeared to be?'

'In what way? Not a Count? Not French? Not rich? What care I? I would be the last one to expose him and I hope you may not either.'

'No, I will not expose him. I thought perhaps you might.'

'Why should I? He does me no harm.' Amelia laughed suddenly. 'I am in no danger of losing my head to that young man because, you see, there is someone. . .' She stopped and laughed. 'But it will do Mama good to think I have.'

'What do you mean? Do you know. . .?' She stopped suddenly because she had heard footsteps on the paving and looked up to see Tom and the Marquis strolling towards them, both smoking cigarillos. They threw them down and ground them under their heels as they approached the girls.

'Miss Thornton,' Tom said, striding forward. 'I searched for you everywhere to claim the dance you promised me and was so blue-devilled when you could not be found, I came out to blow a cloud to console myself. I found his lordship on the same tack.' He grinned up at the Marquis who was at least half a head taller than he was. 'He had lost Lydia, you see.'

'His lordship knew I had gone to lie down,' Lydia said, trying not to meet Jack's searching eyes.

The Marquis bowed to both girls and addressed himself to Lydia. 'I learned you had returned to the ballroom, Miss Wenthorpe, and, if you recall, I had earlier intimated that I would claim the honour of a dance.' He sighed theatrically. 'I was told you seemed to be searching for someone and hoped it might be me. . .'

'I was looking for Miss Thornton,' she said. 'And we were having a private conversation.'

'Oh, have we interrupted?' Tom said, gaily. 'But you girls can have a coze at any time. We claim our partners, do we not, Jack?'

Jack did no more than smile; he was gazing down into Lydia's eyes as if he were Dr Mesmer, inducing such a trance-like state in her, she could not move. 'I. . .' She began and then stopped. What had she been going to say? I am a fool? I am more than a fool, I am a fraud, not fit to be in polite society, not fit to be noticed by anyone upright and honourable? And my brother, who seems to have made a friend of you and calls you by your given name, is even now doing his best to stop me from blurting it all out. She knew without be able to take her eyes from the Marquis's face that this was true; Tom was fidgeting beside her. Why should he be so concerned, when to all intents and purposes the charade was at an end? He did not know of Douglas Fincham's new demands—unless Frank had told him. But, if he had, Tom would never have agreed to them. Would he? *Would* he? She heard retreating footsteps and knew her brother was taking Amelia away, presumably to go back to the ballroom, and still she stood looking into the dark pools of the Marquis's eyes.

As the moon came out from behind a cloud and lit her face with its soft light, he took her hands in his and held her at arm's length. Her eyes were bright, so bright, he could almost have sworn there were tears on her lashes. That the oh, so level-headed Miss Wenthorpe could be moved to tears was something which affected him strangely. He wanted to take her in his arms and comfort her, to tell her there was nothing so bad they could not overcome it together. The music of the ballroom seemed a million miles away, a background to a moment when time stood still. He did not speak. He did not even smile. Only his eyes conveyed his message, and it was one Lydia did not understand.

She felt as though she was wrapped in a cocoon, a world where nothing and no one else existed. She looked from his eyes to his full mouth and slightly parted lips, over his strong jaw to his throat where a quickening pulse beat just above his stiff uniform collar. She lifted her face and looked once more into his eyes. They were still regarding her as if to commit every feature to memory, drawing her face, line by line, in some corner of his brain to be brought out at a later date, perfect in every detail. Lost to any sense of time and place, she felt as though she was floating, without limbs, floating up into the star-filled sky with nothing to anchor her to the earth but the firm grip of his hands. She clung to them.

They did not kiss; it was not a moment for kissing. He knew that if he bent his head and put his lips to hers he would break that timeless moment. As the strains of a waltz reached them from that far-off other world of harsh colours, loud voices, intrigue and gossip, he slipped one arm about her waist. Slowly, without taking their eyes from each other, they began to dance. With skirts swaying about his long green-clad legs, she allowed herself to melt into him, to become moulded into one being with him. It was as if the music were playing for them alone, and she did not want it to stop; she wanted it to go on forever. But it did, all too soon, brought to an end by the flourish of the orchestra and the polite applause from the ballroom. He stopped and brought her hand to his lips. She shivered.

'Thank you,' he said softly, as if he was thanking her for more than a dance.

She gathered herself together at last. 'I think we should go back indoors.' Her voice was a little shaky. 'Tom and Miss Thornton have returned, and if we are missed. . .'

'We did not come out here together and we need not return together.' He sounded so normal as he tucked her hand under his arm that she believed the moment had been of little importance to him. 'I will escort you to the door and then stay and smoke another cigarillo.'

'Thank you, my lord.'

'You do not mean to disappear again, I hope?'

'Disappear? No, my lord. I am quite recovered.'

'I am glad to hear it. You do not suggest to me a young lady given to fits of swooning.'

'I am not,' she said. 'It never happened before. . .'

He smiled down at her. 'Then it must have been something very serious to make it necessary for you to flee the ballroom earlier this evening. I hope it had nothing to do with my arrival.'

'Good heavens, no!' she said quickly.

'So! You did flee and the headache was false.' He stopped and turned towards her. 'Miss Wenthorpe, if there is anything troubling you, anything at all, I beg you acquaint me with it. If I can be of assistance, I should consider it an honour. . .'

Her trill of a laugh echoed falsely. 'Now, why, sir, should you be forever suggesting something is troubling me? It is not very flattering, you know. There is nothing on my mind beyond choosing which partners to dance with and whether to have the wine or the champagne.'

'Are you so empty-headed?' he asked and then answered himself. 'No, I think it has something to do with the Comte de Clancy. . .'

'The Comte de Clancy.' Did she sound as breathless as she felt? 'What is he to me?'

'Forgive me, but I had thought he was very close to you indeed.'

She thought her shaking hands would betray her and her voice was strained with the effort of keeping it light. 'A mere cousin, and one, I may say, I cannot remember ever having met.'

'He is French, is he not?' he queried, deciding to play her game until he found out the reason for it.

'Yes,' she said, unwilling to say any more.

'But not brought up in France?'

'No, Canada.'

'But I have heard talk of gold and jewels hidden in France.'

'Tattle, my lord, mere tattle.'

'You do not believe there can be any substance in the story, then?'

'What I believe is of no consequence.' Oh, why was he persisting with this inquisition? She did not want to talk about the Count; she wanted to keep everything as it had been a few moments before, when they had been so close, so at one with each other. Now he had introduced a discordant note and spoiled it all.

'But it is of consequence to me,' he said.

She turned on him, angry now. 'Why?'

'Why?' He seemed to be considering the question. 'Because, among several other things, I am concerned for Miss Thornton. . .'

'Miss Thornton!' She stared at him in astonishment and then her heart nearly stopped beating. He cared for Amelia Thornton and was jealous of the Count. And Amelia herself had intimated that there might be someone else. Could it be the Marquis? Was Amelia deliberately trying to make him jealous by allowing the Count to pay attention to her? She had succeeded admirably if she was, more than she realised, for Lydia herself was consumed by the little green monster. It would be laughable if it did not hurt so much.

'She is too young and innocent to be treated so shabbily,' he said.

'By whom, my lord?'

'By the Comte de Clancy. Whom did you think I meant?'

'I am not responsible for the actions of my relatives,' she said, stung to a reply she was immediately ashamed of. 'Do not come to me with your complaints.'

He smiled, but it was the smile of the tiger. 'I would go to the Count himself if I could find him,' he said. 'But he is a very elusive gentleman. Now you see him, now you don't. I had hoped you would put me on his track.'

'I am afraid I cannot help you,' she said coolly as they stopped at the door. In order to give the appearance of observing the proprieties it had been left sightly open and a shaft of light lit the terrace. 'I have no idea where the Comte de Clancy might be found.'

With this whopper, she stepped into the room, where her aunt still sat at the card table with her cronies. She had a pile of coins at one elbow and a half-empty glass of wine at the other. It crossed Lydia's mind that if her aunt had been doing her job as chaperon conscientiously there would have been no ticklish exchange with the Marquis which had put her in such a quiver. But neither would there have been that earlier silent moment, stretching to eternity, and the waltz in the moonlight. She had—though she could not tell exactly when it had happened—fallen head over heels in love with the Marquis of Longham, and the realisation had come almost simultaneously with the knowledge that his affections were engaged elsewhere and he had only been flirting with her. He had no business lowering his famous hauteur and allowing her to see the real man—no business at all; he should have stuck to calling her a hoyden and delivering lectures on her behaviour; that way she would still be heart-whole. Raventrees beckoned to her irresistibly; there she might learn to forget.

The evening dragged on and ended without her being able to speak to Amelia again and Tom seemed to be avoiding her for he had partners for every dance until the time came to take their leave. She could not even talk to him on the drive home because of their aunt's presence, and as soon as they arrived he gave a huge yawn and took himself off to bed. It was not until they met at the breakfast table that she was able to tell him of Douglas Fincham's blackmail and her determination to return home as soon as possible.

Unconcerned, he continued liberally spreading blackberry conserve on to his bread and butter. 'Oh, Lydia, do stop prosing on, there's a good girl. You know you can't go home yet and the evening was a prodigious success. Mrs Burford puts it all down to the mysterious Count. You were exquisite and I have no doubt could carry it off much longer.'

'I could not! And I will not! Douglas Fincham must be silenced. For good.'

He glanced up at her and smiled. 'Murder? Really, Lydia, I had not thought you capable of that.'

'Oh, don't be so idiotish. You know what I mean. Mr Fincham could continue blackmailing indefinitely. . .'

'It will only be another month.'

'And another and another.'

'No. It is double or quits and that will be an end of it.'

'Double or quits!' Her voice rose in a shriek. 'Do you mean...? Have you...? Oh, no, not even you would behave so shabbily...'

'Shabbily, Lydia? Why, it is a great compliment to you. Not even the great Mrs Siddons could do better, believe me.'

'If you were not my brother, I would...'

He licked blackberry conserve from his fingers, one by one. 'But think how dull life would be if I were not.'

She could think of no words to express the anger and frustration she felt. He took her so much for granted that he could not even conceive that she would not do as he asked, but this time he had gone too far. Much too far. She left the table and slammed out of the room.

She had not cooled down by the time she had changed into riding dress and taken one of the mounts from the stables, flung a saddle on it and galloped out of the mews. Scrivens's cry of 'Wait, Miss Lydia,' fell on deaf ears.

If she had not been a good horsewoman, she would have sent more than one pedestrian flying and entangled herself with several carriages and carts before she had gone a hundred yards, but she was a fearless rider and her mount used to her ways, so that all that happened was that she left the pedestrians shaking their fists and the coach drivers shouting abuse, and a few minutes later she turned into the park, almost oversetting a landaulet which was coming out of the gate. The carriage was hauled to a stop by the driver but Lydia could not have stopped if she had wanted to. It was the last straw as far as her stallion was concerned; he bolted with her and she needed all her wits about her to stay on his back.

With her head low over the horse's neck, the ground became a blur as it passed under her. The sound of hoofbeats thundered in her ears and branches whipped past her face as she fought to control her mount. On and on they sped, until the crowds were left behind. She did not see the fallen tree across the path, nor did she hear the sound of other hoofs. A warning shout from somewhere behind her came too late as the horse refused to take the obstacle; she was suddenly airborne and then the ground came up to meet her. With a bone-crunching thump she found merciful darkness.

The first sensation she had when she began to regain her senses was that she was lying somewhere soft and warm and that something had touched her lips, something light, like a leaf or a moth. There was a mist before her eyes which made everything indistinct, but slowly the blur resolved itself into the handsome features of the Marquis of Longham. His head was so close she could feel the warmth of his breath on her cheek and he was regarding her with an expression which was almost like... No, she would not allow herself to go on; he was only showing concern.

'Oh, you little fool,' he said, but he made it sound like an endearment. 'Are you hurt?'

She lifted her head and realised he was kneeling on the ground and she was leaning against his thighs with her head on his arm. 'I do not think so,' she murmured, sinking back again, too comfortable to want to move. 'My lord, how came you here?'

He smiled and brushed a twig from her hair, steeling himself to resist the temptation to lower his head and kiss her slightly parted lips a second time; if he succumbed when she was conscious enough to know what was happening, nothing would ever be the same again. She would either think him an incorrigible rake and never speak to him again or she would assume that he meant to marry her, and he was not prepared for either interpretation. 'I was returning from a ride and saw you enter the park as if all the demons of hell were at your heels. So did a great many other people, including the occupants of that landaulet you nearly overturned. I collect you owe them an apology.' This was more like the Marquis she knew, giving her a rake-down. 'Don't you know better than to ride like that in traffic?'

'Of course, but my horse. . .'

'He is cropping not two yards away,' he said. 'Once he had rid himself of his burden, he had no inclination to continue. Why were you so foolish as to ride an animal too powerful for you? And where is your groom?'

She could not be such a rabshackle as to let Scrivens take the blame. Reluctantly she sat up. 'I rode out by myself. There is nothing to that, I often do.'

'In Suffolk perhaps it might be allowed, but in town?' His voice was censorious. 'I think not, Miss Wenthorpe.'

'I can do without a jawbation from you,' she said and though she spoke sharply she knew he was right.

It was too much to hope that there was no one who knew her among the people who had seen the incident. 'You are not my guardian.'

'If I were,' he retorted swiftly, 'I would make sure you had more care for the safety of your mount.'

She scrambled to her feet and dusted down her habit. 'Oh, there was I thinking you cared that I might be hurt and all the time you were only concerned for the horse. Well, you may save your sympathy for either of us. I shall ride him back.'

'No. His fetlock looks bruised. Tewkes has gone to fetch a carriage to take you home. Besides, you are still too shaken. Do you think you can walk to the end of the path? It is too narrow here for a vehicle.' He took her arm to help her.

She shook herself free, stooped to pick up her hat and strode off ahead of him. Half amused, half annoyed, he shrugged his broad shoulders and followed her. She was the most infuriating female he had ever come across, alluringly feminine at one moment with big soft eyes and tender lips that made a man forget all propriety, and almost mannish the next. She was a bruising rider and had a deft pair of hands with the ribbons of the phaeton, he had noticed, and he would not be at all surprised to learn she was a crack shot as well. He supposed it was being brought up in a male-dominated household. Why her father had not engaged a female companion for her he could not fathom, and as for her aunt. . . He stopped to smile at the vision of Mrs Wenthorpe which came to him; the aunt was so eccentric as to be a positive antidote. How could the poor girl be expected to find a husband? As soon as an eligible male put in an appearance he would either take her for a hoydenish flirt of the kind who abounded in the hazy *demi-monde* on the fringe of polite Society and not treat her seriously or he would be frightened off by her masculine accomplishments. Unless, of course, he could outdo her. Somehow the thought of that amused him.

She turned and noticed his smile. 'I am glad to see my mishap diverts you, my lord,' she said.

'Not at all. I was thinking of something else.'

Or someone, she thought; someone like Amelia Thornton, petite and feminine with big blue eyes and golden curls, who would never put a foot outside the door without a female companion and a groom to accompany her and would never dream of galloping. No wonder he smiled. 'It is hardly gallant to have your mind otherwhere when you are with a lady,' she said, then, unaccountably, laughed. 'But then I am not a lady but a tomboy, isn't that what you said? And now I have convinced you of it.'

'No more than before.' His voice had lost its bantering tone. 'But I can't think why you see the necessity. I liked you best as the gentle shepherdess. Now, there was a lady.'

She was silent. Why did he have to remind her of the ball? Speaking of the shepherdess also brought the Count to mind and she did not want to be reminded of him. For a man who did not exist the Comte de Clancy seemed to be everywhere; he was in her head, in Tom's hopes, part of Douglas's greed and his name was on everyone's lips. She had created a monster and the monster would destroy her.

A closed carriage, driven by Tewkes, came along

the path and stopped. Jack hurried forward to open the door and let down the step and, when she had climbed in and the door shut again, jumped up to replace Tewkes on the box. 'I'll drive,' he told him, picking up the reins. 'You walk the horses back.'

As if one scolding were not enough, as soon as the Marquis had left her in the care of her aunt, Lydia was subjected to another. 'Such conduct will not do,' that good lady said, wagging her closed fan at her niece. 'Riding out alone is bad enough to make everyone think you fast, but then to compound that by galloping and falling off. . .'

'I did not fall, I was thrown, and no one saw me except his lordship and I do not believe he will tattle about it.' Lydia smiled in spite of her aching bones. 'The Wenthorpe reputation for horsemanship is still intact.'

'I was not referring to your reputation as a rider,' her aunt cried, throwing up her hands. 'It is your conduct which is at fault. I cannot think what came into you, rushing off like that. Scrivens said you would not wait for him.'

'I was in a hurry.'

'To meet the Marquis, no doubt.'

'I did not know he would be there. I wish it had been anyone but him.'

'Do you, now?' Mrs Wenthorpe said knowingly. 'I wonder why?'

To which her niece responded by bursting into tears. This was so untypical that Mrs Wenthorpe was quite taken aback but as Lydia would not tell her what ailed her she naturally assumed her niece was in love with the tall young nobleman who had brought her home and there had been a lovers' tiff. She smiled knowingly. 'Oh, do dry your tears, child,' she said, putting her arm round Lydia's shoulders. 'You will make your face all blotchy and it is not the end of the world. The young man has invited us to join his party at the theatre tomorrow night and supper afterwards and you can make up your quarrel then. I am sure all can be resolved.'

Lydia sniffed. 'Aunt, if you think I will be seen in the company of that top-lofty, stiff-rumped, odious man, you will have to have second thoughts, for I will not go to the theatre if he is to be there and I will certainly not have supper in his company.'

'Why ever not? What has he done to upset you so?'

'Nothing but hurl insults at me.'

'Insults? He has insulted you? Then, of course, he will apologise.'

'Not he. And I will not give him the opportunity.'

'But Lydia, how did he insult you? I cannot believe he is so wanting in gentlemanly conduct.'

'I won't hear another word on the subject, Aunt, so you may save your breath. Besides, tomorrow I want to call on Lady Thornton and Miss Thornton.'

'You will do no such thing! I will never darken her doors again and neither will you.'

'Why not?' It was imperative that she finish her talk with Amelia and if her aunt had a compelling reason for cutting her ladyship it would make it decidedly awkward.

'I have known Letty Thornton ever since we were girls together but that does not give her the right to criticise me in that sly fashion,' her aunt said. 'She said some very strange things to me at the ball, blaming me for keeping up a family feud when the poor Count is so young and all alone in the world and other such foolish talk which I did not understand but which I am sure was meant to be insulting. Letty Thornton must be going off her head to be taken in by that young man. He is no more the Comte de Clancy than I am the Queen of Sheba and so I told her. I will not stoop to call on her again until she comes to her senses and I will be obliged if you will not call on her daughter either. Goosecaps, the pair of them.' She paused, for Lydia had gone very white and looked about to faint. 'Are you ill, child?' She helped her niece to a chair and pulled the bell-rope by the fireplace. 'That fall has shaken you more than you realised. Why did you not say, instead of letting me ramble on? I must send for the physician.'

'No, Aunt, I am perfectly well. I will lie down until dinnertime.'

A footman arrived and was sent in search of Lydia's maid and when Betty arrived Lydia was placed in her care. 'There is a paregoric in the chest in my room,' Mrs Wenthorpe instructed her. 'Give Miss Lydia a draught and see that she rests until dinner.'

The scolding was forgotten as Lydia was put to bed and cosseted like an invalid. It did nothing to make her feel any less guilty. The hateful masquerade had affected her aunt now and that was the outside of enough. She would confess all and hope for forgiveness. She would do it after dinner when they were comfortably sitting in the withdrawing-room over the teacups.

Even then fate conspired against her. Dinner was to be *en famille* and at six o'clock she returned downstairs dressed in a green silk gown over an eau-de-Nil slip and made her way across the hall towards the small dining-room, just as a footman announced Mr Burford.

Mrs Wenthorpe had not yet come downstairs and Lydia went forward to greet him. 'We are about to dine,' she said, as he bowed to her. 'Would you care to join us?'

'Thank you, but I am expected at my club. I came for a private word with Tom. And you, too, if I could get you both together without Mrs Wenthorpe.'

She sent the footman to find her brother and then led the way into the library. 'You look very mysterious,' she said, managing to smile now that her decision had been made. 'Don't tell me that odious Comte de Clancy has been giving you trouble.'

'Not exactly.'

She was instantly serious. 'How not exactly?'

Tom came strolling into the room, dressed for dinner except for his cravat. 'I say, Burford, you do choose the most awkward times to come calling. I had half got the wretched thing tied to my satisfaction and had to leave it. I've already ruined three and Barber is losing patience with me. How does Jack Bellingham do it, I wonder?'

'Never mind your neckcloth, Tom,' Frank said, drawing a letter from his coat pocket, while Lydia mused on a mind's-eye picture of the Marquis tying a cravat with long, lean fingers which could be gentle too. 'Just tell me what you make of this. It was addressed to the Comte de Clancy at Burford House.'

Tom took it and read it. 'Oh, I say,' he said, then read it again, while Lydia stood impatiently tapping her foot. 'Oh, I say, what a turn up!'

'What is?' she demanded, snatching it from him. 'Let me see.'

'It has come to our notice that you are trying to trace a quantity of family jewels, left in France,' she read aloud. 'If you would care to call at our offices at your convenience, we may have something of interest to tell you concerning these jewels. Signed Charles Wilmott, Attorney.' She looked up at them. 'It must be a hoax. I'll wager Douglas Fincham is behind it. Throw it away.'

'But what if it's genuine?' Tom said.

'How can it be? We invented the whole story, remember?' She was feeling irritable and miserable enough without Tom acting as if the Count and his jewels really existed. 'If it isn't Douglas Fincham bamming, then someone else is putting us to the test and I will have nothing to do with it.'

'We can't simply ignore it,' Frank put in. 'Wilmott's is a genuine law firm, that much I know, and they would not lend their name to anything havey-cavey.'

'Then return the letter, say the Count has gone to France and cannot be contacted.'

'In that case we should not have broken the seal,' Tom said reasonably. 'And the de Clancy family *was* real; just supposing. . .'

'Just suppose nothing,' she snapped. 'I will not pose as the Count again.'

'But aren't you in the least bit curious, Lydia?' Tom went on implacably. 'After all, we might learn more of Mama's family, might even find real long-lost relations.'

'Then you go, if you are so interested,' she said, refusing to admit that she herself was curious. 'Tell them you are in charge of the Count's affairs in his absence.'

'They are lawyers, Lydia, they will not believe that without written instructions and if the story of the family feud has also reached them they will not divulge whatever information they have to me.'

'They can't have any, there is none.'

'We won't know that unless we go, will we? Oh, come on, Lydia, what harm can it do? If it looks as though he has seen through us, we'll own it all a hum.'

'Promise?'

'You have my word on it.'

'I think we should tell Aunt Aggie.'

'No!' the young men said in unison.

'But she knows more about the de Clancy family than we do. Besides, she is up in the boughs over Lady Thornton's treatment of her and all over the Count. She told me she thought the Count was an impostor. We cannot leave her in ignorance any longer.'

'Tomorrow,' Tom said. 'After we have seen the lawyer, we might have more to tell her. It might be good news. Say nothing tonight.'

Why, oh, why, she asked herself later, did she let

him talk her into it? She should have stuck to her guns. The only consolation was that this was not a public appearance of the Count; no one but the lawyer need see her. But even in that she was wrong.

The first person they saw when they left the house next morning was the Marquis of Longham descending from his curricle at their door.

'Good morning, Wenthorpe,' he greeted Tom cheerfully and then looked coolly at Lydia, who became absurdly conscious of her polished hessians and close-fitting beige pantaloons which revealed rather more of her well-shaped legs than she liked. She saw his gaze roam from these up over her full-skirted frockcoat to the cravat at her throat, something which had taken her an age to tie in the latest oriental knot. She felt her cheeks flame as he lifted his eyes to her face. 'Count,' he said. 'What a pleasant surprise to see you here. I had thought you had left Burford House to go to France. I hope this may mean the rift with the family has been mended?' Lydia was conscious of the hint of sarcasm in his voice as she returned his greeting with an inclination of her head.

'It was never a very serious thing,' Tom said quickly before Lydia could speak.

She forced herself to smile and give the Count's light laugh. 'I stay with my cousins at Wenthorpe 'ouse for one day more, then I go to France.'

'Of course.' Jack bowed stiffly from the waist. 'I did not mean to pry. Is Mrs Wenthorpe at home?'

'Aunt Aggie?' queried Lydia, almost forgetting her role. 'You wish to see Aunt Aggie?'

'Well, no,' he admitted. 'It was Miss Wenthorpe I

wanted to speak to.' He paused, looking directly into Lydia's eyes and making her wish the ground would open up and swallow her. 'I came to see how she goes on after her. . .her mishap and to apologise for my conduct. We had a slight difference of opinion and I had hoped to make amends. . .'

'Apologise?' Tom queried. 'I am sure no apology is necessary. On the contrary, my sister is excessively grateful for your assistance. Is that not so, Maurice?'

If he had been standing nearer, Lydia would have kicked him. Instead she was obliged to smile at the Marquis and answer. '*Mais oui*, I believe she did say something about the 'elp of your lordship.'

'But I am afraid you cannot see her this morning, Jack,' Tom said. 'She is not fully recovered—the shock, you know. She is so looking forward to the play tonight and would not for the world miss it if she can help it, so she decided to stay in bed until this evening to be sure of being well enough to attend. You understand?'

'Of course,' he said, looking at Lydia. 'Will we also have the pleasure of your company at the theatre, Count?'

'I fear not,' Lydia said. 'I 'ave to travel to Dover tonight. We catch the first tide tomorrow.'

'What a shame!' Jack said with a twinkle in his eye which was not lost on Lydia. 'I had hoped we might have an opportunity for that talk we spoke of.'

Tom looked puzzled, but Lydia smiled. 'Oh, la, I 'ad that forgot. *Je regrette*, it will 'ave to wait.'

'Of course,' he said, touching the brim of his brown beaver with a kid-gloved hand. 'I shall look forward to it.' He climbed back into his curricle and took up the reins. 'Will you tell Miss Wenthorpe I called and that I am looking forward to seeing her at the theatre tonight?' And though he addressed himself to Tom it was at Lydia he looked as he spoke.

'Of course,' Tom said, grinning. 'I am sure she would not for the world disappoint you.'

'Good day to you, de Clancy. I shall look forward to seeing you on your return.' He flicked the reins to set the horses moving. 'Good day, Wenthorpe.'

'What does he want to talk to the Count about?' Tom asked, as they watched him go, then set off down the road, arm in arm like the two young men they purported to be.

'The de Clancy family. He asked to have some conversation with me at the ball.'

'Why? What is it to him?'

'I do not know. Either he has seen right through my disguise or he knows there is no Comte de Clancy and he is playing with me like a cat with a mouse. He says he would like to help me but I think he means to denounce me.'

'Of course he will not. He believes in the Comte de Clancy, as everyone does. Your disguise is perfect. As for what he thinks of Lydia, it is clear the man intends to offer for you.'

'Oh, for goodness' sake!' she said, stamping her foot. 'It is bad enough playing your April gowk games without being hurled at the head of that... that rake. I have taken an aversion to him and if you mention his name again I shall refuse to go a step further.'

'Very well,' he said meekly, having been confirmed in his belief that his sister was in love. 'But do not stamp in that fashion; it reminds me of nothing so much as a spoiled young lady and I shall have to revise my opinion of your ability to sustain the man.'

'Then let us abandon it at once,' she said quickly.

'After we have seen this lawyer fellow,' he said, taking her arm and walking her swiftly in the direction of Westminster where Charles Wilmott had his offices.

CHAPTER SIX

IF TOM had not been with her Lydia would have turned and fled as soon as she found herself in Charles Wilmott's office. It frightened her with its air of legality, its shelves of heavy books, its piles of papers on every available space and its smell of candle wax and ink. A big desk was set in the middle of the room, behind which sat a young man with fair curly locks and broad shoulders. He looked up from studying some papers as they entered and rose to greet them. 'I am Charles Wilmott,' he said, moving forward with hand extended though it was obvious from his puzzled expression that he was not sure which of his visitors was the Comte.

'I 'ave my cousin, Thomas Wenthorpe, with me,' Lydia explained, shaking his hand and bowing. ''E will perhaps 'elp me if I do not understand the Engleesh.'

'Of course. Please be seated.' He pulled forward a couple of chairs and retreated behind his desk again. 'Thank you for coming so promptly.' He paused, shuffling papers, then looked up and smiled. Lydia decided she liked his smile and at any other time might have enjoyed talking to him, but now she could do nothing but fidget and wish herself anywhere but where she was. She forced herself to lean back in her chair and cross her legs in a nonchalant pose.

'I 'ave leetle time,' she said, playing with her quizzing glass. 'I 'ave to go to France.'

'I may be able to save you the journey,' he said. 'I believe you were going there to recover some jewels?'

'*Oui*,' she admitted guardedly.

'Where in France?'

Lydia looked at Tom, but he was busy studying the ceiling and no help at all. She said the first thing that came into her head. 'Fleurry; it is a leetle village between Toulouse and Bordeaux. I 'ave never been there, you understand, but *ma mère* 'ave spoken of it.' That, at least, was true; her mother had often been homesick for the little village where she was born and had told her children that one day she would go back. Sadly the dream had never been fulfilled.

'De Clancy is a very old French family, is it not?'

'Oh, yes,' Tom put in suddenly. 'My mother was very proud of her antecedents, although the family refused to acknowledge her after she became an actress. It caused her great sorrow. She always hoped they might be reconciled, but it was not to be.'

'Is that the reason for this family dispute I have heard about?'

Tom seized the opening thus provided. 'Yes, of course. So silly. What have Maurice and I to do with quarrels which happened before we were born? We are the best of friends, is that not so, Cousin?'

'*Mais oui*,' Lydia said, uncrossing and re-crossing her pantaloon-clad legs. 'But, *pardonnez*, what is it to you, *monsieur*?'

'I come to that. Can you describe the family crest?'

Lydia felt trapped. She looked again at Tom, hoping fervently for a smile and a nod which meant they could reveal their deception, but now he was studying his fingernails. 'I 'ave only seen it once or twice,' she said, remembering a pair of silver-backed hairbrushes belonging to her mother. They had had a design etched on them which might have been a crest. 'I cannot remember *exactement*, but it 'as a stag and a falcon. The falcon 'as its wings so.' She held out her arms. 'Both 'ave coronets.'

'Good. Good. What would you say if I told you I had seen it recently, here in England, on a fob?'

'I should be surprised.'

'Why?' demanded Tom. 'Your father, my uncle, may well have sold pieces when he came to England on his way to America. He would have needed the rhino for the journey and his new life, don't you think?'

'It was not sold in this country,' the lawyer said. 'It was taken from the knapsack of a dead French soldier. We believe it had been plundered. . .'

'We?' queried Lydia, thinking suddenly of Douglas Fincham and his threat to find the real Count.

'My client, a gallant officer and a true gentleman, has asked me to try and restore the find to its rightful owner.'

'A fob?' queried Tom, while Lydia digested the information that it could not be Douglas after all; he had never been a soldier, let alone a gallant one. 'I wonder why he bothers? To the victor belong the spoils and all that.'

'It is more than one piece, it is a whole cache of jewels and gold plate, though, as yet, I have only been privileged to see the fob. . .' He stopped and looked from one to the other, puzzled by their reaction. The Count was showing a decided lack of enthusiasm and the gleam in Thomas Wenthorpe's eye was one of avarice; Charles had seen that light in too many eyes to be mistaken.

Lydia was the first to come to her senses. 'It cannot belong to me,' she said firmly. 'There must be two de Clancy families. *Mon père* took all he 'ad to Canada. 'E left nothing behind.'

Mr Wilmott looked puzzled. 'But the story. . .your visit to France. . .everything I have heard. . .'

'A tale made up to gain entry to the *ton*,' she said.

'You are not the Comte de Clancy?'

'No,' said Lydia and,

'Yes,' said Tom.

Tom looked daggers at Lydia and then turned back to the lawyer. 'What my cousin means is that the title is assumed. The family name certainly is not.'

'Oh, I see.' Charles Wilmott smiled at Lydia. 'But the story of the jewels may be more true than you imagined. All I need is proof of your identity and then I will arrange for you to see the whole collection and you may be able to identify it. Have you papers? Old letters? Other articles of jewellery which might match?'

'I do not think so. I wish you to forget it, *monsieur*. If our silly game 'as led you to believe we are the rightful owners of the property, then I am sorry. Tell the gallant officer 'is honesty does him credit, but the plunder is 'is.' She almost forgot her accent in her anxiety. 'I wish you would forget the whole affair.'

She bent to pick up her beaver hat from the floor where she had put it and stood up. 'I bid you adieu, *monsieur.*'

Reluctantly Tom rose to follow her to the door. He paused and looked back at the lawyer. 'I will talk him round.'

As soon as the front door had closed and they found themselves on the step, he turned on his sister in annoyance. 'Really, Lydia, you are a sapskull; those jewels rightfully belong to us. Our mother was a de Clancy and we would have no difficulty proving that.'

'Not without admitting the Comte is a complete fabrication and involving Papa. Forget it, Tom.'

'You said you wished the Count would come to an untimely end and that is what he will do.'

'Oh, most certainly; at any rate, he must disappear, but that has to be the end of it.'

'But with the Count out of the way. . .'

She managed a faint smile. 'Oh, so we are plotting murder, are we?'

'Don't be such a pudding, Lydia. You talk as if the man were flesh and blood.'

'Oh, don't you see?' she cried, so angry and frustrated that she had allowed her voice to rise and was receiving some surprised glances from passers-by. 'To everyone else he is real and to inherit what is his you would have to provide proof of his death to the lawyer. How do you propose to do that when he does not even exist?'

'I'll think of something.'

'For two pins I would have told Mr Wilmott the whole truth instead of only half of it. I wish I had now. Tom, what we are doing is criminal and I wish you had never talked me into it.'

'It was you hit on the idea of using the de Clancy name, not me, and you who described the crest. And I ain't letting a fortune like that go begging. Mama was a de Clancy and if there are no other relatives then I am the true heir to the fortune and if I can secure it I will be free of Douglas Fincham and can pay all my debts.'

It was no good; she could not continue to argue with him on the step where they were in danger of drawing a crowd. She clapped the beaver on her Brutus wig and hurried down the street to find a hackney, impatient to return home and throw off the hateful disguise.

He set off after her. 'Think, Lydia,' he said, too self-centred to know when to keep silent. 'Just think what it will mean. You can return to being Miss Lydia Wenthorpe and enjoy the rest of the Season. You have yet to make an appearance at Almack's; I collect Aunt Aggie said vouchers had arrived from one of the patronesses—I forget which but it is of no consequence. And she is moving heaven and earth to get you into one of the Queen's Drawing Rooms and there is your own come-out ball. With the extra blunt we could make it an affair to remember.' He paused, smiling artlessly. 'Longham will offer for you and you will end the year a marchioness.'

'No one will offer for me,' she said bitterly. 'Not that I would have the Marquis of Longham if he did.'

'Why ever not?'

'Because he is. . .' She stopped, unable to put her illogical reasoning into words. 'Oh, you are an unfeeling, insensible thatchgallows,' she snapped. 'And, what is worse, you have made one of me too. I am not fit to be anyone's wife. I shall go home to Raventrees at the earliest opportunity and become an ape leader.'

Unabashed, he grinned. 'If you expect me to believe that tarradiddle, then you must think me a bigger souse-crown than you are yourself. It is obvious to anyone but a complete codshead that you are wearing the willow for Jack Bellingham.'

'I am not! And if you dare so much as mention his name again, Tom Wenthorpe, we will have a serious falling-out.'

He grinned and shrugged his shoulders, but at least she had managed to silence him. If no one mentioned the Marquis, then it might, just might, be easier to stop thinking about him.

The object of their discussion was at that moment driving himself to Chelsea in his curricle, musing on the strange behaviour of the Wenthorpe brother and sister. He could, to a degree, understand Tom trying to gammon his friends for a lark, especially on April Fool's Day, but what he could not understand was why Miss Wenthorpe should be a party to the deception, perhaps even its instigator. It was not the behaviour one would expect from a well brought-up young lady in her first Season. He had called her a hoyden, but he had not really meant it, and now she seemed determined to prove him right. He was curious and strangely hurt, as if it was him she were trying to gull. Nor could he fathom the reason for it. He promised himself that he would solve the riddle later and resolutely put his mind to the business which had brought him to London in the first place and to Chelsea today. Drawing up at the faded door of a tall, narrow house, he jumped down and handed the ribbons to his groom. 'Walk 'em up and down a bit,' he said. 'I'll not be long.'

Finding documentary evidence of a wager made half a century before was, he had soon discovered, more difficult than he had supposed. The records of the well-known gambling clubs went back many years and it had been diverting to read in their betting books of the extraordinary things people staked their money and possessions on, not just cards and horse racing, but whether Lord A would be married before the Earl of B, which of two spiders would catch a fly in their webs first, or the speed with which raindrops ran down a window; even what colour a certain gentleman's waistcoat would be the following day. Fortunes had been won and lost in these puerile bets but nowhere was there any mention of the wood on the Longham estate. He had concluded that the wager, whatever it was, had been made at Longham Towers or in its vicinity and he would have to resume his search there.

After his last meeting with Charles, it had occurred to him to ask Littlejohn if he had ever heard anything of a wager. Apart from Tewkes, who went everywhere with his master, Littlejohn, the head groom, was the only one of the Longham servants to accompany him to London. The man had been in the Duke's employ all his working life, as had his father and grandfather before him; if anyone knew any old stories about the wood and those who lived on the neighbouring estate, he would. Jack had sent Tewkes to fetch him from the mews where he lived over the stables.

'It were allus called Harker's Wood,' the groom had said, running his fingers through his sparse gingery hair. 'On account of the family who lived in the house t'other side of it in the old days was called Harker. That was long afore Mr Grimshaw's time, o' course, Mr Grimshaw 'avin' been there only since the beginning of the war. About the time you went away, sir. Sir Bertram Harker was a right crabby old man, used to drive us boys outa the wood with an old sporting gun.' He chuckled at the memory. 'I recall one time it backfired, set his beard afire and knocked him off'n his feet.'

'So the wood belonged to him then. When was that?'

'Oh, fifty year ago, at least. I were a lad o' six or seven.'

'The same age as my father?'

'Oh, aye, he and me did often play together, afore he were sent away to school, that were. Course we weren't s'posed to, him being the old Duke's heir and me naught but the head groom's son.' He smiled again, revealing a broken tooth. 'When he came back, things were different; we hardly met 'cept in the stables.'

Jack could readily imagine that. 'So, the wood changed hands in my grandfather's time?'

'That seems the way of it.'

'Do you know how it came about? Did the old Duke buy it? Or could he have won it with a wager?'

'I can't say as I know for sure, sir, but your

grandfather weren't any too free with his blunt and Sir Bertram was known for a gambler. It could be.'

'Were they enemies?'

'Not then. Thick as thieves, they were. Hunted a lot together, went to the races together. Raced each other sometimes.' He paused. 'When Sir Bertram died, the house was put up for sale to pay his debts but it didn' go and had to be rented out, then it stood empty, let go to rack and ruin, 'til Mr Grimshaw took it over in '08 or '09.' He scratched his head again. 'Sir Bertram had a daughter, I recollect, but she married and moved away.'

Jack had been disappointed, not so much at the likely loss of the land but at the thought that Ernest Grimshaw might have bested him. 'It looks as if I must come home by Weeping Cross,' he had told Charles later the same day.

'There may be a note of the wager in the archives at Longham Towers,' Charles had said. 'Or Grimshaw's deeds, though I doubt you'd get a look at those.' He had paused, stroking his chin thoughtfully. 'We must find the daughter. She may know something of it.'

It had taken Charles three weeks to discover that the daughter had died long since, but there was a granddaughter, a widow, who now lived with her son in genteel poverty in rooms above a shoemaker's shop in Chelsea. It was to see Mrs Henrietta Griggs that Jack had driven to Chelsea, with Littlejohn up behind him on the tiger's seat. Tewkes had been left to attend to the laundering of six shirts and a dozen neckcloths, and the polishing of three pairs of boots. He had grumbled, assuming his beloved Captain could not be trusted anywhere without him, but Jack had insisted that clean laundry was essential to his well-being and if he did not look in prime twig at the Drury Lane theatre that night the failure would be laid at his valet's door. And besides, no one but Tewkes knew how to get the mirror shine on his hessians that everyone envied. The flummery had the desired effect and Tewkes had grudgingly allowed Littlejohn to take his place.

Henrietta Griggs, having been apprised of the visit by a letter from Charles, received him politely but coolly. She was six and twenty, or thereabouts, and a little too thin. Her grey cambric dress was very simple, though well-cut, and her stiff white cap with its black ribbons was worn over mousy hair scraped back into a coil at her neck. She would have been plain, but for good bones, fine eyes and a well-modulated voice which soon dispelled this unfavourable image.

'May I offer you refreshment?' she asked, taking his hat and gloves and laying them on a small table just inside the door. 'Tea? Coffee? Some wine, perhaps?'

'Thank you, tea would be welcome.'

She went to a door at the end of the tiny hall and called to someone to bring the tea tray, then led the way into a small drawing-room whose main piece of furniture was a pianoforte in a window alcove. A boy of about five was playing on the hearthrug in front of a tiny fire. At his mother's prompting he rose and went to sit at a dining-table on the far side of the room, which was spread with a cloth and laid out with paper and paints.

'He likes to draw,' his mother said, gazing at him fondly. 'You do not mind if he stays with us? He will be no trouble.'

'He is welcome,' Jack said, realising that the child was to be his mother's chaperon. 'I shall not impose on your time for long. I believe my lawyer has acquainted you with my errand?'

'In part, yes. Do please be seated. I believe there is some dispute about the ownership of some land, though I doubt I can resolve it for you. I have never been to Longham and I never met my grandfather.'

'Did your mother never speak of him?'

'Rarely.' She smiled. 'She had, I believe, expected a good dowry but her father died about the time of her wedding—I am not sure which event came first—and it was then discovered that not only was there no portion coming to her, but the house and land had to be sold to meet his debts. And even that was not as extensive as she had believed it to be. For someone whose expectations had been high, this was a particularly bad blow. It caused a rift with her husband, my father, which was never healed. He left her a year later.'

'I am sorry to re-open old wounds. . .'

'Oh, they are not my wounds, my lord. I don't remember my father. My mother and I managed tolerably well on our own. She was a fine musician and I have inherited that gift, at least sufficiently to earn a modest living as a music teacher. My father turned up at Mama's funeral but there was nothing for him and I was a stranger to him. He went away again immediately afterwards.'

A skinny little maid appeared with the tea tray, which she put on a small table at Mrs Griggs's elbow.

'Why was the land not as extensive as your mother had hoped?' he asked, watching her pouring tea with long-fingered, delicate hands. 'Could it have had anything to do with Harker's Wood?'

'That was only one of many such disappointments,' she said, handing him a cup of tea. 'My mother told me that when her father died she discovered the land on which the wood stood had been lost in a wager with a neighbour, a horse race or something of the sort. I am afraid she was incensed...'

'That I can readily understand. But was she sure that she had no redress? Was anything written down?'

'My lord, why do you wish to know? It is so long ago that surely there can be no doubt about its ownership now? And, forgive me, it is so small a thing compared to the rest of your...the Duke of Sutton's estate.'

'Oh, it is not the value of the land itself that concerns me, Mrs Griggs, but the fact that it has been usurped from under my father's nose. He is not well, you understand, and I think it was a dastardly trick to take advantage of that.' He smiled and set his cup down. 'I need proof it belongs to the Longham estate.'

'Is there nothing in the estate records?'

'Nothing has come to light as yet.' He smiled. 'My father is not the best of record-keepers. I had hoped you might be able to help me.'

'And if you find proof, what then?'

'Why, then we shall turn the fellow off. He is

ruining the wood by indiscriminate felling and not a new tree has he planted. It looks like a barren desert where once it had been full of wildlife. We are quite near the east coast and it had used to shield the village and the villagers' crops from the gales coming from the North Sea. Sir Bertram Harker was a countryman; whatever kind of a scapegrace he was, he would not have cut down the trees without careful re-planting and he knew my family would not either. Now the whole neighbourhood is up in arms and blaming my father for doing nothing about it. *I* intend to do something, Mrs Griggs.'

'But you need to prove your title to the land?'

'Yes.'

She smiled. 'I have a boxful of papers and correspondence between my mother and the family lawyer from the time of my grandfather's death. I do not know why I kept it. I suppose I thought that one day I might read it all and put it into order. . .'

'Mrs Griggs, you will oblige me immeasurably if you will fetch it out and look through it. If you find anything, anything at all about the wood, would you make it available to me?' He hesitated before going on. 'I will recompense you generously for your time and trouble.'

'That is quite unnecessary, my lord,' she said coolly. He realised he had made a serious error of judgement; she would regard payment as an act of charity or the result of a guilty conscience on his part. 'I will do what I can.' She set down her cup on the tray and rose to her feet, bringing the interview to an end. 'If I have any success, I will inform Mr Wilmott.'

Almost reluctantly he rose and took his leave. She was, he decided as he drove back to town, a courageous and independent woman who had shown none of the resentment he had expected. After all, she could have cut up rough and said the land or its price should have been part of her mother's portion; she could have refused to see him, let alone help him. If he should win his case against Grimshaw with her help, then he would find some way, acceptable to her, of making amends for the shortcomings of their respective grandsires.

It seemed that one of his problems looked a fair way to being solved, so perhaps the other might take a step forward. Not that the ownership of a haul of gold and jewels was a particular problem; if Charles solved the mystery of the crest, then he would naturally do his best to reunite the owner with his belongings, but if it were not possible, then he could console himself that he had done all he could and accept his good fortune with an easy mind. He began to feel more optimistic and it was in that frame of mind he went to his club for nuncheon, had a hand or two of whist and then returned home where he found a note from Charles asking him to call because he had not only traced the crest, but had spoken to a Comte Maurice de Clancy, who might turn out to be the true owner of the jewels. He had asked the young gentleman to provide proof of identity before proceeding further.

'De Clancy!' Jack lifted his eyes from the letter and stared into the gilt-edged mirror above the fire in his library and smiled suddenly at his reflection. Of one thing he was sure: the Comte de Clancy could not prove his identity. But why had the Wenthorpes chosen that name above all others? Had they known about the jewels? Was it not so much a harmless prank as a criminal deception to lay their hands on a fortune? He did not want to believe ill of either of them, but what other construction could be put on their behaviour? He could not understand why other people had not seen through the disguise; it was as plain as a pikestaff to him who the Comte de Clancy really was. And why involve pretty little Miss Thornton? Was she their dupe or part of the plot? He could call on her and try to find out, but how could he do that without betraying Lydia? For some reason he was reluctant to acknowledge even to himself, he did not want to do that.

He could almost see Lydia's reflection beside his in the mirror: her dark hair, curling over her ears, her laughing violet eyes, the upward curve of her mouth, the proud set of her head, her long neck and white shoulders. And what no mirror could reveal: her spirit, her humour, her spunk. He remembered that waltz in the moonlight and his offer of help. She had almost laughed in his face. Furious with himself for his gullibility, he screwed the letter up in his hand and cursed the fate which had made him decide to bury that dead French dragoon before the carrion got to him.

He roused himself as Tewkes came in, carrying a pair of hessians which rivalled the mirror for their shine. 'Here's your boots, Captain,' he said. 'And if you don't stir yourself and change your rig, you'll be late.' He paused when he noticed the letter in his master's clenched fist and his thundercloud looks. 'Not bad news, I hope?'

'What? Oh, no. It seems we might have found the owner of the jewels.'

'Oh.' Then, 'I'm sorry for that, sir.'

Jack sighed. 'So am I, Tewkes, so am I.'

'I did say you should let well alone, now didn't I? But what's done is done, as they say, so you might as well forget about it.'

But that was one thing he could not do, he told himself, as he went up to his dressing-room to change into evening clothes. He could not forget, nor forgive someone for making a fool of him, not to mention half of the London *ton*. It would serve her right if she were to be exposed.

Lydia herself would not have quibbled at this estimation of her just deserts; she felt beastly. As for facing the *haut monde* from a box at the theatre, it was the last thing she wanted to do. But as Tom patiently pointed out when she said she would not go, who was there to make a connection between Lydia Wenthorpe and the Comte de Clancy?

'The Marquis of Longham,' she retorted.

'Fustian! You are making a Cheltenham tragedy out of nothing at all. You are over-sensitive because you have taken a fancy to him and he to you. . .'

'Don't be so vulgar! And far from liking me he holds me in aversion.'

'Then why did he call this morning to apologise to you and assure himself that you would be at the theatre tonight?'

'Curiosity. He has an idea about the Count and wanted to catch us out.'

'But he didn't, did he? And if he has any suspicions, which, give me leave to doubt, you will not allay them by refusing his invitation after he has taken prodigious trouble to bespeak a box when almost every performance is sold out.'

Lydia could think of no reason that her aunt would believe for her absenting herself from the outing and, besides, she really did want to see the famous Edmund Kean on the stage. Grumbling, she agreed to go and took herself up to her room to change.

She took especial trouble with her appearance and it was over an hour later when she returned downstairs to join her aunt and brother for the drive to the theatre. She had dressed in a gown of deep pink gauze with tiny puffed sleeves over a rose taffeta slip. The neckline and high waist were outlined in tiny rosebuds and seed-pearls and a gossamer scarf was draped over her bare arms. A ruby necklace, pink satin slippers, elbow-length gloves and a mother-of-pearl fan completed an ensemble she knew set off her dark hair and clear complexion to perfection. She did not suppose it would weigh with Lord Longham in the least, but she was determined he should not find her out of countenance tonight. She would show him that she could be as well-bred and ladylike as the best and she would behave with absolute decorum; nothing would evince the slightest need to criticise.

The Marquis of Longham rose to greet them as they were shown to his box a few minutes before the rising of the curtain. He looked magnificent in black satin knee-breeches, a black long-tailed coat and a white brocade waistcoat, across which hung a silver watch-chain and a large fob. Smiling easily, he came forward to take Mrs Wenthorpe's hand and usher her to a seat. Then he turned to perform the same office for Lydia, but the warmth had faded from his eyes and gone was the twitch of amusement from his mouth; there was not even a hint of mockery. He was perfectly civil, perfectly correct, but cold as charity, as he took her hand and bowed over it. Her own smile froze on her face and she uttered an involuntary, 'Oh,' as he straightened his back and she was able to see the detail on the fob he wore. The stag and the falcon were etched there as clearly as they had been on her mother's hairbrushes. She found herself staring at it, her mind so tumultuous with the thought that here was Mr Wilmott's client, the 'gallant officer and true gentleman', she did not, at first, realise he had spoken.

'I beg your pardon?' She sat down heavily in the chair he pulled forward for her.

'I said, I hope I see you recovered from your fall?'

'I did not fall, I was thrown,' she responded mechanically. 'And apart from a bump on the back of my head which ached abominably at the time I am none the worse.'

'I am glad to hear it.' He paused, then to her consternation added, 'I had the pleasure of meeting your cousin, de Clancy, again this morning. I asked him to convey a message to you.'

She lifted startled eyes to his, but his expression was bland and she forced herself to speak calmly. 'Something about an apology, I collect.'

He smiled. 'Yes. I had no right to speak as I did when you had been hurt. In fact, it is not my place to criticise you at all on your conduct or which mount you may ride.'

If that were all he had to criticise she would have been content, but his pointed reference to the Count made her more than uncomfortable. She forced herself to answer him. 'Think no more of it, my lord. I own I was at fault, as my aunt was quick to point out when I arrived home.' She laughed, but it was a cracked sound, without merriment. 'I shall conduct myself with more seemliness in future. I would not want my papa to think my case was hopeless.'

'Oh, never that,' he murmured, as the orchestra struck up the overture. 'I cannot believe the lively Miss Wenthorpe is without offers. . .'

'None that I would entertain,' she said, as the curtain opened and the audience began a frenzied clapping. Let him think on that!

The play was good and Edmund Kean magnificent, but Lydia could not have reported on the plot, nor described the costumes, nor repeated a single line of the dialogue, because her entire attention was taken up with speculating on how the Marquis of Longham came into possession of the fob and whether there was, indeed, more of the same in his keeping. Had he seen through her disguise and invented the jewellery to catch her out? But if that were so, where had he acquired the fob? Had he really found it on a body? She shuddered at the thought and stole a glance at him. Did she imagine it, or did he look darkly brooding, sinister even? He was certainly not smiling, even though the audience was laughing at some droll remark made by one of the players. He was attending to the events on the stage no more than she was.

Long before the interval, she wished the evening at an end. Of one thing she was certain: any hope she might have entertained that he might, one day, come to love her as she loved him was at an end. By her own foolhardy actions she had put herself far below his touch.

To the accompaniment of applause, the interval curtains closed across the stage and the new gas lamps were turned up to fill the auditorium with their smoky glow. Jack went to the door to send for refreshments for the whole party, and Tom, who had been sitting behind Lydia, leaned forward and whispered in her ear. 'I say, Sis, have you seen Longham's fob?'

'Yes.'

'It is, isn't it?'

'I believe so.'

'Then he must be. . .'

'The honest soldier? Yes.'

'Oh, lord, Sis, what now? If I had known it was he. . .' He stopped suddenly as Jack returned, followed by Mrs Burford and Frank who had been occupying the adjoining box.

That good lady was her usual talkative self and, having dismissed the play out of hand with half a dozen words, went on to say how glad she was to see them and to know that the family were once again all in accord. Mrs Wenthorpe, who did not know what to make of this, replied tartly, 'Why should we not be in accord?'

'Well, to be sure, I am the last one to dwell on it,' Mrs Burford said huffily, accepting a glass of champagne from the Marquis, who was listening in rapt attention, 'even if the Count did leave my house somewhat abruptly. If it was to mend a rift in his own family affairs, then I, for one, applaud it. But I was sorry to see him go.'

'Carrie Burford, just what are you prosing on about?' Mrs Wenthorpe demanded. 'If you are talking about that man-milliner you introduced at your ball as the Comte de Clancy, then you are a bigger sapskull than I took you for. He is a nobody.'

'Oh, then I have mistaken the matter,' Mrs Burford said, colouring to the roots of her hair. 'I should not have mentioned it. But I did wonder if he had received his letter before leaving for Dover. . .'

'How should I know?' demanded Agatha, out of all patience.

'Yes, he did,' Tom put in quickly, seeing that Lydia had been deprived of speech. 'Frank gave it to him.'

'Mama, I told you I had,' Frank said, aggrieved. 'One would think I could not be trusted to carry a letter now.'

'Oh, but you cannot blame me for being interested in the young man,' his mother went on. 'He is such a romantical figure and if he regains his fortune, which was what the letter was all about, for Frank told me so, he will become one of the most eligible bachelors in town this Season, don't you think? Why, Lydia, he might offer for you. . .' She stopped suddenly because the Marquis chose that moment to choke on his champagne. 'Is anything wrong, my lord?'

'No, indeed,' he said, wiping his eyes on a lace-edged handkerchief. 'The bubbles, you know. . .'

To Lydia's immense relief the conversation was brought to a halt by the dimming of the house lights, which necessitated Mrs Burford and her son returning to their own box.

But that was not the end of it. The subject was returned to at supper, which the Marquis had arranged at a hotel not far from the theatre. While they ate soup *à la* Charlotte and fillets of Turbot, removed with glazed ham and ducklings in an orange sauce, Jack, pretending to an idle curiosity, commented, 'Mrs Burford is a great gossip, is she not? Do you think she invents half of it?'

'Course she does,' said Mrs Wenthorpe. 'Caroline Burford is a notable gabble-grinder and a credulous gull to believe everything she is told. Why, she must have known that having a costume ball on April Fool's Day would encourage pranksters.'

He was silent for a moment and Lydia began to hope that he had given up the subject, but when Mrs Wenthorpe turned to speak to Tom he had, out of politeness, to address himself to her, sitting at his side. 'I am persuaded you did not find the play to your liking, Miss Wenthorpe, and for that I am sorry. Perhaps we should have gone to Covent Garden instead?'

'Not at all. I wanted to see Edmund Kean. He is every bit as good an actor as they say he is.'

'You had not seen him before?'

'No.'

'I had thought you might be a frequent playgoer—a connoisseur, in fact.'

Startled, she looked up from the dish of Rhenish cream in front of her to meet his gaze and then looked away again. She would not give him the satisfaction of asking him why he had thought it. She knew and he knew she knew. 'My mother had an interest in the stage,' she said. 'She often talked of it and, of course, we learned some Shakespeare in the schoolroom, Tom and I, hardly grounds for supposing us to be knowledgeable on the subject.'

'Then you were bored by the play.'

'Not in the least, my lord.'

'But you were not paying attention.'

She smiled. 'Perhaps I was overcome by the honour you did us by inviting us into your box. I felt I was the one on display.'

'And very prettily you display, Miss Wenthorpe. I was the envy of every young blade in the audience.'

If she had not felt so miserable, she might have been pleased enough by the compliment to flirt a little, but it did not matter what he said—every word was a barb, every sentence held an innuendo and she knew he was still playing with her in the way a fisherman played in his catch, letting out the line and then, when the fish was exhausted, reeling it in. She might dive and try to swim away, but inexorably he would land her. She applied herself to eating so as not to look at him, but she was acutely aware of his presence beside her, his size and strength, his masculinity, the way his eyes and voice made her feel weak with longing. She wondered what he would say and do if she confessed all. She had already tasted his anger and his sarcasm; his enmity would be unbearable. But it was inevitable; she had better make up her mind to that. He had made it very clear that he disapproved of gamblers, hoydens and young ladies who behaved without any sense of propriety. The Count had gone to France, from where he would never return, but it was too late for Lydia Wenthorpe to set things right with the Marquis because of the visit to the lawyer and that fob. Was it real? Or was it a paste replica made purposely to trap her?

'How long have you known Mr Burford?' he asked.

'What?' She came out of her reverie to find him looking closely at her. 'Oh, Frank? Forever. The Burfords have been country neighbours of the Wenthorpes for at least two generations. Why do you ask?'

'I wondered why the Comte de Clancy should stay at Burford House, when he is a cousin of yours.'

She fumbled with her napkin. 'You heard the story.'

'Yes, but your aunt seems very displeased by it and she does not seem to be a lady to bear a grudge for long; she is far too sensible. It seemed to me that the feud might not be between the Wenthorpes and the de Clancys but between Mrs Wenthorpe and Mrs Burford? I collect your aunt does not approve of Mr Burford as a suitor?'

For a moment she was taken aback and very nearly smiled at the thought of Frank offering for her, but recovered herself to reply haughtily, 'Really, sir, that is hardly a matter that need concern you.'

'Oh, but it does. If Burford's constant escort is displeasing you. . .'

'Displeasing me?' She was genuinely annoyed with

him now; what right had he to question her? 'On the contrary, my lord. Mr Burford is a gentleman and he would never do the least thing to upset me. And if I did not like his company, I would choose another's.'

'I beg pardon,' he said, smiling and proving he was not in the least sorry. 'You do right to set me down. I excuse myself on the grounds that my interest is only for your happiness.'

'I assure you I am perfectly happy.'

'Then I must accept that.' He paused and then, as if to bely that by adding to her discomposure, he went on, 'I once offered my help if you should have need of it and, though you declined it, rest assured that the offer still stands.'

'Thank you, my lord, but, even supposing I need any assistance, I should apply to my family.'

He smiled. 'Yes, but families can be the very devil, sometimes.'

'Yours is?' She felt on safer ground by turning the subject.

His smile turned to a rueful grin. 'My father is not in the best of health and he finds attending to matters on the estate sadly wearying. I find I must go home. I have an engagement in the morning, but shall leave tomorrow afternoon.'

'Indeed, I am sorry.' She tried to convey by her tone that his presence or otherwise in London was a matter of indifference to her, but succeeded only in showing by her heightened colour and slightly shaking hand that she was far from indifferent. If he was out of town, then she would be safe from his all-too-perceptive eye for a little while, but all the same his going would leave a void in her life. It was as if her last bulwark had been removed and there would be no one left to lean on if things got really bad. And she knew from experience how comforting leaning on him could be. Tom, brother or no, would be of little use in a tight corner, and Frank was only marginally better.

'I had hoped to have some conversation with that elusive French gentleman before he left for France,' he said. 'Now it must wait.'

'I do not think he intends to return.'

'No?' He lifted one quizzical eyebrow. 'Mrs Burford seems to think otherwise. And he would hardly abandon a fortune in jewels. . .'

'It was a mistake. The jewels were not his.'

'You surprise me,' he said in all honesty. If the masquerade had not been for the purpose of taking possession of the loot, why had the Comte been conjured up? What devious game was she playing now? 'I thought that was the reason he was in London.'

'And I would wish him in Jericho,' she said. 'If you cannot find a more interesting topic of conversation, we may as well be silent.' She was immediately mortified by her rudeness and stammered an apology.

'No, you are quite right,' he said. 'As a subject of conversation, the Comte de Clancy is a dead bore. Tell me, have you read *The Corsair*? I don't think Lord Byron will ever better it, do you?'

The evening ended with a discussion of the notable literature of the day, but Lydia had little to contribute and was glad when the meal came to an end and their carriage was called up to take them home.

It was a silent journey; everyone seemed to be immersed in private thoughts and disinclined to chatter. Tom, who had seen the strange looks his aunt had been throwing at him and Lydia, especially when the Count was mentioned, guessed that an explanation was about to be demanded, and took himself off to White's as soon as he had seen his aunt and sister safely indoors.

He was right. Instead of allowing Lydia to go straight upstairs to bed, Mrs Wenthorpe required her niece to attend her in her sitting-room where she bade her sit down. 'Now I ain't missing a sheet and I ain't cabbage-green,' she said, sending her dresser away to find someone to bring them hot chocolate. 'There is something havey-cavey going on and I want to know what it is. You and Tom are in a scrape and it's all to do with Frank Burford and that fly-by-night flat-catcher who calls himself the Comte de Clancy. I'm not budging from this chair until you have told me, so you may as well confess.'

Her niece's answer was to throw herself on her knees at her aunt's feet and burst into a torrent of tears. It was some minutes before she was composed enough to do as she was bidden and then she was taken completely by surprise when, instead of the severe scold she had expected, she heard her aunt chuckling with unsuppressed delight. 'Oh, what a Canterbury tale, to be sure,' she said, wiping her eyes. 'And it serves Letty Thornton right and Carrie Burford too. But there's no doubt you've got yourselves into a coil and there's nothing for it but I shall have to help you out of it. Now go to bed, child, and tomorrow we will put all to rights.'

Lydia rose and kissed her aunt, before making her way to her own bedchamber. She felt a great deal better for her confession but whatever her aunt did it would not put things right with the Marquis. He would never love her now. Throwing off her beautiful gown as if it had been no more than a rag, she flung herself between the sheets and wept as if her heart would break.

CHAPTER SEVEN

'YOU will tell Miss Thornton the truth,' her aunt said next day as they drove to Park Lane. 'But I do not think it is in the least necessary to tell her mama. I do not care to have her think I am a flat of the first water. I shall have to swallow my pride enough as it is to call on her.'

'I am sorry, Aunt,' Lydia said for the hundredth time. 'I never thought. . .'

'No, that is just it, you do not think, but I can forgive you, for I am persuaded that it was Tom and Frank Burford who were at fault.'

No, it is not fair to blame them entirely, I was the one who thought of it first.' She paused, but when her aunt did not reply went on, 'What will you tell Lady Thornton?'

'I shall endeavour not to tell her anything but if I have to I shall own the Count is your cousin on your mother's side and I erred in thinking the rest of the family had perished. You have sent him away and we must hope he will be soon forgotten. I have told Tom that I expect him to make a clean breast of all to his father.'

'He will not like doing that.'

'No more he won't, but I believe he will do it.'

'And Mr Fincham? He will call Tom out for a welcher.'

'If he does, it will be one service my scapegrace

nephew cannot ask his sister to do for him,' Mrs Wenthorpe said with some asperity. 'It is time that young man stopped hiding behind your petticoats and behaved like the gentleman he is supposed to be. And so I told him this morning. I rose especially early to do so.' She smiled suddenly. 'Not that you are without fault. He has come to look on you as a brother, not a sister, which is hardly to be wondered at when your behaviour is so hoydenish. You will please bear that in mind in future.'

'Yes, Aunt.'

'If we can keep all quiet, then no harm will be done to your prospects of making a match.'

'It is too late; I am sure Lord Longham knows. He has already rung a peal over me about gambling and riding out alone and wanting to drive a high-perch phaeton.'

'How very uncivil of him!' her aunt said, with a chuckle. To her way of thinking it was a sure sign of his lordship's interest. 'But, you know, there are other pebbles on the beach.'

'And there is that fob,' Lydia went on, ignoring her aunt's last remark; now was not the time to explain that other pebbles did not interest her. 'I am sure he decided to wear it last night to catch us out.'

'That is a something else again. If there is a lost fortune, it must belong to someone. Might as well be Tom. Your papa can confirm the de Clancy family history and identify the crest. The rest will be up to the lawyers.'

'That means Mr Wilmott will have to be told there is no Comte de Clancy.'

'Naturally he, above all people, will have to know.'

'And he will tell Lord Longham and. . . Oh, Aunt, I shall not dare to look his lordship in the face again.'

'Fustian! Lawyers are paid to hold their tongues and, as for Longham, whatever you may say about him, he is not a gabble-grinder.'

Lydia gave up. Her aunt had taken command and reduced everything to black and white, right and wrong, but her feelings for the Marquis could not be thought of in those terms. She shut her eyes, remembering the dance on the terrace and the feel of his arms about her waist. Oh, it was too bad of him to make her feel so soft and ready to yield, when he had meant nothing by it. Two minutes later he had been his customary, cold, haughty self.

They arrived at Thornton House without exchanging another word, and were received by Lady Thornton, who was too well-bred to comment on the early hour. 'Do be seated,' she said, then added almost triumphantly, 'I am sorry my daughter is not here, Miss Wenthorpe; she has gone riding with the Marquis of Longham. Will you take tea or coffee?' This last addressed to Agatha who seated herself next to Lydia on a sofa and replied that coffee would be very acceptable.

'I could see no harm in it,' their hostess went on, pulling the bell-rope by the handsome marble fireplace in her morning room. 'Amelia is well-chaperoned by her abigail and a groom. Besides, his lordship is a man of consequence and his address is excellent, not at all like his rake of a brother, in spite of what the tattlers say.'

'There is gossip about him?' queried Mrs Wenthorpe, looking at Lydia with a twinkling eye.

'How glad I am that Lydia has not developed a *tendre* for him.'

'Oh, it is nothing to refine upon,' her ladyship said and then began to do just that. 'He has come back to England after serving gallantly in his country's service to find his brother dead and his father missing a sheet. . .'

'The poor man can hardly be blamed for that,' Mrs Wenthorpe put in.

'No, indeed. He has a fortune from his mother, so he is not dependent on his father, which is a good thing, but. . .' She paused to order coffee from the maid who had answered her summons. 'Where was I?' If Lydia had hoped the interruption would change the subject, she was doomed to disappointment. 'Oh, yes, Longham. He has taken over the estates and practically made a pensioner of his father, who may not do a thing or spend a single groat without his permission. I do not doubt he has a reason: he must, after all, save the house and land from ruin, but I feel for His Grace, indeed I do.'

Mrs Wenthorpe murmured something which could have been assent but could equally have been the opposite, and Lydia remained silent, wondering why they stayed, when Miss Thornton was not at home. But if they left, they would only have to return so that she might fulfil her errand, but how she wished they did not have to spend the waiting time talking about the Marquis of Longham. Anything would be better than that.

'And the worst of it is,' Lady Thornton continued inexorably, 'there is talk of a court case.'

'Oh?' Mrs Wenthorpe lifted her eyebrows in an

enquiry; this was news to her, for she had thought she was abreast of all the latest *on-dit* about the Marquis of Longham.

'There is a Mr Grimshaw who has lately come to town and is by way of being a neighbour of the Bellinghams and he accuses his lordship of all manner of iniquity. I am persuaded he is nothing but a mushroom who has sprung up from nowhere, though he does seem prodigious plump in the pocket. I do not know the whole and would not repeat it in front of Miss Wenthorpe even if I did, but it is most scandalous, I can tell you.' She sighed and went on. 'Bits of muslin I can believe, but to lie and cheat and wrest a person's land from him with threats is something I cannot believe any gentleman of quality would do.'

'No, indeed,' said Mrs Wenthorpe, thoroughly confused.

'And now that he is the Duke's heir, he must needs make a good connection and I have been wondering if I ought to allow him to pay his addresses to Amelia. The Comte de Clancy has left town but Amelia is sure he means to return and she has quite set her cap at him. I am not at all certain that I would be wise to encourage him. After all, my dear Agatha, you repudiated him.'

'So I did,' Mrs Wenthorpe said. 'And very uncivilly, for which I am come to beg pardon.'

'But is the Count who he says he is?' her ladyship went on as if she had not heard her.

Lydia looked at her aunt, who seemed to take a long time answering. 'He is a de Clancy, but more than that I cannot vouchsafe. He is certainly not a gentleman.'

Lydia's amusement at this careful honesty faded when Lady Thornton said, 'Then I shall encourage the Marquis of Longham.'

Her daughter arrived back from her ride at this moment with his lordship in tow, and Lydia, seeing Amelia's sparkling eyes and flushed cheeks, came to the conclusion that the Marquis had been paying her pretty compliments, and once again the little green monster took over and it was all she could do to smile and answer him civilly when, after paying his respects to Lady Thornton and Mrs Wenthorpe, he turned to her with a look in his hazel eyes that was slightly mocking, slightly reproachful, and bowed. 'Your servant, Miss Wenthorpe. I hope I see you well?'

Declining an invitation to stay for the refreshment which was then being brought into the room, he explained he was setting out for Longham Towers almost immediately, and took his leave. Lydia watched him go with a mixture of relief that she would no longer be subjected to his searching scrutiny and desperation that he had gone thinking ill of her and there was no way she could put the matter right.

As soon as the footman had closed the door on him Lady Thornton dismissed the maid and began asking her daughter where his lordship had taken her, what he had said to her and her replies, and whether she found him amiable, so that Lydia was left with the impression that the young lady had found him very amiable indeed.

'Did he say he would return in time for the Countess of Boreton's ball?' her ladyship asked, but before her daughter could reply turned to Mrs Wenthorpe. 'Amy Fincham comes out this year, though she is hardly out of the schoolroom. Amelia will put her quite in the shade, especially if the Comte or Longham comes up to scratch.' Then to Lydia, 'Will you go, Miss Wenthorpe?'

'Of course she will go,' Mrs Wenthorpe put in as Lydia hesitated. 'The invitations arrived days ago.'

'It will be a glittering affair, though it will not surpass our ball,' her ladyship went on. 'We held that early and set the standard, don't you agree?'

'Oh, yes,' Mrs Wenthorpe said with a twinkle. 'The earlier in the Season, the better, when the eligibles have not yet made any offers.'

'Oh, how true!' Her ladyship seemed unconscious of being teased. 'It is not so hot either, and the fashions are fresher. Not that Amelia is not always dressed to a shade. She has a new gown for the Finchams' which is particularly pleasing, enough to make any waverer come to the mark; a heavenly blue, so flattering to Amelia's fair complexion. . .'

'Oh, may I see it?' Lydia asked, being nudged into speech by her aunt's bony elbow. 'Do show it to me, for it would never do for me to dress in the same colour and style.' She turned to Amelia. 'Could we not leave your mama and my aunt to have a comfortable coze together?'

Amelia, who was frequently embarrassed by her mother's pretensions, readily agreed, and the two girls took themselves off to Amelia's bedchamber, where the gown was taken from its tissue and displayed. While Lydia was agreeing that it was, indeed, very fine, her mind was busy wondering how she could set about opening the subject of the Comte de Clancy when Amelia unwittingly helped her.

'Mama thinks that I am being too particular and should have made a greater push to encourage an offer by now. . .'

'I recollect that when we last spoke you told me you wanted your mama to think you had developed a *tendre* for the Comte de Clancy.'

'So I did and you tried to warn me off him. . .' she laughed. 'I am out of all patience with Mama over it.'

'Surely she does not want you to accept the Count's suit? I do hope not because. . . Oh, Miss Thornton, you have been cruelly deceived.'

'Not I.' She laughed. 'Did you think I was fooled? No, Miss Wenthorpe, not above two minutes, though I own I was a trifle miffed. I did not want to make a scene on the ballroom floor—that would have been most improper—and afterwards, when I told F. . . Mr Burford that I was sure my partner had been a woman, though I did not know who it could be, he explained all.'

'Oh, how relieved I am!' Lydia exclaimed. 'Will you ever forgive me?'

'Of course I forgive you, and since I have had time to think about it I admire your cleverness. While Mama is busy watching the Comte de Clancy—what a romantical name!—she does not see what is really happening under her very nose.'

'But she has just said she would encourage the

Marquis of Longham, so she cannot have been truly blinded by the Comte.'

Miss Thornton uttered a shriek of amusement and sank on to her bed. 'Oh, Miss Wenthorpe—may I call you Lydia? And you shall call me Amelia. We are to be friends, are we not?' Lydia nodded and she went on, 'I know I should not be disrespectful of Mama but she is truly the most stiff-necked snob in Christendom. It is not as if I need a fortune, for I don't, and I am determined to marry for love.'

'Love? You love the Marquis of Longham?'

'The Marquis? Good gracious, no, though I'll allow he has been very attentive and if his interest has been engaged then I am sorry for it. We should not suit, you know.'

Lydia let out her breath in relief, but as quickly returned to melancholy when she realised that being rejected by Miss Thornton did not necessarily mean the Marquis would turn to her, and she was not at all sure she liked the idea of being second-best. 'But you said there was someone. . .'

'So I did. I shall tell you who it is if you give me your solemn promise not to tell a soul.'

'I promise.'

'It is Frank Burford. We are truly in love, but Mama will not even let me consider him.'

'Why not?'

'She thinks he is too young and irresponsible to settle down. And he has no title. If she were to hear of his part in this masquerade of yours, it would only confirm her low opinion of him.'

'I shall certainly say nothing of it and neither will my aunt.'

'Your aunt knows?' Amelia asked in astonishment.

'Yes, I was obliged to tell her last night. She knew something was wrong, you see, and she made me promise to tell you. . .'

'Then you must think of some reason why you could not do it. Lydia, I do not *wish* to be told.'

'I'm sorry, I do not understand.'

Amelia patted the bed beside her. 'Do sit down and let me explain.' When Lydia obeyed, she went on, 'You know, the arrival of the Comte was a godsend; Mama was beginning to suspect something was in the wind. . .'

'In the wind?'

'With Frank and me. We mean to elope.'

'You are funning me?'

'No, indeed I am not. But everyone will think it is the Comte de Clancy who has carried me off.' She paused, but before Lydia could overcome the astonishment which had struck her dumb she went on, 'Oh, pray, don't look so startled, it is simplicity itself. The Count will go to the Fincham ball and just before midnight he will stand up with me. I shall complain of the heat and we will wander into the garden. Mama will not chaperon us too closely. We will slip out of the gate and find the post-chaise which Frank will arrange. He will be waiting for us at the posting inn in Watford where he will have hired a private room. When we have eaten a meal, he will go to see if the horses are ready and you will change back into petticoats and creep back to the coach without being seen. I will join you a few minutes later and then we will be off again. From then on, you will be my companion and we will be travelling under the escort of my brother, Sir David Daventry. The Count will disappear into thin air and if Papa comes after us, for assuredly Mama will make him do so, he will be quite put off the scent.'

'You cannot mean it!' Lydia said, jumping to her feet. 'Whatever made you think I would consent to such a farrago?'

'Why, Frank said you would do anything for a dare. It was his idea and I think it is a prime one. It is foolproof, Lydia, just so long as you continue to play your part.'

'But the scandal when it all comes out. . .'

'No one knows you and the Comte de Clancy are one and the same. I'll wager if any were to suggest it they would be laughed out of court. He is such a top-of-the-trees *man.*'

'And afterwards?'

'The Count will never be seen again, unless you want him to be, of course, and once Frank and I are married Mama will come about.'

'But you will not be received anywhere,' Lydia insisted. 'Think of your parents, think of Mrs Burford. Oh, the disgrace will be terrible. Miss Thornton—Amelia—you must not do it.'

'Oh, don't be so Friday-faced, Lydia. I thought you would be our friend and stand buff for us. Frank looks on you as the sister he never had; he told me so when I told him I thought he was being too familiar with you.' Every other word was attended by an anguished emphasis. 'It is not so much to ask.'

'It is a great deal. I have been mortified with worry and guilt and so relieved to tell you the truth. . .'

'You only felt guilty because you thought you were

deceiving me and that was only proper, but now I am to be a part of the masquerade it is altogether different.' She smiled and drew Lydia down beside her again. 'All I ask is that you become the Count, just once more.'

'But if your Mama knew how much you love Frank, surely she would relent?'

'Not she. If the Count fails to return she will make me marry the Marquis of Longham. You can have no idea what she is like, Lydia. She will refine on and on about my ingratitude, how disappointed Papa will be if I do not make a match, how much my come-out has cost and the humiliation of having a daughter who failed to find a suitable husband when she has every advantage. It will be never-ending. And I shall give in simply to silence her.'

'If Lord Longham knew that, he would surely not offer?'

'He will not be able to stand against Mama either. I am my father's only child, Lydia, and my portion will be considerable. If Lord Longham were to marry me, all his problems would be solved.'

'His problems?'

'His inheritance has been plucked clean by his own father and brother and he must make a good match to come about.' She paused. 'It would be a disaster, Lydia. I should lead him a dog's life and make him dreadfully miserable.'

Lydia smiled wanly at the idea of the Marquis of Longham living under the cat's paw. But she knew her dowry could never match Miss Thornton's, and if that was of prime importance what chance did she have? And Miss Thornton, with her golden curls and blue eyes, was very pretty. She looked up to find Amelia looking at her with a sparkle in her eyes as if she could read her thoughts.

'Oh, I shall have to flirt with him a little because the Comte has gone to France and until you make him come back I must put Mama off the scent...'

'That could be dangerous,' Lydia said, remembering the moonlight waltz; that had certainly been dangerous for her peace of mind. 'His lordship is an accomplished flirt and he might take you for a...' She stopped, confused.

'How do you know that?' she demanded, then noticing Lydia's anguished look, 'Good heavens! You are wearing the willow for him yourself.'

'Gammon!' Lydia did not normally blush easily, but now she found her cheeks flaming. 'He is top-lofty and conceited and domineering and uncivil and...'

'And you love him.' Amelia laughed. 'You know, if I marry Frank, I cannot be made to marry the Marquis. You must save him from me. If it makes you any easier about it, I will undertake to tell his lordship that I persuaded you to help us and he will not blame you at all.'

'If you do that, he will certainly try to stop us.'

'Goose! I shall say nothing until after we are married and then if he cares for you at all he will do something about it.'

'No, Amelia, it isn't only that...' She stopped; better say nothing about the jewels and the visit to the lawyer, though she had a fair idea that the whole of London would know about it very soon.

'It will mean your brother's release from his wager

too, don't forget,' Amelia went on relentlessly. 'I should not like anyone's blood on my conscience. . .'

'Blood?'

'Is Mr Wenthorpe any good with sword or pistol? How would you feel if he killed Mr Fincham?'

'Relieved,' retorted Lydia.

Amelia laughed. 'Well, yes. But supposing it was your brother who was killed, what then? Surely you would do anything to prevent that?'

Lydia hesitated. Could she do it? To save Tom? Or the Marquis of Longham from Amelia? 'If I come at all, it will be no further than Watford.'

Amelia smiled. By making her demands so excessive that Lydia was bound to concentrate on those, she had managed to get her tacit agreement to the first and most important part of the enterprise. How very clever Frank was to think of that! 'The first change of horses after Watford,' she said. 'I will engage an abigail there to go on as my chaperon. I have told Frank I would not go without one and he would never compromise me.'

'He will have done that the minute we set off.'

'But we will be married before we return and the whole thing soon forgotten. Please don't fail me now. I shall die if I cannot marry Frank.' She paused and laid a hand on Lydia's arm. 'It is nearly a month to the ball so you have plenty of time to make up your mind. Promise me you will think about it.' Lydia nodded and she added, 'Now let's go back downstairs.'

In a daze Lydia followed her back to the drawing-room where Lady Thornton was still debating the relative merits of the Comte de Clancy and the

Marquis of Longham, triumphant that two such eligible men should be vying for the hand of her daughter. It was a conversation which amused Amelia and troubled Lydia and she was glad when her aunt said it was time for them to leave.

'I never met such a noddicock,' Mrs Wenthorpe said of her ladyship when they were safely in their carriage and on their way to Portman Square. 'It is to be hoped the subject of the Comte is allowed to die a natural death now, for I am heartily sick of his name.'

Her aunt was no more sick of it than Lydia herself and what to do about Amelia's request she did not know. She told herself over and over that she would not do it, that Amelia would have thought better of it by the date of the ball. Eloping was such a direful step to take and the whole plot would not have disgraced a Drury Lane farce. Perhaps if she did not bring up the subject again, then Amelia would abandon the idea.

But once the Comte de Clancy had been purposefully banished from her mind the vacant space was taken by thoughts of the Marquis of Longham. He had obviously decided London Society did not please him and she was not sure if it was because she had given him a disgust of her or because he had received no encouragement from Miss Thornton; or perhaps there was some other reason entirely.

In the following weeks, Lydia made a determined effort to pay attention to her social life and the other young men whom she had barely noticed while the tall figure of the Marquis was to be seen about town. She went to routs and breakfasts and once to

Almack's, which was a sad disappointment, drove her phaeton or rode sedately in Hyde Park with Scrivens at such a respectable distance that he thought his mistress must be ailing, and walked in Green Park with whichever of her admirers fancied his chances. And one afternoon she and her aunt drove to Hyde Park in the phaeton to witness a balloon ascent. Tom, who might have accompanied them, told them he was going to Manton's to try out some new pistols, which set her thinking about duels and bloodshed and quite spoiled the outing for her.

It was a sunny spring day; the sky was blue, and trees green with new leaf and clumps of daffodils glowed in the grass beside the carriageway. Lydia matched the day with a straight gown of primrose-yellow silk, decorated under the high waist with green velvet ribbon. Her chip-straw bonnet was tied on with green ribbon and trimmed with silk primroses. Her tall figure was striking enough to draw admiring glances from the crowds who squeezed themselves against the ropes which ringed the area where the colourful balloon was anchored. Behind those on foot, rows of carriages gave their occupants a grandstand view of the proceedings. Half a dozen men had taken most of the morning filling the balloon with hydrogen gas and by the time the Wenthorpes arrived it was almost fully inflated. As they watched, the two men who were to fly it climbed into the basket while dozens of others held the ropes that held it earth-bound. Then, with a roar of flame, the huge silk monster began to strain against the ropes, the anchor man released it and, accompanied by cheers, it soared into the sky. Lydia stood up in the phaeton to watch it as it drifted with the wind over the tree-tops of the park, becoming smaller and smaller until it disappeared from sight.

She was about to sit down again when, at the edge of her vision, she caught sight of the Marquis of Longham standing near the roped-off enclosure. She turned to look more closely. He was wearing knee-breeches and top-boots and a frockcoat of tan cloth with brown velvet facings. But it was not his clothes which surprised Lydia but the fact that a young boy, in nankeen breeches and duffel-coat, was sitting astride his lordship's shoulders with one hand firmly planted on the crown of his lordship's beaver and the other waving at the disappearing balloon. He was obviously happy and comfortable on his perch, held securely by his lordship's hands about his ankles. Beside them stood the slim figure of a young lady, neatly dressed in pale blue and white striped cambric with a matching pelisse and a plain straw bonnet tied with a blue ribbon. She was undoubtedly the child's mother and on familiar terms with the Marquis, for she turned and spoke to him and they looked at each other and laughed.

Lydia's knees buckled and she subsided on to her seat in a daze. She remembered Lady Thornton's reference to 'bits of muslin' and wondered why she should be so surprised that this particular piece of gossip should be true. She stole another glance at the Marquis's companion. She looked respectable, and whoever heard of a bit of muslin who took her child with her on an assignation with her lover? They seemed more like a happy family group, and more dangerous to her peace of mind for that. When the balloon could be seen no more, he lifted the child down and all three began to walk towards the gate, the man and woman with the child by the hands between them. The sight of them was too much for Lydia. With a strangled sob, she grabbed up the reins.

'Have a care, child,' her aunt remonstrated, as the horses turned sharply in the mêlée of departing carriages and they found themselves wheel to wheel with a yellow-painted barouche containing Lady Thornton and Amelia. The occupants of both carriages exchanged greetings and, as neither could move in the tangle of traffic, all but the brooding Lydia chatted about the balloon ascent.

'As a form of conveyance it is worse than useless,' Lady Thornton said. 'All the morning in preparation and then a carriage needed to get one from the point of descent back to civilisation.'

This seemed unanswerable, and the conversation progressed to future engagements and the Fincham ball in particular, which was now only three days away.

'Have you heard from the Comte de Clancy?' Amelia asked Lydia, leaning towards her with the smile of a tiger.

'No.' Lydia cast a terrified look at her aunt; it was too much to expect that she had not heard, for Miss Thornton had spoken quite clearly. She tugged on the reins but it served no useful purpose; they were stuck until the carriages in front of them had moved.

'I have. He has written to say he will be returning in time for the Finchams' ball and hopes to have the honour to be my escort. I do believe he has been successful in his venture into France, for he tells me he has something particular he wishes to impart to me. Can it be that he has recovered his fortune and means to propose, do you think?' She smiled wickedly. 'Shall I accept him?'

'You should not put any great store on what he says,' Mrs Wenthorpe said waspishly, looking daggers at her niece. 'Lydia knows better than most how little he can be relied upon.'

'There!' Lady Thornton said to her daughter. 'Did I not tell you you would be better fixing your attention on Longham? At least he is an Englishman.'

'If the Comte does not return, then I shall,' Amelia said, looking hard at Lydia. 'His lordship is certainly a very handsome man and a marchioness is superior to a countess, after all.'

'Perhaps his affections are already engaged,' Lydia said, fighting to control her own feelings as well as the frightened horses; she was furious with her so-called friend and almost in tears over the Marquis parading his *cher-amie* for her to see. 'Or perhaps he is secretly married. I perceive him over there.'

'Where?' Amelia twisted in her seat.

Lydia pointed with her whip, her unhappiness making her voice unnaturally high. 'There, with the young lady and the little boy. A pretty picture they make, do they not?'

'Oh.' Amelia studied his lordship's companion for a moment. 'She is hardly *haut ton*. She looks like a soldier's wife.'

'I collect the Marquis was a soldier,' Lydia said.

'Oh, I know he is not married, he told me so, and if that is one of his barques of frailty then it is very ill-judged of him to be seen with her here. I have a good mind to call him over and ask to be introduced.'

'You will do no such thing!' her horrified mother exclaimed. 'You will not even notice him.'

'Too late, Mama, he has seen us.'

Lydia took her attention from her horses in order to confirm this and in that instant the greys saw a narrow opening between the barouche and a tilbury and started through it, jerking the reins from her grasp. They managed to squeeze through the space but the phaeton became stuck and before Lydia could recover the ribbons they were rearing and neighing and passing on their panic to the other horses until a mass stampede seemed imminent. Drivers and grooms yelled at each other while their passengers cried out in terror; carriages banged together and wheels locked. Into the pandemonium rushed the Marquis of Longham. In no time he had positioned himself between the heads of Lydia's horses, grabbed their snaffles and calmed them sufficiently to have them standing still. Then he picked up the reins, put them back into her hands and closed her fingers over them, holding the grip for seconds longer than he needed if all he wanted to do was ensure she had regained control of the greys. His touch sent a shiver through her from finger-tips to toes. It was like fire, followed by ice, and she nearly cried out. She wanted to throw herself at him, to ask him to climb up beside her and take her away, anywhere where they could be alone together and she could explain herself. Ashamed of her weakness, she jerked away from him, almost upsetting the horses again.

'Hold 'em!' he commanded, and turned his attention to disentangling the tilbury from the barouche so that their respective drivers could take them away.

'Are you hurt, my lady?' he asked, coming to the side of the barouche. 'Miss Thornton?'

'A little shaken, that is all, my lord,' Lady Thornton said, looking towards Lydia who was now apparently holding her two greys quite calmly. 'If you had not been near by I believe we should have been overturned and it is no thanks to that silly chit that we were not. She is incapable of doing anything without making a mull of it and should never be allowed to drive a phaeton.'

'Oh, I do not think you should blame Miss Wenthorpe,' he said, making Lydia's cheeks flame with embarrassment. 'Something frightened the horses.'

'I am glad to see you returned to town, my lord,' Amelia put in loudly enough for Lydia to hear. 'I do hope that means you will be coming to the Fincham ball.'

'Yes. And hope to have the honour of standing up with you, Miss Thornton. Will you save me a waltz?'

She gave a trill of laughter. 'Why, yes, if the Comte de Clancy does not claim them all. He will be returning especially to escort me; did you know?'

His hesitation was only momentary. 'No, I did not, but I shall look forward to meeting him again.' He bowed to both ladies, Lady Thornton nodded to their driver and the barouche moved slowly out of the crowd, followed by the tilbury. He stood and watched them thoughtfully for a moment and then returned to Lydia.

The smile with which he had favoured Amelia faded and he looked at her with a hard glint in his eyes which made her tremble. Tom had been putting off going to Raventrees and their father could not have communicated with Mr Wilmott or the Marquis, so it could only be that her tormentor had guessed the identity of the Comte and was furious that he intended to reappear. But why did that make her feel so illogically angry with him? She busied herself with the reins and avoided looking at him.

'The cattle are calm enough now,' he said, addressing Mrs Wenthorpe. 'I would drive you home but. . .'

'Oh, do not trouble yourself,' Lydia put in quickly. 'I can manage easily. Please return to your friend; she is looking quite lost.'

He turned to look at Henrietta, who was standing uncertainly a little way off. Lydia flicked the reins and before he could turn back again she had put the phaeton about with a dexterity which would have drawn an admiring comment if his lordship had not been too preoccupied to notice it. In a minute she was bowling out of the gate.

He returned to Henrietta and offered his arm to walk her back to the road where he might find her a hackney.

'Was anyone hurt?' Henrietta asked.

'No, not at all,' he said, then lapsed into silence and she was too sensible to interrupt his thoughts again.

He had returned from Longham after talking to his father and wading through a mountain of papers and documents, none of which had been put into any sort of order. One year the wood was not included in the estate accounts and the next it was, but there was no record of a sale having taken place, nor of it having been handed over as the stakes in a wager.

His father had been foxed most of the time and out of temper and told him curtly not to waste his time on pin-pricks when finding an heiress would be more to the purpose. He was growing old, he said, and he needed to see a grandson before he finally stuck his spoon in the wall. Edward had been on the point of proposing to the Earl of Winton's eldest when he'd wound up his accounts and if Jack did not make haste and procure himself a wife he would find himself having to take his brother's leavings. 'And I am persuaded you would not like her,' he had added maliciously. 'She has a face like a horse; comes of living on the back of one, I suppose. The only good thing about her, apart from her dowry, is her seat on a hunter. And *that*, I can tell you, is broad enough.'

'I will find my own bride, sir,' Jack had told him stiffly. 'And it makes no difference to my intention of bringing Grimshaw to book. There is something very havey-cavey about that man.'

His father's continual nagging was enough to drive the most dutiful son away and there was nothing to keep him in Essex; he'd returned to London to find a note from Charles telling him that he had heard from Mrs Griggs. She had enclosed a letter from her grandfather to his agent which instructed him to change the boundary fence of the manor grounds to exclude the wood because the land had been acquired by the Duke of Sutton. Jack had lost no time in going to see Charles and examining the letter. Here was the proof he needed and he gave the lawyer instructions to proceed with an injunction against Grimshaw. Then he had gone to see Mrs Griggs to offer his thanks and, if he could prevail upon her to accept it, some recompense.

'I am glad the letter was of some use,' she'd told him, showing him into her tiny drawing-room and offering him refreshment. 'But I could not accept a reward.'

'Your grandfather lost his wager and the land was handed over, but. . .' if she thought there had been dishonesty, then she might reconsider '. . . I, too, have found evidence. . .'

'Then you did not need mine?'

'Oh, indeed, I did. This concerns the wager itself. It was won, no doubt of that, but. . .' he paused '. . .there are ways to slow a horse down.'

'No, my lord.' A bright pink spot had appeared high on each cheek. 'It all happened too long ago. If you really wish to make restitution, then you should leave the land to Mr Grimshaw.'

'No. You see, my father is not well enough to fight his own battles and I am sure Grimshaw's encroachment would not stop at the wood. If I had not returned when I did. . . But you do not want to hear about that. The whole thing must be distasteful to you. But I must make amends. . .'

'You do not care about the land or the wager at all, do you?' she had said suddenly. 'It is only the thought of losing you cannot stomach.'

He had laughed at the uncomfortable truth. 'I have offended you.'

'Not at all.'

'Then let me do something for the boy.'

She would not accept money and that was how he'd come to suggest the outing to Hyde Park to see the balloon ascent. He had not stopped to look into his motives or he would have realised that it was his annoyance with his father and, to some extent, Lydia, and not his innocent grandfather which had prompted his generosity. How could he take a bride when the only woman he wanted for a wife was embroiled in some devilish plot to relieve him of his plunder? It wasn't as if he wanted the jewels; he was doing his utmost to return them to their rightful owner. He smarted under a dual grievance—his father's insistence on him marrying and Lydia's perfidy.

He had taken Miss Thornton out riding to discover if she was a party to the deception but she had chattered on to him about the Comte de Clancy in such a way that he had been convinced of her innocence. Poor child! What would she do when she learned the truth? It would serve Lydia Wenthorpe right if he were to cut the Count out with Miss Thornton and put an end to her capers but he knew the dangers of that. He would lay himself open to an attack from Lady Thornton on behalf of her daughter. He had considered the idea of offering for Miss Thornton only as long as it took him to think of Lydia in his arms. Damn his father! He had never taken the slightest interest in his younger son before the death of the elder, who had been cast more in his own mould, and now he demanded instant obedience. He had a good mind to propose to Mrs Griggs to spite him! She was cool and restful and undemanding. And not at all like Lydia Wenthorpe!

He had just decided it would be grossly unfair to her even to think of such a thing when he espied the tall figure of Lydia standing up in her phaeton like some golden Greek goddess in a chariot, standing out from the lesser mortals who surrounded her. He had watched her until the boy's insistent cries of, 'Look, sir, look!' had forced him to remember his duty.

Later he had seen the two carriages, side by side, with Lady Thornton and her daughter speaking animatedly to Mrs Wenthorpe. Lydia, he had noticed, sat silently beside her aunt, as if impatient to be gone. And then her impatience had overcome common sense and she had tried to leave—impossible in that crush, of course; he could not imagine why she had attempted it. As soon as he had helped to free the carriage, she had driven off and left him staring after her like some gauche schoolboy given a put-down. She was unpredictable, perverse, wilful and utterly infuriating, and he loved her to distraction. There was nothing for it; he would have to confront her and *make* her tell him the truth; someone had to show her the folly of what she was doing.

Mrs Wenthorpe was, at that moment, doing her best to do just that. 'I am very displeased, Lydia,' she said, as soon as they had taken off their bonnets and gone into her sitting-room. 'I hope you can enlighten me as to how Miss Thornton is still under the impression that there is a Comte de Clancy. And how she came to receive a *letter* from him. I cannot understand her Mama allowing her to receive letters from gentlemen.'

'That was a whisker, Aunt. There was no letter. She was bamming me.'

'Why?'

'I. . .' She paused, remembering her promise of secrecy. 'I think she may be displeased with me.'

'You may be sure it is nothing to my displeasure. You have let me down sadly, Lydia, and your dear papa too. As for your coming out and making a good marriage, I think that is out of the question now. I have come to the conclusion that I must own my failure and send you home at once.'

Lydia had been thinking the same thing, but she could not bear the thought of her father's hurt if she went home in disgrace. 'Oh, Aunt, it would break Papa's heart. I want to go home, indeed I do, but if I go suddenly without saying why everyone will gossip, you know they will. Can we not think of a reason for me to go which will not cause any raised eyebrows?'

'The announcement of your engagement is the only thing that will serve, my child, and that seems as far away as ever. I never met such a contrary miss when it comes to the social graces. Don't you know how to attract a man?'

'It seems not,' Lydia said, thinking of Jack Bellingham. If she had tried just a little harder, if there had been no masquerade, if Tom had not persuaded her to visit the lawyer and made matters ten times worse, would he have come to love her? It was a question she could not answer and it did no good even to think about it because what was done was done and there was no undoing it.

'Is that what you truly want?' Her aunt peered closely at her niece and saw the pallor of her complexion and the bleakness in her eyes, and her annoyance turned to compassion. 'It would not be a clanker to say you were ill,' she said. 'You do not look at all the thing.'

'I have the headache. It was the noise and the horses trying to bolt and. . .'

'The Marquis of Longham. You have been a fool, girl, don't you know that?'

'Yes,' said Lydia miserably.

'Then you will go home where the country air may do you good. If a certain person has anything in his cockloft at all, he will come after you.'

'I do not wish him to come after me,' Lydia said, regaining some of her spirit. 'He seems perfectly happy with what he has and I will not be one of those wives who turns a blind eye to her husband's peccadilloes simply because he has bought her on the marriage market. I would rather remain single.'

Her aunt laughed, knowing she was thinking of his lordship's companion in the park. 'Gammon! You will come about. Now, before you set off for Suffolk we must decide what to do about this fiction you have perpetrated.'

'I'll put an end to the Count myself, Aunt,' Lydia said, suddenly making up her mind. 'He'll disappear, I promise. Please give me a few more days.'

She did not tell her aunt how this was to be achieved, but she was still so full of an inexplicable and ungovernable rage with the Marquis and annoyance with Amelia, not to mention worry about Tom and Douglas Fincham, that she could not think beyond her desire to do something utterly crazy. There was no hope for her now, but if it was to be the end then she would go out not with a whimper but a bang!

CHAPTER EIGHT

Mrs Wenthorpe made no move to persuade Lydia to attend the ball and, believing her niece intended to have a quiet evening at home and go to bed early, she had decided to visit her friend, Mrs Davies. She was expected to return about half-past nine, by which time Tom and the Comte de Clancy would have left for the Finchams' mansion in Kensington. But Lydia was taking so long dressing, Tom had come to her bedchamber door. 'What are you doing in there, Lydia?' he called. 'Aunt Aggie will be back any minute.'

'I'm almost ready.' She sat on her bed to put on white dancing pumps with silver buckles.

She had decided to dress entirely in white—white stockings, white satin breeches fastened below the knee with white ribbons; white brocade coat trimmed with white braid; a white satin waistcoat embroidered with silver thread and a pristine shirt and cravat in which nestled a single diamond pin. 'No one will forget Maurice, Comte de Clancy, after this night,' she murmured, going to the mirror. Her reflection showed her a rather pale, dissolute young man with plump cheeks and the shadows of sleeplessness about the eyes. She smiled and, placing a white silk high-crowned hat at an elegant angle on her golden wig, she opened the door to her brother, who stood and stared at her with his mouth hanging open.

'So?' she enquired in the Count's voice. ''Ow do I do?'

He walked slowly round her. 'So this was what all the secret shopping was about. You will stand out like a beacon.'

'So I 'ope.'

'I trust you know what you are about,' he said. 'But I begin to think this mummery has addled your upper works.'

'If Mr Fincham wants a show, he shall have one,' she said in her own voice, handing him a small valise and leading the way downstairs. 'Has the hackney arrived?' They dared not involve the servants by taking their own carriage and Betty, assured that her mistress was going to bed early to catch up on the lost sleep of the previous weeks, had been given the evening off. The rest of the indoors staff were below stairs and the hall was deserted.

'I mean to go home to Raventrees tomorrow and put it all before Papa,' he said, stealthily opening the side-door. 'So if you want to cry off. . .'

'I do not want to cry off,' she told him. 'I started it and I shall finish it.' She marched ahead of him to the gate and on to the road where the carriage waited. 'I shall finish it in a blaze of glory. And tomorrow I'll return to Raventrees. My Season is finished.'

'Oh, Lydia, I am truly sorry; it's all my doing. . .'

She gave the jarvey the direction and settled herself on the seat beside her brother. 'It is of no consequence. I never liked the idea of the Marriage Mart anyway. I shall stay quietly at home with Papa and become an ape leader.' She smiled suddenly.

'But I shall have a night to remember, a night when I fooled the whole *ton*, a night when I helped two people in love to attain their dream. . .'

'And lost your own,' he said miserably. 'I think I shall tell Bellingham.'

'You will do nothing of the sort!' she rounded on him. 'It is nothing to do with him.'

'Nothing?'

'Nothing.'

There was no more to be said and they continued without speaking again until they were just short of the Earl of Boreton's mansion where a lonely figure stood on the corner, muffled in a huge overcoat. Lydia ordered the driver to stop and silently handed over her valise.

'You are late,' Frank said. 'I was afraid you had changed your mind.'

'No, though I'm not sure I shouldn't,' she said.

'Make sure you are not late; the chaise won't wait.' He paused. 'I am counting on you to bring Amelia safely to me. Tell her. . .tell her I love her.'

'Tell her yourself,' she said, laughing, then to their driver, 'Carry on.'

The Earl of Boreton who, with his wife, son and daughter had been standing at the head of the stairs to greet their guests, had decided there would be no more latecomers and they might as well join the dancers, when Lydia and Tom arrived. They turned back and all four stood transfixed at the sight of the white-clad Comte de Clancy as he handed his hat to a footman, crossed the marble-floored hall and made his way up the magnificent curved staircase with his cousin at his side.

Douglas was the first to recover. Smiling silkily, he moved forward and bowed before the Count and introduced him to his parents and sister, all of whom said how pleased they were that the Comte had honoured them with his presence.

Lydia made an elegant leg. 'The *honneur* is mine,' she drawled in the Count's affected accents. Then she stepped into the ballroom and stood just inside the door, surveying the scene through her quizzing glass in a languid pose. It was between dances and everyone was either promenading round the ballroom in pairs or standing in little clusters talking, but as soon as the Comte de Clancy was announced all conversation died away and the whole assembly turned to look at this vision of pristine manliness. Deliberately she scanned the sea of faces, looking for one particular one, but could not see him. Supposing he did not come? Would that make the evening any easier to live through? Or harder? Could she go back to Raventrees on the morrow never having seen him again? It seemed she must.

'A real out-and-outer,' Douglas whispered, coming to stand beside her. 'If you last the night out, then I fear I may have lost my wager.'

She turned and lifted one dark arched brow to him. 'And will you then concede defeat?'

'Naturally.' The bet had lost its appeal as far as he was concerned. He was more interested in a cache of gold and jewels. Mrs Burford, being the gossip that she was, had set the whole of London talking about the Comte's visit to the lawyer and everyone knew that a soldier had brought the de Clancy jewels back to England in his knapsack. Highly exaggerated stories were being spread about their worth and how the matter had come to light. Douglas had his eye on the prize. He could denounce Lydia as an impostor but then she would blab about his blackmail and it would not guarantee that he would end up with the loot. Judging by her lavish costume and that diamond pin, it had already been handed over to her and his best course was to relieve her of it; she could hardly make a furore over its loss. How to do it was the thing most on his mind as he stood beside her watching the men taking their partners on to the floor for the next dance. He smiled suddenly as he spied Lady Thornton making a beeline for them, pulling Amelia by the hand. 'Here comes your great test, my dear. For your own sake, I hope you succeed.'

'Count,' Lady Thornton said breathlessly. 'How nice to see you here. And looking so magnificent.' She turned to her daughter. 'Do you not think so, dearest?'

'Yes, Mama. Top-of-the-trees.'

Lydia bowed.

'And Amelia is in looks, don't you think?' Lady Thornton demanded, ignoring her daughter's discomfiture.

'I 'ave never seen a lady more *ravissante*,' Lydia said, then, before her sense of the ridiculous could overcome her, she added, '*Mam'selle*, will you do me the *honneur*?'

Amelia dropped a curtsy and bent her head, more to hide her laughter than in modesty, and then allowed herself to be led on to the floor. I am glad to see you in such outstanding twig,' she whispered.

'The scandalous Comte de Clancy will be easily described.'

'I wish he had not come. Every minute I expect to be exposed.'

'Fudge! You are magnificent. Now I shall make sheep's eyes at you and you must try to look like a man in love.'

As soon as the orchestra began to play, Lydia realised it was a waltz, and though she had been practising she found the man's steps very difficult and they could hardly keep from bursting into hysterical laughter. 'I think we had better take a stroll before we let the cat out of the bag.' Amelia said at last.

Lydia was glad enough to agree and put up her arm to escort her partner from the floor. They found a couple of chairs beside a potted palm, out of sight of everyone, and sat down. 'Shall I do the agreeable for appearances' sake and fetch you some lemonade?' Lydia asked.

'Later. I want to talk.'

'You have changed your mind?' Lydia asked, more in hope than expectation.

'Not at all. Did you see Frank?'

'Yes, he says all is arranged. The chaise will be ready at midnight at the side-gate and we must not be late. For my part, the sooner we can leave, the better—before Lord Longham arrives.' It was not possible to think about what she was doing without that peer coming into her mind and sticking there like glue despite all her efforts to oust him.

'What has it to do with his lordship?'

'You have heard about the jewels, haven't you?'

'Everyone has. What is that to the point?'

'He has an interest in the Comte de Clancy. . .'

'But not in Miss Lydia Wenthorpe.' Amelia laughed. 'Oh, dear, how mortifying for you. But I promised to tell him everything and I shall keep that promise, though as he has not come I doubt he can be really interested.'

There must be some truth in that, Lydia thought, admitting to herself that all the time she had been dressing she had been thinking of his possible reaction when he saw her not merging into the background in black pantaloons and tailcoat but in gleaming white from head to foot. Surprised? He might well be. Full of admiration for her acting? Perhaps. Regretful? What might he regret? His top-lofty attitude towards her? His invention of the jewels? He *had* invented them, she told herself over and over; the story of finding them on a dead French soldier was too far-fetched to be believed. If his fabrication was meant to be the answer to hers, it had failed, because she had no intention of claiming his loot. But there were other things he might be sorry for. Was he sorry he had come after her when her horse bolted? Had he taken advantage of her insensibility to kiss her and now wished he had not? And there was that waltz and the disturbing way he had looked at her. Above all, had he regretted that?

If the Marquis of Longham regretted anything, it was not the dance on the terrace, nor the kiss he had given her when she'd lain unconscious in his arms; her closed eyes and slightly parted lips had been too tempting to resist. Would it have made any difference if she had known about it? he asked himself, as he dressed for the ball. Would she have confided in him? By hedge or by style, he intended that she should do so tonight, even if he had to beat it out of her—or kiss it out of her. If she told him everything, then they could go forward in a relationship he knew would be stormy but which would be entirely delightful. If she persisted in playing the Comte, then it would be an end of all his hopes and he might as well marry the Duke of Wilton's horsey daughter. He sighed heavily and picked up his cravat just as Tewkes knocked and put his head round the door.

'There's a lady called to see you, Cap'ain. . .'

'Lydia,' Jack murmured, because she filled his thoughts and he could think of no one else.

'No, sir. Mrs Griggs. I told her you weren't receiving, but she won't go away.' He paused. 'The lady's in what you might call a quake. Got her lad with her too. I put her in the drawing-room.'

'Very well. Tell her I will be with her directly.'

Tewkes disappeared, and Jack finished tying his cravat in greater haste than such an operation normally demanded and hurried down to greet his visitor.

She was sitting on the edge of one of the Chippendale chairs with her hands clasped in her lap. She wore a dark cloak with a hood which had fallen back from a face so pale, he thought she might be about to swoon. Beside her stood her son. 'I am sorry to come here like this,' she said, springing to her feet as soon as he entered the room. 'But there was no one else I could go to.'

'Please sit down again, ma'am,' he said, with every

appearance of patience though he was far from feeling it. Lydia's disgrace could be complete by now and he nowhere on hand to prevent it. 'Tell me what has happened.'

'I had a visit from Mr Grimshaw this afternoon. He is the most objectionable man I have ever come across; the things he said about you I cannot repeat. . .'

Jack smiled grimly. 'I can imagine.'

'He told me I must withdraw my support in your forthcoming lawsuit or I would be sorry I had ever meddled in his affairs. He said. . .' She stopped and took her son's hand. 'He hinted the boy would he harmed. My lord, I am sure he means it. I came to ask you to drop the case.'

Jack paced up and down while Tewkes poured two glasses of wine, one of which he took over to Mrs Griggs. She was about to refuse, but then changed her mind and took it, gulping at it gratefully.

'I'm sorry, I cannot do that,' Jack said slowly. 'It would not end there, you know. It would only make him think he was invincible and he would go on, adding insult to injury.' He stopped his pacing to take a glass from Tewkes and stand opposite her. 'But I promise you no harm will come to you or to the boy. I will put a stop to Mr Ernest Grimshaw's antics if I die in the attempt.'

'You will not call him out? Oh, please, my lord, don't do anything so foolish.'

'I will do whatever is necessary, ma'am,' he said coolly. 'Now, I suggest you return home. . .'

'My lord, I dare not go back. I am sure he has set men to watch me and I am afraid. . .'

'Then he will know you came here.' Heaven help me, he thought, if her visit gets out, I might have to offer her marriage after all. Aloud he said, 'Give me a moment to think.'

'Cap'ain, you could take Mrs Griggs to Wenthorpe House,' Tewkes said. 'Mrs Wenthorpe can be trusted to look after her until you can make other arrangements.'

Jack turned to him. 'Does Mrs Wenthorpe not go to the ball?'

'I believe not, Cap'ain, nor Miss Wenthorpe neither.'

'But I'll wager the Comte de Clancy is there,' Jack murmured under his breath, and then aloud to Henrietta, 'Will you allow me to take you to Mrs Wenthorpe while I seek out Grimshaw...?

He stopped suddenly as Tewkes, who was on the point of leaving the room again, coughed. 'My lord...' Tewkes only used his employer's title when he knew he might receive a severe put-down. 'My lord, the man is not a gentleman; you cannot call him out. It's not done and you know it.'

'No, but...'

'But there is more than one way to kill a rat,' Tewkes went on. 'I know something what might make the devil scuttle back to his hole...'

Jack eyed him suspiciously, while Henrietta looked from one to the other; the Marquis seemed to allow his servant a great deal of freedom and yet she could not doubt the respect each had for the other. 'Out with it, man.'

'Certain bits of paper have come into my possession...'

'Fetch them.' He paused. 'No, tell Littlejohn to bring the coach to the door first. The *closed* coach,' he added. 'And then fetch the papers.'

Tewkes scuttled away and soon returned, handing a sheaf of crumped papers to his lordship. 'The coach will be at the front of the house in five minutes, Cap'ain.'

By the time the carriage was ready, Jack had acquainted himself with the gist of the documents he had been given, which consisted of orders, invoices, bills of lading and dunning letters. 'So that's where the timber went,' he said. 'He was selling it to the dockyards at a huge price as seasoned wood.'

'But not all to our dockyards,' Tewkes said. 'You'll see most of it went to French ports; Napoleon's new fleet was built with English oak. In my book that's treason.'

Jack smiled. 'Not the whole fleet, my friend, but more than enough. This puts a whole new complexion on Master Grimshaw's activities. Bellingham grievances fade into insignificance.'

'And that's not all,' Tewkes put in. 'He was owling.'

'Owling,' repeated Henrietta who had been sipping her drink while she watched the two men. It was almost as if she had been forgotten. 'You mean catching owls?'

Tewkes laughed. 'No, ma'am, owlers were people who smuggled wool to France during the war. Did you know half the French military uniforms were made of British wool?'

'But that's dreadful!' she said, suddenly understanding what she had got herself involved in. 'No wonder he did not want to be brought to court over a little piece of land.'

'And here's something else,' Jack said. 'A message. "Latour. Hollesley Bay, midnight. 6th March. Three flashes to come in, six to abandon." Doesn't say which year, though.'

'Latour's a French name,' Tewkes said, stating the obvious. 'I reckon he was harbouring spies. His house is not far from the coast, only the other side of that wood.'

Jack looked up from his reading. 'I assume I am not supposed to ask how you came by these?'

'Why, Cap'ain, they sort of fell into me hands. I was looking for something about the wager...'

Jack grinned; he had a fair idea that his servant had been doing a bit of housebreaking while they were at Longham Towers but he would not force him to lie by asking him. 'Why did you say nothing before now?'

'It seemed to me I was the best one to deal with that thieving cove, my lord, not being so perticlar as you about doing the honourable...'

'I never heard anything so...' Jack stopped, remembering Mrs Griggs. 'I will deal with you later. Now we must hurry.' He turned to Henrietta. 'I have an engagement this evening but, if you permit it, I will take you to Mrs Wenthorpe first.'

She was reluctant to go, but even more reluctant to return to Chelsea, and they set off for Wenthorpe House in the old coach. He smiled as he helped her into it; he had told Lydia he might yet find a use for it and now he had—to convey a lady secretly from his lodgings. He hoped sincerely that she had not been seen arriving and that Tewkes was right when he said Mrs Wenthorpe would help them.

Agatha, who had only a few minutes before returned to the house, belonged to the old school—nothing ever surprised her. She sent for a servant to prepare two adjoining rooms and something for her guests to eat, filling in the waiting time with inconsequential chatter which did nothing to disguise the fact that she was more than a little distracted. As soon as Mrs Griggs had taken her son up to their rooms to put him to bed, she turned to the Marquis.

'Why did you take Mrs Griggs to Hyde Park, you foolish boy? Don't you know what people are saying about it?'

'I can guess,' he said laconically.

'Lydia is convinced you are a rake. It is because of that I think she is going to make a thorough cake of herself. I dread to think what the outcome will be.'

'What is she going to do?'

Mrs Wenthorpe drew a deep breath. 'She left me a note saying she was going home to Raventrees tonight.'

'Tonight!' He had been sure she was going to the ball and was more than a little taken aback. 'How can she have gone tonight? Who has she gone with and how? She would never go alone, would she?' He paused. 'Would she?'

Mrs Wenthorpe sighed. 'I would put nothing past Lydia, my lord. When I first read her letter, I thought perhaps she had persuaded her brother to take her, but I know Tom intended to go to the Fincham ball and remove to the country tomorrow...' She stopped to gulp from a glass of brandy which stood on a small table at her elbow. 'I believe she has gone to the ball dressed as. . .'

'The Comte de Clancy.'

'So you did see through her disguise.' She smiled crookedly. 'She was sure you had. I never saw it myself so I do not know how good it is.'

'Very good indeed,' he said, then added, 'Except to someone who knows and loves every single feature of her capricious face.'

'Oh. So you do love her, then?'

'Can you doubt it? In spite of the fact she has set me up as a complete flat. What I do not understand is how she came to hear about the jewels before I had ever said a thing about them myself.'

'That looks bad, I own, but you must believe she didn't know about them, not until your lawyer wrote to her. . .to the Comte, that is. She never meant to involve you. It was a prank that got out of hand and nothing to do with you.'

'Then why, in the name of heaven, did she choose the name de Clancy? I did not even know it myself until my lawyer traced the arms.'

'It was her mother's name. Part of the story she told was the truth. There was a de Clancy family and they did live at Fleurry, but as far as I know all but Nanette—Lady Wenthorpe, that is—perished. I believe she only escaped because she was such a good actress; she left France through Spain dressed as a French soldier. It was where she met her husband; his lordship was on a diplomatic mission at the time. If there were other survivors, I never heard of them. Lydia was sure you had somehow come by the fob and invented a cache of jewels to catch her out.'

'No, there is a substantial fortune. If I had known Lady Wenthorpe's name was de Clancy...' He paused. 'I will give the find to Lord Wenthorpe when I take his daughter home.'

Mrs Wenthorpe's expression brightened. 'And about time too. Now, why don't you go and find her and put her out of her misery?'

'I intend to. Are you sure she has gone to the ball as the Count? You don't think she may have found some means of leaving town?'

'No, she went to the ball, I'll stake my oath on't; though what was afoot I do not know. She gave her maid the night off but Betty's beau let her down and she came back early. She saw Lydia and Tom getting into a hackney and came to tell me the minute I came in. Oh, if only I had stayed at home, I could have stopped her. I was about to order the carriage to take me to Kensington when you arrived, though what I could do to save the situation I have no notion. I suppose I should have tried to shield her by pretending I believed in the Comte de Clancy.' Her lined old face suddenly creased into a wicked smile. 'I must confess it would give me a great deal of satisfaction to gull Letty Thornton, but not at Amelia's expense, nor yours, my lord.'

'It appears that your niece does not have the same scruples, ma'am,' he said laconically. 'But in spite of that she must be rescued from the bumblebath she has fallen into.' He smiled and added, 'Though not before she has confessed the whole to me.'

'Are you so cruel that you want to see her squirm?'

'No, but I wish her to be open with me or there will be no dealing together.'

'She is stubborn.'

He laughed. 'I know that, ma'am. But we must waste no more time. Will you leave all to me?'

'Yes, and glad to.'

He thanked her for sheltering Mrs Griggs and hurried back to the coach. 'Horse Guards,' he ordered Littlejohn, climbing in beside Tewkes. 'And spring 'em.' The next minute they were lurching through the streets at breakneck speed, considering the amount of traffic still about.

'Ain't you going to the ball?' Tewkes asked, hanging on to the strap.

'Later. First we pay a visit to the Colonel.'

The Colonel under whom both had served in the early part of the Peninsula campaign was now working at the Department of Military Knowledge at the Horse Guards, but at that time of night it took some time to run him to earth, which they did eventually at Watier's, a club notorious for its deep gambling. He was reluctantly prised from the gaming table and came to an ante-room ready to give the rightabout to anyone who had the temerity to call him from so important an activity. Seeing the one-time officer whose gallentry he had so often commended, he forgot his annoyance, greeted him warmly and asked him to join the play, which Jack politely refused before losing no time in putting the evidence of Grimshaw's traitorous dealings into his hands.

'Latour,' he murmured. 'So that's how he came and went.' He looked up at Jack. 'He was well-known to us as a spy and we knew he had come to

England on several occasions, but we could never catch him. He covered his tracks too well. If this Grimshaw fellow was his contact, then he has a great deal to answer for.'

'What will you do?'

'Arrest him. I'll send the Runners after him.' He paused. 'Unless you want the pleasure of bringing him to book. . .'

'Thank you, sir, but no. I am unforgivably late for an engagement. I will leave it to you. . .'

The Colonel smiled and tapped his nose. 'A lady, heh? Nothing else would keep you from the chase.'

Jack grinned. 'I must go. May I suggest you act swiftly, sir? He may miss those.' He pointed to the papers in the Colonel's hand. 'If you need me again, I shall be at your service.'

'But not tonight, heh? Oh, well, you are not in the army now, so I cannot detain you. Be off and enjoy yourself.'

Jack came smartly to attention, bowed and hastened back to his coach. 'Earl of Boreton's,' he ordered Littlejohn, jumping in the coach and settling himself beside Tewkes. 'Now for the Comte de Clancy. Let us pray we are not too late.'

It was past the hour when even latecomers were usually admitted and there was only a footman, half asleep in a chair by the door, when they arrived. Jack threw his hat into the man's lap, making him wake with a start, and bounded upstairs unannounced.

He had hardly been in the ballroom five minutes, searching for the figure of the Count, when he was accosted by Lady Thornton. 'There you are,

Longham,' she said, tapping his arm playfully with her closed fan. 'You are prodigiously late.'

'Yes,' he said, peering round over her head for Lydia among the crowds of colourfully clad dancers. 'But I am here now.'

'And a good thing too. The Comte has gone a good way to stealing a march on you and has already danced twice with Amelia. Have you seen him?'

'Not yet,' he said grimly.

'Then you are in for a surprise. I declare I have never been so startled.'

'Oh?' Jack lifted one eyebrow in enquiry, wondering if she had seen through Lydia's deception, but decided she had not, or she would not have continued to refer to Lydia as the Comte. 'How so?' he asked, mildly.

'You'll see.'

'But that is just it, I cannot see her. . . I mean Miss Thornton, of course.'

This slip of the tongue persuaded her ladyship that the Marquis's mind had been on her daughter all along and she felt suitably gratified. 'La!' she said, tapping him again with her fan. 'Your head is so full of *l'amour* you are paying no attention to me. And why not? I give you leave to go and find her.'

He bowed and hurried away. After ten minutes he had established that the Comte was not in the ballroom and widened his search to the supper-room and the conservatory. Had she left? Had she gone to Raventrees after all? Who would take her? Not her brother for he was dancing and apparently enjoying himself in the most unconcerned fashion. If he had not been so preoccupied with finding Lydia, Jack would have dealt him a facer; he was sure that young man had been the cause of all the trouble.

He found Lydia at last, sitting on a sofa in the window of the book-room, lost in thought. She had not seen him and he stood in the doorway a moment to watch her. The room was lit by a single candle which she had probably brought there herself and she looked almost ethereal in that sparkling white costume; her face was uncommonly pale and her eyes seemed darker than usual, more deep-set and misty. Definitely misty, he told himself; she was on the verge of tears. Good God, that would give the game away if anyone saw her. He took a step nearer. 'Lydia.' His voice was no more than a murmur, but she started up as if she had been shot and her hand flew to her face in a very feminine gesture.

'Oh, my lord, it is you,' she said, forcing herself to be calm. To be discovered was bad enough, but to be discovered by the Marquis was enough to throw her into a panic. After Amelia had left her to dance with the other young hopefuls who had filled her card, Lydia had danced and flirted and danced again and been the centre of a galaxy of young ladies, but after her second dance with Amelia her bravado had deserted her, and she had scuttled away to hide herself until the time came to claim her partner for that all-important supper dance. 'You 'ave me taken with surprise,' she said, sinking back on her seat and reverting to the character of the Count. 'I did not know you 'ad arrived.'

'Evidently not,' he said, seating himself beside her. 'Would the Comte de Clancy have come himself if he had known?'

'Why should 'e not?' She was amazed at her coolness considering he was sitting very close to her indeed and she could feel the warmth radiating from his muscular torso. It would be so easy to lean against him, to put her head on his shoulder and turn traitor. ''E 'ad the invitation.'

'You are not afraid of being exposed?'

Her hands were shaking so much she could not keep them still. She thrust them into the pockets of her coat and leaned nonchalantly against the sofa-back. 'Exposed, my Lord Longham? I do not know what you mean.'

'Oh, I think you do,' he said. 'What I do not know is the reason for it.'

'For what?'

'Perhaps this is what you are after?' He unclipped the fob from his waistcoat and dangled it in front of her face. 'This and all that goes with it.'

'No!' she said, shrinking back from the jewel swinging like a pendulum before her eyes. 'Keep your spoils, my lord, I have no interest in them.'

'Not interested in a fortune! Now I had heard that was why the Comte recently went to France—to find a fortune in jewels which was all the time in this country.'

'The jewels do not exist,' she snapped. 'And if they did, a man as supposedly on his uppers as you are would not scruple to keep quiet about them and not try to return them. I do believe you invented them.'

'There is no need for me to invent,' he said, then smiled as if cajoling a child. 'You have done enough inventing for both of us. And I am glad you have decided to spit out those cheek-pads and drop that ridiculous accent.' He put the fob into his waistcoat pocket. 'In truth, there is quite a cache of jewels but they shall go to Lord Wenthorpe and he may do with them what he wishes.' He paused, watching the look of consternation cross her face, to be followed by another of sheer obstinacy. 'Now we have disposed of that irrelevance, will you please tell me just what your game is?'

She blinked away her tears; tears were for women and children and the Comte de Clancy was a man; at least he would remain one until she reached Watford.

'I am waiting,' he said.

She looked up at him, her misery plain on her face, but she managed a cracked laugh. 'As you say, a game, my lord, no more than an April Day jest.'

'This is May, and you will forgive me if I say it is no jesting matter but a cruel deception. I thought at first it was aimed at me, but now I discover it is Miss Thornton who is the butt of your humour, and that is worse. Miss Thornton is a gentle person, a delicate young lady. . .'

'And I am not?' she retorted with some heat. 'Oh, I know you think I am a hoyden of the worst order, so you do not need to deny it.'

'I have no intention of denying what is so patently true.'

'There are worse things than being a tomboy. . .'

'Indeed there are. Footpads and highwaymen, pickpockets and flat-catchers. . .'

'I am not a criminal!' she cried, stung to anger and quite failing to see the light of amusement in his eyes. 'And you are a fine one to talk of deceiving people. You pretend to be the pick of the Season. . .'

He laughed. 'I have no such pretensions.'

'Do you deny you are looking for a wife?'

'Most certainly I deny it,' he said, smiling at her. 'I have found the woman with whom I wish to share my life.'

'Oh.' She was silent for a moment, thinking of Amelia. Would he be very disappointed when he discovered he could not have her? 'Does she know you have your little bit of muslin tucked away for your amusement when the honeymoon is over?'

'Little bit of muslin? Now where can you have learned such a term?'

'You forget, I am so like a man that everyone takes me for one.'

'Yes,' he said softly, resisting the urge to put up a finger and trace the outline of her troubled face. 'I had forgotten because you don't look at all like a man to me, not even in that rig.'

'Don't change the subject!'

'Ah! The subject. What was it now? Something to do with why you have been gammoning Miss Thornton and half the world with this wretched masquerade.'

'No, we were talking of you.'

'And my little bit of muslin. Really, my dear, you must learn to be a little more discreet. . .'

'And so ought you. Fancy bringing her to Hyde Park and showing her off in front of everyone! It is not as if she is anything special.' It seemed as if the little green monster was sitting on her tongue and speaking with her voice and she could not stop him. 'She looked very ordinary to me.'

'Mrs Griggs is very special,' he said, getting to his feet and making an effort to control his anger and keep his voice low. 'She is a true lady. And if I were not a gentleman, I would. . .' He paused, thinking of how he would enjoy a rough and tumble with her. She might kick and scratch but she could be tamed.

'Call me out, *monsieur*?' she queried, cocking one eyebrow up at him and adopting the Count's voice again. 'I would 'ave to choose pistols for, un'appily, I 'ave not the skill with *l'epée*.'

'I should put you across my knee and spank you and make you apologise to Mrs Griggs, except that I would certainly not want her to know what you had said of her.'

'Why did you not bring the lady to the ball?' she demanded. 'Does she know of your intentions towards Miss Thornton?' She laughed harshly because he was looking at her with a strange expression on his face which betokened an outburst of anger beyond anything she had ever provoked in her father and she found herself suddenly very afraid. 'Which one of them are you deceiving most?'

'Neither.' He ground the word out from clenched teeth.

'You need not flatter yourself that Miss Thornton will accept you,' she went on, unable to stop. 'She agrees with me that you are the most odious, the most disagreeable, the most unprincipled man she has ever met.'

He disconcerted her by throwing back his head and laughing aloud. 'How glad I am to know that!'

Taking her shoulders in his hands, he pulled her to her feet and gave her a shake. 'Now stop trying to put me off the scent with talk of Mrs Griggs. If you want to know where the lady is at this moment, she is at Wenthorpe House, enjoying a comfortable coze with your aunt.'

'Aunt Aggie!' Was there no end to the surprises he could spring on her?

'Yes.' He paused. 'Your aunt was about to come here when I called...'

'But she thinks...'

'You are on your way to Raventrees. No, she doesn't; your maid saw you leaving the house and was concerned enough to tell Mrs Wenthorpe how you were dressed. I persuaded your aunt to allow me to come in her stead.'

'Oh,' she said miserably. She might have known he would not have come on his own behalf.

'So you see I am not here because of Mrs Griggs or Miss Thornton but because of you and this charade of yours.'

'Aunt Aggie told you?'

'She did not need to. Were you foolish enough to think I would not recognise you?'

In spite of herself she was curious. 'When did you realise it was me? Was it at the fair?'

He laughed. 'No, it was dark, if you remember, and I was feeling too bruised and knocked about the head to think of anything except my bed.'

'Why did you fight? Tom said it was because you are a devil-may-dare like me.'

'Is that what you call it? Yes, perhaps you are

right. But perhaps I did not wish to see your brother beaten to a pulp. . .'

'So you took the punishment instead. How very magnanimous of you!'

'You do not believe me?' he queried, tilting his head on one side to look at her with a crooked smile.

'Of course not. Why should you do such a thing?'

'What would you have said if your brother had taken a thrashing and you knew I could have stopped it, but held myself back?'

'Oh, do not gammon me into thinking you did it to please me. Why, as far as you knew, I was not even there!'

'If I had not been there,' he said, 'if your brother had taken up the challenge, what would have happened?'

'I dare say he would have given a good account of himself,' she lied. It was far more comfortable talking about Tom than about the Comte de Clancy and she found her taut nerves beginning to relax. She pulled herself up sharply; that way lay disaster.

'Perhaps. But if he had been beaten, would that have put an end to the Comte de Clancy? I've often wondered.' He paused to smile at her. 'Without Tom there would not have been a Comte at all, would there?'

'No, I suppose not.'

'Why did you do it?'

She looked up at him defiantly. 'It was a challenge.'

He laughed. 'Like riding in my coach?'

'Yes.'

'But far more dangerous. You risked your reputation and your future for an hour or two's excitement.'

'I do not need you to ring a peal over me for it,' she said sharply. 'I am not unaware. . .'

'Then why go on with it? If it is not for the de Clancy jewels, what can have induced you to come here tonight? And in that rig. You might as well have put a notice in the *Morning Post*.'

'Oh, do you not like it, my lord?' she asked, flicking a speck of dust from her pristine white sleeve. 'Now, I thought it just the thing for going courting.'

'Let me take you home. At once.'

'No.'

'Would you prefer that I denounce you, here and now?'

'You wouldn't.'

'Try me.'

He would, she decided. 'I. . . I cannot go with you.'

'Why not?'

'I cannot tell you; it is not my secret. Oh, please say nothing. We are harming no one. . .'

'We?'

She hesitated then went on, speaking slowly and hoping to convince him, 'I cannot tell you anything except that after tonight the Comte de Clancy will disappear for good and, please God, he will be forgotten. You must trust me.'

'I seem to recollect asking you to trust me, but you found you could not. Why should I oblige you now?'

She risked looking up into his face and had a moment of indecision; he was gazing at her with an expression that was more of pain than of anger. Was there hope for her after all? Would he understand? Could she make him see she had to go through with the masquerade just once more, just for tonight, to please someone else, even if it meant displeasing him? She looked into his eyes and felt as if she was drowning in a warm sea. He was silent, watching her, refusing to save her. And the next moment she was in his arms and his mouth was on hers.

She tried to push him from her but he held her fast and then as his lips parted hers and the kiss deepened she ceased to struggle and forgot everything in the pleasure and the pain of it. She felt soft and yielding and would have fallen in a heap at his feet if he had not been holding her upright. She found herself clawing at his back, pressing herself against his muscular torso, feeling his thighs against hers. It was madness, but she did not want it to stop. While he held her like that nothing could come between them. 'Let me take you home.' His voice was low and sensuous; it caressed her.

'I don't want to go,' she murmured.

'Why not? Surely you do not want to go on with this charade now?'

The change in his tone brought her to her senses. Could she confide in him? Dared she? But he would put a stop to the elopement if she did; Amelia would never forgive her and Frank would be waiting in Watford. He had said he was counting on her to deliver Amelia to him safely and he would be beside himself with worry. 'I cannot. Frank is expecting. . .'

'Frank! You mean Frank Burford?'

'Yes.'

'What a clunch I have been!' He pushed her from him. 'I've been blind.'

'No!' She looked up at him in despair; whatever she said, she made matters worse. 'You do not understand. . .'

He looked down at her from his great height and his lip curled. 'Oh, I understand very well. I understand there is to be an elopement. You must have thought me a prime jobbernot.' He bowed. 'I wish you happy, Miss Wenthorpe.'

'Oh, you. . .' The case clock against the wall struck midnight and put a sudden stop to whatever it was she meant to say. It was too late for explanations; it had always been too late. 'I have to go. Perhaps one day, my lord, you will find it in your heart to forgive me.' Before he could stop her, she had darted away, leaving him staring after her.

CHAPTER NINE

THERE was no time to think of the consequences of that strange conversation or that heartbreaking kiss; she had to put Jack Bellingham from her mind, now and for always, and find Amelia. She hurried back to the ballroom, forcing herself to behave calmly. A new dance was about to begin and Amelia was busy staving off the attentions of two would-be partners. Seeing Lydia, she smiled and hurried to join her.

'Where have you, been, Count?' she cooed. 'I thought you must have forgot we were engaged for this dance. Now I do believe the sets are all made up.'

'Then let us walk, *ma chère*,' Lydia said, smiling and offering her arm. 'It is 'ot in 'ere, is it not?'

They forced themselves to walk slowly towards the door and down to the ground floor. People were milling about down here too, so their stately promenade continued until they were in the garden and out of sight of other strolling couples, when they began to run.

'If the coach has gone, I shall never forgive you, Lydia Wenthorpe,' Amelia said as they reached the side-gate. 'And neither will Frank.'

The travelling chaise stood on the corner. The driver was already up on the box ready to leave. ''Bout given you up,' he muttered, as they scrambled inside. ''Arf a minute more and I'd ha' bin gorn.' He cracked his whip and they set off through the night-dark streets at a ruinous pace.

'Do you think anyone will come after us?' Amelia asked. 'How long before we are missed?'

'With luck, not until the ball ends at dawn, and it will be an hour or two after that before they realise what has happened and organise a pursuit.' If the Marquis of Longham does not put a spoke in the wheel, she added, silently, sitting back in her seat and closing her eyes. She would say nothing to Amelia of her encounter with him; it would only put her into a panic and there was nothing to be done about it. Besides, she was still shaking from that devastating kiss and she did not want to talk about him.

He thought she was eloping with Frank and, thinking about it now, she remembered him quizzing her before about Frank, and her evasive answers. If only she could have stayed to explain, if only she could have told him she loved him, but it would have made no difference; he did not return her love. She was everything he most disliked in a woman; he had kissed her only to punish her and oh, how bitterly, how sweetly it had hurt! Amelia, white-faced and apprehensive beside her, was more to his liking, petite and graceful and so very feminine. When Amelia and Frank were married he would know the truth, and what would he say when he realised she had been instrumental in helping the elopement and taking Amelia from him? It would be one more thing to add to her crimes as far as he was concerned.

The paved streets and mansions of the rich gave way to humbler brick homes, strung out on either side of the road, and then they were travelling in open country between hedges and fields and occasional wooded areas. Amelia was silent and Lydia was consoling herself with the thought that tomorrow she would be safely at home in Raventrees when the crack of a pistol and a shout startled them both.

'Surely it cannot be Papa already,' Amelia whispered, looking paler than ever.

Lydia leaned forward to look out of the window as their driver hauled their team to a stop. They were being held up at gunpoint by a rider in a thick black coat with a kerchief over his mouth and chin. His accomplice, who was unmounted, was a rough-looking fellow in fustian breeches and a thick leather jerkin, with a wide-brimmed hat pulled down over his eyes. He was aiming a pistol at their driver. 'Would you believe we are being held up by toby men?'

It was like a set piece and, drained of all emotion, she watched with a kind of uncaring detachment as the man in the cloak dismounted and approached the carriage. Her first thought was that Lord Longham had followed them and decided to teach them a lesson by frightening them out of their wits. She would give him a rake-down if he had. But no, this man was too short and somewhat plump. 'Your jewels!' he demanded in a grating voice. 'Hand 'em over or I let fly with this.'

In true ladylike fashion Amelia gave a little cry and fainted across Lydia's lap; the Marquis would have appreciated this evidence of femininity, Lydia decided; she had never felt less like swooning. 'You 'ave frightened the *ma'm'selle*,' she said calmly in the Count's voice. 'She 'as fainted clean away. Put up that pop gun.'

'This is no jest,' he said, pointing the pistol at her. 'Hand over the jewels or you die.'

While Lydia was wondering whether to defy him, Amelia moaned and opened her eyes. 'What happened?'

'This gentleman of the road wishes for our jewellery, *ma chère*.'

'Oh, then we must give it to him.' She sat up to undo the clasp on her pearl necklace. The man grabbed it from her and turned to Lydia. 'Now you.'

'I 'ave only this.' She took the diamond pin out of her cravat and handed it to him.

'That will not do. I want the de Clancy jewels.'

After the initial surprise at this demand, Lydia looked up and laughed at him. 'Surely, *monsieur*, you 'ave not been 'oaxed by that—'ow do you say?—Banbury tale?'

She wondered what he would say if she told him that not only were there no jewels, there was no such person as the Comte de Clancy, that she was a woman and that Lord Longham was, even now, denouncing her to Lady Thornton. Before many hours had passed Lord Thornton or his agents would be on their trail. She had only to keep him talking until help arrived. The idea of aiding an elopement had flown right out of her head. 'You have ridden post for a pudding,' she said, trying to sound unconcerned. 'I advise you to abandon a quest which can only lead to the gallows.'

Infuriated by her apparent lack of fear, he pulled

open the door and dragged her from her seat, then reached in and grabbed Amelia's arm. 'You too.'

Amelia, sobbing now, tumbled out beside Lydia and they stood and watched helplessly as he took their cases from the boot and emptied the contents over the road. When that revealed nothing he started on the carriage, pulling out all the cushions and looking under the seats. 'You will find nothing,' Lydia said. 'You are a fool to believe gossip about fortunes that do not exist.'

He turned angrily towards her. 'Oh, they exist. Now pick that up and put it back.' As they bent to obey, he added, 'Everything. I want no clues left behind.' When they had done he returned the baggage to the boot and flung the cushions back into the coach. 'Now, get back in.'

'Will he let us go?' Amelia whispered as they obeyed.

'I doubt it. We can identify him.'

'Then he will surely kill us.' She began to sob hysterically.

'He hasn't the courage.' She smiled and patted Amelia's hand. 'They haven't found the jewels and now they cannot agree what to do with us. Listen to them arguing like a couple of fishwives.' She looked past Amelia to the other side of the road. It was still dark but she could make out a ditch and a hedge and beyond that a field. 'We could get out this side and make a run for it while they are making up their minds.' She unfastened the door carefully. 'Tell me, what are they doing now?'

Amelia overcame her fear sufficiently to look out on the nearside. 'Talking. The big one in the jerkin is climbing on to the box. The other is pointing his pistol at our driver. Oh, he will shoot him!'

They heard his voice. 'You. Get down. You can go home by shanks's pony.' Their driver lost no time in obeying, but before Lydia could persuade Amelia to put her plan into action the cloaked man had hitched his horse to the back of the carriage and joined them. No sooner had he taken his seat than the chaise gave a lurch and they were on their way again, driven by the accomplice.

'Where are you taking us?' Lydia asked, while Amelia sat hunched beside her, unable to speak. 'I doubt you mean to convey us to our destination, but I would be very much obliged if you would.'

'If you do not have the jewels, then you are going to meet someone who has. Wenthorpe, perhaps, or the Marquis of Longham. It makes no odds.' There was something about his cracked laugh that was familiar.

'You think we are going to meet Longham?' She forced a smile; if only it were true; if only his lordship were somewhere at hand. 'You could not be more wrong.' She leaned forward and whipped the cloth from his face, then laughed at his consternation. 'You are the biggest souse-crown in Christendom, Mr Fincham,' she said. 'You, above all people, should know why the Comte de Clancy's jewels were invented. I needed the story of a fortune to play the part properly.'

'Oh, but they are real. I heard your welcher of a brother telling Frank Burford so. If you do not know where they are, Tom does.'

'Then find him and ask him. I promise you we are

not going to meet him. All you have done is tumble upon an elopement, no more, no less. Are you not afraid someone will come after us? I assure you Miss Thornton is. If you stay with us, you will be caught. . .'

'Two women eloping!' He went into gales of maniacal laughter.

'I am glad you enjoy a jest,' Lydia said. 'Now, stop the coach and let us go. We will say nothing of this night's work, if you do.' She made a dive for the pistol in his hand but his grip tightened and he pushed her roughly back on to her seat.

'If you try that again, I shall be obliged to shoot you,' he said. 'I have nothing to lose, after all.'

'And will your accomplice agree to that?'

'Jake? He will do as he is told.'

Lydia was not so sure about that; the big man had seemed the more nervous of the two, but she kept her thoughts to herself and the coach tumbled on through the night. Dawn was turning the eastern sky a rosy hue and the dark shadows on either side of the road were taking on the definite outlines of trees, hedges and haystacks when they turned off the high road on to a narrow lane. After several minutes they turned again on to what was little more than a cart track and they found themselves being thrown from side to side as the wheels slid into muddy ruts. Lydia decided it was time to take possession of their abductor's gun. She would need to be careful he was not given the opportunity to use it, either on them or to alert the driver who was cracking his whip and urging on the horses with a choice selection of epithets.

Before she could do anything the coach stopped

suddenly; throwing her forward. She made to grab the gun, but Douglas was alert to his danger and knocked her back against the door which had not been properly closed. It flew open and she tumbled out into the ditch which ran alongside the lane.

The air was suddenly pierced with Amelia's screams. Douglas slapped her hard to silence her and jumped down to examine the inert figure.

'You've killed her,' the driver said, scrambling down from his perch. 'I didn't come into this to do no murder.'

'Fustian!' he said. 'She's only stunned. Help me take her inside.' He turned to the now silent Amelia, who peered down from her seat, looking faint enough to fall into the road beside her friend. 'Get down, Miss Thornton, and go indoors.'

Slowly she turned her head and saw that they had come to the end of the lane and a small farmhouse stood not twenty yards away. She watched in a trance as the two men picked Lydia up between them.

'Go on,' Douglas said. 'Go in front and open the door. And no tricks.'

Now her hysteria had subsided, Amelia had become numb. She walked unsteadily to the door and pushed it open. The room they entered was very simply furnished. There was a table, four chairs, a sideboard and a settle on which they put the unconscious Lydia. Amelia ran to kneel beside her.

'Look after her,' Douglas commanded her, and, to his accomplice, 'Pen and paper, if you have such a thing. I must write a letter.'

The cottage was apparently Jake's home; he went to the sideboard drawer and found writing materials before turning to stir up the fire and set the kettle on the hob. Douglas sat down and wrote quickly. 'That should do the trick,' he said, folding the paper and putting it in his coat pocket. 'Stay and guard them till I come back. And keep an eye on the tall one.' Then he strode out of the house, unhitched his horse and rode back down the track.

Jack had stayed in the library after Lydia left him. He was furious with her, with Frank Burford, with Tom Wenthorpe, but most of all with himself for allowing his feelings to overcome his sense. How blind he had been! How easily fooled by the depths of those violet eyes into thinking she might care for him. He had been right the first time: she was a hoyden, an eccentric, too mannish for words, beyond consideration. Burford was welcome to her. His thoughts ran on in this vein for some time, but he could not convince himself. Belittling her did nothing to ease his hurt or help him to forget the taste of those soft lips. She had wanted him then, he could have sworn to it; she had responded to the pressure of his mouth, had kissed him back with all the passion of a woman in love. But what did he know about women in love? Nothing, he told himself, nothing at all. None of the women he had known—and some had been skilful lovers—had been in love with him, nor he with them. Damn them all!

It was some time before he remembered Mrs Wenthorpe; he had promised to extricate Lydia from the coil in which she had embroiled herself and instead had behaved like a clod and made her run from him. Whatever he felt about her or his own foolishness, he must rouse himself and do what he could to keep his word. Reluctantly, he returned to the ballroom.

Lydia was nowhere to be seen; neither was Miss Thornton or Frank Burford. The only actor left in their little drama was Tom Wenthorpe waltzing with Amy Fincham. And that young man's unconcern incensed him even more. He forced himself into a languid pose, though anyone who knew him well would have realised that his hazel eyes missed nothing.

'Well, did you find her?' Lady Thornton appeared at his side just as the music came to an end and Tom offered his arm to his partner for the customary promenade around the room.

'Yes, my lady, but now I have lost her again.' He gave a rueful smile, aware of the irony in his answer.

'Pity. I would much rather it had been you and not the Comte.' She paused, idly watching Tom and Amy. 'I saw them go out into the garden. It was some time ago now. They may still be out there. If you want to cut the Frenchman out, you had better do something about it.'

'Yes. Will you excuse me, my lady?'

'Of course.' She tapped him with her fan. 'Call tomorrow. I'll make sure Amelia receives you.'

'Thank you.' He bowed and hurried across to Tom and Amy. 'Your pardon, my lady, I need a word with your partner.' He grabbed Tom by his sleeve and propelled him into a corner.

'I say, Longham, that's a bit much,' Tom said, aggrieved. 'You were monstrous rude to Lady Amy and you are pulling my coat out of shape.'

'It's nothing to what will happen if you do not tell me where your sister is.'

'Lydia? At home, in bed, I shouldn't wonder.'

'You know she is not. She was here earlier as the Comte. Now where has she gone?'

'How should I know? She don't tell me everything.'

'She's gone to meet Frank Burford, hasn't she?' He shook the young man angrily. 'Hasn't she?'

'Yes. But with Miss Thornton. . .'

'Where?'

'Watford, I think.'

'Has your travelling coach been repaired?'

'Yes, but you are surely not going after them in that?'

'No, you are going home to Raventrees in it as soon as you leave here.'

'Why should I?'

'If you want to come out of tonight's adventure with a whole skin, that is what you will do. You will also ask your aunt to call on Lady Thornton and set her mind at rest; her daughter is safe and sound at Raventrees with Miss Wenthorpe where you took them on leaving the ball. She is to say she has confronted the Comte de Clancy who has admitted he is an impostor and has prudently decided to disappear. Do you understand?'

He refused to listen when Tom tried to justify himself, and went into the garden. An exhaustive search revealed no sign of Lydia or Amelia, though a small side-gate was banging back and forth as if someone had failed to close it properly. He went on to the lane which ran beside the mansion. There were fresh wheel marks and hoofprints in the mud as if a carriage and horses had been standing some time. He smiled ruefully and returned indoors to fetch his hat and take leave of his hostess, then he called for his carriage and returned home. Half an hour later he had been shaved and changed from his black brocade evening coat and pantaloons into buckskins and brown coat and was heading north in his curricle accompanied by Tewkes.

It was almost dawn by the time they left the town behind and were dashing through open country, past meadows and farms, over bridges and through villages, at a rate which made even the normally placid Tewkes cry out for him to have a care. To begin with it was easy to track the chaise the girls were using simply by describing the Comte's distinctive dress at the tolls they passed through. Why Lydia should have taken Miss Thornton with her and arranged to meet Frank at Watford he did not know, nor did he intend to tax his brain with it, any more than he would waste time wondering why Lydia had gone as the Count and in that white rig. It was either an act of extreme recklessness or there was some deeper reason for it. He was trying to make up his mind which it could be when the trail went cold. The coach had passed through the toll at Barnet but the next tollkeeper could not remember a young man dressed in white, though he had let two or three carriages through.

'She could have put on a cloak or an overcoat,' he said to Tewkes. 'We'll carry on to Watford.'

There was a coach standing in the yard of the Green Man when they arrived in that town but it belonged to a fat alderman and his wife on their way to Dunstable. They went into the inn and found Frank Burford in the back parlour, pacing backwards and forwards in a ferment of worry and indecision. The look of relief on his face when the door swung open changed to dismay when he saw Jack. 'Longham! What are you doing here?'

'I came to stop you making a fool of yourself and ruining a lovely young lady. Where is she?'

'She isn't here,' Frank said morosely. 'She must have changed her mind.'

'No, she did not do that,' he said grimly. 'The ladies left as arranged. Are you saying they have not arrived?'

'They're not here, are they? They should have come hours ago. I thought her mama must have discovered what was afoot and kept her close or persuaded her. . .'

'Wait a minute,' Jack said slowly. 'Did you say her *mama*?'

'Yes. Lady Thornton. She does not approve of me, you know. . .'

Jack suddenly threw back his head and laughed. 'Of all the sapskulls. . .'

'I beg your pardon.' Frank said stiffly. 'There ain't no call for you to say that. I might not be a pink of the first water, but. . .'

'Oh, not you, my dear fellow, I was referring to me.' He was grinning like a schoolboy. 'I thought it was Miss Wenthorpe who was eloping.'

'Lydia! With me? Good lord, what a comical idea!' He paused. 'You said they left as arranged?'

'They might have been a trifle late.' He smiled. 'I am afraid I detained Miss Wenthorpe.'

'And you did not pass them on the road?'

'No.' He turned to leave. 'We must go back and look for them.'

'You don't suppose Lord Thornton followed them and has taken them home?'

'No, I do not.'

'Then they must have lost their way. Or overturned or been waylaid. Oh, I should never have let them come alone... If anything has happened to them...'

Jack stopped to look back at him. 'Well, are you coming or not?'

'Of course I'm coming.' He followed Jack into the yard, but just as they were about to get into the curricle the innkeeper came hurrying out to them, waving a piece of paper. 'Beg pardon, sir,' he said, addressing Jack. 'Are you the Marquis of Longham?'

'Yes.'

'This came for you about half an hour ago, my lord. I was busy in the back room getting breakfasts for the next stage and didn't see you arrive. I was told to give it to you personally.'

'How did anyone know you would be here?' Frank asked, watching Jack unfold the letter and skim through its contents.

'Someone evidently does.' He turned to the innkeeper. 'Who brought this?'

'A boy. Said he'd been paid a sixpence by a man who stopped at the toll on the edge of town. Would there be anything else, my lord?'

'Nothing, thank you.' The innkeeper went back

inside and Jack handed the missive to Frank. 'Here, read it.'

'"Miss Wenthorpe and Miss Thornton will be returned to you unharmed in exchange for the de Clancy jewels,"' Frank read. '"If you do not have them with you, you are to send for them and wait at the Green Man for instructions."' He looked up. 'What do we do now?'

Jack's appearance of calm belied the tempest of worry and anger inside him. His imagination painted a thousand lurid scenarios of the two girls in the clutches of unscrupulous scoundrels. How would they cope? Lydia would not panic, he decided, but she might attempt something foolish to free them and force their abductor into violence. If that happened... He stopped himself; thoughts like that would not help. 'Their coach must have been halted between the last toll and here,' he said. 'The horses would have been pulled up sharply and may have marked the road. The villains—I doubt there was only one—would have been waiting somewhere in hiding, behind a hedge or among trees, and almost certainly mounted. They may have abandoned the carriage or taken it with them. We must look for signs.' Then as Frank seemed disinclined to stir himself he added, 'Come on, man! I am not staying here to wait on a kidnapper's convenience.' He sprang into the curricle and turned to Tewkes. 'You wait here in case there are more messages.'

Ignoring the servant's grumbling at being left out of the chase, they set off, driving slowly and stopping frequently in order to examine the road at every point where a vehicle might have been halted or to ask at dwellings if anyone had seen the coach with its distinctive occupants.

'This is going to take all day,' Frank said after getting down for the third time and finding nothing of significance. 'Perhaps we should have waited at the posting inn as the letter said.'

'You think I should pay the ransom?'

'The ladies are surely worth a few paltry jewels.'

'Oh, they are worth every grig and groat, but. . .'

'The de Clancy jewels do not exist, then?'

'They exist, and I accused Miss Wenthorpe of masquerading as the Comte to get her hands on them.'

'What a mull! Amelia will never marry me now.'

'And you will be well served, sir. You are an incompetent bungler. I could almost wish the Comte had been a real person and taken her from you.' He checked himself suddenly and smiled. If Lydia were a man it would be his loss. 'Why, in heaven's name, did you cook up such a crank-brained scheme?'

'Lady Thornton would not countenance me. It was all on account of my wild behaviour as a student, pranks and so forth. Made a bit of a reputation. All behind me now, of course. I have a decent income, a country estate and a town house and every prospect of settling down, but her ladyship would not have it. I had to think of something or Amelia would have been forced into a marriage she hated. Maybe with you.'

'Impossible,' Jack said laconically, as they climbed back into his curricle. 'But why involve Miss Wenthorpe?'

Frank's expression momentarily lightened. 'She made such a capital fellow.'

'It was your idea?'

'Well, yes, but I wouldn't have thought of it if Lydia hadn't puffed herself up to play the man. And she thought of the name herself.'

'You had better tell me the whole. From the beginning.'

Before they had gone another mile, Jack was in full possession of the facts. Poor Lydia! To have been forced into the masquerade and then to have him scolding and misunderstanding her on top of everything, it was no wonder she had run from him. But what courage! What resourcefulness! And what a fool he had been! He could not wait to tell her so and a great many other things beside. Pray God she was safe; that they were both safe. 'You may thank providence I am fully occupied in tooling this pair,' he said when Frank had finished. 'I am mightily inclined to draw your cork, and if anything has happened to either of them I most certainly shall.'

'Lydia will look after them both.'

'She is not a man, for you to put such a burden on her,' he said furiously. 'She is a woman, strong-willed and capable, it is true, but a woman for all that—beautiful, graceful, capricious but entirely delightful.'

Frank looked at him in surprise. 'Good God! You. . .'

'Yes, and if one hair of her head is harmed you shall answer to me for it.'

Frank had nothing to say to that and they rode on in silence until Jack pulled up at a hedge tavern which was set a little off the road with a yard and a tumbledown stable beside it. 'We'll ask here.'

They left the carriage and went inside. It was low-ceilinged and dirty. 'This ain't fit for pigs, let alone young ladies,' Frank said, as if the kidnapper would take account of that. 'Good heavens! Fletcher!' This last was addressed to a man who was eating breakfast in the taproom though it was nearer noon than breakfast-time.

'Mr Burford!' he said, rising.

'This is my coachman,' Frank explained to Jack before turning back to his servant. 'Where is Miss Thornton and. . .the young man?'

'I don't know. The high toby took them. They had guns; I couldn't stop 'em. They took me coach and left me to walk. I've tramped leagues, and what with me boots plaguing me and me empty stomach rumbling I couldn't go no further. "Martin," I sez to mesself, "You ain't goin' another step 'til someone comes along with a vehicle to take you up." So, here I am.'

'Do you know which way the coach went?' Jack asked.

'Straight up the road.'

'Then come along and show us where it happened.'

Reluctantly the coachman left his ham and eggs and followed them out to the curricle where he clambered up behind them and once again they turned in the direction of Watford.

'I shall soon know every blade of grass on this stretch of road,' Frank said. 'If there had been any signs we would have seen them before now.'

Twice Fletcher stopped them and assured them it

was the spot and twice he owned himself mistaken, but a third descent from the carriage revealed hoof and wheel marks and, more significantly, a scrap of white lace and a silver shoe buckle. Their spirits rose as they walked beside the horses, following the tracks to where they turned down a lane. From there they followed the scent like bloodhounds, picking out a particular hoofprint until they found themselves on a very bumpy track at the end of which they could see a small house and a wisp of smoke.

'We had better approach on foot,' Jack said. 'There's no telling what they might do if they see us coming.' He turned to Fletcher. 'Draw the rig into that field and wait with it. We may need to leave in a hurry.'

Douglas, watching from an upstairs window, cursed. He had not expected to be found so quickly. He should have shot that driver and not listened to Jake, but it was too late for that now; he had to get the women away. He crossed the room to the back window. There was a garden and beyond that a field and across the field was another road. He ran downstairs.

The two girls were sitting side by side on the settle. Amelia was calmer and Lydia was fully conscious. She thanked providence that the muddy water in the ditch had cushioned her fall, though she had a lump on the back of her head which was throbbing unmercifully. Her beautiful suit was ruined but that was of little consequence; she had come to hate it.

'Come on, both of you,' Douglas said. 'We're leaving.' He turned to Jake. 'Tie their hands and gag them and be quick about it.'

'So, someone is coming,' Lydia said, guessing the reason for his haste and wondering who it might be. She opened her mouth to shout a warning but before she could make a sound a dirty cotton handkerchief had been forced between her teeth.

As soon as both girls had been securely tied, Douglas ordered Jake to destroy all evidence of their stay. 'You ain't never seen us,' he said, flinging half a dozen sovereigns on to the table. 'Act the innocent.' Then to the girls, 'Come on. This way. And make haste.' He pushed them in front of him out of the back door and across the yard.

He took Lydia's arm, knowing Amelia would follow, and hauled her, stumbling, along an overgrown track alongside the field. By the time they reached the road on the far side, Lydia was fighting for breath and her wrists were hurting. She kept grunting in an effort to make him realise her predicament.

'I'll untie you if you promise to behave,' he said.

She nodded.

He took the gag from her mouth and untied her. 'I'll have my pistol handy and I won't hesitate to use it if you try anything.'

'Now what are you going to do?' she asked, wishing she could have a drink to clear the taste of the filthy handkerchief from her mouth.

He ignored her and released Amelia. 'Now, both of you, walk ahead of me that way.' He pointed with the gun.

'Where is he taking us, do you think?' Amelia whispered as they obeyed.

'I do not know. I don't think he does either. He didn't expect visitors.'

'Who was it, do you think? Could it have been Frank? He'd be out of his mind when we didn't arrive.' She paused. 'Or Papa perhaps?'

'Perhaps.'

'If it is, will that man Jake tell?'

'I doubt it. He won't want to hang for his part in it.'

'Stop talking.' Douglas's voice came from just behind them. 'Just walk.'

'You have cooked your goose now,' Lydia told him without looking round. 'You will be on the run for the rest of your life.'

'With your ransom I can afford to go abroad. So, we will find another hiding place for you until I can collect it.' He chuckled. 'You will write a letter to Longham begging him to comply with my instructions.'

'Lord Longham! Don't be absurd!' Was he being absurd? Would the Marquis have followed them? She could think of no reason why he should; she had been so upset when he found her in the book room and even more so when he kissed her that she had hardly known what she was doing, but surely she had not let slip anything about an elopement, had she? Would he have followed? She could not imagine that proud, implacable man doing the bidding of a kidnapper, especially to help her, whom he despised. On the other hand, his lordship had not denied he had a *tendre* for Amelia, so perhaps he would hand over the jewels for her sake. But did they exist? She had only his word for that.

They heard a carriage coming up behind them and Douglas stepped into the road and held up his hand for it to stop.

A portly red-faced man in a green frock coat put his head out of the door. 'What's afoot?'

Douglas walked round to speak to him. 'Our coach lost a wheel and we started to walk, but the lady can go no further.'

'Where are you making for?'

'St Albans.'

'This ain't the road for St Albans.'

'No. Ninny that I am, I thought it was a short-cut and now we have lost our way. I'd be much obliged to you, sir, if you would take us up.'

The portly man looked thoughtful as if the request needed a great deal of consideration, but at last he said, 'Very well, get in. But make haste.'

The girls were only too glad to comply. Riding was infinitely better than walking and if there was some way they could let the man know their predicament then he might help them.

'I must thank you, sir,' Douglas said when they were settled in their seats and on their way. 'I do not know what we would have done, if you had not come along. My name is Brotherton, by the way.'

'I mean to stop in Watford for a change of horses, Mr Brotherton. 'I'll put you down there.'

'Oh, that will be wonderful,' Amelia said, thinking of Frank. 'Of all places it is the best.'

'I do not advise Watford,' Douglas said calmly. 'The horses there are nothing but skin and bone. I'd go on to St Albans if I were you.'

'How can you say that?' Lydia put in. 'The Green Man 'orses are as good as any to be 'ad.' She turned to their rescuer. 'Your beasts look done for. It would be a sin to ruin them for an extra few miles.'

'You are right. Watford it is.'

Lydia gave Douglas a triumphant grin; he scowled back at her and the coach rumbled on. Everyone was silent.

'I have it now!' Amelia exclaimed suddenly. 'It's Mr Grimshaw, isn't it?' He looked startled and she added, 'We met at Lady Winter's soirée. Don't you remember?'

He smiled humourlessly. 'You have the advantage of me, I am afraid.'

'Miss Thornton,' she said. 'I was with Mama.'

Silently he cursed. 'Lady Thornton, to be sure.' He turned to Lydia. 'Then who are you?'

'The Comte de Clancy,' she said promptly. If anyone was on their trail, then that name should help them.

'De Clancy,' he murmured. 'I've heard that name somewhere.'

'Everyone 'as,' she said. 'It is a fine French name.'

'French, of course,' he said thoughtfully, wondering where the young pup's loyalty lay. He was probably an *aristo* and a man-milliner at that, useless in a tight corner.

'Are you making a long journey, *monsieur*?'

'Scotland. I have friends there.' He laughed suddenly, remembering how badly he had misjudged Longham and that woman, Griggs. He had felt sure they were lovers, especially when she had rushed off to the man's rooms the minute he had delivered his ultimatum. If his men had not been on their toes and warned him of the visit to Horse Guards, he would, even now, be in custody. How Bellingham had learned about his wartime activities he did not know.

Flight had been his only recourse; there were people north of the border who were not so loyal to the English crown who would shelter him. And after all that to be sharing a coach with someone who recognised him! 'Needed to get away from town for my health's sake,' he went on, telling himself not to panic.

As they passed through the toll on the edge of the town, Douglas smiled easily. 'I should be mightily obliged, sir, if I could prevail upon you to let us continue with you to the next stage. We will not delay you here by leaving the coach.'

Grimshaw had been thinking hard and his thoughts had been running along the same lines; if the Runners were close behind him, then the presence of his passengers might be providential. He would make the man get out and see to the changing of the horses, while he stayed hidden. 'My dear fellow, of course,' he said. 'I am rather gouty and would welcome your help in making sure we have good horses and they are changed swiftly. If I can prevail upon you. . .'

'Delighted to be of service, sir,' Douglas said. With luck Jake would have delayed Longham and Burford and they would not yet be back in Watford. That they would return when their search proved abortive he did not doubt. It was their only link with the girls. He could leave a note for Longham and then find somewhere to hide his prisoners while he sent someone to collect the ransom. Perhaps Grimshaw. That was it; he would make use of the man. He had heard of him; if the rumours he had heard were true, he had no liking for the Marquis of Longham and would welcome an opportunity to do him down.

They drew into the yard of the Green Man, which was bustling with activity. A stage had just drawn in and the passengers were passing into the inn while the ostlers and grooms set about changing the horses. As Douglas jumped down, Lydia went to follow him, but he turned and pushed her back into her seat. 'Stay there. We have no time to waste.' He smiled at Grimshaw. 'The Count fell into a ditch, as you can see, and he can think of nothing but his spoiled looks. If he gets out he will delay us by taking a room so that he can change his clothes. Such vanity! I pray you detain him or we shall lose valuable time.' He disappeared, leaving the girls facing Grimshaw.

Lydia tried to rise but he reached out and grabbed her arm, forcing her back into her seat. 'You heard what the man said. You must stay here quietly with me.'

She sank back on to her seat and stared at him. Had they jumped from the frying-pan into the fire? She did not like the look of his little button eyes which glinted at her with a menace which was far more frightening than Douglas's juvenile threats.

'Please let us go,' begged Amelia. 'We are being held against our will.'

'Is that so?' He smiled a pudgy, humourless smile. 'It makes no odds.'

The horses were changed, Douglas returned and they were on their way again in a matter of minutes. Lydia's spirits sank to their lowest ebb since their capture. Now they were leaving any chance of rescue behind them for no one would have expected them to have gone beyond Watford.

Amelia began to cry.

'Stop that!' Douglas snapped, pulling out his pistol. 'I cannot abide watering pots, and that sniffling will make me lose all patience. Would you have me use this?'

Grimshaw, seeing the gun, looked startled and then he began to laugh. He laughed so much his fat belly wobbled and tears streamed down his round cheeks and lost themselves in his many chins. 'Oh, dear,' he said, wiping his eyes on a large green kerchief. 'This is a pretty kettle of fish.'

Douglas, who hated being the object of such merriment and whose nerve was already at breaking-point, turned the weapon on him and told him to shut his maw. 'It's no laughing matter,' he added. 'And you, too, will do as you are told.'

'By you?'

'Yes.'

Grimshaw smiled. 'Then I should inform you that I know for a fact that the Runners are not far behind us.'

'Runners?' Douglas repeated in dismay, but recovered himself quickly. 'Surely they did not send Runners after the silly chits. They were trying to elope, you know.'

'They're not after them, my dear fellow, but me. I only took you up to give me some cover if we should be stopped and questioned. If I'd known we were, as you might say, in the same boat, I might not have been so willing.'

It was Lydia's turn to laugh. 'Why, *monsieur*, what 'ave you done?'

He smiled across at her. 'Nothing but try to keep

what is mine and make a living, not easy in these troubled times, harder still in wartime.'

'What kind of living?' Douglas asked.

He laughed. 'Importing and exporting.'

'Contraband,' Lydia said, correctly interpreting his euphemism. 'And in wartime. Is that not treason?'

'Depends whose side you are on,' he said. 'You are a Frenchman, you should understand. I'd have done all right and none been the wiser if the Marquis of Longham hadn't died...'

Lydia's heart missed a beat and then began to thump so fast she could hardly breathe. She thought she might faint. 'Dead?' she whispered, as the colour drained from her face. 'He can't be...be dead.'

'You knew him?'

She nodded, hardly aware of the others in the coach, that Amelia had cried out in dismay and Douglas had uttered a furious oath. Her life seemed to have stopped right there and then, in a coach halfway between Watford and St Albans. On either side of the road the life of the countryside went on as if nothing had happened. Men continued to work in the fields and the birds still sang. But they did not exist for her. She remembered the feel of his lips on hers, warm and alive. How long ago had that been? A lifetime and yet only a few hours. What could have happened in so short a time? 'How?' she asked in a whisper, forgetting her accent.

'Took a fence. Jug-bitten, he was, though that was not unusual. Head hit a rock. You must have heard about it...'

'Drunk!' she cried. 'I do not believe it. He was perfectly sober when I left him last night.'

'Last night!' He laughed suddenly. 'I ain't talking about the present Marquis. I meant his brother. Died three months ago. Jack Bellingham is a different kettle of fish altogether. He ain't like his father, nor his brother; he don't turn a blind eye for a little golden grease.'

Lydia found herself shaking like an aspen. Of all the silly mistakes to make, but it had served to bring her to her senses. He was alive! She would not give him up for want of a word. Please God, if she came out of this bumblebath safely, she would go to him; she would find him and try to make him understand. 'Was it the present Marquis who sent the Runners after you?' she asked, forcing herself to smile.

'Probably. It was only by chance I heard of it.'

'And will he come with them?' Oh, let him find us, she prayed; make him see that I am not a hoyden past redemption, that I am a woman with a woman's heart and as effeminate as he could wish. Oh, let it not be too late.

'Maybe, maybe not.'

'No,' said Douglas suddenly. 'He ain't with your Runners, Mr Grimshaw, that I promise you.'

'Good, then we are allies,' Grimshaw said, settling back in his seat. 'Now we'd best put our heads together and decide how to proceed.' He would find somewhere on the road where he could persude them to get down, a lonely spot where their bodies would not be found for a very long time. His coachman would help him; he was in too deep to refuse. There was too much to lose to be squeamish now.

CHAPTER TEN

JACK tooled his curricle into the yard of the Green Man behind Frank's coach, which was being driven by Fletcher. The man they had found at the farmhouse had been difficult at first and denied all knowledge of any abduction, but a search of the house and outbuildings had soon revealed Frank's hidden travelling chaise. Faced with this evidence and with a little persuasion, he had told all he knew, but that was little enough and certainly did not include what the kidnapper meant to do next or where he was taking the ladies. He had simply been hired by a flash cove, whose name he did not know, to help him lift a haul of gold and jewels, but there hadn't been any and all he had out of it was a paltry four guineas. It certainly wasn't worth risking the nubbing cheat for. If Jack had thought for a minute that a thrashing would have extracted any more information, he would have administered one, but he was fairly sure the man did not know. He gave him a severe set-down with a warning of the peril he was in by consorting with criminals and, because he did not want to be put to the trouble of taking him into custody, had left him where he was. There had been nothing for it but to go back to Watford and wait for the kidnapper's next communication.

It had already arrived and was given to them as they crossed the yard, but it told them nothing, except that the young ladies were safe and they were to wait until they heard from the writer where to take the jewels. The innkeeper had not seen the man who left the note; he had been far too busy. Questioning the ostlers and grooms produced no further information; all swore they had had their hands full seeing to the several coaches that had called. Jack went in search of Tewkes, for surely he had been on the look-out, but he was nowhere to be found, either in the inn or the yard. His absence was puzzling; it was not like Tewkes to go off like that without a word.

'What now?' Frank asked.

'I need fresh horses.'

'I bespoke a team for the coach, you may as well have them,' Frank said, morosely. 'I won't need them now.'

While the horses were being changed, they went into the dining-room of the inn and Jack ordered pork chops and a glass of porter each.

'You're never going to booze and peck while Amelia and Lydia might be in mortal danger,' Frank said.

'Supper was a hellish long time ago,' Jack retorted. 'And they are in no danger as long as we stay calm. The man wants his ransom, don't forget.'

'You've done nothing about sending for the jewels.'

'He doesn't know that.' It was important to stay cool, if only to counterbalance Frank's tendency to panic. 'I wish I knew what had become of my man.'

'Oh, I say, there he is,' Frank said, catching sight of Tewkes through the window. 'And he's riding my bay.' He left the table, followed by Jack, and hurried into the yard where Tewkes was dismounting. 'That's my mount,' he said to him in aggrieved tones.

'Yes, sir, sorry sir.' He turned to his employer. 'I was in the yard, keeping a watch like you told me, and this here shay arrives and who should get out of it but Mr Fincham.' He paused, but neither interrupted. 'I thought it was queer seeing's he was at his sister's ball last night. He was in a rare hurry and ordered the horses to be changed in double-quick time; very free with his blunt, he was. I was goin' over, careful, like, to see if he was alone when the landlord called me back to ask where you were. He had another letter, said the fellow in the shay had given it to him, but by then it had gone. Then I remembered where I'd seen that coach...' He stopped, his eyes alight with triumph. 'It was at Longham. It was ol' Grimshaw's.

'Grimshaw's. Are you sure?'

'Yes, Cap'ain.'

How, in heaven's name, had those two come to be in partnership? Would Grimshaw have kidnapped the girls to ensure his freedom from arrest? It put a whole new complexion on things. Grimshaw was dangerous, far more dangerous than that young pup, Fincham. Jack swore imaginatively and at some length, which made Tewkes smile; this was more like Captain Bellingham of old.

'There weren't no riding horses except the one Mr Burford had come on,' Tewkes said. 'So—begging his pardon—I took it and rode after them to see where they went. I'll swear they're making for St

Albans. I've found a short-cut that'll bring us out ahead of them, if we go now.'

'Then why are we wasting time?' Jack said. 'Let's be off and God help you if you are wrong.'

All three ran to the curricle but they could not get out of the yard because the mailcoach was coming in and blocking the entrance. Two men jumped from it almost before it stopped.

'I'll eat my hat if they ain't Runners,' Tewkes said.

'Thornton would never have sent Runners after Amelia, would he?' Frank said.

'No, I am sure he would not.' Jack knew he could trust Mrs Wenthorpe to play her part to prevent that. These men were hunting a different prey, but he wished that Lydia and Amelia had not become part of the chase, which would undoubtedly become public knowledge; he had hoped to avoid giving the scandal-mongers anything to stir their broth with. He jumped down and hurried over to the newcomers. 'Are you looking for Ernest Grimshaw?'

'We are indeed,' one of them said, eyeing Jack up and down. 'Who are you?'

'The Marquis of Longham. I set the authorities on to the man.'

'Then you can identify him when we catch up with him,' the man said. 'We thought he'd be making for the south coast to join his French friends, but no, he runs north.' The man smiled and tapped his nose. 'But we're two downy birds and hedged our bets. Trouble is we lost him when he turned off the main road. Nothing for it but to keep stopping and making enquiries. He'd have to change his horses somewhere or run them into the ground.'

'He changed them here,' Jack said. 'If you come with me, I think I can promise you will have your man in the space of a few hours.' He paused. 'But there is something you could do for me in return.'

'Depends,' the man said.

Jack explained what he wanted and five minutes later the curricle containing Jack and Frank, with Tewkes up behind, left the inn, followed by Frank's travelling coach, driven by Fletcher and with the two Runners as passengers.

The occupants of Grimshaw's carriage were heartily sick of each other's company and no one had spoken for miles, but Lydia's mind was busy with escape and discarding one plan after another. They were travelling too fast to consider jumping out and she could still feel the bump on her head from falling from the other coach, and that had been practically at a standstill. Besides, Amelia would not consider doing anything like that and she could not leave her. Nothing could be done until they arrived at their next stop, the Peahen in St Albans.

'I 'ave the 'unger,' she said, as they rattled into the town. 'Do you think we may 'ave something to eat while the 'orses are changed?'

Douglas had felt pangs of hunger himself and agreed on condition the girls did not speak to anyone and did nothing to attract attention to themselves, though he was doubtful about the Comte's filthy white suit. 'Perhaps you should change,' he suggested.

''Ow?' she asked. 'We left our baggage behind in the other coach.'

'Then wear my cloak.' He took it off and draped it round her shoulders as they came to a stop in the yard of the posting inn. 'Remember I have my pistol and I shall be right behind you.'

'And I shall take care of your fair friend,' Grimshaw said, as his coachman came round to open the door and let down the step. But it was not the coachman.

Amelia gave a little scream and flung herself into Frank's arms, nearly knocking him off his feet. Lydia, who had not seen who it was, thought this was another of Douglas's tricks and turned in her seat to try and take the gun from him. While they struggled, Grimshaw took the opportunity to jump down on the opposite side. He found himself face to face with the Runners who seized his arms and hauled him away. True to their promise to the Marquis, they did not interest themselves in who else might be in the coach, though there was an interesting commotion coming from its interior.

Lydia was kicking and clawing, fighting with all her strength, her fury making her glassy-eyed and deaf to everything except her own laboured breathing. She did not hear anything of what was happening in the yard. She wanted that pistol and she meant to have it. Someone shouted and grabbed her legs. She kicked out and heard a grunt of pain.

'Damn you, will you come out of there?'

She was hauled out backwards and set on her feet. 'Let me be!' She turned on her assailant, arms flailing. 'You. . .you. . . Oh!' She stopped and stared. Jack was standing with feet apart, ruefully stroking his chin where a red weal was already appearing.

He smiled. 'You've a kick like a mule, Monsieur le Comte. I would not for a minute envy anyone who tried to hold on to you.'

She was speechless. She had been longing for him to come, and now he was here, all he could do was laugh at her and address her as the Count. And there were dozens of people in the yard, all crowding round and agog with curiosity, assuming she was one of the criminals and enjoying her humiliation. It was not at all how she had imagined their reunion would be. She pulled herself up short. But of course it was typical of him not to take account of her feelings and she was as big a ninny as ever. Nothing had changed. 'You should mind your own business,' she snapped, covering her distress with words. 'I nearly had his gun and now he's getting away.'

This was true. Douglas had taken advantage of the situation and had turned Grimshaw's coachman off the box and climbed up there himself. He flicked the whip, but the inn's staff had already begun the routine of changing the horses and all that happened was that they broke away from the shafts and trotted up the road without him. The spectators enjoyed the joke hugely and even Lydia found herself smiling as the Runners took him into custody and appropriated the coach to take their prisoners back to London.

'Let him go,' Jack told them.

'Let him go?' Lydia could hardly believe her ears. 'After what he has done? You can't mean it.'

'Indeed I do.' He smiled and those hazel eyes of his bored into hers, making her heart beat in her throat and almost stopping her breath. She felt like screaming and stamping her foot and beating his chest with her fists, anything to let loose the confused emotion she felt and stop him looking at her in that searching way of his. He knew how she felt about him, she could not disguise it, so why did he not have pity on her and turn away? And after all she and Amelia had been through he proposed letting that evil Fincham go free!

'Why? You surely do not condone what he did?'

'Certainly not, but can the Comte de Clancy afford the ignominy?'

'Poof!' she said, and stared in bewilderment as he threw back his head and laughed aloud. 'What have I said that is so comical?'

'Poof! Do you know the Comte de Clancy and Miss Wenthorpe say that in exactly the same way? Now, I wonder why that is?'

So that was how he knew! 'You've been playing a game with me all along, haven't you?' she said. 'You knew right from the first and yet you said nothing until last night. I hate you for that. Do you hear me? I hate you, hate you.' It was a terrible effort to hold back the tears.

'It is you who were playing the game, my dear Count, and you would not have thanked me for spoiling it, would you?' He smiled. 'Please don't look so down-pin; it is all over now.'

'Yes, I suppose it is,' she said dully, looking across the yard to where Frank and Amelia sat on a bench, completely absorbed in each other. Oh, if only she and Jack could be like that! 'What will they do now? It's surely too late to go on with the elopement.'

'Elopement!' he exclaimed. 'How can you have come by that extraordinary idea? No one here would be so foolish as to risk a scandal by eloping, would they?'

'Then what. . .?' Oh, he was infuriating but she did not doubt he had managed all.

The crowd was thinning; there was little more of interest to see. Jack moved closer to her and took her arm, much as a man would take the arm of another man for a stroll. His touch was enough to set her quivering with desire and yet he seemed not to notice it. 'You were magnificent and brave, a valiant soldier,' he said, guiding her towards Frank and Amelia. 'Now we must set all to rights. Be patient, our time will come.'

She looked up sharply but he simply smiled in an enigmatic way and spoke to Frank. 'What reason did you give for not going to the Fincham ball?'

Frank looked up, surprised at the question and not a little annoyed at the interruption. 'I said I had been sent for on an urgent matter to do with my country estate.'

'It's near Hertford,' Amelia said. 'We were going there after we were married.'

'What kind of business?' Jack continued to press Frank.

'I don't know.'

'Think about it. It's important you can tell people what it was.'

'There has been some unrest among the labourers on the Home Farm, so it could be that, though my steward is certainly capable of taking care of it. What has that to do with anything?'

'Everything. It is time you faced up to your

responsibilities if you want Lady Thornton to change her mind about you.'

'She will never do that now. I have made a complete mull of everything.'

'She will come about if you behave like a responsible suitor and not a young scapegoat,' he said. 'I think you should go home at once and see to your estate, show yourself as a caring landlord and employer. If anyone should enquire, you went there yesterday and have been there ever since.'

'What about Amelia?' He took her hand in his. 'We should be married.'

'So you should, but not in this havey-cavey way. Take your coach and go home.'

'You must think me a prize rake-shame if you think I will abandon Amelia. . .'

'You are not abandoning her. You are putting her into my care.'

Lydia looked from one man to the other; surely the Marquis was not, even now, hoping to take Amelia for himself? Was that what he had meant when he had said 'our time will come'? Why couldn't Frank see the danger?

'I can't let you take her home to face her parents without me.'

'I'm not taking her home, I am going to take both young ladies to Raventrees.' He heard Lydia gasp behind him and turned to smile at her. 'Miss Thornton is going to stay with Miss Wenthorpe for a se'enight or two. Tom is already there, together with the Wenthorpe coach. As far as the world is concerned he took her and Miss Thornton there immediately after the ball ended. There never was any question of an elopement. The flight was planned between you to frighten Lord and Lady Thornton into listening to their daughter's wishes.'

'Who will tell them that?' Lydia asked.

'I am persuaded Mrs Wenthorpe has already done so.' He smiled. 'Of course none of them knows about the kidnap, which is why I did not want Fincham detained. With luck he will see the error of his ways and go abroad for a long tour and there will be no gossip. But we must waste no more time. Burford, say your goodbyes to Miss Thornton and be on your way. I'll see what I can do to persuade Lady Thornton that you are a changed character, but it will have to wait a se'enight or so, for I've business of my own to see to.'

Lydia watched as Amelia went with Frank to his coach, then turned back to Jack, undecided whether she ought to be grateful or angry. She was glad for Frank and Amelia, of course, but Jack, because of the capable way he had handled everything, had made her seem so helpless. And that, she supposed, was what she did not like; it proved how weak she was, how incapable of playing the man when it really mattered. She might have fooled Lady Thornton and one or two others, but she had failed none the less. Why, then was he still addressing her as if she were the Comte?

'You arranged all this before you left London,' she said. 'While we were talking, while you were. . .' She stopped and blushed crimson, remembering that kiss. 'Of all the unwarranted interference, the conceit of it. . .'

'Yes, my darling, someone had to save you from

your own folly.' He smiled, knowing what she was thinking and understanding her completely. 'Do you know, I have never much liked the Comte de Clancy? I really do not wish to kiss him again and yet, I fear, I shall have to if you stand there like that.'

'Like what, my lord?' Had he truly called her 'darling'?

'Tousled and troubled, bright-eyed and beautiful beyond anything a man could ever be. Certainly too lovely for my peace of mind. And let us have no more "my lord"; my name is Jack.'

Her heart began to sing. 'Jack,' she said softly, making it sound like a caress.

'Oh, Lydia, if you do not want me to make a complete ass of myself, go away.' He laughed suddenly and there was no steel in his eyes now. They were liquid pools of light, drawing her towards him. And yet he had told her to leave him.

'Go away?'

'I took your valise from Frank's coach. You will find it in room three. Go and change before I forget myself completely.'

Joyfully she found a chambermaid to show her to the room and quickly changed into a cambric slip striped in light and dark shades of blue topped with an open gown of pale blue muslin, over which she wore a matching pelisse, embroidered with roses. She had packed it because it was the sort of dress she could wear in the country and it was to Raventrees she had intended to go today. But to be going there with the Marquis! Oh, if only. . . He had called her 'darling' and gazed at her with a soft look in his eyes; there had been no contempt, nor aversion in them. It was almost as if he loved her. Could it be true? But he had looked at her like that before. Had it meant anything then? Did it now? She hurried her toilette, thankful that her hair was easily brushed into shape; delay in rejoining him would be unbearable. She had to know the truth, once and for all.

He was waiting for her in the inn's back parlour, which was miraculously empty of patrons. She hesitated in the doorway, unsure of herself. He stood with his back to the fireplace and watched her. How could anyone mistake this vision for a man? He smiled and took a step towards her. 'Lydia once more. All woman. *My* woman.' He took a step towards her. 'Come here, my love.'

Her feet seemed to fly as she ran into his arms to be enfolded against his broad chest and held there so tightly, the breath was almost driven from her body. 'Don't do that again,' he murmured. 'Don't ever give me a fright like that again. If Fincham's pistol had gone off. . .' He stopped to hold her at arm's length, looking down at her with dancing eyes. 'And I never went to see the Comte de Clancy again, do you hear me?'

She could not answer because he had covered her mouth with his own and the joy of it spread through her from the top of her head all the way down to her toes. This man, this big, handsome, infuriating man, was all she wanted, would ever want. He let her go at last, simply because neither had any breath left. She laughed suddenly.

'Share the jest,' he commanded.

'I was remembering the Comte creeping about the

corridors of Burford House, trying to be in two places at once. You thought I was fainting and carried me to Miss Whiting's room, remember?'

'How could I forget?'

'I wanted to tell you the truth then. All along I wanted to tell you. That was the night I realised I loved you. When we danced on the terrace. . .'

'Oh, I fell in love with you long before that. It was the first time we met. You were so practical and matter-of-fact and not at all concerned that you might have been killed when the coach overturned. I knew you were no ordinary young lady.'

'No, you said I was a hoyden.'

'I am sorry, my darling. Will you ever forgive me?'

She reached up and pulled his face down to hers and kissed him again. 'Is that answer enough?'

'And now will you answer me another question?' He held her away from him to look down at her. 'Will you do me the inestimable honour of becoming my wife?'

'Oh, yes, yes, my darling. You must speak to Papa at once.'

He laughed. 'I already have. Two weeks ago. He told me if I thought I could tame you, then I was welcome to try, for he had never been able to.'

'What a whisker!'

'It's the truth, I swear it. And I shall tame you like this.' And he kissed her forehead, her cheeks, one by one, her ears, her throat and her lips, and he kept on kissing her until Tewkes came in and told them bluntly that if they did not let the landlord have his parlour back right away they would have to buy the whole place.

Laughing, they made their way out to the curricle where Amelia waited for them. There was little room for three, but they squeezed in beside her, Tewkes climbed up behind and they pulled out of the yard, heading towards Raventrees and home.

MILLS & BOON®

Historical Romance™

LADY JANE'S PHYSICIAN
by Anne Ashley

A Regency Delight

Lady Jane Beresford visited her cousin, but her enjoyment was marred by meeting Dr Thomas Carrington. Tom's blunt attitudes irritated Jane out of her own good manners! But he knew, if she didn't, that an Earl's daughter was far above his touch…

UNTAMED HEART
by Georgina Devon

A Regency delight! ❦ Book 1 of 3

Lizabeth Johnstone was shocked by her primitive reaction to Lord Alastair St. Simon. He should be every woman's dream, but he wasn't *hers* for Alastair was responsible for her younger's brother's death. Her stubborn refusal to accept help left him with only one alternative—they'd have to get married…

On sale from 6th August 1999

Available at most branches of WH Smith, Tesco, Asda, Martins, Borders, Easons, Volume One/James Thin and most good paperback bookshops